CAPTAIN

Thomas Block

D0063747

ISBN: 978-1470158972

An ebook edition of this novel is also available at most online retailers

Other Books by Thomas Block

(see the author's website at http://www.ThomasBlockNovels.com
for details)

Mayday
Forced Landing
Orbit
Airship Nine
Skyfall
Open Skies

To the memory of those captains from a bygone era of airline flying; my heartfelt thanks for everything you selflessly shared with me.

And to Sharon, who continues sharing with me.

Throughout this novel, a few short quotations and a number of historic references to the late Dr. Viktor E. Frankl were utilized. His history and personal trials and tribulations are well known and documented, and the short quotations cited in the novel were originally from Dr. Frankl's quintessential and enormously creative work, "Man's Search For Meaning" (first published in 1946 in Austria and still readily available today). I am very grateful to Dr. Frankl – a leader in the study of modern psychiatry and its underlying structures and concepts -- for creating such insightful material.

Build then the ship of death, for you must take the longest
journey, to oblivion.
And die the death, the long and painful death that lies between
the old self and the new.
D.H. Lawrence

PROLOGUE

The fire was directly behind them and catching up. Ray could not only feel the on-rushing hot and acrid air that rolled over them from behind, but he could sense the flames and, every now and then, would catch a glimpse of that holocaust when he dared peek over his shoulder. "Hurry," he said as he and Katie ran down the long, narrow valley in northern Italy that was being engulfed in a wildfire.

"Ray, I'm frightened." They continued running along the only exit path available to them. Katie faltered and stumbled, her breathing heavily labored.

"Keep running. Almost there. I can see it. The next bend in the roadway." Ray felt Katie's fingers as they, literally, dug into his hand. She was moving slower, and he was pulling her as best he could, urging her along, trying to reach the only chance they had against the monstrous wildfire that had trapped them in this long and narrow valley.

"I can't...keep going..." Katie said as she nearly fell.

"You can!" Ray pulled on her arm to steady her, and she regained her balance. She continued moving forward with him. "Almost," Ray said. "There it is! The airport!"

"Where?" Katie asked, breathlessly.

"Straight ahead. Behind that row of trees." There it was, the small Italian airfield that Ray had somehow known about, nestled in the bowels of this narrow valley, its single blacktop runway positioned parallel with the high valley walls on either side. It would be their only chance to get out of this valley alive. As Ray had remembered, there was a single row of small Italian airplanes parked at the far end of the airfield. "A little further."

"Yes...Okay..."

Katie was keeping up with him, so all that was left was to pick a suitable airplane to make their escape. But as they neared the row of parked aircraft at the deserted airfield, Ray realized that the small airplanes parked on the line — a dozen or more — were the same type. "Single seat sport planes, every one of them!" Ray shouted back at her. "Damn!"

1

"I can fly one. I can do it, if you show me." Katie ran past several of the tiny Italian airplanes, glancing at each and, for some reason, going on to the next.

The airplanes were identical, and they had very small cockpits with only one seat. There was no way to get two people into one airplane. "You'll have to fly your own," Ray said. "Can't both fit into one."

"I can do it, Ray," Katie said as they stopped at one aircraft in the middle of the pack. Katie popped open the cockpit canopy and peeked inside. "You need to show me how to get it started. The cockpit labels are in Italian, can't read them."

"Get in." Ray boosted her into the tiny cockpit. While she strapped herself into the pilot's seat, Ray pointed to various controls as he figured them out. "Mag switch, starter, fuel selector, throttle. The control stick is normal, like the one you've used in the Cub at home. Wheel brakes on the floor, next to the rudder pedals. Use your heels. Put this headset on and use the radio once we get going. Press this button to transmit."

"Okay." Katie glanced around the unfamiliar cockpit. "Ray, I can do this. Get yourself into the next airplane." Katie pointed toward the aircraft to their right. "Hurry. The fire is almost here."

"I know." Ray closed the canopy on Katie's airplane, jumped from the wing and ran to the next aircraft in the line. As he climbed in, he could see the wall of flames as it worked its way around the turn in the road that was not a half a mile from them. The outflow of hot air had gotten stronger, and it was blowing directly down the short runway. That hot wind would shorten their takeoff roll, but it meant that they had to take off directly toward the enormous fire that was racing toward them. As Ray started the engine of his airplane, he could see that Katie had already started the engine of hers. "Can you hear me?" Ray asked on the radio.

"Yes," Katie answered. "Ready." She paused, then transmitted, "Ray, you go first, I'll follow."

"No." Ray could see the problem they'd be facing. The only runway they could use was directly toward the towering flames and mounds of billowing smoke, and it was getting closer with each passing moment. He needed to get Katie to make the first takeoff so she could clear that maelstrom with room to spare;

2

if he were to cut into the top of it, he stood a better chance than she did of wrestling the airplane through that smoke, the flames and the heavy turbulence. "You go, I'll follow behind you."

"Ray, you first — please!" Katie pleaded into the microphone.

"Okay." There was no time to argue. Ray pushed on the throttle and the Italian airplane jolted forward. "Follow me," he transmitted. "Stay close."

"I am."He glanced over his shoulder and could see her aircraft, only thirty feet or so behind his. "When we get to the far end of the runway, I'll swing around," Ray transmitted. "I'll add full power and roll straight down the runway. You wait ten seconds – no more than that – then do the same. Use eighty on the airspeed indicator as a takeoff and climb speed; that should be safe."

"Okay."

"Keep transmitting while you're making the takeoff so I know how you're doing." Ray knew that Katie found comfort in using the radio, in talking about what she was doing, as if that electronic link to someone else provided her with more hands and eyes in the cockpit, and with more skill. "Let go of the transmit button if you need me to answer you."

"I understand."

"Here I go," Ray said into the microphone. "Push up the power in ten seconds."

"Right."

Ray concentrated on his own takeoff. Rolling directly toward that wall of flame and smoke was disconcerting, but there was no other way. The Italian airplane leapt off the runway at 80 on the airspeed indicator, as he figured it would. "Eighty works fine," Ray transmitted. "Start your takeoff."

"Here I go," Katie announced.

Ray steered his airplane as steeply as he dared. He would, barely, clear the flames and smoke. He was clearing it by hardly more than inches, and the turbulence was severe. That meant that Katie wouldn't clear it, and the turbulence would be worse.

"Off the ground...climbing...Ray, the flames, the smoke...right in front of me...it's above me...Ray...Ray..."

In the background, behind her terrified words, Ray could hear the loud ringing of an alarm bell. It was, evidently, from inside her airplane, some sort of fire bell or overheat or smoke warning built into this Italian sport plane. Her airplane was on fire.

"Ray...Ray...I'm going down...Ray..."

But he couldn't answer her because she had kept her finger on the transmit button while she was losing control. He couldn't say anything to her, couldn't give her any advice – if there was any advice that he could give, any advice that would save her. *Oh, my God....* Ray kept hearing her frightened, pleading voice with that loud, shrill ringing of the fire bell in the background....

Finally, the ringing penetrated his conscious mind. Ray realized with a start that it was, in fact, the telephone beside his hotel bed that was ringing. "Hello?" he said, after fumbling around and finally picking up the receiver. What he heard on the other end was an electronic voice: it was the automated wake up call for 8:00 am that he had requested when he checked into this small hotel north of Rome late the evening before.

Ray got out of bed, stepped into the bathroom and splashed cold water on his face. His stomach was churning from the remnants of that bizarre dream, a nightmare that had seemed so damned real, and from the memory of Katie's frightened voice. *Put that out of your mind. Right now. You've got to.* Ray splashed more cold water on his face, then left the bathroom.

He went to the telephone and picked it up. When the front desk answered, Ray verified that his previous night's instructions were being carried out and that the hotel had arranged for a taxi to take him to Rome's Airport at 10:00 am. That would give him two hours to shave, shower, pack and have breakfast. "The taxi will be ready at ten?" Ray asked.

"*Si*," the front desk operator answered. "I have the instructions right here. This taxi service, he's a very dependable. The ride is short, twenty minutes at the most. You will have no problems."

"Thank you. *Gracie*," Ray said.

"*Prego.*"

Ray turned and headed to the bathroom. He had spent the past sixteen days driving through northern Italy, going only to places he had never been before, places that he had never taken Katie to. His friends — the few friends that he would speak to

4

about this very personal subject — said that a change of scenery would be helpful, and so would new areas to explore and enjoy. It would get his thoughts going in a different direction. They had been right, it had.

Some. But not much.

Ray glanced at the one novel and three magazines that he would be taking on the flight. That, plus the one self-help book that he had impulsively grabbed from that bookstore shelf before leaving on his trip to Italy, the book he had bought one afternoon when he had aimlessly wandered around Manhattan on a shopping trip while his head was throbbing and the memory of Katie's face was hardly below the surface of his thoughts.

As Ray had suspected, the words in *Dealing With Anxiety and Guilt* were totally dead to him. Even after he had forced himself to finish that self-help psychology book, the words remained stone dead: as dead as Katie was.

Got to let it go. Those words had become his recurring mantra for some time, but they also had done little to help. Mouthing those words had done almost nothing to ease his pain, nothing to erase those constant, gnawing memories and the periodic dreams and nightmares. Ray sighed, then shook his head as he looked directly at himself in the bathroom mirror. He knew that Flight 3 from Rome to New York was going to be a long ride for him today.

Book One

The natural function of the wing is to soar upwards and carry that which is heavy up to the place where dwells the race of gods.
—Plato

When once you have tasted flight, you will forever walk the earth with your eyes turned skyward.
—Leonardo da Vinci

Chapter One

Wednesday, January 20th
Fiumicino Airport, Rome, Italy
12:25 pm, Central European Time

Captain Jack Schofield stepped into the cockpit of the widebody Consolidated 768 jetliner, put his flight bag on the floor then placed his gold braided captain's flight cap on the shelf above the sidewall coat closet. He took off his uniform jacket and carefully hung it up.

Jack took a moment to look at himself in the small mirror above the coat closet. If it weren't for his receding hairline, he knew that he didn't give the appearance of being 46 years old — like his wife Lori often said, he had those sparkling, mischievous eyes and that infectious smile. But today, after Monday night's long flight from New York to Rome that began with that one hour mechanical delay plus the periodic bouts of en route turbulence, and then his distorted sleeping patterns at the hotel in spite of having nearly thirty hours off in the Eternal City, Jack felt beat up.

Yesterday's Rome weather of cool winds, low clouds and passing rain showers had cut short his late afternoon walk from the Villa Borghese, down the Via Veneto and back to the hotel. He had, as usual, succumbed to his love of good Italian cooking and eaten too large a dinner. After that, he couldn't sleep well.

Now, facing a nine hour and fifty minute nonstop flight to New York, Jack was feeling old. Jack knew that the International flying he'd been doing — constantly flying across the backside of the clock and across six time zones — had taken its cumulative toll. The hell of it was that he was doing his piloting at high altitudes in a comfortable widebody jetliner, and he could only imagine what those old timers must have felt flying these routes in DC-7s, DC-6s and Constellations that flew down low through shit loads of weather. He shivered at the thought.

Maybe, he said to himself for the hundredth time, he should go back to domestic flying. Except for the smaller paycheck, Lori would like it better. That was a vote in favor.

But the negative vote was overwhelming: it would be like giving up command of the Queen Mary to run a tugboat pulling a garbage scow up a river. Jack sighed, then turned to the other two pilots sitting in their flight chairs. "Peter, you got the checklist going? I got hung up at the boarding gate."

"Yes." First Officer Peter Fenton, sitting in the right-front co-pilot's seat, glanced at the captain. Peter pointed to the lower instrument panel. "Got the routing into the computer. We're verifying the entries."

"Good." Jack maneuvered past where Second Officer Linda Erickson sat in the center of the cockpit, aft of the two primary pilot seats. The printed Trans-Atlantic flight plan was on a clipboard she held in her hands. "Hope you're watching him, Linda. Peter likes to throw a few odd entries in to keep me on my toes," Jack said.

"Really?"

"Last time he had the computer take us to Moscow instead of New York." Jack smiled at Linda, mostly to show off that legendary smile of his. Lori would've clobbered him if she ever caught him being flirtatious, as innocent as he knew it was, but Linda was both an attractive young woman and a competent pilot. With the usual female pilots at Trans-Continental, you got one or the other of those traits, but never both. Linda knew what she was doing around airplanes, and she had cute, short blonde hair, beautiful blue eyes and her own bright set of picture-perfect teeth. Jack knew that tossing a flirtatious smile in her direction was the prescription for improving his disposition.

"No Moscow this time, skipper." Linda answered. "He's got New York punched in."

"Really? Peter's not up to his usual antics?" Jack glanced at his young co-pilot who was pretending to be engrossed in his navigation computer programming and was, as usual, ignoring the wisecracks. Peter Fenton was, as everyone who flew the International routes for Trans-Continental Airlines knew, meticulous and inflexible in executing his assignments. He was the last co-pilot who would try a practical joke, which made the idea of it even more hilarious. "Peter, wasn't it you who typed the wrong alternate airport last time we flew together and the computer wouldn't accept the routing because we'd run out of fuel over the South Atlantic?"

Peter moved his eyes slowly from the computer screen and faced the captain. "Don't think so," he said in a low voice and with a deadpan expression. Even though he knew that Jack was only toying with him, Peter didn't appreciate it. He prided himself on being careful and in verifying every detail of what he was doing. Hell, if anyone in this cockpit were capable of sending the navigation computer out of its fuel range and toward the South Atlantic, it would have been Jack Schofield. As far as Peter was concerned, the old farts like Schofield were yesterday's news; every one of them followed proper procedures only when someone in authority was watching. None of those old-school characters had sufficient flight discipline to suit Peter; every one of them were anachronisms. "I do the routing inputs exactly the way the book says," Peter answered with a forced smile. "You must be confusing me with someone else."

"You know, I think you might be right. It was someone else." Jack turned back to Linda. "I stand corrected." He then added, "You folks finish the preflight crap while I do my housekeeping chores." Jack turned in the captain's flight chair and began to organize the maps and personal items from his flight bag. "Then we can get to personal stuff. I need to tell you who I ran into at the gate. I also want to tell Peter about the Italian police captain — I think he's a captain — and what he told me about how the *aeroporto polizia* feel about having a person of Peter's status onboard."

"Really?" Peter shot a quick glance at Jack, then turned to his computer screen while he tried not to show much interest.

"Yes, indeed." Jack grinned; he knew that he had Peter on the hook. This would be fun. "Finish the checklist, then I'll tell you. I'll get us coffee." Jack pushed the flight attendant call button and picked up the interphone handset. "Hey, Tina, how about three coffees for your hard working cockpit crew? Whenever you get a chance." He put down the interphone and returned to the pre-flight setup routine. He went through the same ritual before settling into the cockpit before each flight: his personal headset, sunglasses, the route charts, the airport diagram for Fiumicino were carefully placed in their proper positions. Finished with that, Jack glanced at the windshield. He frowned. "The Italians know how to cook, but they sure as hell don't know how to clean windows."

9

Linda, who had finished with her part of the routing computer check, looked at the captain's windshield. It was somewhere between clean and dirty. "Saw the ground service guy working on the windows while I was doing the walk-around. Want me to call them back?" she asked.

"No. If we told them the windows were dirty we'd create a major international incident."

"Not to mention the major delay," Peter added. If Schofield wanted extra windshield cleaning, he should have gotten to the cockpit earlier — it would be like him to delay the flight over something as insignificant as smears on his windshield. Peter finished with the computer inputs and sat back in his flight chair. "We'd get more success by asking the Italians to change an engine than to wash the windows again. They would take that request as a direct insult."

"Right you are again," Jack said. He looked at his co-pilot who, as usual, wore a stern and serious expression – a compatible match to his thin face and short black hair. "Then, rather than risk that International incident, we'll go to the New World with a dirty window. Peter, find a rain shower between here and New York to wash it off."

"Not likely, considering the weather." Peter tapped his hand on the stack of flight papers sitting on the console between them. He resisted the urge to ask Schofield if he had bothered to read the weather reports. Instead, Peter broke his own promise of not appearing to give a damn and asked, "Since you brought it up, what did that Italian police captain say about the armed flight officer program? Naturally, I'm curious."

Gotcha. "The police captain surprised me by being supportive." Jack pointed toward where Peter had placed his .40 caliber pistol, in its holster, on his side of the cockpit. "I expected the police to be protective of their turf, but this guy seemed happy to have the anti-hijacking help. Matter of fact, the guy was surprised that the co-pilot and not the vessel's *commandante* would be the pilot onboard with the weapon."

Peter nodded; this was a subject he enjoyed talking about. "He doesn't know the TSA. Hell, if it wasn't for the end result, I wouldn't have done it myself." But Peter knew that he was lying; having official government approval to carry a weapon onboard an airline flight was too personally important to not have done whatever they asked.

Peter glanced at the pistol that the TSA had issued him — it was, literally, a badge that signified his importance to this flight, to the passengers and to the airline. Feeling chatty since they were now talking about something important, he turned to the captain. "They won't tell us officially, but I heard that eighty percent of the Federal Flight Deck Officers on the International routes are co-pilots."

"Sure." Jack waved his hand in a gesture of dismissal. "How you guessed the proper answers to their psychological bullshit questions is beyond me. How you find the patience to comply with their procedures is another mystery."

"Well, it's not been completely..."

"Yes, it has been," Jack said, interrupting Peter before he could finish. "I find it insulting that they make you do this crap on your own time. I couldn't tolerate their nonsense — which is what I suspect the TSA management is hoping for. I'd bet you ten to one that they're amazed that some of you managed to jump through their hoops."

"Well, maybe." But Peter wasn't surprised that he, personally, had managed to be accepted into and to successfully complete the FFDO training program. Secretly, he was happy that pilots like Jack Schofield wouldn't be considered. Even though a good deal of the criticism of how the program was setup and administered was valid — every one of them agreed that the government was actively creating obstacles rather than doing what was necessary to encourage pilots to become armed flight officers — the end result was what Peter had hoped for: he had become a duly-certified armed flight officer, and that was a feather in his cap. The legal right for a pilot to carry a weapon onboard an airliner was a hard-won battle, and the new change that added select International routes to their mission profile was even longer in the making.

"Peter, let me ask you a question," Linda said.

"Sure." Peter swivelled around in his flight chair to face her.

"Is it the Department of Homeland Security that's the parent organization?" Linda asked. "The Transportation Safety

Administration — the TSA — is a small part of that government agency? Is that right?"

"That's right," Peter answered. "Homeland Security is the boss, but it was the TSA that I worked with to get into the program and be trained."

"I heard that the testing done by Homeland Security had lots of screwy questions in it," Linda said. "Someone told me that the questions were deliberately designed to get airline pilots to fail."

"Yes, indeed," Jack answered before Peter could reply. Jack laughed loudly, then added, "Here's one of those instances. I heard this first hand. They would ask the pilot applicants if they'd like to be fighter pilots. Well, since a good number of airline pilots had been active military fighter pilots at some point in their aviation careers, they would naturally answer yes. Truthful answer, right?"

"Yes, but…"

"But *nothing*. The TSA bureaucracy — or maybe it was the masterminds at the omnipotent Department of Homeland Security — had determined that a yes answer to that question indicated an overly aggressive personality and, hence, that pilot was immediately disqualified from being part of the program." Jack laughed again. "What nonsense, typical of a government agency."

"I don't remember that question," Peter said defensively. While it was like Schofield to run down a viable program that he didn't stand a snowball's chance in hell of getting into, some of what he was saying was true. Sometimes he was right, but, so what? Right or wrong, Schofield was still a pain in the ass. "I heard that those sorts of questions were part of the first testing standards, but they were dropped."

"Not dropped as quickly as the pilots who answered yes to them." Jack smirked at Peter, then added, "I rest my case." He enjoyed goading his super-serious co-pilot whenever the opportunity arose, and this armed flight officer nonsense was exactly what the doctor ordered.

Peter silently returned to his computer screen while Jack continued to watch him. In a strange way, Jack liked Peter. The young co-pilot was, technically, knowledgeable and competent and he was also skillful when it came to physically handling the airliner. But he was very uptight and he was constantly worried about every single thing and every minor detail. He was the sort of pilot who saw only the small picture, never the big one – which meant that he was the epitome of the new breed of airline pilot the company was hiring these days. "Peter, you've got to admit that the TSA has a deep-seated institutional opposition to the idea of armed pilots...they want only *their* people under *their* control up here with weapons. If the budget allowed, they'd have a sky marshal on every flight."

Peter looked up from the computer screen, debating whether or not he would glorify Schofield's asinine opinions with an answer. Finally, he did. "The TSA can't afford Sky Marshals on every flight. That's why I'm here."

"Very illuminating. I thought you were hired to fly airplanes," Jack said.

"That, too." Peter held Schofield's eye for a long moment; he was about to say more — maybe too much more — when Linda tapped him on the shoulder. "Yes?" he said, turning to her.

"Peter, here's something else I've heard," Linda said, trying to sound neutral but also trying to defuse what she thought was a negative situation building between these two. She didn't need to spend the next ten hours sitting between two pilots who were at each other's throats. "I heard that pilots with active gun experience were turned down," Linda said, trying to take some of the pressure off Jack and trying to turn this building confrontation into an academic discussion. "Did you hear that?"

"Actually, yes. I did."

"That seems curious. Do you have any previous gun experience?" she asked.

Peter took a deep breath; he couldn't decide if she was ganging up on or asking a logical question. Finally, he answered. "Not really. Not that previous gun experience matters. For me, I've done some target shooting." Peter squirmed slightly; that was another part of the FFDO program that he had heard, that many of the pilots who had a great deal of firearms experience and training had been turned down without explanation. If you applied and they turned you down, you weren't allowed to ask why. Even pilots who had one time been policemen or military officers were dropped from the program without any reason. "A friend of mine has a .22 rifle and I went to his place in the country. We did some shooting. The last time was maybe a year ago. But, like I said, having gun experience doesn't matter."

"Doesn't matter?" Jack said, rising slightly in his flight chair, his voice rising also. "Experience doesn't matter, is that what you're telling us?"

Peter turned back to Schofield. "I only meant that we had this comprehensive training course. That's how we got certified."

"Really? How long was the training period?" Jack asked.

"One week."

"It must have been a hell of a week, Wyatt Earp."

"It was intense," Peter said, ignoring Schofield's sarcasm. "I felt I learned everything that I needed to know."

"Well, I hope so." Jack glanced down at the panel clock. 12:29 local time. The agents would start the boarding process soon, and he wanted his coffee. He was about to call the flight attendant station on the interphone again when the cockpit door opened. "Tina, great timing. I was thinking about that coffee."

"Coffee is served," Tina Lopez moved forward into the cockpit with her tray of three coffees. "Black for the captain, cream and sugar for you two," she announced. All three of the pilots reached for their cups. "The boarding should start any time. The agent tells me it's full in the back, half empty in the front. We should have the door closed by departure time."

Jack took a sip of his coffee. He looked at Tina, who was the senior flight attendant. She was the quintessence of the best of her Spanish heritage, with her dark wavy hair, her dark eyes and her full lips. A real looker and — if that wasn't enough — also a nice lady to work with and a smart lady. Then there was also that other thing that would become a player today. A big player. "Did you see the manifest? Did you notice who's riding on a vacation pass in first class?"

"No."

"Someone you know very well." Jack paused for effect, knowing what the name would mean to her. He then added, "Ray Clarke."

"Oh." Tina stood absolutely motionless, and absolutely speechless. A avalanche of thoughts and feelings were tumbling through her.

14

"Ran into him at the boarding gate," Jack said to break the silence. He knew that her reaction would be something like this. "He's been here on vacation in Italy for a few weeks, going home today."

Tina tried to keep her expression neutral. She took half a step backward. "Haven't seen him in quite awhile," she stammered, not knowing what else to say. "Not since before he retired."

"That's been awhile," Jack answered. He knew damn well the two of them weren't a number any more and hadn't been for quite some time – the airline scuttlebutt had sent that message loud and clear. "Ray's been retired, let's see, nearly two years now."

"Yes. He retired on his fiftieth birthday. It was in February, two years ago." Tina paused. An entire range of thoughts raced through her head at the same time. "How did Ray look?" she asked, trying to sound non-committal, and knowing damned well that Jack would see right through her.

"Exactly the same. He hasn't changed." Jack took another sip of his coffee. "I didn't get much time with him at the boarding area, but he did say that he was enjoying himself, that he didn't miss any of this, that he was glad that he took the early retirement offer." Jack paused, then shook his head slightly. "I know that he didn't retire because of what happened to Katie," he said, broaching what he knew was a delicate subject, "but that disaster didn't help his mental state. It was one more reason – maybe the main reason – for him to be away from this place. Tragic."

"Yes." Tina thoughts were filled with images of Katie. "Absolutely tragic." Katie had died on a hot, steamy day in August, and Tina would never forget Ray's voice when he called her that afternoon to tell her the horrible news. Ray's wife – Tina's best friend – had tragically died that morning in an airplane accident. Tina knew that she would never get over Katie's death, or, for that matter, any of the things that happened afterward. Wordlessly, Tina turned and began to leave the cockpit.

"One more thing," Jack added. "Once everyone gets settled in the cabin, please escort our retired captain to the cockpit so that he can, with my compliments, join us here for the takeoff."

"Jack, that's absolutely not allowed under the new security..."

Jack put his hand up. "Peter," he said with a forced smile, his words coming out in a slow and deep voice, "please hold that thought for a moment." He turned to the flight attendant. "Tina, tell Ray that I — that all of us — would be most honored by his presence here on the flight deck for our takeoff from Rome."

Tina nodded. "Certainly." She turned and quickly left the cockpit.

"Now," Jack said, facing Peter again, this time with no smile whatsoever, "what were you trying to tell me?" There was, in addition to his stern expression, a slight edge in his tone. Jack knew damn well where this conversation was going, and he intended to head it off *right now*.

"Only that the security rules don't allow for this," Peter answered. "The fact that this man was once a captain here doesn't matter, not as far as the security rules are concerned. He isn't allowed in the cockpit. I can show you in the book." Peter began to reach for his manual.

"Peter," Jack said firmly, pointing a finger at him. "Put a sock in it." Jack glared at Peter for a moment, then slowly began to shake his head. "That's exactly what's wrong with this security bullshit, with this airline and with this whole fucking country, for that matter. Pardon my French," Jack said, as he glanced back toward Linda, then at his co-pilot again. "The man who — to use your own terms was once a captain here — was one of the finest pilots that this company ever had. He worked as a pilot here for almost thirty years, and he personally taught me more than I ever learned anywhere else. He was a direct link to the original men who flew those old airliners, captains like Maynard Lyman and Edwin Johnson."

Peter sat in silence, knowing full well what would be coming next. He had opened the floodgates by simply pointing out what the current rules were, and now he was going to be drowned in verbal bullshit.

Jack took a deep breath, then continued. "It was this evolving bureaucratic craziness that took Ray Clarke down, although it was the death of his wife that certainly finished the job. But I'm here to tell you that Captain Ray Clarke will be invited to sit in any cockpit that I'm in command of until they force me out of this seat, like they did to him. He will be coming up here for the takeoff, and all of you will make him feel very, very welcome, too." Jack paused, then added slowly, and in carefully chosen words, "Do I make myself clear?"

"Yessir," Linda answered immediately.

Peter shrugged a lukewarm acceptance, then turned away. *I hope you get caught, you sonovabitch,* he thought. *Then it'll be your ass.* But Peter did have enough common sense not to say any of those thoughts out loud. Instead, he looked out the co-pilot's side window at the loading activity on the ramp area around them. He knew that it was going to be one hell of a long flight if he had to sit up here with those two old bastards. They'd reminisce all the way across the fucking North Atlantic.

Chapter Two

Flight Attendant Tina Lopez stood in the first class galley of the Consolidated 768, her hands moving nervously as she fussed with a stack of napkins. She was waiting for the passengers to make their appearance in the jet bridge that connected the aircraft's forward entrance door to Rome's terminal building number five.

The other flight attendant in the first class galley, Annette Riley, was looking over the paperwork that the boarding agent had laid on the galley counter a few minutes earlier. "This new terminal building in Rome makes things run smoother, don't you think?" Annette asked as she flipped through the computer printouts.

"Yes. Better," Tina answered distractedly. She was only half listening to Annette, who was saying something about the number of families in the coach section and something else, too.

"So, what do you think?" Annette said, in a louder voice.

"What?"

"Yes or no?"

"I'm sorry, I didn't..." Tina glanced at what Annette was pointing at on the paperwork.

"Fred Lyle. He's in a middle seat in coach between two families. We're going to have eight first class seats open. How about if I move him up after we close the door?"

"Fred Lyle? The New York flight attendant?" Tina looked at the printed sheet where Annette was pointing. She hadn't noticed the male flight attendant's name on it earlier, although she had looked long and hard at the name of Ray Clarke.

"Yes. You've flown with Fred, he's the one who speaks Italian and French. I saw him in the terminal when I was at Duty Free. He told me that he and his current boyfriend Allan — Allan's a domestic flight attendant in New York, but you might not know him — were touring Germany and Italy for the past ten days. Allan had to go back to work a couple days earlier, so now Fred's headed to New York by himself. He's got a London trip tomorrow night." Annette paused and looked at Tina. "Okay if I move him to first class after we close the door?"

"Fine."

"Good. You know how Fred is, too damn cheap to pay for the upgrade. But we like him well enough. I'd like to do this, he's always helpful and friendly."

"Yes. Absolutely. Take care of it."

"Be right back. I'll tell Nancy and she'll tell Fred as soon as he gets onboard that we'll be moving him forward. Don't want him to get too settled." Annette stepped out of the galley and toward the coach section of the airliner. "It's a nice thing for those two families in coach. Puts an empty seat between them."

"Right." Tina nodded, then watched Annette walk away. Tina glanced up the corridor of the jet bridge. Still empty, but she expected that the first class passengers — technically, marketing called it Business Class, but the crew called it First Class — would appear any moment. Ray would be one of them. Tina hoped that she didn't look as nervous as she felt.

She had, more or less, put Ray Clarke out of her mind. But with him about to board, all she could think about was him, about what they've done together, about what they'd meant to each other. The words, emotions, snippets of episodes were flashing through her mind like a movie run at double speed.

"Hello?"

"Hello, Tina. This is Ray...I'm sorry...I'm really sorry to say this. Tina, I have bad news. Horrible, horrible news."

Tina had stood with the telephone pressed to her ear, dumbfounded. She didn't utter a sound or, as best as she could remember, take a breath. She knew from his words and from his tone that this telephone call had to be about Katie, about Ray's wife and her very best friend.

"I'm sorry that I have to say this on the telephone, but I...didn't want you...to hear...from anyone..." Ray's voice was hesitant, as if by not saying the words they wouldn't be true. She could hear that he was almost too choked up to continue.

"Ray...what...?"

Ray cleared his throat. "Katie is dead." He paused, the silence that now filled the telephone line hanging over them like an impenetrable shroud. "Katie is dead..." he said again, his voice trailing off.

"What? How?"

"The airplane. She went to the airport this morning. To practice takeoffs and landings. I offered to go with her, but she wanted another solo session."

"How could it happen...what happened?" Tina heard her own voice as if it were someone else who was asking the question. None of this was real or, more accurately, it was far too real. Her mind was a blank, and her voice sounded as if it weren't her own.

"Don't know. Not for sure. Not yet. One of the witnesses said he heard popping sounds after she lifted off — she had already done four or five takeoffs and landings — and then the noise level suddenly changed and then the airplane rolled to the left and then it crashed inverted off the side of the runway. It happened in a few seconds. Just a few seconds. Engine failure...she didn't get the airplane's nose down...like I told her...so many times..."

Ray had stopped talking, but she could hear him, hear him breathing on the other end of the open telephone line.

"Ray...oh, Ray..." Tina began to cry...

"Excuse me, Miss. Where's this seat?" The man in a sport jacket gestured with his boarding card.

"Oh. Sorry. You snuck up on me." Tina forced a smile toward the passenger and took his boarding card. "2F. Second row on the right." She handed back the boarding card and pointed toward a seat in first class. After that, she began to systematically deal with the lineup of passengers making their way into the cabin.

Tina knew that Ray would be boarding at the end of the First Class group, ahead of the coach passengers. She spotted him when he was a half-dozen passengers from the entrance door. He was a tall man, slightly over six foot, and he obviously hadn't gained a single ounce over the 190 pounds that he weighed since she and Katie first met him on that San Juan flight ten-plus years ago. His reddish-brown hair had grown longer and fuller since his retirement. He had broad shoulders and those penetrating hazel eyes. Finally, it was Ray's turn to come onboard. He stepped across the threshold.

20

"Well, how about that for good fortune? Hello, Tina." Ray forced a thin smile on his lips. "A real surprise," he said, fumbling for his next words. "A pleasant surprise," he added after a few more seconds. "Jack didn't tell me you were onboard." Ray paused, then added, "Guess he wanted me to see that for myself."

Tina wanted something clever to respond with, but she couldn't think of a single blessed thing. "Good to see you again. Great, actually." She laughed, then reached forward and closed the short distance. She hugged him, then stepped back. "Been awhile."

"Yes. It has." Ray glanced at his boarding card; it had become a map with the route for his escape. "It says seat 4A."

"4A," Tina repeated. She was going to wait until later to announce what she'd already decided a few minutes ago, but she found herself blurting it out then and there. "Seat 4B is empty. I'll sit next to you. Later. We can talk. We can catch up." Tina pointed to the cabin. "Don't get settled. I'm supposed to escort you to the cockpit. Jack *insists* that you sit up front for the takeoff. You know how he is."

Ray nodded. "I figured Jack might want me up front," Ray answered neutrally. He moved past her but as he did, he stopped and laid his hand on her shoulder; he knew that he had to do something of the sort, to say something of the sort. "Glad we'll be getting this chance to talk. We'll have the opportunity later. I'll drop my bag at the seat and come back for my cockpit visit."

"Fine," Tina answered. "We've got a ten hour flight, there's plenty of time." She smiled, but her feelings were completely fragmented. "Come back and I'll take you to the cockpit."

"Okay."

Tina watched Ray walk away. She wanted to keep talking to him and, at the same time, she felt that she shouldn't. She shouldn't even *want* to talk to him. Not after the way he treated her. She knew that she should just let it go, that she should just forget him, that Ray was no good for her.

But even as the idea formulated in her thoughts, she also knew that it was a hollow and meaningless thought. Forgetting Ray would certainly be prudent. But it was impossible, and she damn well knew it. Tina forced herself to turn to the lineup of coach passengers who were assembling at the entrance door.

As the passengers continued to enter the airliner, Tina's mind was on Ray and their shared history. She continued with her boarding duties, but her thoughts were focused on a another time that seemed decades ago, and on another place that felt like it was in a different galaxy. Paris in September. Cloudy and rainy. The two of them had taken an ambling afternoon walk through the city and had stopped at the Museum d' Orsay.

◇

In the cockpit of Trans-Continental Flight 3, the crew had completed the first of their checklist routines in preparation for their departure. Jack glanced at his panel clock. "Fifteen minutes, if they decide to get us out on time," he said.

"Sounds like the boarding is finished," Linda said. "If either of you want more coffee, this might be a good opportunity."

"Not me," Jack answered. "How about you, Peter?"

"No. One's enough." Peter looked out the cockpit window. He gestured out toward where a countless number of airport vehicles of every size, shape and color — tugs, baggage carts, buses, cars, trucks, scooters, tractors — seemed to be in endless motion in every direction around them. "Rome amazes me, but what amazes me most is this airport," Peter said. He decided it was time to make small talk with Jack since there was no reason to have that awkward silence between them for the entire flight. Besides, Schofield was tight with enough of the flight department supervisors to make real trouble if he wanted to.

"Rome's airport amazes you more than the city itself?" Jack said. "Okay, I'll bite. Why?"

"It looks like the airport just opened for business every time I fly here. There's craziness from one end of this airport to the other. It's a wonder they get any of the proper things on the correct airplanes. Look at that maintenance truck, he cut off that string of baggage carts. Everyone's frantic. Constantly."

Jack glanced in the direction that Peter was pointing. "It does look like a carnival sideshow. Dodge 'em cars." Jack

22

laughed. "I'm not sure that it's more amazing than, say, walking to the Trevi Fountain or the Spanish Steps late at night, but it certainly does have its moments. Hell, this ramp action is a microcosm of Italian life. Everything is steeped in either *un minuto* or *presto*, followed by *rapidamente*."

"You sound like a native," Linda said. Now that things were going well between the two men, it was a good to encourage them. "How much Italian do you speak?" she asked.

"Enough to order my dinner and get a taxi," Jack answered. "Hey, did I tell you about the taxi ride I took with Scott Reynolds last year, when he was still a co-pilot. You know Scott?" he asked Linda.

"No," Linda answered. "Don't know him."

"No matter." Jack turned more in his seat toward Linda since he knew that there was no love lost between Peter Fenton and Scott Reynolds — they were as far apart in temperament and outlook as two co-pilots could be. Peter wouldn't be interested in Scott Reynolds anecdotes.

"I've heard the Rome taxi story. A good one," Peter said. "Actually, it's a classic."

Jack glanced at Peter in surprise."I'm glad you liked our Rome taxi story, but I thought you didn't like Scott," Jack said.

"He's okay." Peter shrugged. "We work together fine."

"That's not what I heard." Jack added, "I heard you were chasing the same flight attendants."

"Not true."

"Maybe not." Jack turned to Linda and began telling the story about the Rome taxi driver. When he got to the punch line, Jack said, "Hey, wazza that'a fast enough for a you?" in his imitation-Italian accent and let out a rolling laugh that filled the cockpit. Linda laughed with him, and even Peter chuckled.

Linda then said, "Speaking of stories, I'd like to hear more about the man I'm about to meet. I heard stories about Ray Clarke, but it's difficult to tell how much is true and how much is fiction. I'd like to hear from someone who knew him."

"Sure," Jack answered. "The best of the old-school pilots — men like those I mentioned before, Maynard Lyman, Edwin Johnson and, eventually, pilots like Ray Clarke who followed directly in their footsteps — made the flights better." Jack paused, then added, "Lots better."

"Really? How?"

Jack noticed that Peter had moved further back in his flight chair, had folded his arms and closed his eyes. Like always, Peter was keeping his head in the sand. Jack turned to Linda. "In those days you might question the captain's decisions, but no one in the crew or on the ground ever questioned his authority." He added, "That's why he's called the captain, and that's why being a captain meant more back then. It doesn't mean much any more."

"You're still the captain of this ship," Linda said in a friendly way. "That really hasn't changed."

"The payroll department says I'm the captain," Jack answered. "But everything else — from inter-office memos on through the operations manuals and FAA enforcement decisions — says the opposite."

"Well, you can make a point for it being necessary back then," Linda said. "In the earlier age of aviation before computers and satellites. Don't you think nowadays a flight needs to be more of a team effort?"

"A loaded question. That depends who's on your team," Jack replied. He glanced over at Peter, who was pretending to be ignoring this turn in the conversation. Now, Peter was leaning forward and reading through the flight plan again. "Regardless of the composition of today's team, the team needs a leader. The team needs to take orders from the captain." Jack had decided, based on the long flight to Italy, that his female second officer was competent, intelligent and was attempting to be cooperative. That's more than he could say for his young and hard-headed co-pilot for whom any idea that didn't come out of an official rulebook wasn't worth considering.

Years ago, Jack began dividing pilots into two groups; those who have faced the unthinkable in flight, and those who have not. He was fairly certain that neither Linda nor Peter have ever had a bad experience in the air. In fact, most pilots could put in twenty or thirty years without being in a true life-or-death situation. Jack himself had been in two such situations, both times as the co-pilot, and both times with obviously good results. Since Linda asked, he was going to give her what she asked for. "I'll tell you a story about Ray and me," Jack said.

"Great."

"More than twenty years ago, with Ray as the captain, and me as co-pilot, we were in heavy icing on a heavy-weather winter approach to Pittsburgh. We had a failure with one side of the wing anti-ice equipment at the worst possible time." Jack added a few technical details, then said, "The summation of the story is, and I quote what Ray said to me while my hands were shaking as we taxied in across the blowing snow in an ice-encrusted airplane. 'You've got to be ready and willing to make quick adjustments in whatever direction your experience and intuition tells you. Any flight is capable of going from completely routine to your worst nightmare in less than thirty seconds."

"Sounds like good advice," Linda said. She wasn't absolutely sure that it was, but she was certain that Jack believed it. That was good enough for her, at least for today.

"Yes." Jack paused, then added, "Ray made the right decisions that damned winter night, which is why Ray, me and 150-plus others lived through it."

At that moment the cockpit door opened and Tina walked in. Ray was directly behind her. "Captain, as you requested. Your cockpit visitor has arrived."

"Ray, I think you know Peter Fenton," Jack said. "But I don't think you know Linda Erickson."

"No, I don't." Ray nodded toward Peter Fenton, then stepped around Tina and extended his hand. "Nice to meet you, Linda. I could hear Jack telling one of his many stories while we were walking up."

"A great story. It's a pleasure meeting you, captain." Linda shook hands with him briefly.

"Don't think the title applies. On top of being yesterday's news, I took early retirement and left you folks holding the bag, so to speak."

"Baloney, Ray," Jack said. "Once a captain, always a captain — and you did more with your thirty years at this horrible excuse for an airline than most people could do with fifty. That's the way I look at it, and I'm sticking with that version. Hell, we're *all* sticking with it, right crew?" Jack stole a sideways glance at Peter, more as a reminder than a dare — but, as far as he was concerned, either interpretation of his gesture would do.

"Yes," Peter answered slowly. "Of course." He smiled weakly at Clarke, then returned his attention to the clipboard on his lap.

"Absolutely, Captain Clarke" Linda said. "Jack told me about a particular flight the two of you had. I look forward to hearing more."

"Call me Ray. And don't believe a damned thing Jack says. If you haven't noticed, he exaggerates." Ray glanced at Jack, wondering if this was the time to ask him why the hell he didn't say something about Tina being onboard.

Linda turned in her seat to face Clarke. She smiled at him warmly. "Well, perhaps he does exaggerate about some stories. Taxi drivers in Rome, for example."

"Hey, that story was the absolute truth!" Jack put his hand up against his chest. "You have stuck a knife into my soul with the unjustified thought that I had exaggerated even slightly."

"Folks, I'm going back to work," Tina announced. "We'll have the cabin door closed in a couple of minutes, so unless you guys are screwing it up on this end, I predict an on-time departure." She took a glance at Ray, then turned and walked out of the cockpit.

Jack cleared his throat, then said to Ray, "Nice lady." He looked at Ray to get a read from his expression; he could easily see that Ray was pissed. "I knew that the two of you had been...close friends," Jack continued. "So I thought you might like the surprise."

"It was certainly a surprise." Ray had the urge to grab Jack by the throat and choke him, but he let that pass. Instead, he said, "Maybe – just maybe – you could've given me a heads-up. Then I would've been prepared."

"There's no sense planning a surprise if it isn't one." Jack could tell that his idea of springing Tina on him cold-turkey had gotten its full and desired effect; what Ray Clarke needed, in his opinion, was a couple of good emotional jolts to get his head back on track. It was an adjustment that was long overdue. Jack gestured toward the empty flight chair in the cockpit. "Ray, sit down. Get comfortable."

Ray sat in the extra cockpit seat, the one directly behind the captain's flight chair and slightly elevated so the observer would have an excellent view of everything in the cockpit. "Don't let me interrupt, I'll enjoy the chance to watch."

"Okay. Settle in. I'll drag the crew through the pre-start checklist."

"Right." Ray smiled. When Jack turned away, Ray took a cursory glance around the cockpit. He actually didn't care a single thing about being in the cockpit of an airliner — as he had vowed, that was a part of his life that was behind him. Behind him forever. But there was no way he would insult Jack, a man who had been a great co-pilot for him in the earlier years and had always been a friendly voice in the crew rooms and on overnight layovers whenever they ran across each other in the years that followed. That was particularly true in that year-plus after Katie's death, until Ray could take the early retirement offer. Hell, Jack and his wife Lori had been at Katie's funeral.

Within a few minutes, Jack and his crew had finished their checklist duties. Jack turned in his flight chair to face Ray, who was sitting directly behind him. "Ray, look here," he said, pointing to the fuel gauges on the center instrument panel. "Extra fuel for mom and the kids. I talked to the fueling guy myself — a friendly sort, I've dealt with him in the past. Anyway, I asked him to pump more than I usually take and it looks like he did even better. I asked him for an extra twenty-five hundred pounds of fuel in each of the main tanks and it looks like he put three thousand pounds extra on each side."

"Good to have the fuel," Ray said. Even though he hadn't been inside the cockpit of an airliner for nearly two years, it had been such a big part of his life for so damn long that he began to respond automatically to the sights and sounds surrounding him. He allowed his eyes to roll slowly over the curved lines of the glare shield, the orderliness of the instrument panel, the outcropping of controls and switches on the center console, the sweeping array of the rows of gauges and circuit breakers on the overhead area. As much as he hated to admit it, the cockpit gave him the feeling of being home.

"Yes, extra fuel is good," Jack said. "You're the guy who made me realize how much sense it made to add extra fuel when you thought you might need it. That had to be, what, almost twenty years ago, when I first flew co-pilot for you."

"Trying to make me feel old, right?"

"You *are* old." Jack turned and playfully punched his friend in the arm.

"That business about extra fuel is interesting. What did you tell him?" Linda asked as she leaned forward to be nearer to the exchange between Clarke and the Captain. This turn in the conversation was exactly the sort of piloting detail that she was on full alert for.

"Ray, your quote, you tell her," Jack said. "Go ahead."

Ray turned to the second officer. She was certainly attractive and, in some ways, she reminded him of Katie. Not this lady's appearance, since Katie had long red hair, a round face and dark eyes, but in her tone: just like Katie, this lady had enthusiasm and sincerity in her voice. "You sure you want to hear tales between ancient aviators?" Ray asked.

"Neither of you are ancient and, yes, I'd like to hear it. Very much. I'm always ready to learn something new about this job," Linda said. While her mission to keep the cockpit atmosphere as calm and tranquil as possible was in effect, she was also being sincere; regardless of what they said in the training departments and the official manuals, Linda knew that there was lots to this job that you had to learn on the spot and under the guidance of someone who really *knew*.

"I pointed out what seemed obvious, that it's better to be a little overweight for the takeoff than to be a little out of fuel for the landing. I learned that from the men I flew with when I was a co-pilot." It was a thought that Ray hadn't considered for some time, and he was happy to see that it still sounded logical after so many years.

"Makes sense. But why is weight an issue?" Linda asked.

"Because this fuel is off the books," Peter added, joining in the conversation. Now that this particular bit of unorthodox and illegal procedure was being publicly discussed, he was sure as hell going to get his own two cents in. "We'll have six thousand pounds more on the airplane than the paperwork shows." His tone was neutral, but his message was unmistakable: *this is not right.* There was nothing about the way that Schofield handled this flight that he liked. This only verified what Peter already knew: that pilots like Schofield and this Ray Clarke were aerial dinosaurs and a threat to the safety and stability of the system.

"Peter is a great believer in proper paperwork and following the book rules," Jack said. "I, for one, think the rule book has nice guidelines in it. But they are not stone tablets handed down from above. They are made by men sitting in rooms, sometimes with other agendas on their minds. Quite often, the rule makers couldn't even taxi the airplane, never mind actually fly it. Hence, on this subject, I would rather face a few seconds of exposure to being overweight for takeoff than to ever run the risk of running out of fuel."

"Hey," Jack continued, turning to face Ray. "Did you see the TV special on that US Airways landing on the Hudson River back in 2009? It was the anniversary of that 'Miracle on the Hudson' — that's what they called the show. The media covered it in the papers, too. We've beaten the subject to death between us, but I'd like to get your view."

"No, I didn't see the show," Ray said. "I did see mention of it being broadcast." Ray omitted saying that he had no interest in seeing it, no interest in seeing anything about airplanes. He had, of his own free will, walked away from that part – and more – of his past life. He was headed in a different direction. The only question he hadn't answered yet was, in what direction? And when in God's name was he going to actually get moving? Even he could see that this transition to this new life – whatever the psyco-babble from that book might actually mean – was taking too long. Far too long. Finally, Ray said, "The crew on that US Airways jet did a great job."

"What's your take on the captain's decision to put the Airbus on the river?" Jack asked. "Worked fine for them. Would you have done the same?" Jack knew Ray well enough to figure out his answer, but he wanted Linda – and Peter, too, for that matter – to hear it.

"I'd like to think so," Ray answered. But he was realistic enough to understand that you never knew for *absolutely certain* what a person would do in a critical situation until it actually happened. There were no guarantees in life – as he had painfully learned for himself. "To be honest," Ray continued, getting back to the subject, "Can't imagine anything else."

"Why?" Linda asked. Again, the cockpit conversation had taken another interesting turn – this was lots better than refereeing an endless squabble between Jack and Peter. "Don't you think the crew had other options?"

Ray looked at her. For some inexplicable reason, he was enjoying this conversation. "The crew had choices — they always do. In this instance, the other options were bad. Faced with calm water on an empty Hudson River or 125th Street in Harlem or those crowded New Jersey suburbs on the way to Teterboro, there was no choice. It wasn't *picking* the landing spot that made the captain and crew into worldwide heros — it was the *execution* of the maneuver. That, and the fabulous crew coordination and the text-book evacuation that followed. Plus good fortune in being rescued immediately."

"You were right when you said 'text-book.' From the reports I've seen, it was strictly by the book," Peter added.

Before anyone could answer, they were interrupted by a voice in Italian-accented English coming into the cockpit from the overhead speakers. "Captain, the door she is' a closed and we are ready for' a push back."

"Ladies and gentlemen, it is show time!" Jack announced in a booming voice. He spun around to face forward in his flight chair and punched the interphone button to speak with the driver of the tug while he motioned for Peter to call Rome ground control to get their taxi clearance.

The Consolidated 768 widebody jet, operated as Trans-Continental Flight 3, was at that moment beginning its nine hour and fifty minute nonstop flight to New York. The record would show that they departed Rome on schedule, with a total passenger count of 197 and a flight crew count of eleven. At 1:03 pm Central European Time when the airliner began to taxi across the ramp on its own power, a good portion of the European Continent and the entire Atlantic Ocean lay between Flight 3 and its intended destination.

Chapter Three

"See how things work out for me?" Jack was taxiing the airliner with the tiller wheel in his left hand while he twisted slightly to his right in order to face his co-pilot. "I'll take full credit for this change in plans," he added. Even though he was facing Peter, Jack was addressing everyone in the cockpit of Trans-Continental Flight 3. "I figured this south wind would pick up before we left. With twenty knots from the southeast, Rome would switch the departures from runway 25 to 16 Right. In time for us to have that extra two thousand feet of runway length, right Peter?" Jack laughed.

"We're not legal, if that's what you're getting at. Not with that extra gas onboard." Peter gestured toward the cockpit fuel gauges. They had, by switching runways, gone from being grossly illegal to being slightly illegal. As far as Peter was concerned, it was like being slightly pregnant. "We're considerably overweight, even with the extra runway."

"But not on paper. That's your biggest concern, right?" Jack laughed again. "The paperwork says we're at gross weight for takeoff, but, hell, we're more like ten thousand pounds beyond what the paperwork says when you realize that the airline uses average weights for passengers. Most of them in the back," Jack said as he gestured toward the cabin door, "have been on pasta their entire lives...did you get a look at them when they boarded!"

"That's not the point," Peter said irritably. Arguing with this man was useless, Schofield was going to embrace whatever whim struck him next. But Peter wanted to be clearly on record of being in strong opposition — he knew that the cockpit voice recorder was getting every bit of this. It was the best way to cover his own butt if anything did happen on the flight, and that was what his verbal pronouncements were about. "I'm opposed to making this takeoff before we burn off the extra fuel so we're at the legal takeoff weight."

"Peter, I believe we understand your objections," Jack said in a friendly tone. "I suggest you get ready to fly."

"You're the boss," Peter answered.

"Exactly my point."

Peter turned his attention to his flight panel and checked the navigation instruments one final time. As far as he was concerned, most of these old guys were nothing but cowboys flying airliners. But Peter knew that his protest would end right here and now, just as Schofield knew it. Peter had no intention of doing anything more, like going to the Vice President of flight George Fisher about this violation in airline procedures. It wouldn't do his own reputation any good and, besides, those old timers stuck together. Hell, they still had that *very* old man – Maynard Lyman — working in the flight management office. Lyman was the epitome of old-school thinking, the king of the old school pilots, and it would be like George Fisher to have Maynard Lyman deal with a co-pilot who complained about a captain they held in high esteem.

"Peter, I think you've missed the point," Jack finally said. "The odds of having a total engine failure at exactly the wrong time on takeoff — we're talking about a window of a handful of seconds — is exceedingly remote."

"But..."

"No buts. The odds of needing the extra fuel is greater. I'm playing the odds." Jack knew that what he was really doing was toying with Peter. It was a little entertainment during the long taxi to the far end of the runway. If the truth be known, he was putting on a show for his mentor, too – a mentor who had also become his friend. All of this was pure fun, a sport. Hell, one of the reasons that Jack had put on the extra fuel today — and put on as much as he did, which was on the high side, even for him — was to get Peter's goat, since the New York weather was clear skies and forecast to remain that way. He didn't need the extra fuel for this particular flight but, hey, it didn't hurt and once again, First Officer Peter Fenton had lived up to his up-tight reputation and Jack's expectations. "Experience has told me that fuel in the tanks is far more important than numbers on paper." Jack glanced over his shoulder. "What do you think, Ray?"

"I've eaten too much pasta myself the last two weeks. With me here, you're overweight for sure." Ray didn't give a damn what Peter Fenton thought of him, but he didn't want to get into crew politics even though his own outlook was far more aligned with Jack Schofield than Peter Fenton.

"I did notice you've put on a few pounds," Jack said. Actually, it was a lie since Ray hadn't changed the slightest since the day he retired. Nor, for that matter, had he changed much in the previous ten, fifteen, twenty years — he was one of those men with nearly timeless features. He had grey hair now, a few strands making a minor display at the temples of his reddish-brown hair, but that was it. Excepting for that one additional change in his appearance from the old days. Ever since Katie's death over three years ago, Ray's face had a constant look of weariness – hell, more than weariness. Basically, he looked like shit. "You surprise me, Ray."

"How?"

"Gaining weight was not something I expected, not with the hit you took on your retirement by cashing out so damn early. I assumed by now you'd be penniless and starving to death."

"I would've on the airline pension. Luckily, I made wise investments along the way. I won't run out of food money anytime soon." Ray smiled at Jack, then glanced at the co-pilot. Peter was ignoring him, which is what Ray expected. He knew that Peter didn't care for him—and vice-versa, for that matter. But none of that mattered, since Ray was a short-term visitor in the cockpit, and there was no need to think about Peter. Ray intended to spend nostalgic time with his old friend Jack – he sure as hell was going to tell him not to pull any more surprises on him in the future – and then go back to his seat in the first class cabin for the remainder of the flight.

"Okay, enough of that," Jack announced, as if he had read Ray's thoughts. "Looks like we're number one for takeoff. Linda,"

"Yes sir," Linda answered.

"Tell the cabin attendants we're ready to launch. Takeoff roll in two minutes. Peter, wrap up the checklist. Let's get this crate to New York."

Peter began reading the final pre-takeoff items while Linda finished alerting the cabin attendants. By the time Jack had taxied to the threshold of the runway, they had gotten their takeoff clearance. "Ciao for now, Roma," Jack announced with a laugh, mostly to amuse himself. "Peter, you got it," he said.

"Got it," Peter answered. As was customary, the captain was letting the co-pilot do the hand flying of the airplane on their return flight to New York since the captain had flown the airplane eastbound. Once the airliner was lined up with the centerline of the runway, Peter pushed the throttles with his left hand while he held the flight control column with his right. The jetliner's two enormous power plants began to build up to full power. Slowly, the heavily loaded jet gained speed as they accelerated down the empty ribbon of concrete that measured more than 2 ½ miles long. Finally, Peter tugged on the control column and a few seconds later Trans-Continental Flight 3 left the ground. "Gear up," he called.

"Gear up," Jack responded. He reached across the center console and picked up the landing gear lever. Within several seconds their tires and wheel assemblies were tucked neatly inside the aluminum skin of the jetliner.

"Climb power."

"You got climb power, kid." Jack edged the twin throttles to a slightly lower setting. "Nice view, huh, Ray?" Jack was pointing to the beach passing beneath them; the blue Mediterranean waters were lapping against the white sand. There were only a few scattered beach goers standing on the sand because of today's wind and cool air.

"Yes. Sure is." Ray glanced at the scenery, then at Peter. The co-pilot was doing a nice job with the hand flying, and the instruments agreed that they were flying exactly on the customary profile. Which was a good thing to be able to do, but it wasn't everything. "We should have an excellent view of Corsica today," Ray said. He was, in some ways, surprising himself at how much he was enjoying this display of airmanship and the sights and sounds of being in the front office once again. A stroll down memory lane. But Ray also knew that memory lane was a place that he was dragged down far too often these last few years. If it were up to him and within his powers, Ray would wipe every bit of his memories completely out of his mind.

"Corsica. Right you are. Always one of my favorites," Jack answered. He glanced over the jet's nose but there was nothing as yet. "Soon."

"Yes." Ray watched as Peter engaged the ship's electronic autopilot. That was another marked difference between the younger pilots and the older ones: the younger ones were far quicker to turn on the autopilots and other computer-driven aids, while the older pilots spent more time holding the airplane's controls in their own hands and using the basic flight instruments. Did that make any difference? Ultimately, probably not.

Ray sat in the observer's seat and watched the altimeter on the co-pilot's instrument panel as it continuously wound upward. Although Ray didn't know much about Peter — he and Fenton had, to Ray's memory, only flown together on one trip several months before Ray's retirement — he suspected from the co-pilot's comments so far and his tone that Peter hadn't changed any in the past two years. He was pure new-school.

Peter was a pilot who was high on regulations, procedures and theory. Like so many of the younger generation, they looked to manuals and computers for the answers. But Ray, when he allowed himself to think about it at all, held onto the belief that procedures and technology were a poor substitute for having a basic feel for a developing situation and doing whatever your gut feeling told you might be the best next move. Sometimes your gut told you to closely follow the book, sometimes it didn't. That was what the pilot was for, although the goddamn government and most of today's airline's management people didn't look at it that way. Not anymore.

Ray shrugged; it was thoughts like those that had made him understand it was time to take that early retirement offer; that, and, of course, the idea of getting away from those constant reminders of his life with Katie. Even that stupid self-help psychology book had told him as much. Ray looked out the windshield. "There's Corsica," he announced as he pointed ahead. "I can see it through the haze."

"Right you are, captain," Jack answered. "You haven't lost your route skills yet."

"Maybe." They both laughed.

"Remind me later to tell you," Jack said, "what the major alterations to the basic airplane have been since your retirement, beyond changing the name from Boeing to Consolidated."

"Sure," Ray answered. "I've read the public relations releases." He glanced around the cockpit and, from where he was sitting, it looked and felt like the cockpit of every one of the Boeing 767s that he had flown for thousands of flight hours. Once again, Ray was surprised at how familiar, how comfortable, how *at home* he felt here in the cockpit. He quickly pushed that thought aside because this was nothing but nostalgia; he wanted to turn the page; in fact, he *needed* to turn the page.

"As you probably heard, Boeing had objected strenuously to these modifications."

"Saw that in the newspapers," Ray answered.

"Right. I think there was talk of court action, but once the FAA approved the proposed Consolidated changes, Boeing was glad not to have their name on the end result. That's what I heard," Jack continued.

"Interesting." Ray began looking around the cockpit more closely. From where he sat, most of the ship was pure Boeing — but he could see here and there where alterations had been made and where new switches had been added. Once those changes were finished, the airplane was officially labeled a Consolidated 768. "Do you like it?"

Jack shrugged. "I like the parts that Consolidated left alone, the straight Boeing stuff. The engine controls are new — that was the biggest selling point — and they are much more automatic in what they do, when they do it and why they do it." Jack gestured toward the rows of engine gauges in the center of the instrument panel. "Frankly, it scares the crap out of me because it seems like a cross between black magic and voodoo," he said. "Flying a giant computer has never been one of my heart's desires."

"Frankly, mine, neither," Ray said.

"We're the first airline to get these Consolidated 768s," Jack said. "We got the guinea pig price — our new management can't resist a bargain."

"The old Boeings were fine, but the 768s are far better performers," Peter said as he decided to interject himself into the conversation. He wasn't going to allow these two to get away with bad-mouthing the newer stuff because they didn't understand it. "The engines have integral electronic engine fuel controllers that are totally automatic. They regulate a number of parameters in each engine far beyond what the old Boeing controllers did, so we get optimum fuel efficiency and a far greater service life. The Consolidated 768 modifications have unquestionably worked well, and it was a great deal for the company to buy the conversions as opposed to shelling out more money for new airplanes."

"That so?" Jack said, as much to keep some conversation going as for any other reason; having Ray up here, having Ray participate in a conversation about airplanes was good for him, as far as Jack was concerned.

"Yes. I read the company's accounting figures," Peter answered, "in the latest stockholder's report. Didn't you read it?

"I don't read comic books or stock holder reports," Jack answered. "And if you believe what our new President and his bean-counters have written, then I have a bridge to sell you."

"Just a bridge to sell me?" Peter snapped back, losing his composure. "Why not have me sell ice to the Eskimos if you're going to use worn-out cliches."

"Listen, Peter," Jack said, ignoring Peter's comeback. He leaned over the center pedestal toward the younger man. "You can't believe anything that people like Brandon Kyle might say or have printed in those official company reports they issue. They've been telling us for the past few years that this company is losing money big-time, yet the airplanes are full. How's that? Hell, he's telling everybody that you're overpaid and under-worked — do you believe that, too? Kyle reminds me of the man behind the curtain in 'The Wizard of Oz.'"

"The wizard of what?" Peter asked.

"Never mind." Jack laughed again, then turned away and busied himself by putting away the Rome departure charts and getting out the en route charts they'd be using next.

"I read the company internal report," Peter continued, not wanting to give up his edge in this nonsensical debate on new versus old technology. Peter turned from Jack and toward Ray. At least this retired pilot didn't raise an idiotic objection every time Peter pointed something out. "Every indication so far is that these new Consolidated 768 aircraft will save both fuel and engine life, as they've been designed to do. They're worth the money."

"The 767s were doing an efficient job," Ray said. "That's what I was told." For some reason, he felt a need to defend the old Boeing that he had spent so many years with, although he didn't want to get into an argument with Peter. The fact that he cared was a surprise to him.

"The 767s were fine airplanes. Consolidated left nearly all the basic Boeing systems installed just as they were," Peter said. "What Consolidated did was to add additional systems, additional layers of automation and computer control above and beyond what the old Boeings were designed with. Remember, the Boeing 767 is an old design that initially began service back in 1982, while this airplane is very modern and very high tech. The Consolidated 768 is basically the old Boeing 767 on electronic steroids."

Ray knew that Boeing had continuously updated the original 767 design over the years, but he wasn't going to say anything that might begin a debate. Actually, he didn't feel like debating with anyone about any subject, and hadn't for some time. That was especially true about airplanes and airlines. "Where I'm sitting, it looks like a Boeing to me," Ray said as he waved his hand around the cockpit. "Makes me comfortable."

"It's a comfortable airplane," Peter answered. "Both the Boeing version and the Consolidated version."

"Right." Even though it had been nearly two years since he had been in command of one of these airplanes, Ray surprised himself by clearly remembering so many of the technical details about the Boeing jet where he had spent thousands and thousands of flight hours. He could see that this Consolidated variation, this modification on that basic trustworthy airliner, wasn't much different in that regard. *Comfortable.* Yes, Ray had been comfortable. Once. Ray sighed, then glanced at the altimeter. It was time. He unbuckled his seatbelt, then announced, "We're out of 20,000 feet, so I'll take your leave and sample that good cabin service I've been reading about in the travel ads."

"Sure. But I want you to come back after you've eaten." Jack patted his old friend on the shoulder as he turned to leave the cockpit. "Don't be late. I've got war stories to swap during the Atlantic crossing. Gossip, too." That was when Jack was going to get more direct with Ray about how he was getting along these days – *really* getting along – and what his plans for the future might be. The conversation after that would depend on what Ray said, but Jack intended to give it to him straight – no bullshit, no tippy-toes. "Peter will be on his cabin break then," Jack added, "since we want him fresh for another of his superb landings in New York." Jack grinned at Peter, who was, at that point, completely ignoring him. Jack turned to Ray. "Okay with you?"

"Certainly." Ray had hoped he could stay in the first class cabin, but with Peter on break and the airliner tucked at cruising altitude, maybe he and Jack could have a pleasant, low-key visit with each other. That was when he would clear up this business about being surprised by Tina. "I'll come back when I'm done eating."

"Great. You can slide into the co-pilot's seat if Linda won't mind. This way, I won't get a sore neck turning around to talk." Jack had already decided that, after Ray returned, he'd have Linda take a cabin break for fifteen minutes so the two of them could have some privacy. Then, if he didn't like what the hell Ray was telling him, he read him the fucking riot act.

"Fine with me," Linda said to the both of them. "I'll sit here when Ray returns. I look forward to those stories." She smiled at him.

Ray laughed. "Tell me that after you've heard them. Then maybe I'll believe you." He turned and stepped slowly toward the cockpit door, as if he were reluctant to leave. Ray had, to his surprise, enjoyed his time up front more than he had expected, and he knew damn well that what he was about to face in the cabin wasn't going to be pleasant. As he put his hand on the cockpit door, Ray stopped for a moment, puzzled.

For an instant Ray thought that he heard something; no, not heard something but *felt* something. Something new, something unusual. It was, he was beginning to realize, a very small vibration – a continuous low frequency pulsation that seemed to be coming *through* the door frame and into the door knob with a discernible harmonic pattern.

Ray turned at the rear of the cockpit; he was going to mention it to the flight crew, but he stopped. Jack was talking casually to Linda, and Peter was fiddling with the autopilot. None of the three of them were taking notice. If they had sensed anything, they would certainly have reacted to it. Ray decided that it must be his nerves, or that fucking anxiety crap like the book said, or....

Ray laid his hand more carefully against the door knob. This time, he could feel nothing. Nothing whatsoever. Whatever it had been had disappeared. Completely. If, in fact, there had been any at all. Maybe a periodic small vibration of that sort was a normal occurrence in this Consolidated version of the old

Boeing. Or, maybe, probably, it was just Ray's imagination – a combination of having been away from the flight deck and its particular noises and sensations for the past two years, and a creation of his own mental baggage that he was dragging along with him like a ball and chain.

Yes, a ball and chain. That was a damn good name for the mental weights he carried, like a reincarnation of an evil spirit. What amazed Ray the most, though, was that he *knew* what the problem was – his fixations about Katie and his endless associations with the past that were irrevocably tied to it. But knowing and verbalizing those associations hadn't made a goddamn difference, in spite of what that book had said. He was, evidently, destined to keep his ball and chain; after all, he had more than earned it. Ray shook his head, opened the cockpit door and walked out.

He headed for the fourth row in first class on the aircraft's left, seat 4A. Even before he reached the seat, Ray was rehearsing his opening lines for the inevitable conversation that he needed to have with Tina when she sat herself down in seat 4B.

Ray sat down and strapped himself in. Tina and the other first class flight attendant — Annette, as he recalled — were standing in the opposite aisle serving the first course on the lunch menu. Tina glanced at him and their eyes met. She gave a little wave, and he waved back.

Ray knew that the two first class flight attendants would work their way around the cabin and be getting to him soon. Shortly after that, the lunch service would be completed and the inflight movie would begin on the individual monitor screens at each seat. With the cabin quiet for the long-haul cruise segment, Tina would come over and the conversation between the two of them would start. Finally.

Ray knew that he had put off this conversation for too long, and he knew that it wasn't going to be an easy conversation. It was going to be painful because, basically, nothing had changed. For either of them.

This was a conversation that Ray needed to have. He shouldn't have waited this long, and ignoring it was no longer an option, thanks to his friend Jack. For a moment, Ray could imagine what would have happened if Jack had, in fact, told him that Tina was onboard Flight 3; Ray probably would've run from the terminal like a scared rabbit and come back for tomorrow's flight, or next week's, or, maybe, never. Then he'd be forced to take up residence in Italy, somewhere far to the north, hidden in the mountains....

Ray laughed when that image flashed across his thoughts: *macho ex airline pilot runs hysterically through the Rome's terminal to get away from pursuing flight attendant.* Ray took a few deep breaths, shook his head, then glanced at his wristwatch, which he had set back six hours to New York time: 7:42 am. By 10:00 am, Ray knew that he and Tina — a woman he had shared so many good and so many bad moments with — would be talking about the things they should have dealt with a long time ago. It would be worse than reading that *Anxiety and Guilt* book. He'd be writing himself into that book as the main subject.

Book Two

Ignorance is the curse of God; knowledge is the wing wherewith we fly to heaven
>—William Shakespeare

I really don't know one plane from the other. To me they are just marginal costs with wings.
—Alfred Kahn, Chairman, Civil Aeronautics Board

Chapter Four

Albert DeWitt stood at the window of what had been his office for the past seven months and looked casually down at the Manhattan early morning traffic twenty-eight floors below. It was a cold, breezy day in New York, with a forecast high temperature to reach the upper twenties. The good news was that the skies were clear and there was no chance of snow.

Albert DeWitt – Al, to his many friends – took a sip from his coffee mug, then glanced at the wall clock. The young lady from the magazine was due to arrive at 8:30 am, so he had time to indulge himself with no distractions because the department secretaries wouldn't arrive until 9:00 am. Other than the interview, Al didn't have much to do except a few special goodbyes since he had covered that sort of thing at the party the department gave him yesterday afternoon. Other than his coffee mug, his pen set and the photos of Alice and the girls, he had cleaned out his desk and taken home his personal items.

Al was a free man. With his pension, his earned stock options and the savings he had accumulated over the years — he had never been much of a spender and had earned a decent salary — he would be financially independent for the rest of his life. The only thing he might run out of was time, but since he was in good health he figured that account had a positive balance to it.

For the first time in forty-four years Al would call the shots for every minute of every day of his life, as soon as this final assignment was behind him. A public relations industry magazine had called two days ago with a surprise request: they wanted to interview Al for a feature story on his long and distinguished career.

Al had been with Trans-Continental Airlines since he was twenty-one years old. He held various jobs and titles, ending up as the Director of Public Relations and Marketing for the last twenty-plus years. The airline had grow from a small company to a large International corporate entity while he went from a young to an old man. It was the only place he had ever worked; today was Al's sixty-fifth birthday.

Al sighed. He turned from the window and faced the desk. Today he was feeling nostalgic about every damned thing he looked at, even that old desk that had traveled from office to office with him. Yet he knew that he shouldn't be such a sentimental old fool, that when all was said and done it was just a goddamn desk. Al smiled, but continued to allow his thoughts to wander.

The only thing missing at the official finish line of his forty-four year career with Trans-Continental Airlines was his wife. It had been four years since her death, yet it seemed like hardly yesterday when their thirty-nine years of shared life had ended. Retiring without Alice at his side was his only regret in his life. A knock at the door brought Al back to the moment. "Come in," he said as he put down his coffee cup.

The door opened. "Good morning, Mister DeWitt. Jennifer Lane from *Public Relations World Magazine.* I've got to start by apologizing for being early. The guard said you were up here, so he told me go right up."

"Glad he did." *Wow.*

Jennifer walked toward DeWitt with her hand extended. "Getting this assignment has been a real pleasure for me. From what I've read, you've had a fascinating career."

"Hardly," Al responded. "But it's had a few interesting moments." He smiled broadly as he took the young woman's hands in his and held them. She had long, flowing red hair, soft brown eyes and an overall appearance of composure and competence. She was wearing a very stylish outfit of black pants and a purple leather jacket. A long overcoat hung from her left arm, with a briefcase slung from a shoulder strap across her left side. One gorgeous lady. "Please call me Al. My friends do."

"Thank you, Al." Jennifer paused, then said, "I apologize again for being so darn early. Everything took less time than I planned. I got a taxi immediately, the driver spoke recognizable English and there was no traffic." Jennifer watched Al's eyes as she allowed herself to ramble on. She had always been good at sizing up a person's response by watching their eyes, and today

44

would be particularly crucial. "It's good karma to start the day with, but that did put me here considerably ahead of schedule."

"Extra time for making this article special. That's good." Al slowly removed his hands from hers. This gorgeous and cutting-edge-sharp lady was one heck of a bonus for doing a simple end-of-career magazine interview. "Good karma for the both of us."

"That would be nice."

"Right." Al gestured toward the wall. "Put your coat on that hook. We can get started. Early is no problem, I have nothing to do the rest of my life."

"Doubt that," Jennifer answered. "From what I've read, you're not the type." Albert DeWitt was indeed a handsome man — a little over six foot tall, slender, with a full head of flowing hair that was considerably peppered with grey, and a neatly trimmed grey mustache that rode above his expressive mouth and those very white teeth. But there was more to it than being a handsome older man – he had an instantly appealing nature about him. That would be useful in the retirement article angle, and it would make everything else more believable. Jennifer hung her coat. "A photographer from the magazine will be arriving between nine-thirty and ten. Is that okay?"

"Certainly."

"Like to get started?" Jennifer reached for a notebook from her shoulder bag. "We've got a very successful career to document, and our audience will want details." She sat in the upholstered chair opposite his desk. Jennifer had a game plan on how to work this man to get what she was after and, so far, the setup had been perfect.

"Coffee first?" Al pointed to the coffee maker on the side table. "Got fresh cream to go with it, none of that powdered junk."

"Yes, thank you."

He stepped toward the office refrigerator beneath the sideboard. "How do you take it?"

"Cream would be nice. I don't like that powered stuff, either."

"Sugar?"

"No."

"Just the way I take it." Al made the two coffees, handed hers over, then sat in the other upholstered chair beside her rather than at his desk. "Where would you like to start?"

"As usual, I'm not quite sure," she lied. Jennifer knew, from her extensive research, that this interview for the public relations magazine would be proper cover for the bigger piece – the high-budget, high-paying exposé for *Business World Media* that they'd been planning for the past several weeks. Her actual assignment was to gather the final material for a mega-feature on what was being called the long rise and the dramatic fall of Trans-Continental Airlines. Stumbling on this retirement article idea a couple of days ago had been very fortunate, and it had turned into her ticket of admission. "As I mentioned on the phone, while I'm learning about the airline I'll be interspersing those facts with your own personal history and your observations."

"Understand," Al answered. "We'll sort of wing it, if you'll pardon the airline-related metaphor."

"Exactly." She smiled. "After the photographer arrives we'll take the corporate shots. Then you and I will take a cab to the airport to get pictures of you with airplanes in the background. We can't do a story about an airline person without visuals of airplanes to go with it." While she was at the airport, she knew what other names she had to wangle an invitation to speak with.

"Sounds like a plan." Al sipped his coffee while he kept his eyes on the intelligent, attractive lady that he would be spending the first day of his retirement with. "Matter of fact," Al said, "as you requested, before we head for the airport I've arranged to spend a few minutes with our President, Brandon Kyle. He's expecting us in his office at 9:15."

"Very nice." Jennifer added, "From what I've read, Brandon Kyle is relatively new at the airline." That was her opening salvo. She had pointedly asked in her telephone conversation with DeWitt if it were possible to get interviews with higher-ups – the President of the airline, in particular. That would be a nice touch for the personality profile. Spending face time with Brandon Kyle was what she wanted – no, *needed* – so that she could get the *Business World Media* piece launched in the proper direction. Using Albert DeWitt as her entry to see

46

Kyle was the only way to get in to the airline President, according to what the insider on the Trans-Continental Board had told them. Kyle and his group were not granting any interviews so their plans would remain below the media's radar.

According to the leaks from their single source at the upper level of Trans-Continental, Kyle and his select group from the Board of Directors had developed an astonishing, aggressive plan: because of mounting financial losses, they would shut down the airline, dismantle it and sell off the pieces for more than the whole *enchilada* was worth as an operating entity. It was, as Kyle would say, the only way to maximize the value for the majority of the debt holders and key financial institutions with the prospects for airline businesses in general looking so bleak for the foreseeable future.

The only losers in this secret mega-bucks deal would be the common stockholders and the airline employees since neither of those groups would be getting much of anything – the common stockholders would get pennies on the dollar, and the employees, zip. The preferred stock holders and the bigger financial institutions holding various company bonds and other financial instruments would be well taken care of. It was also rumored that the upper-crust executives would be getting a *huge* golden parachute from this deal – a deal that was supposed to come down in the very near future. The insider information being fed to them would be the crux for the upcoming *Business World Media* blitz.

"Yes, Brandon Kyle is relatively new. He replaced our previous President three years ago."

"And he came directly from some large truck leasing conglomerate?" Jennifer asked, although she already had every detail of Brandon Kyle's corporate life nailed. "My understanding is that he had no airline background whatsoever, which is quite a counterpoint to your own career. As you know, most marketing people float through a great many industries in their working lives," Jennifer said, continuing with the setup exactly along the strategic lines that she had mapped out.

"That's what I hear," Al answered.

"Right. Which is another point that makes you unique." Jennifer had decided that the key to this Albert DeWitt interview for *Public Relations World Magazine* would be his stability. She would, in fact, actually be doing that personality interview and the PR article – a small one, of course – in addition to her main objective of getting the very first coverage on the upcoming dissolution of the airline. Jennifer would use that angle – stable employees trapped in an unstable corporate jungle – in the exposé on Kyle and his cohorts in the *Business World Media* coverage. "You not only remained in one industry, but you also stayed with a single company. That, in itself, is unusual. What can you tell me about that?"

Al paused, then shrugged. "I guess I like airlines. Trans-Continental was a good one."

"Was?" Jennifer perked up; here was her first opening.

After a delay of a few moments, Al grinned. "Did you hear me say 'was'? I was pretty certain that I had said 'is.' Yes, I'm positive of it. Trans-Continental *is* a good airline."

"Then 'is' it indeed will be." Jennifer nodded and made a notation on her pad. , She knew enough not to push it. Not yet, anyway, so she focused back on her cover story. It was obvious that the key to Albert DeWitt would not only be his stability but also his maturity and elegant grace. That would make a good counterpoint to the cold efficiency of a hatchet man like Brandon Kyle, and she could work that into the main story, too. Another bonus. "How did you like the corporate decision to move the upper executives to Manhattan this past summer?"

"The President made the argument that it made good corporate sense. Manhattan is where the financial and corporate business opportunities are." Al purposely omitted what he normally added when talking to his close friends, that the airline's new corporate offices were – coincidentally, of course – lots closer to Kyle's Manhattan penthouse apartment.

"So you agreed with President Kyle's decision to separate the corporate executives from the operations environment?"

"Don't recall that he asked me." Al sat back and smiled; being officially retired was giving him more wiggle room than he had ever had in his career, although up until a few years ago he hadn't needed much. Vernon Wells, the previous airline president, had been steeped in the airline business and had been with Trans-Continental for twenty-plus years. He was a smart man and a nice man. Al had gotten along nicely with Vernon Wells, and he was sorry to see him forced out.

Brandon Kyle had taken over almost three years ago after that special stockholder uprising and soon thereafter the new president began making his Wall Street style moves. Since then, the airline had been in a metaphorical tailspin at jet speed. They were spending money like drunken sailors, and the losses were mounting. The corporate move to Manhattan was a *huge* expense, and a frivolous one. Al felt that Kyle was, in one arrogant bundle, everything that an airline president shouldn't be. Although he was tempted for an instant by his new sense of freedom — Al was, after all, no longer an employee of Trans-Continental Airlines — his basic corporate instincts prevented him from saying anything impetuous or controversial during a press interview.

"So," Jennifer said, leaning closer to Al, "I saw indications that many of the old time airline folks don't think much of President Kyle or his recent corporate moves in reference to long-time employees and even this corporate upper echelon move to Manhattan. What's your opinion?"

Al paused, then said, "You're asking this for the article, for the record?"

"Certainly."

"Then here's my quotable comment — I was happy to do my part to make these transitions called for by the new President as efficient as possible."

"I see." Jennifer waited a moment, then added, "Tell me this. If it had been up to you, would you have moved the Trans-Continental executives to Manhattan?"

"Easy answer. Wasn't up to me."

"Good answer." Jennifer made a note on her pad, but in her mind she was beginning to shift gears. This man was sharper than she thought he would be. Working through her cover story to get into the information she had come for might take longer than she had expected.

"Right." Al took a sip of his coffee, then added, "The only possible answer." Looking at her, he could see the twinkle in her eye and that growing little smirk at the corners of her lips. He had the feeling – a feeling that she was distinctly conveying – that they were purposely engaged in communications at two levels. As Al well knew, the entrapping smile of a beautiful young woman could be summoned up specifically for making an older man feel comfortable and special. Usually for a specific reason, too. At the moment he didn't know what that reason could be. "Kyle and his people have their business priorities," Al said. "They make the rules. I call the subsequent plays for the Public Relations and Marketing departments. Up until yesterday, that was my job. That's exactly what I did. It was what they paid me for. No more, no less."

"You're being too modest." Jennifer picked up her coffee cup and took a long sip. "The coffee is good." Jennifer paused. Her instincts told her that, maybe right now, it was time to push a little. "I think I hear you telling me something." She paused again, then said, "What do you really think about Brandon Kyle? Outside of this interview, off the record."

"Off the record?" Could she be trusted? Certainly and obviously not. But, Al wondered, aside from this little sporting game where they were each trying to outfox the other, did it make any difference what he said, now that he was officially retired? I mean, who ultimately cared what Al DeWitt's opinion was?

"Yes. Off the record. I was wondering. Between the two of us. A sort-of heads-up for me."

"Fine. Then here's my off the record answer." Al paused, smiled, then added, "He's a jerk."

Jennifer laughed. "Well, that certainly says it all." She put down her coffee cup, picked up her pad and made a short notation.

"Hold it," Al said. He knew that he needed to protest or she might catch on to what he was doing, how he was giving the appearance of allowing her to toy with him when, in fact, he was the one who had thrown out the bait and was doing the trawling. Al's internal radar had been lit to full bright; he had a strong feeling that this overqualified lady was not here to do a simple end of career interview. She was up to something. It would be an interesting challenge to find out what it might be. "Time out. No fair." Al pointed to the pad. "You said that comment was off the record. I need to hold you to that."

"What I wrote was about you."

"Me?"

"Yes. Personal notes." Jennifer knew that she was going to do something like this; to her surprise, what she had written

50

had been easy to come up with because it appeared to be true. She turned her pad and pointed to the bottom entry. "There. Read for yourself, if you can make out my chicken scratching."

Al looked at the pad. Written at the bottom, were four words in her flowing handwriting: *honest, sincere, mature, gracious.* "Very kind of you."

"Very truthful." Jennifer smiled warmly. "Now," she announced as she turned the pad around so she could write, "I need to ask for additional details about your personal life." For a fleeting moment, Jennifer thought about Doug — her ex boy friend of three years whom she had broken up with this past October. If she were to describe Doug in four words, they would be *dishonest, insincere, immature, graceless.*

"You'll discover my personal life has been pretty ordinary," Al said. He waited for more.

"Personality interviews need to launch with what you might think are ordinary details. You can never tell which of those details would be a focus point," Jennifer answered, using another of her canned phrases. "I know some from what I've read, but I do need to touch on the tragic death of your wife. That was four years ago from cancer, correct?"

Al nodded. "Yes."

"Your two daughters?"

"Wonderful girls. Grown and married. Stephanie and Carol. Stephanie is divorced, but it was for the best…"

"Let's hear more about them." Jennifer glanced at the wall clock behind her, then looked at Al. She smiled softly. "You can provide me with the details of your personal and family life now," Jennifer added. She was being sincere. Now that she had met him, she knew that the cover piece she was doing for *Public Relations World* could be an interesting and insightful profile of a pleasant and competent man. That was icing on the cake, and it would help soften the sensation that their *Business World Media* group was only out for blood. "Good background material to get the article going. Makes for good reading."

"Okay."

"Besides," Jennifer said, gesturing over her shoulder, and with an added hint of lightness and mischief in her voice, knowing full well that she had gotten the two of them to where she wanted. "I see we've got plenty of time until we're due upstairs to meet President Jerk."

Chapter Five

From the thirtieth floor of the new Trans-Continental Airlines executive offices in midtown Manhattan, William Wesson glanced out the window and allowed his thoughts to drift while he waited for the airline President to get off the telephone. Wesson knew that he had played his part well since he had signed on as the Vice President of Legal Affairs for Trans-Continental almost two years earlier and, since then, he had unquestionably become Brandon Kyle's team captain. Now, all he had to do was to take the rest of the ride. Along with Kyle and the other insiders on the Trans-Continental Board, William Wesson would soon be a very rich man. Retiring before he reached fifty years of age had been a great personal goal to have, and it now looked very attainable.

"As always, it becomes a matter of timing," Brandon Kyle said as he hung up the telephone and turned to Wesson. Kyle rubbed his hands, walked over to his deep-cushioned office chair and sat down. "With the new President of the United States taking office today, I expect that very soon we'll be seeing the first displays of that aggressive economic agenda we were planning on. Everything is on track."

"Right."

The inter-office buzzer on Kyle's desk telephone console sounded. "Excuse me," Kyle said as he reached for the handset. "Yes?" He paused a moment, then said, "Fine. Send them in." He put the handset down. "We've got company."

"Who?"

"I may have forgotten to mention this minor interruption. As you know, our esteemed Director of Public Relations and Marketing, Albert DeWitt, officially retired from Trans-Continental yesterday. I had to break away from a conference call with our senior board members – our special team members – to attend his farewell party."

"I heard about his retirement." Wesson had worked directly with Al DeWitt on a few small projects in the past several months. But Wesson had been careful to remain at arm's length from the man because he knew that Kyle didn't care for him. Besides, DeWitt would already be retired before the final aspects of Kyle's plan to break up the airline could be put into place. The Director of Public Relations and Marketing was a non-player in the bigger scheme of things. "Is DeWitt coming?"

"Yes. With a reporter from a trade publication. They're doing a feature article on him."

"Reporter?" Wesson looked quizzically at Kyle.

"I know what you're thinking," Kyle said. He smiled. "My instructions on absolutely no media contact by any of our special team members remains in full effect. I simply offered to say a few parting words about DeWitt's exemplary career and his forty-four years with Trans-Continental. Got my notes on my desk," Kyle said as he reached for a packet of papers sitting on his in-box.

"I understand," Wesson answered, even though he didn't understand. Kyle had been emphatic with everyone on the special team – Kyle's own term for the insider's group that was engineering this top-secret corporate maneuvering – that they were forbidden to talk to any media person about any subject whatsoever until the corporate financial deal was locked down.

"William, greet them while I glance through the notes."

"Sure." Wesson rose from his chair and stepped toward the door as it opened.

Al DeWitt stepped in, with a young lady behind him. "Hello, William. Didn't know you'd be here. Allow me to introduce Jennifer Lane," Al announced.

"Pleasure to meet you," Wesson said. He stepped toward the lady with his hand extended. "I'm William Wesson, Vice President of Legal Affairs. President Kyle told me about the upcoming interview. We're certainly excited about it. But I didn't catch the name of the magazine." The two of them shook hands, and Wesson did everything he could to not openly stare at her; the woman was a knockout.

"*Public Relations World Magazine*," Jennifer said. "We're pleased to include comments about the retirement of Mr. DeWitt from both you and President Kyle." She smiled at Wesson who, to her, looked like someone that central casting had sent over to play the part of the company lawyer. He had that corporate attorney look, a strange blend of intensity and vacuousness, and her instincts told her that this man was a big part of whatever was going down at Trans-Continental – in fact,

54

his name was on her list. She would make a point of getting pictures of him, too – he would be good grist for the *Business World Media* coverage. "We won't take much of your time, but I'd like to chat with you, also."

"Take all the time you'd like," Brandon Kyle announced as he stepped from behind his desk and toward the group. "With any of us. Although I don't believe any of us have enough time to list the things Albert DeWitt has done for this airline in his enormously long career. This company is certainly going to miss him." Kyle patted DeWitt on the shoulder.

"This is our president, Brandon Kyle." Al ignored the pat on his shoulder; whenever he was with Kyle, Al knew that his bullshit monitor was going to get a real workout. He turned to Jennifer. "Mr. Kyle came to my office party yesterday and gave me a gold watch and his best wishes." Al pulled out his new gold pocket watch, glanced at it, then put it away. "A nice gift, although in retirement, I'm not sure I'll be checking the time much."

"You will. You're not hibernating, you're retiring," Jennifer said, making general conversation while trying to feel out the best direction to go next. These next few minutes would be critical, she had to move cautiously. "You'll find something that will call for that new watch soon enough."

"Nice of you to say that," Al answered. "Don't know what I'll do next, if anything."

"I'm certain you'll find something suitable," Kyle said to inject himself into the conversation. While he was standing there, a clever idea popped into Kyle's head: he could make a small gesture which would get him a nice mention in a national trade magazine. With what was on the horizon for the airline, a smattering of good personal PR wouldn't hurt his credibility, and the gift itself might help deflect any notion of what they were about to do. "William and I were talking about when would be best to present Albert with his additional surprise. Looks like you've provided the opportunity."

"Yes," Wesson answered. He took a half step forward, being careful not to edge past his boss, either physically or conversationally. Wesson had no idea what this was about.

Jennifer reached for her pad. "I'm honored to be part of this breaking news event," she said. Jennifer knew, from studying his history, that Brandon Kyle had the requisite credentials for modern corporate America. He was 56 years old, wore an expensive suit capped off with a designer tie, he had gone to the right prep schools and business schools, and had worked at various management levels in different industries. His oval face, sculptured hair, pursed lips and wire-rim glasses created the proper image. Yet somehow, in person, he seemed smaller than the aura he had created about himself – not physically, but in the stature of his personality. Small. Like Doug.

Jennifer had the suspicion that what Kyle was about to say was a load of crap being spread specifically for her benefit, but she could tell from the expression on Al's face that he had no idea what it might be. That, alone, might provide an opening for her. "Go ahead."

"I was hoping to have the actual documents before you arrived," Kyle said, "but they're not ready. I'll make a verbal presentation." Kyle made a mental note to have his secretary get something in writing, suitably elaborate, worked up as soon as DeWitt and the reporter left his office. Kyle stepped up to DeWitt and grabbed his hand. "Albert, because you've worked so diligently for this airline for the past 44 years, we are proud to present you with this extra retirement present on behalf of myself and the Board of Directors: two first class positive-space travel passes good for the next year for unlimited trips anywhere in the world that Trans-Continental flies, for you and any companion of your choice. We sincerely hope that you'll take the time to use it."

"Thank you. Thank you very much." Al wasn't sure that he wanted to travel anywhere at this juncture in his life — he had seen most of the world from an airliner's window seat the past forty-four years — and he didn't have anyone to travel with, either. But he had to admit, it was a nice gesture. If it hadn't come from Brandon Kyle, it would have been even nicer. "I'm honored."

The office door opened and the man who was the magazine photographer walked in, escorted by Kyle's secretary. "Roger Corbis from the magazine," the secretary announced. "I knew you'd want him to come right in."

"Yes, Nancy. Perfect timing," Kyle said. He stepped around DeWitt and put his arm around him. "This is a definite photo opportunity."

The photographer glanced at Jennifer, who gave a subtle nod. "Let's have the two of you gentlemen move to your left," he said as he took a camera out of its bag and began making adjustments. "Won't take but a few minutes." He began clicking off pictures while he instructed the men to turn this way and that.

Jennifer watched the action. Eventually, she would get in a few of the pictures herself, and getting those photographs would be a part of her *prima facie* evidence package that the interviews with Kyle and Wesson had, in fact, taken place. Jennifer took notes here and there, but she knew where this part of the article – both articles – would be headed. Once the photographer was finished, she'd interview each of these corporate bigwigs separately. During the interviews she would push them, but not too much. They might complain later that their comments were fabricated or taken out of context, but, hell, who could really tell at that point – right?

But for Al DeWitt, it was a different story. Here was a real gentlemen who was proving himself to be sharp and intelligent, who had spent his entire life working at one company, and who had evidently done a damn good job of it. Writing that short personality profile about Al DeWitt would be an easy thing to do.

Chapter Six

Captain Maynard Lyman sat at the desk in his office. Through the open doorway to the next room he could see the man who was seated at the inner office desk. "George, did I remind you that Al DeWitt is coming over with that magazine reporter this morning?" he called out. "Be here any minute."

"What? Captain George Fisher took his eyes off the never ending paperwork that ran across his desk like a swift river. He glanced at his assistant in the next room. "What did you say?"

"That you should put a fresh battery in your hearing aid." Lyman paused, then added, "Hard to believe that I'm old enough to be your father, and you're the one who's going deaf."

"Selective hearing," George answered. "I only hear what I consider worth listening to."

"Then you should hang on my every word," Maynard said in that slow monotone of his. He smiled at the man in the adjacent office who was, technically, his direct boss.

George nodded toward his friend. "Right. I'll check my hearing aid later. Tell me what you said."

"Al DeWitt. Be here any minute."

"You reminded me. Twice, matter of fact. You told me to expect them at 10:00." George glanced at the wall clock: 9:58. "Your memory is failing faster than the rest of your body."

"Certainly is." Maynard smiled and waved his hand in a gesture that showed that none of that was a concern to him. Matter of fact, it was a topic the two of them often discussed. "My body's going to win this race by losing. I predict that I'll remember my own name when I breath my last."

"I'd cover that bet the other way," George answered as they continued their customary bantering. "I base that on what you did with that stack of memos about the parallel approaches to San Francisco".

"Those? It was bullshit," Maynard answered.

"But it was *necessary* bullshit."

"Now, what you just said, now that's top-grade manure. Everything in those memos from that unqualified group of know-it-alls on the west coast wasn't worth a damn. None of it deserved to be commented on, never mind saved."

"Well, you might be right about those particular memos on the San Francisco approaches," George answered after a slight pause. He had already decided that Maynard had, as usual, been right. When it came to airline flying, Maynard had an incredible way of seeing right through whatever fog might be laying over a question; he had x-ray intuition.

"Glad you agree, although it's late to do otherwise. I shit-canned the whole file yesterday."

"Should have checked with me first," George said, although he didn't mean it and he knew that Maynard knew that, also. Maynard didn't need to check with George about anything, not as far as George was concerned.

"Guess I forgot."

"You forget lots of things. I hope you're not getting too old for this paper-shuffling job." While they often joked about it, George was increasingly concerned that the legendary Captain Maynard Lyman was showing his age. Regardless, he had the respect and complete trust of the pilot group, and that went a long way in getting things done around this place. Besides, Maynard needed this administrative job after he pissed away most of his lump-sum pilot's retirement ten years earlier by handing it to those three-piece suits hawking bad investments. Being a legendary genius with an airliner didn't mean you had a lick of sense about finances and money schemes. History showed the opposite as far as many airline pilots were concerned.

"Never too old for this job." Maynard stood up behind his desk. "This job calls for no memory, no intelligence and no ambition. You're going to have a hell of a time finding a replacement as well qualified as me."

"Certainly will. You are uniquely qualified." George sat back in his office chair, smiled, then made a small hand gesture for his friend to keep coming into his office. In reality, George knew that Maynard was incredibly qualified for this special assistant job because of his personality and his history. Even though Captain Maynard Lyman hadn't actively flown an airliner in more than fourteen years since his retirement, he knew his stuff and he could communicate it to the rank and file pilots better than anyone. "I'm glad Al wanted to include us in his end-of-career interview. You've got to admire him, he's a prince of a guy. The only straight shooter on the corporate side of the house. How he puts up with the craziness inside the Puzzle Palace," he said, using their private name for Trans-Continental's corporate offices in Manhattan, "is beyond me. He deserves his retirement." George paused. "Remind me not to say that when the reporter gets here."

"I'll cover your flank."

"Right." George looked closely at Maynard, who seemed to be aging a year or more with every passing month. The lines on his face were deeper, his white hair was sparser than it had been, and that ever-present thin smile on that round face of his seemed to be evaporating. "Sit down. Let's talk about what we should say to this reporter."

"Don't worry." Maynard sat in a chair in front of George's desk. "Al will take care of us. He'll steer the conversation along safe lines. Always does."

"Probably." George nodded, but his thoughts were on the man in front of him. Maynard was a wonderful guy who had once been a truly great airline pilot and would always be a trusted companion. For those reasons and many more, George periodically pleaded with the company President and the Board of Directors to add something to what was left of Maynard's pitiful retirement annuity. "How are you feeling? You look pale." Actually, he always looked pale these days.

"Okay. A little tired, maybe."

"Right." George almost had a special deal for Maynard approved when Vernon Wells was booted out and Brandon Kyle took over. Now, that was in doubt — hell, so was Maynard's job, for that matter. If George hadn't convinced Kyle that Maynard's contacts within the pilot group would be valuable in the upcoming labor negotiations, Kyle would have replaced him with a kid getting half the salary.

What would happen next was anyone's guess, and George had done everything he could for his old friend, a man he had often flown co-pilot for during his own early and most impressionable years with the airline. These days, with Maynard's help, George had kept an inside track on developments and kept a semblance of peace in the increasingly hostile atmosphere between the pilots and management. This airline had turned into a lousy place to work after thirty-plus years of being exactly the opposite. George sighed.

"Something troubling you?"Maynard could read every one of George's gestures and moods, even with what others called that inscrutable face of his.

"Not really."

"You sure?" Maynard looked at his friend. George was fifty-eight years old, and God had been particularly generous by giving him the vitality, physical strength and good health of a much younger man — characteristics that Maynard didn't have himself, even at that age. Other than George's bald head — which he had handled in his usual aggressive manner by shaving it clean — George Fisher was the picture of a powerful man, both physically and emotionally. It was a trait he used to good advantage, but he was careful not to overuse it. That was one of his biggest strengths, and Maynard admired him for it.

"I was thinking about the mandates from Kyle," George said. "I don't know how I'm going to break this news to the pilot group without pissing them off. This could get real ugly very fast."

"You'll think of a way, then I'll talk to a few people. Besides, Kyle might back off some."

"Fat chance. They're up to something, I can feel it. It's not going to be good."

"Never is." Maynard paused, then said, "You need a break." He pointed to the stack of papers on George's desk. "You need to consider these complexities while you're away from here. Take a flight tomorrow night, I can cover this place." Another factor that separated Maynard from George was that Fisher still held a valid FAA pilot's license and medical certificate and was legal to be in command of one of the airline's jets to Europe whenever he wanted. As the Vice President, he could pick any trip he wanted. Maynard envied that enormously.

"Went to Madrid two weeks ago."

"Three weeks ago." Maynard hadn't turned a wheel in revenue service since his retirement, although he had flown several test and ferry flights for the first few years because that was a legal option. His first heart attack ended that, and flying was something that he missed. It wasn't the same as it had been in the old days, but not doing it at all... "Pick up the trip to

London tomorrow night. Go see one of matinees in the city and you'll be back here Friday afternoon. When you come back to this hell-hole on Monday morning, I swear that everything in this crappy office will be ship-shape."

"Maybe." The outer door to their office area opened and Al DeWitt walked in. Behind him was an attractive lady, and a man holding a camera bag trailing behind her. "Come in, Al. We were talking about you."

"George, this is such a pleasure. Thanks for taking the time. Allow me to make introductions." Al DeWitt completed the formalities. Everyone shook hands, then the photographer began taking photos of the three men.

"I understand that you'd like photos of Al with one of our aircraft in the background," George said. "I've checked. We've got one 777 and one Consolidated 768 on the maintenance ramp. Al, you go with the photographer, before the maintenance department decides to take the wings or engines off."

"Okay."

"Jennifer, you stay and we'll talk. I'll straighten out the lies Al has probably told you."

"I'm getting nervous about this," Al said.

"Didn't you get your retirement check yesterday?" George asked.

"Yes."

"You're not an official employee anymore? Then there's nothing to worry about," George said. "Nothing I'll say will put a stop-payment on it."

"Okay. I think."

"Maynard will go with you. He'll make sure you get what you need. He speaks that peculiar dialect known only to mechanics, if it becomes necessary," George joked.

"A man of many tongues," Al answered. He patted Maynard on the shoulder. "I do want a photo of me and Maynard together." Al turned to Jennifer. "This man is another of the long-time employees. He's been with this company as far back as anyone can remember. He was an active pilot for nearly forty years, and has worked here in the office a dozen more."

"Really? More than half a century with one company? Incredible." Jennifer made a notation on her pad; this would fit nicely, particularly in the *Business World Media* piece. "So, you flew for the company until…"

"Mandatory retirement was age sixty," Maynard said. "Now, it's sixty-five. In their infinite wisdom, the Federal Government taketh, and then the Federal Government giveth."

"I remember reading about that change," Jennifer said. "A number of years ago."

"Yes."

"You work here as assistant to Captain Fisher?"

"I do. Try to keep him out of trouble. I fix the spelling and punctuation in his memos. A full time and thankless job."

"Jennifer," Al said, "ask Maynard to tell you his airline stories, when he was flying the old Boeing 707s and the Lockheed Electras — and even the piston airliners before that, the DC-6s and DC-7s." Al glanced at Maynard, then at Jennifer. "Maynard's got one hell of a story about landing a DC-7 in a snowstorm with only two engines running out of the four engines he started with. That particular incident earned him a special award from the company and the government."

"Hold it,"Maynard said. "The lady is here to interview Al, not me. I'm not giving any interviews. I only give interviews on Mondays."

"Let's get to it folks," George said. "Before the maintenance department moves those airplanes. That'll screw everything up."

"Right. But absolutely no pictures of me," Maynard said as he began to walk toward the door. "Can't be recognized. I'm in the Federal witness protection program, for impersonating a useful airline employee these past several years." Everyone laughed.

George waited for Maynard, Al and the magazine photographer to leave the room, then said, "Let's get to your questions." George sat at his desk and gestured for Jennifer to sit across from him. "What would you like to know?"

Jennifer had read about George Fisher, the Vice-President of Flight – he was definitely one of the people on her list. He was an old-school airline employee, so she doubted that he could be part of Kyle's rumored insider group. But there was one way to find out. She would throw some oil on the fire. "First, what did you think of President Kyle's decision to move the corporate offices to Manhattan?"

"Whoa." George raised his hand. "I thought we were here to talk about Al DeWitt's career."

"This is about Al's career. It's about your career, and, now that I've met him, about Maynard Lyman's very significant career." Jennifer knew that using some of the truth at this point would not be a bad idea. "It's about a workplace where people start when they're young and stay their entire working lives. I've met three of them and, I have to say, I'm impressed with each of you. What I'm looking for here is a thread." Jennifer paused and waited, a pen in her one hand, a writing pad on her lap. She knew enough to let him think about it, to simply wait.

George was silent for a full minute. The attractive young lady who sat in front of him remained quiet and her facial expression remained neutral. She was waiting for George Fisher, the Vice President of Flight Operations for Trans-Continental Airlines, to say something in response to her direct question. "Jennifer, I would guess that you're not really looking for a thread here," he finally said. "What I'm guessing is that you're looking for a tear in the fabric."

"Perhaps I am." She smiled. This man was a smart cookie. "Perhaps I can sense one already."

"And perhaps you're right. But where is this going? What is the real object of this interview?"

"You mean, am I looking for real gut stuff, versus a fluff personality piece?"

"Yes."

"You're a smart man," Jennifer said. "I don't have to answer that. We both know the answer." For an instant, Jennifer wondered if now was the time for her to say something specific about *Business World Media* and her real reason for being at the airline. No, she decided. Not quite yet. "Any article I do," she continued, "will have more impact if I talk about the real world and not some make-believe world." When she had finished with that teaser, Jennifer watched George's eyes closely; what she saw in them told her that *right now* was the time to add more. "I would think that people like you, Maynard and Al – people who have this airline world in their blood – would want this story to be told. The real story, not the fluff."

64

"Yes. That's what we'd want," George answered. He looked at her while he fiddled with a pencil on his desk, turning it over in his hand several times. What had started as an innocuous personality interview on Al had made a sharp turn up a totally different road. But maybe this new road could become a highway. "We'd want the real story to be told. But only if it was told the right way. An honest way."

"I'll tell it the right way," Jennifer answered. "That's a promise."

"I have no earthly reason to believe you," George said. He paused, then added, "But, for whatever reason, I'll go along with your request." George had months ago decided that he owed Brandon Kyle and the Puzzle Palace bastards nothing. Even less than nothing. "Start with this anonymous tip on the tear in the fabric that you've sensed. I'll begin by telling you about the corporate nonsense these last years that's turned a great airline into a shadow of its former self and has caused this company to lose money. We're losing money as if we were trying to."

Book Three

Superior pilots are those who use their superior judgment to avoid those situations where they will need superior skills.
—Anonymous aviation axiom

The emergencies you train for almost never happen. It's the one you can't train for that kills you.
—Ernest K. Gann

Chapter Seven

More out of boredom than any other reason, Captain Jack Schofield had the weather reports and forecasts from their flight planning session in Rome spread across the center pedestal between the two pilot positions on the Consolidated 768 jetliner. "Just as well we're on this random south routing today, we wouldn't see much of the Canadian coastline," he said to the other person on the flight deck.

"Right," Peter answered absently, not paying attention to what the captain was saying. He knew that Schofield couldn't sit quietly for more than fifteen minutes without saying something to fill that dead air, and it was worse with Linda on her rest break in the cabin and only the two of them in the cockpit. Jack always did it, and Peter always found it annoying.

"There's no shipping traffic this far south." Jack looked out the cockpit window and scanned the empty sea around them. "Nothing." This portion of the flight was a drag; there was nothing to do and hardly anything to look at. Jack gathered the weather reports from the pedestal and put them to the side.

"Uh, huh," Peter mumbled. He knew from experience that no real answer was required. Instead, he went back to the clipboard on his lap. He was rechecking his figures for their next position report. It would occur at a longitude of 20 degrees west, in twenty-five minutes.

"Yeah, Canada is covered with low clouds and snow. All the way to New England. Nice to see a good forecast for New York," Jack said.

"Right," Peter replied. He knew that it made no difference what answer he gave, just so some sort of sound came out of him. That would keep Jack happy. This moron of a captain was rambling on and his nonsensical babbling was making Peter more than ready to get back into the cabin for his scheduled rest break in forty minutes. Then Peter would have piece and quiet.

With nothing else to do, Jack began to methodically look out the cockpit windows, beginning on the left side, then the center windshield, the far right, then the left side again. There were a few scattered clouds below them, but they were the visual exceptions. What was in his view was the featureless and endless Atlantic Ocean. He sighed, then turned to Peter. "Empty. Nothing. We're alone out here. It looks like we're the only humans on this part of the planet." When he saw that Peter wasn't going to respond, Jack turned away and looked out the windshield.

The vast Atlantic, which Jack knew was frigid cold this time of the year, stretched as far as the eye could see. From up high, the ocean looked like a placid swimming pool that stretched for hundreds of square miles beneath them. Down low, he knew that there would be large waves, big swells and continuous currents. It was not a hospitable place, and, because of that TV special, he thought for a moment how lucky that US Airways pilot had been in 2009 when his double engine failure occurred above the calm Hudson River and not over the tumultuous Atlantic.

Jack pushed those thoughts out of his mind. He turned to Peter. "Hey, I see from the weather reports that our new President William Taylor is going to have good conditions for his inauguration." Jack tapped the forecast sheet in his hand. "As long as he doesn't mind wind and cold. But no rain or snow. Do you know what time the inauguration begins?"

Peter looked at the captain. Since a specific question had been directed at him, Peter knew that he was expected to provide a response. "Saw it in the newspaper." He glanced at the clock on the copilot's panel. "The inauguration ceremony should start in an hour, at eleven-thirty. A few hours of parades. After that, the inauguration Balls. There are a dozen parties, with Taylor and his wife stopping at each of them. The parties begin at eight pm."

"He got a dozen party invitations for the same night? That proves how popular a guy he really is."

Even Peter had to smile at that one. "Guess so," he answered.

"Hey, let's see how good the weatherman was with the Washington forecast," Jack said. He reached for the center console where the controls for the satellite messaging center was.

Jack typed in a coded request, then pushed the button. "We'll find out if this Federal employee will keep his job. Forecasting clear skies and having it rain on inauguration day is grounds for immediate dismissal."

"Probably."

Jack glanced at the satellite receiver's screen. Sometimes these message requests took several minutes to be completed, sometimes they came back instantly. There was no rhyme or reason to how long a given request might take, excepting that the ones that you needed *right now* would take nearly forever. It was like waiting for a teapot to boil. Most of the stuff going on inside these electronic boxes were more hocus-pocus than science, as far as Jack was concerned. "Hey, look," he announced a few seconds later. He pointed to the screen where the reply to his request had flashed on. "The satellite link is operating at the speed of light today."

"What's it say?" Peter asked, although he really didn't give a shit. Politics of any sort was another area he didn't care about.

"The weatherman can keep his job. The Washington, DC weather at ten o'clock was scattered clouds, twenty-six degrees Fahrenheit and a northwest wind of fifteen to twenty knots. Brisk but workable."

"Good."

"So, how we doing on the flight plan?" Jack asked. It was a rhetorical question because he knew the answer: he had glanced at the flight plan a short while earlier.

"Couple of minutes ahead of flight plan. A few hundred pounds less fuel." Peter looked at Jack for an instant, then back at the paperwork in his lap. He didn't need to say more because they both knew damn well why the airplane had burned more fuel than the computer flight plan had predicted. The laws of aerodynamics were inescapable: they would burn additional en route fuel to carry that unnecessary extra fuel — the unauthorized 6,000 pounds of jet fuel that Jack had added in Rome — that they were lugging along for almost ten hours of flying. That extra weight had to be pulled through the same sky as the airplane, the passengers and the cargo did, hence, the additional costs of energy and fuel to carry it. That was another reason why it was foolish to carry extra fuel, it costs the company money.

Jack saw the look and knew exactly what Peter was hinting. He laughed, then said, "Peter, it's okay if we spend more on fuel." He tapped his finger against the gauges on the center panel. "What we don't spend in fuel, the company will spend on perks for management."

Peter looked at Jack again. The man's comment had been so off the wall that Peter couldn't think of a response. He turned back to his paperwork.

"Or management will give themselves bigger bonuses after they lower the pay for everyone else."

Without looking from the paperwork, Peter answered dryly, "There's absolutely no indication of anything of the sort. Not even a rumor."

"Not what I heard," Jack said offhandedly, then turned in his flight chair and was reaching for a magazine on the cockpit floor when he felt something. Something unusual, something strange. A deep rumbling, a vibration of some sort. Jack turned and sat upright. "Hey, you feel that?"

"What?" Peter looked up.

"Vibration. Some kind of vibration." Jack's eyes made a quick pass of the instruments in front of him. Everything was where it was supposed to be. "Increasing. Maybe."

"Yeah." Peter sat upright. As much as he normally discounted anything Schofield had to say, the man could be right about this. Peter put the clipboard down, then laid his hand against the cockpit side window "I feel it. Seems to be going away. More like the rumble in a pressurization duct. Maybe one of the valves is in the wrong position, or loose or something."

"Maybe." But that's not what Jack thought. He had felt a hint of this same vibration an hour or more ago, although it seemed to be less back then and he hadn't mentioned it. At that time, before he could focus on the vibration, it had disappeared. Now, it was back. It didn't seem threatening, but when you were seven miles up and midway across 2,000 miles of cold Atlantic Ocean, then no unusual news was the best unusual news. It was the *only* acceptable news. "Still feel it. Reduced, but it's there."

"Well...possibly," Peter said, as he carefully studied the cockpit gauges. Every indicator was normal.

Jack laid his hand against the engine throttles. He could feel that same vibration there, but by now he could feel it most everywhere. It seemed to come and go in waves — small waves, true, but waves nonetheless. Unusual vibrations. He looked carefully at the rows of engine gauges on the flight panel, studying each one. That's when he noticed the slight movement of the needles. "Here."

Peter's eyes followed the captain's hand. Now, he could see the quiver in the fuel flow indicators — they were moving in a cyclic, almost imperceptible motion across a small portion of the scale. "Both of them," Peter said, as he gestured toward the two individual fuel flow indicators. "Lock step with each other." The co-pilot paused. What he was seeing on the cockpit instruments was that both of their giant turbojet engines were doing a slight rhythmic surging. The amazing thing about this unusual display was that they were doing this strange surging *absolutely together*. "That's impossible."

"Apparently not." Jack picked up the flight deck interphone that would connect him to the cabin. He held it in his hand for a long moment while he thought over the situation. Jack wasn't overly concerned about what he was seeing and feeling, but he wasn't particularly happy about it, either. His first reaction was to call for Linda to come back to the cockpit so that he had the entire flight crew at their stations, but now he had second thoughts. Jack lowered the interphone handset into its cradle.

"More than likely, this means nothing." Peter said. "The needles could have been doing that all morning and we wouldn't have noticed. Some sort of minor indicator problem with the fuel flow sensing circuits. See," Peter added as he tapped his finger against the gauges. "They've settled. The gauges are rock-solid again."

"They are," Jack agreed.

"It was a minor anomaly," Peter added. He sat back in his flight chair and reached for his clipboard to prepare for the routine position report he would be making soon.

"Right." *Anomaly*. Jack frowned, since that was one of the electronic wiz-kid words that he had learned to hate. *Anomaly* was a ten-dollar way of saying that they couldn't explain what the hell was going on with their fancy gadgets. Jack let his eyes run slowly over the panel instruments. "Keep an eye on those fuel flow gauges," he said to Peter.

71

"Okay."

"And if the indications get more erratic, we'll contact maintenance on the satellite link and see if they have any suggestions." What Peter had said about the fuel flow circuits was correct — that the gauge for each engine was showing a customary and steady reading. Jack had to agree that everything on the instrument panel of Trans-Continental Flight 3 was where it was supposed to be, and there was no reason to think that it wouldn't remain that way. If you took a picture of this Consolidated 768 panel at that instant, it would be a snapshot of a strictly routine North Atlantic crossing. Everything, as the wiz-kids liked to say, was nominal.

It was a minor vibration that had quickly gone away. The fuel flow gauges were a coincidence. Nothing more. Jack glanced at the flight deck interphone; no, he would leave it where it was. He scanned the instrument panel, this time carefully, his eyes locking on each instrument in turn. Everything was absolutely, completely normal. Jack sighed. He sat back in his flight chair. Peter must be right, it's only one of those anomalies, that's all. We'll just wait and see. Jack certainly wasn't going to become an alarmist at this stage in his career – and especially not with his friend and mentor Ray Clarke in the cabin.

Chapter Eight

After crossing Corsica a few hours earlier, Flight 3 had continued northwest across the Mediterranean Sea until they had reached the southeastern coast of France. From there, the flight continued on a diagonal course across the French countryside, and eventually exiting the western coastline south of Brest. All that had occurred a while ago. Ray sighed, then sat back in his seat in the first class section of the airliner.

His thoughts weren't on the flight's progress or their routing to New York. Instead, no matter how hard he tried otherwise, his mind was stuck on those events from his past that seldom left him, and on that unexpected and long-postponed event that he now had to deal with. He asked himself for the hundredth time that day why in hell he couldn't get those constant, debilitating thoughts out of his head. Even if Katie's death had been his fault, he knew damn well that there was nothing he could do to change the horrible facts. Nothing.

Ray finished poking at his lunch, then glanced out the cabin window. There was only the surface of the sea below, and he knew that the only thing they would see for next five-plus hours was the featureless Atlantic Ocean until they made their initial landfall over North America near Cape Cod. That would put them slightly over an hour from their New York landing. Ray pushed his window shade shut, then looked around the first class cabin.

Including him, there were a total of twelve passengers scattered around the twenty-four first class seats. The oversized leather recliners were arranged in four rows of six, with an aisle separating each pair of seats. Behind him and the closed curtain that separated first class from coach were, he had been told, 186 passengers: as usual, the flight had departed with a full house in the coach section.

Sitting to Ray's right, on the other side of the wide cabin in seat 4E, was Second Officer Linda Erickson. She was in the crew rest seat in the cabin, on her break. Earlier she had been flipping through a magazine. Now, she was taking a nap — standard routine.

To Linda's right, at window seat 4F, was a tall young man that Ray had been told was a flight attendant for Trans-Continental, who was also flying on a vacation pass as Ray was. The young man had earlier been chatting with Linda, but the next time Ray looked at them, the young man had pulled down his window shade, propped a pillow on the sidewall and was also asleep.

Ray turned to the window and partially raised the shade again. They were, he had earlier been told by Jack, flying further south than the published North Atlantic tracks that Ray had usually flown. Nowadays, the computers selected this sort of random-route when the factors — wind, weather, temperature, aircraft weight, comparative costs of fuel — were considered.

Computers. Electronics. Ray shook his head. The gadgets packed into the cockpit of a modern airliner had started out as helpful aids but somehow, they wound up being more in command of the ship than the flesh and blood pilots. These boxes of circuit boards were, in a manner of speaking, making the decisions — and most of the time, the computers didn't bother to bring the pilot into the decision loop, they spoke directly to each other.

This subtle alteration in the pilot's job and duties was well underway before Ray had retired from Trans-Continental, and it was another part of the change in the airline flying job that he didn't miss. A modern airline pilot could occasionally eavesdrop on what the electronic equipment might be saying, but that was all the pilot could hope for. Ray knew that, at least for him, there was no way to understand the language these computers spoke in — it was the modern equivalent of speaking in tongues.

At that moment, something caught Ray's attention. A vibration. There it was again, a slight resonant vibration passing through the airframe. It was a subtle but distinct vibration, one that he could actually hear — no, not actually hear, but certainly feel. It was, he was certain, the same vibration he had felt earlier when he was leaving the cockpit. Ray sat motionless, trying to get a feel for the vibration as his pilot's instincts went automatically into high alert. He was trying to figure out what it might be an where in the hell it might be coming from.

This minor vibration was passing through the airframe in subtle waves, and it was doing so continuously. Ray sat upright

74

and laid his hand against the window's inner pane. As he did, the vibration ceased.

Gone. Now there was nothing. Nothing at all. Ray moved the palm of his hand to different portions of the wall surrounding the window. Nothing. The vibration was gone. Definitely gone.

Ray sat back and tried to analyze the vibrations that he had felt. They didn't seem threatening, and they certainly were minimal. That, plus the fact that none of the regular flight crew seemed to have noticed them. He had guessed that it was probably the air conditioning valves. Some sort of new functional pattern for them, a new routine. The Consolidated 768, he decided, must be different than the 767 and the valves are making periodic automatic adjustments. It was probably computer driven.

Ray sat back and shook his head. Automatic adjustments. Computers. Most of the other pilots thought that these changes, all of this *progress*, was somewhere between fine and fabulous because it made their day to day chores easier. Ray didn't feel that way and hadn't for a long while. The job had, in his opinion, been dumbed-down to where the captain of a widebody jetliner was expected to be hardly more than a figurehead. The only good part of these changes were that they weren't his concern any more. Those reasons – and the memory of Katie and the emotions attached to that – were why he wasn't in command of an airliner.

Ray glanced at his wristwatch: 10:38 am, New York time. As Jack said on the public address system a short while earlier, their estimated touchdown time at JFK was 4:34 pm, which was slightly ahead of schedule. Less than six hours to go. Those remaining flight hours didn't mean much to Ray; the next half-hour did.

He looked up, toward the first class galley. He could see that Tina was finished with her duties and was about to take her break. She would be taking her break in seat 4B, next to him. They would, finally, be having that talk. There was no way to put it off. In his heart he knew that he shouldn't avoid it, that he had left that option behind when he stepped onboard this flight. *Macho ex airline pilot seen running hysterically through the Rome's terminal to get away from pursuing flight attendant.* Ray laughed at himself once again, although in his heart he knew that none of this was a joke – or, perhaps, more accurately, it was the cruelest joke he'd ever been a part of.

Ray had already vowed that this time he would deal with Tina completely and irrevocably. None of this, he damn well knew, would go away by ignoring it. It was, Ray thought, the same way he had managed to ignore what he now suspected was a small but recognizable hint of a growing problem in the Apache's left engine, the way he failed to act on any of the clues that should have been more than obvious to him, until it was too late. Until it had cost Katie her life. He had run and rerun those last half dozen flights he had taken in the Apache in his mind until he was now certain that there had been discernible clues coming from that failing engine but he had not acted on them. He had done nothing – nothing except to turn the airplane over to her. Ray shivered, then tried to force his thoughts in a different direction.

Yet the harder he tried, the more it haunted him. Ray knew that he couldn't get it out of his mind by saying words or reading words. That damn psychology book had pointedly said that a burden of guilt – whether the guilt was warranted or not – could take a person down. What that book hadn't said, at least not in any way for Ray to get a handle on, was how to put those things behind you. Ray didn't want to ever forget Katie, but, at the same time, he very much did. But he couldn't. He couldn't.

Ray squirmed in his seat while that well-worn pattern of thoughts ripped through his mind like a tornado across a prairie. The worst part was how outside factors could suddenly push the memory of Katie – his guilt, his anxiety – to the forefront. But unlike those examples in that psychology book, Ray was not dysfunctional.

Ray could, unlike many of those men and women that had been written about in that book, go through normal routines in a normal manner. His day to day world was intact. But while he went through his daily motions, Ray felt as if he had been hollowed out, as if he were carrying a hole – a black hole – within himself. He was not dysfunctional, but he was definitely haunted. Yes, haunted was the right word for it. Ray was carrying a ghost deep inside him, a ghost that was haunting him with memories, distractions and nightmares. There was no way to drive that ghost out, at least no way that he had found so far.

What brought Ray back to the moment was the sight of Tina walking toward him. She came down the first class aisle, then stood beside him. "Ready for company?" she asked, pointing to the empty seat next to his.

"Of course," he lied.

She slid into the seat, then twisted around to face him. "Having you onboard has been a wonderful surprise," Tina said. For the past few hours she'd been deciding how to handle this, and the more she thought it over the more she felt that the two of them could start over again. Tina was certain that she could make Ray happy, and she was *absolutely positive* that Ray could do the same for her. For that reason, she was going to be very upbeat. "This is a great opportunity for both of us."

Ray exhaled slowly. He looked at her face. A waterfall of emotions flowed over him. *Tina. Katie. Paris.* "Don't know where to start," Ray said, and he was being truthful. He didn't know where to begin, and he dreaded where the conversation would be headed. If there ever was a screwed-up gang of associations in his mind, it was the combination of his thoughts, his memories and his emotions about Tina and Katie.

"None of the past matters," Tina said as her opening line, the one she had rehearsed repeatedly for the past hour. "If there's anything you want to say about it, go ahead. I don't need it. We were enormously emotional back then. Understandable." Tina put her hand on his arm. "Talk about any of that if you'd like. Or we could talk about now. About today. About tomorrow. About the future."

"That's the problem," Ray said. He kept his eyes fixed on her face, even though he wanted to turn away. He knew that he had to just say it, there was no other way. Yet he continued to sit silently.

Tina could see that she was pushing him too hard and too quickly, but she couldn't help herself. "Wait. Both of us take a deep breath here." She kept her hand on his arm. "There's six hours of this flight left, and Annette will cover galley calls. Let's take our time. Think long and hard about what we're feeling, about what we're saying." Tina smiled, squeezed his arm, then let her hand slide off him and drop onto the small table between the two first class seats. There were no passengers near enough to overhear them, but they were both keeping their voices low.

"Okay." Ray nodded; he knew that he needed time to think, time to consider what he was going to say and then time to phrase it precisely the way he wanted it to sound. He owed her that much. Matter of fact, he owed Tina much more than he was capable of giving. That, in a nutshell, was the problem. Ray wasn't capable of giving anything, not any more. Not to Tina, maybe not to anyone.

He turned away, raised the window shade and glanced down at the ocean below. Even though he had gone over this a hundred times since he boarded the flight and saw her, he still couldn't find the right words. He had begun to realize that there were no right words.

The two of them sat in silence. Tina knew that she had said too much and said it too fast at this, their first meeting in such a long time, but she was making up for the time they'd been apart, and making up for the fact that she had given up hope. Now, even after his abrupt departure from her life nearly two years before, she could see that nothing had changed for her, that nothing had been altered in the slightest. Tina had loved this man for some time, and still loved him today.

Paris. That rainy, cloudy afternoon. The Museum d' Orsay. But that was not where it had started, that was where it had abruptly ended. It had ended that very afternoon in the museum when they had first kissed, and, later at the hotel that night when they made love. That night was the first time they made love, and it was also the last time. By then, Katie had been dead for thirteen months.

Tina sighed, then glanced at Ray. He was turned toward the window, staring at the ocean that was seven miles below. She decided to leave him alone, to give him more time. She turned away from him and allowed her eyes to close.

Tina knew that she had, at first, loved Ray for exactly what he was to her: a wonderful friend, a great man to be around, and the eventual husband of her best friend in the world. Ray and Katie had been there for her when Tina had married Renaldo. Ray and Katie got married themselves a year later, and both of them had been there for her when she divorced Renaldo three years after that. Then, it was the three of them again, flying

78

together whenever they could. After Katie's tragic death, Tina continued to fly with Ray, at first to help him with his pain. She also tried to help him with his guilt, which was enormous and unjustifiable.

Katie's death had not been Ray's fault. Everyone agreed on that — everyone but Ray. He wouldn't hear any of what she or anyone had to say on that subject — he steadfastly took the blame for her death. Ray had been home at the time, and what killed Katie on her solo practice flight was a sudden and catastrophic engine failure on their personal airplane that no one could have seen coming. It happened so quickly that Katie couldn't react fast enough to save herself.

The experts that Tina had talked to had agreed, and every one of them said that there was no way on earth for Ray to have known that the left engine's crankshaft was about to separate. But not Ray. He told Tina that he should have seen it coming, that he should have seen some developing trends, some small clues, something. He had failed to protect her, and it was his stupidity that had killed her.

As time went by, Tina continued to fly trips with Ray and spend time with him on the layovers in Europe. Slowly, she began to love Ray for the man he was, and for the man that he could be for her. It was, she knew, the same reasons that Katie had loved Ray so enormously. Tina opened her eyes and turned back to him. It was time to break the silence. "Ray, let's give ourselves…"

"No, Tina." He turned from the window and faced her directly. "I'm going to say it. No other way. I should have said this two years ago because I knew it then. I didn't have the courage. I wasn't thinking clearly."

"We can find a way…"

"No." Ray didn't know how to deal with this because Tina was a wonderful lady. But he couldn't be around her — even now, so far removed from those direct associations with Katie. He knew now that he'd never be removed from any of them, not with her. "It doesn't work for us. There's too much in our past." He had to work at keeping his voice down; he glanced around the cabin and was happy to see that nobody was paying attention to the two of them.

"Please, Ray…"

79

"Let me talk," he said, in barely more than a whisper. "The problem is me, not you. Not you at all. Not you in the slightest. But I'll never get over it, and when you're around, it's like what little bit I can push aside bubbles up into me. It grabs hold of me and won't let go. It's like being dropped into hell." Ray exhaled again; he had, to his surprise, said it in a few short sentences. It was far more blunt than he intended, but there was no way around it.

"Ray, I..."

He could see that there was a tear forming in the corner of her eye. "Tina, please understand that the problem is mine. Totally. None of the problem is yours. I never should have allowed Paris to happen..."

"Paris was wonderful. Don't try to ruin that for me."

"I'm not trying to ruin anything. I'm trying to tell you the truth."

"You're not giving yourself a chance." She paused, wiped away the single tear with her hand, then faced him. She hadn't given any thought to the possibility that Ray might react to her this way, not after so long. "You're not giving *me* a chance."

"Can't." Ray turned away from her and looked down at the Atlantic Ocean again. He sat silently for awhile, then finally said, "It's impossible for me. Can't do it." Ray turned back to face her. "I wish in God's name that I could. But it's too painful," he continued. "Seeing you again drags everything up, even the little bits from our pasts that I can sometimes push aside. I can't function like this, and I've known that for a long time. It wouldn't be fair to either of us."

Without another word, Tina got up from her seat and walked toward the first class galley. She stepped inside the galley area and drew the curtain closed behind her.

Ray, who was now totally numb inside, turned back to the window and looked blankly down at the cold ocean below.

Chapter Nine

It was thirty minutes later when Annette Riley went into the first class cabin to get Ray Clarke. "I was sent to escort you to the cockpit. Captain Schofield has requested that you come up."

"Certainly." Ray was not surprised that Jack was sending for him since he had seen the second officer leave her crew rest seat and walk to the cockpit a short while earlier. It was time for Peter Fenton's scheduled break period, so Jack wanted Ray to sit in the co-pilot's seat for some story swapping between them. Ray had already decided to not mention anything more about Jack keeping Tina a secret from him; that was something that he'd just as well not think about again. Ray unbuckled his seatbelt and followed the flight attendant forward.

As she moved down the left aisle of the first class cabin and toward the cockpit door, Annette could see that Tina was standing in the first class galley as she had been when they got the interphone call from the cockpit a short time earlier. But, now, she had turned away. Annette knew that something had gone wrong for Tina; she had seen the tears and seen the change in her behavior after she returned from the first class cabin earlier. Clearly, it was something between her and this retired pilot, although Annette didn't know what. Annette didn't know Tina well enough to ask. "Here you are," she said to the retired pilot as she took out her cockpit key and unlocked the door. She stepped aside so he could go forward.

"Thank you." Ray entered the cockpit quietly, the cockpit door closing and locking behind him. He stood a moment at the rear of the flight deck, since he could see that the three crew members were in conversation. Jack was gesturing toward something on the instrument panel and saying something to Linda, who was sitting in the second officer's seat behind and between the two forward pilot stations.

Jack turned and saw that Ray had entered the cockpit. "Ray, come up. Sit here behind me," he said as he patted his hand on the extra seat in the cockpit directly behind the captain's flight chair. "We've had some interesting things happen awhile ago. I'd like your opinion."

"Oh?" Ray slid into the observer's seat behind the captain and fastened his seatbelt out of habit. He could see that there was something going on between the three of them, that they had been in an operational discussion. "What's the situation?"

"Damned if we know." Jack let out a nervous laugh, then added, "Be happier if we did. What we've had," he continued, his arm moving in a sweeping motion across the instrument panel, "are impossible indications. Peter likes to call them anomalies. That means he can't explain them, either."

"Because they're nothing more than minor and random variations," Peter answered. But there was a hint in his voice that he wasn't absolutely certain himself. "Minor indication problems," he said, emphasizing the first word. "Very minor."

"Maybe." But Jack did have to agree that whatever they had seen that was out of sorts earlier had completely vanished, as Peter had predicted. Maybe Peter was right.

"Tell me more," Ray said. He looked over the instruments on the panel and could see that everything was precisely where it was supposed to be. "Some sort of problem?"

"No. Not exactly." Jack prided himself on not being an alarmist in the cockpit — a good trait he had learned years ago — so his automatic response was to downplay events. Still, something about this business had him on edge. "Peter noticed it first, at the same time we noticed that minor vibration."

"Yes, the vibration." Ray knew exactly what Jack was talking about. "A low rumbling. I felt it, too – maybe a half hour ago?"

"Exactly. Peter's guess was that it was something wrong with the air conditioning duct work or with the valves themselves. None of that would amount to much since we've got lots of backup in those systems."

"Seemed unusual to me, but I figured it was something new to the 768 fleet." Ray paused, then added, "I felt it a few hours earlier, when I was leaving the cockpit. Briefly."

"Didn't feel that one. But I did one other time. Also briefly." Jack glanced at the instrument panel. At the moment, all was well. "The only thing on the gauges when we felt the vibrations were very minor fluctuations in the engine fuel flow indicators. The fluctuations — a rhythmic up-and-down of less than a needle's width — seemed to stop when the vibrations did.

But the weird part was that it was happening to both engines at exactly the same time, in exactly the same rhythm. It's as if we had only one of our EEEC computers controlling both engines."

"Is that possible?" Ray asked. These electronic additions that Consolidated had added to the old 767 to make it into a 768 was a component that Ray had no knowledge of. But it didn't seem reasonable that one computer would be allowed to control more than one engine.

"No, it's not possible," Jack said. "Not according to what we were taught. There are two fuel control computer systems, one dedicated to each engine. The two of them do have some sort of software linkup so that both computers are aware of the aircraft's total situation at every given moment, but it's strictly for informational exchange only. There is absolutely no way that the left computer can control the right engine, or vice-versa. Like I said, that's what they told us."

"Seems reasonable," Ray said. "Can't imagine the FAA would approve any hard link between them."

"Which means that this is a coincidence," Peter said. The co-pilot, who had been going through his aircraft manual, closed the book and slipped it back into his flight bag. "What we've got here is a vibration in the air conditioning system, and, at the same time, some sort of very minor indication problem that's affecting both fuel flow sensors. Maybe a loose terminal strip or a bad ground. Anyway, we didn't notice the needle movement until we started looking around during the vibration. Maybe the vibration itself is what caused the fuel flow indicator problem. Maybe it shook the wires that were already getting loose."

"I guess it's certainly possible," Jack said. He then turned to Ray.

Ray slowly nodded his head in agreement. "A reasonable answer. As reasonable as anything at this point." He wasn't totally comfortable with what the co-pilot had said, but he couldn't come up with any other possibility. "Maybe."

"Okay, then it's settled," Peter said. "We can officially categorize this occurrence as an anomaly." The co-pilot had a wry smile on his face. "So, with your approval, captain, I'm headed to the cabin for my rest break. Linda can transmit the 30 West report in a few minutes — I've got it prepared."

Jack thought over what he said for a moment, then finally answered. "Okay."

Peter began to unstrap the holster that held his .40 caliber pistol from around his waist. As required by the complex TSA rules, he would return his anti-hijacking weapon to its locked compartment in his flight case before he departed from the cockpit, since no one else in the cockpit was authorized to use it.

"Have a nice nap, Peter," Jack added. "Linda, you can stay where you are and I'll have Ray slide into the co-pilot's seat when Peter..."

Before Jack could finish his sentence or Peter could rise up from his flight chair, a sudden and violent vibration grabbed hold of the airliner and began to shake it from the insides. Everything in the cockpit was nothing but a blur, and it was getting worse with every passing second.

"Christ!" Jack spun around in his flight chair and looked at the instrument panel. At that instant, the engine instruments were going absolutely crazy — *winding upward, both sides,* in a headlong dash to put out more and more engine power.

"Power!" Linda shouted. She pointed at the instruments. "Both engines! Running away!"

Jack grabbed the throttles and yanked them fully aft. To his disbelief, nothing whatsoever happened to stem the runaway of both their engines. It was as if the airliner's throttles were no longer connected to the engines out on the wings, that each of the giant engines had a mind of their own or, more accurately, *one* mind controlling *two* engines. "No response!" Jack yelled, as much to himself as to the others. He had both of the jet's throttles all the way back to their idle positions, yet the powerplants continued to surge ahead with more and more power output. They were now going beyond full power.

"Temperatures!" Linda pointed at the very important exhaust gas temperature gauges in the center of the instrument panel; both of them were into their red zones and rising as each of the engines continued to produce more power — far more than they'd been designed for. "Going to overtemp! Both of them!"

By now, various warning bells and alarms were going off in the cockpit, and the instrument panel had become bright red with a dozen warning lights as various operating limitations were being exceeded. But the one that caught Ray's eye was the airspeed: it had, because of the additional engine power being produced, gone through its normal limit and was climbing quickly beyond. "Airspeed!" Ray shouted over the noise of the alarms. "Jack, get the airspeed down! Get the nose up!" The aircraft's rapidly increasing airspeed had, in a few seconds, become their most crucial flight parameter. All sorts of really bad things would happen if they didn't keep that airspeed from going higher.

Without answering, Jack grabbed hold of the flight controls, disconnected the autopilot — which had been holding the aircraft straight and level at their cruising altitude — and yanked rearward on the control wheel. The big jetliner immediately pitched upward at an alarming angle. It was the only way Jack knew to get their excessive airspeed back into limits, by using this excess power to go straight uphill — like a runaway skier might turn up the mountain to get unwanted downhill speed under control.

"For Chrissake, get the power back!" Jack shouted as he continued to wrestle with the flight controls. He knew that he was headed for deep trouble because when the airliner went beyond its service ceiling, then the wings would stall and they would begin to fall. "Do something!"

Peter sat rigidly in his flight chair, his both hands in a death grip on the armrests, his eyes wide, his heart pounding, his mouth wide open as he saw in absolute disbelief that *both engines were running away!* It was an impossible occurrence, a pure incredible nightmare. Peter's mind was locked on one circular pattern of thoughts, that there was no procedure for this impossible failure, no procedure whatsoever...they were going to die...there was no procedure...Those final elements of cognitive thought and the training and the flight experience that Peter's conscious mind was trying to call on was quickly pushed aside by the overwhelming, extreme fear that now burst out of his subconscious mind and had grabbed hold of him as if it were a savage animal taking its next meal. Peter had – within a handful of seconds – been devoured by an unbridled panic and was now firmly entrenched in a state of pure terror.

"Altitude!" Linda shouted. She glanced at Peter in the co-pilot's seat. His eyes were wide and he seemed absolutely frozen with fear. Paralyzed. She looked at the altimeter on his flight panel: 37,000...38,000...all she could do was to watch the numbers winding up. She knew that, at this aircraft weight and their flight conditions, when they went much above 39,000 feet, the thin air would mean that low speed stall and high speed buffet would merge into one number. When that happened, the wings would stop working and they would stop producing the needed lift. Then the giant airliner would become nothing more than 150 tons of metal plummeting headlong toward the ocean.

Ray could see how dire the situation was, and he knew for certain that, unless the engine power was brought back immediately, they would die. He looked at the co-pilot, who was wide-eyed and totally motionless. He was frozen in a deep panic. "Peter!" Ray shouted, but there was no response from the co-pilot.

Peter could hear nothing and feel nothing. Nothing beyond being overwhelmed by an implacable alien force. The fear circuits of his subconscious had taken over and his conscious mind had been shut down, locked out, frozen shut. He was now short of breath, had become soaked in sweat and was overwhelmed by an immense sense of helplessness. Mercifully, the sense of time had stopped for him.

Ray turned from Peter and to the flight panel. He knew that he needed to do something, even something drastic. Cut the power, cut it in half. He attempted to reach forward to activate the fuel shutoff lever to the left engine, which was the closest one to his outstretched hand. But Ray's seatbelt, his shoulder harness and the motions of the airplane prevented him from moving far enough forward. Ray was stopped with his fingers several inches away from where the fuel control shutoffs were.

"Linda!" Ray shouted over the noise of the warning bells as soon as he realized that she was within reach of the fuel cutoff levers. "The fuel shutoffs! Grab one and..."

Then, as quickly as it had begun, the enormous vibration that was severely rattling the airframe suddenly and completely ceased. At that very instant, both of the engines began to spool back and settle toward their flight idle settings, which is where the manual throttles had been positioned by Jack shortly after the nightmare had begun.

Jack immediately pushed the control column forward to level the aircraft, then allowed the airliner to descend back down to thicker, more useable air. He glanced at his altimeter the moment before they had reached the apogee of their uncontrolled ride upward: 40,100 feet. He knew that a few hundred feet more, or a thousand at the most, and they would've stalled out and spun straight down.

But they hadn't. Gingerly, the captain pushed the manual engine throttles forward to their normal position and immediately saw that both of the engines were now operating as they were supposed to. One by one, the alarm bells that filled the cockpit began to silence themselves and the red warning lights on the instrument panel began to blink out. By the time the airliner had descended to 35,000, the indications on the instrument panel were normal. Amazingly, the ride back to their normal cruising altitude was done with complete silence between them, without any of the four of them uttering a single sound.

"Christ Almighty," Jack finally said. It was the first words he had spoken since shortly after their uncontrolled climb had begun. "What the hell happened to us?" he said in a thin, nervous voice, mostly to himself.

◇

Tina had been standing at the right rear of the first class cabin of the airliner when the loud vibrations and the initial runaway of both their engines had begun. She was in the aisle and talking to Fred Lyle who was in seat 4F. "What's that?" she said loudly as the commotion began.

"Oh, no!" Lyle grabbed his armrests as the Consolidated jetliner began, after several seconds, to pitch upward at an increasingly alarming rate. "Oh, God!"

Tina spun around and began to try to move quickly back to her crew station adjacent to the first class galley. Clearly, something was wrong, bad wrong. She had to get back to her crew station and get herself strapped in.

But the increasing motions of the airplane, and the sudden vibrations began to toss her from side to side and made her forward progress through the cabin nearly impossible. Rather than fight it, she grabbed the back of seat 3E, pulled herself around and into it, and quickly fastened her seatbelt. This was not just something bad, it was something *really* bad.

She looked out the window to her right and could see what her senses were telling her; that the airliner was pitched up at an ungodly angle and still climbing. She had enough years of experience to know that the engine sounds weren't right, either, that they were louder and almost frantic sounding.

The passengers in the first class section were seated and were, at the moment, sitting quietly — they were too startled to even react yet to whatever this developing emergency was. From behind the curtain that separated first class from coach, Tina could hear shouting and screaming. Clearly, the coach cabin was at a marked level of chaos.

Tina turned to her left. The passenger in that seat, a doctor as she recalled from the manifest, was looking at her. "Seatbelt!" she shouted at him.

"Yes, I have it." Dr. Lee Frankel gestured toward his fastened seatbelt. "This is not good," he said, in a clear voice.

"Hang on." Tina could see a few things — pillows, blankets, books, drink glasses, a dessert plate — rolling around on and across the aisles, but otherwise their condition in the forward cabin seemed to be secure enough to ride out whatever this was — as long as it didn't go on much longer. "Everyone! Seatbelts! Hang on!" she shouted as loud as she could. Her years of experience and her gut feelings told her that this was going to end — one way or the other — in a short time. She had been in bad turbulence many times in her career, but this, somehow, seemed different. Much worse. "Hang on!"

Then, as suddenly as it had started, it stopped. The engine noises and the vibrations reduced themselves dramatically, and so did the wind noises. The aircraft began to pitch nose-over to a normal flight attitude.

"Recovering," Dr. Frankel said, again in a loud and clear voice. "The pilots are getting us to normal flight again." He pointed toward the window to Tina's right, where the horizon line was once again level and then, tilted slightly up to indicate that the aircraft was headed down. "See?"

"Yes." For an instant, Tina's thoughts were on how calm the doctor had looked and sounded throughout this incredible event. Amazing. She knew that she wasn't calm and she probably hadn't sounded calm, either. Tina turned her attention to the airplane itself and their flight condition.

Other than a slight sensation of weightlessness for a few seconds as the jetliner transitioned from nose up to nose down, the sensations of flight and motion had returned to normal. Even the engine and air noises from the air conditioning ducts returned back to what Tina knew were normal for cruise. She could feel the airplane level out. Everything seemed stable.

Tina waited a few seconds to make certain that this normal flight condition would last, then she unbuckled her seatbelt and jumped up. "Everyone! Stay where you are, keep your seatbelts fastened! Stay calm!" she announced in the most authoritative voice she could muster, considering how rattled she was.

This past time — how long was it? Thirty seconds, one minute? — seemed like it had been an hour. Two hours. Tina moved quickly toward the cockpit door, to find out what had happened. Even more importantly, she needed to find out what would be happening next.

Chapter Ten

Tina opened the cockpit door with her key and pushed it inward, not knowing what she would see. Much to her surprise, the sight in front of her was nothing beyond what she normally saw whenever she opened the cockpit door in flight: everything appeared calm and orderly. The three men and one woman sitting in the cockpit were absolutely stoic in their flight chairs, all of them facing forward toward the instrument panel and the windshield. The pilot who was actually flying the airplane – Captain Schofield – was making only occasional small movements with his one hand resting on the control column, his other hand on the ship's throttles. The fact that it took so little movement on the pilot's part to make such a big airplane do so much had always amazed her – and had always frightened her some, too. Now, she had even more reason to be frightened.

From a distance of several feet behind them, nothing appeared to be wrong – as if nothing horrific had occurred to the flight, as if this section of the airliner hadn't gone through the same ride from hell that the cabin had. Incredible. Tina could hear a conversation going on between the pilots, but she couldn't make out the words. "Captain," she announced in a loud voice to announce her presence, "do I need to be doing anything?"

Jack turned half-around in his seat, although he continued to hand fly the airliner. "No," he said. Then he quickly changed his mind. "Wait." He paused while he considered his options. "Yes," he finally said. "You can get the cabin preparations going. Come here. I'll fill you in. You pass the word to the rest of the crew, then tell the passengers on the PA. Don't have time to make announcements."

"Certainly." Tina took a few more steps forward and stood beside Ray, who was seated in the observer's chair directly behind Jack. Tina and Ray glanced at each other for an instant – both of them too numb from the wild maneuvering they had been through to say anything to each other – then Ray turned his full attention back to the gauges on the instrument panel. Tina couldn't tell what he might be thinking, and she certainly had no idea of what had happened to cause such a horrible ride for even that brief time. This experience had so far been both bizarre and frightening, to say the very least. She asked the captain, "What happened? They're going to expect me to tell them. I'll need to say something."

"Tell them it was an engine problem." Jack paused again, then added, "It's now under control." He glanced at the engine instruments, expecting that they might be making a liar out of him very soon. Instead, the gauges continued to show that all was okay. "But also tell them we're going to divert. Right now. As a precaution. To the Azores." Jack turned slightly toward the co-pilot, who hadn't spoken a single word since the ordeal had begun. He was sitting rigidly in his flight chair, not moving. "Peter, tell air traffic control we're declaring an emergency," Jack said in a calm voice, although his insides were churning. "Tell them we're diverting from our present position direct to Lajes. We're south of the normal flight tracks, but make it clear that I'm not waiting for a re-clearance. Turning south right now."

With that, Jack put the airliner in a mild bank to the left so they would be headed in the general direction that he knew the Azores would be. With his free hand he reached toward his flight computer and, after typing in the proper airport code and pressing a button, their cockpit navigation display screens showed a magenta course line that was the direct heading toward the Azores. Jack made a slight adjustment to the airliner's flight path to line up with the computer-generated navigation line, then announced, "Four hundred seventy-four miles to the airport at Lajes" as he read what the display was telling him. "Less than an hour of flight time at this airspeed." He turned back to the senior flight attendant. "Secure everything in the cabin. Get ready for landing. We'll alert the cabin when we're ten minutes out."

"Yes Sir." Tina paused. "Should we do anything more? Should we have the passengers put on life jackets?" she asked.

Jack didn't answer immediately. He knew that he needed to stay calm, think clearly, and not begin overreacting. That was crucial. Finally, he answered, "No." He paused again, then added, "if that changes I'll let you know. Immediately."

"Right." Tina turned and walked out of the cockpit, closing and locking the door behind her.

"Jack," Ray said as he tapped the captain on the shoulder. "I think Peter is having a problem." He pointed to Peter, who was still sitting motionless in his flight chair. His eyes were opened wide and he was facing the instrument panel, but it didn't seem as if he was actually looking at anything.

"Peter?" Jack could now see what Ray was telling him: the man was paralyzed; he had been paralyzed by fear. "Peter!...Peter!"

"I...I..." Slowly, Peter turned away from the instrument panel and toward the captain. "I...can't...believe this...none of it...not possible..." His eyes were still wide and his mouth hung slightly open. Peter could feel his heart pounding heavily in his chest, although his vision – which had narrowed as if he had been standing at the end of a long and dark tunnel – was slowly beginning to brighten up. "I can't believe...this could happen...to us."

"Peter, get hold of yourself. Did you hear what I said about our diversion, about calling air traffic control?"

Peter paused, then turned his attention slowly from the captain on his left to the retired pilot sitting behind him. Finally, he looked at the captain. "No," he said hesitantly. "I...I don't think I heard it."

Jack repeated his instructions slowly and clearly; he now knew that he was dealing with a man on the verge of a complete panic attack. As he had suspected, Peter was one of that large group of pilots who had never actually faced a dire life-and-death situation — and now, suddenly, he was facing one. Worse yet, it was a situation that was supposed to be impossible, according to the books and everything they knew about this airplane.

Jack turned in his flight chair to look at the third member of his cockpit crew: although he had heard Linda shouting to him during the actual event, she had been sitting quietly since that incredible dual engine runaway had ended. "Linda, how are you doing?" he asked.

There was a silence for a few seconds, and then she said, "Damn nervous. That was one hellishly wild ride," she answered. Linda brushed aside some strands of her blonde hair that had fallen down across her forehead and put on a weak smile. "I sure hope you're not planning on another of those roller coaster adventures. I don't like theme parks."

"No problem," Jack answered. He exhaled slowly while he got his own thoughts and his own emotions into check. "Your ticket's punched. It's only good for one ride a day." At least she was okay. Jack glanced back at Peter. The co-pilot was busying himself with the flight plan and a chart, evidently getting ready to make that diversion call. He was taking far too much time checking stupid details when he should have gotten the first radio message out, but Jack was afraid to push him too hard or too fast. He was obviously in an emotional turmoil. Jack decided to let him make the radio call at his own pace since it would focus his attention. He would just give Peter a slight nudge. "How's that radio call coming?"

Peter took his eyes off the paperwork in his lap and looked at the captain. "Radio call...yes...I'm...almost ready...almost..." he answered in a trembling voice. His thought patterns were beginning to settle back into his well-learned habit patterns. He would recheck the figures first, then give them a position, then give them an estimate....

"Fine." Jack nodded his head. "There's no rush making that radio report. Everything is running fine." The captain's free hand gestured toward the instrument panel while he tried to keep his voice positive and reassuring. "Everything is back to normal, everything is going to be fine."

"Fine...right...yes...fine..." Peter answered hesitantly. He didn't want to think about the failure, only about the job he had been given to do.

"Yes." Jack was trying to sound as positive as he could, since the last thing he needed was for his co-pilot to mentally collapse on him. He had seen an episode of a full-scale panic attack once in his life — ironically, it had not been on an airplane but on a pleasure boat where a fire had broken out — and it was not a pretty sight. He knew from the conversations afterward and with his talks with other people that a panic attack could be noisy and obvious, or it could be hardly noticeable and deadly quiet. But the end result was the same: a different part of the person's brain – a basic, more primal portion – had taken total control of them. Once it began, it was said that a person could stay that way for hours. "Transmit that report when you're ready. Okay?"

"Okay," Peter answered tentatively. He turned his attention back to the paperwork in his lap, which seemed to comfort him.

"Jack, can I make a suggestion?" Ray asked.

"Hell, yes."

"There's something we need to do."

"Which is?"

"Let me explain myself first." Ray pointed to the engine gauges. "What we saw here was, according to the books, impossible. We can pretend that it didn't happen that way, but it did. From a technical point of view, we've found ourselves in uncharted waters."

"I agree with that." Jack continued to steer the airliner directly to the airport in the Azores, the only place that he could land this jet within a thousand miles of their current position. The weather at Lajes was forecast to be a low overcast with rain showers, but well above their operational limits, so that made it a good choice. A great choice, actually, since it was on dry land. Ditching might have been a viable option for that US Airways flight in 2009, but there was a world – no, a galaxy — of differences between the Hudson River and the Atlantic Ocean. Not to mention the possibilities of a timely rescue, which were less than zero out here.

"Since we've seen the impossible," Ray continued, "that might mean that the next thing we see is the totally unexpected." He noticed that the co-pilot had suddenly put down the microphone that he had picked up and, instead of making that radio transmission, was now watching him intently. Ray ignored Peter and continued with his explanation. "I don't need to remind you that we only have two engines and that, somehow, they managed to lock themselves together. I know that it's impossible and you know that it's impossible, but it happened. We saw it."

"Right." Jack nodded. He could see where Ray was going with this.

"My instincts during that double engine runaway," Ray added, "were that if we had only one of the engines going nuts, then we'd have more time to get the ship under control before we pushed the airframe operating limits too far. Better yet, we'd have the other engine in reserve if we couldn't get the runaway engine into normal operating range in time. We need to shut down one of our two engines, right now."

"Wait! What are you saying!" Peter's voice started out loud and it quickly rose to nearly a shout. His eyes were glazed over and both his hands were visibly shaking. "Everything's okay now," Peter yelled as he pointed at Jack. "You said it yourself!" Peter then turned to face Ray.

Ray saw that the co-pilot's expression had turned from being sort of tuned out to a combination of overwhelming fear and unbridled rage. Those emotions had gotten hold of him and he was clearly on the brink of completely losing what little control he had left. "Try to stay calm," was the only thing that Ray could think of to say. "I'm presenting a possible option to the Captain, that's all."

"Yes, Peter," Jack said. "Calm down. I know that this is stressful. It's stressful for all of us. It's understandable, but you're not thinking clearly."

"*I'm* not thinking clearly! Have you gone nuts? Both of you!" Peter was shouting again, now his entire body trembling. "You told us everything is okay, and he wants to voluntarily shut down one of the engines? Then, if we had even a small problem, we'd have no running engines! There's absolutely *no procedure* for anything like this in the operations manual! No procedure!"

"Peter, I know this." Jack didn't know what to do next, except to let the co-pilot continue to vent. Maybe by letting him rant he would, like opening a valve on an over-pressurized steam boiler, get this irrationality out of his system. "I think Ray might be right. If we shut down one of the engines, we'd have it in reserve if…"

"No! It's unauthorized!" Peter answered in a shout. There was no way he could allow anything like this to happen to them, to happen to him. Those engines were the only thing that were keeping him out of the water, keeping him from dying. "I can't believe that you could be considering that sort of crazy idea from this totally unauthorized person!"

"Peter, please…"

"Get him out of the cockpit!" Peter pointed at Ray with a trembling hand. His vision was beginning to narrow again, and his heart felt like it was about to explode out of his chest. As the memory of the fear he had felt during that last wild ride flooded over him, his entire body began to shake. Peter began to suddenly understand the complete situation, that they were trying to kill him…that this unauthorized man in the cockpit was trying to kill them, trying to kill him…."Get him out of here!"

Jack didn't know what to do about Peter except to let him yell. He turned away from the ranting co-pilot and back to Ray. Maybe if he ignored Peter. "Ray, I see what you mean. Do you think it matters which engine we shut down?"

"No, it shouldn't. They're in identical condition, from what we can tell." Ray pointed toward the fuel control levers on the center pedestal between the two pilots. "Academic choice."

"Wait!" Peter rose in his flight chair as much as his seatbelt would allow. He had to save them, he had to save himself, he couldn't allow anything like that wild ride to happen to them again. He had to stop it before they made the situation into another pure nightmare – he couldn't face going through another bout of sheer terror. "This is suicide! We're over the middle of the fucking North Atlantic Ocean in January and you want us to voluntarily shut down one of the engines, even though the captain's admitted that everything's okay?"

Linda leaned slightly forward in her flight chair. "Peter, please try to calm yourself and listen to what they're both saying..."

"You *are* nuts! Both of you! Maybe all three of you!" He had to stop them. He had to. Peter fumbled on his right side, then pulled out the .40 caliber H&K automatic pistol that he had been in the process of locking away in his flight bag when the engine runaways had begun. He pointed the pistol directly at Ray. Peter could see that it was this unauthorized man in the cockpit who was the crazy one, the one who was trying to get them killed. "I knew you shouldn't be up here, this is some kind of goddamn..." Peter paused for an instant before he shouted out the single word that had popped into his head, the one word that somehow tied all of this horror together. "Hijacking! That's what you're doing! Unbuckle your seatbelt! Get up from that chair!" Peter shouted. His extreme fear had turned from frozen passiveness to pure rage. "If you don't, I'll put a goddamn bullet in you!"

"Put that gun away, you moron." Jack didn't know what else to do at that point except to get as forceful as he dared; clearly, trying to reason with Peter while he was in this condition was not going to get them anywhere. Maybe he would respond to Jack's official authority as captain of the ship. "You listen to me, you little bastard. I'm the captain here, I'll make the decisions, and I'm not going to tolerate any insubordination. I see what Ray is saying, and he's absolutely right. We need to shut one engine down. We need to shut it down right now." Jack continued to hand-fly the airliner on a southerly heading.

"No! Absolutely not! There's no procedure for this!" Peter looked at the captain, and then back at Ray. The retired pilot had released his seatbelt and had stood up directly behind the captain's flight chair, as he had been ordered to. Peter understood what would happen to him, happen to all of them if he didn't continue to prevent it. "I don't give a shit if you're the captain, this man's got you in some kind of trance or something," he said to Jack. "He's hijacking this airplane. That's it...he's hijacking it, or trying to commit suicide with it — and you're letting him do it!"

"Stop ranting, Peter. You're frightened, that's all," Jack said, once again trying to sound completely calm and matter of fact. "Get hold of yourself. I'm the captain and I'm telling you to quiet down. Right now. Put that gun away."

"No. It's a suicide thing," Peter continued as a new thought entered his mind, a new thought that had come out of same subconscious portion of his mind that his other fears had sprung from. The cogent and reasoning portion of his mind had already shut down, and he was now reacting completely to the overwhelming impulses of fear that had absolute control over him. Fragments of panic-induced thoughts were flooding through his brain, yanking his emotions and perceptions in haphazard, disjointed directions. "His wife committed suicide. Now he's trying to do the same. He hates the airline, that's why he quit. Now, he's trying to get revenge on us. He's trying to kill us. He's trying to kill me."

"None of that is true," is all that Ray could say in response. He was working hard to keep his voice low and as calm as possible, and he, too had no idea how to deal with the irrational co-pilot. Peter, with his hand visibly trembling and his face covered with sweat, continued to point the pistol directly at him, so Ray knew that he dared not make any moves whatsoever. "My wife's death was an accident. You can ask anyone in the crew who knew her. Tina, the senior flight attendant, was her best friend. It was almost four years ago. I left my job for other reasons — I retired early, that's all." Maybe, Ray hoped, one of the others would be able to disarm the co-pilot, who was totally out of control and could be jeopardizing their only chance to keep the airliner aloft if their mysterious engine problems returned. One of them had to do something, and they had to do it quickly.

"Get back in the cabin, both of you! I'm taking over." Peter knew that there's no other way. He released his seatbelt so he could move further away from them, then reached forward with one hand to dial in the hijacking code on their satellite transmitter. He then picked up the microphone. "Mayday, Trans-Continental Flight 3 is being hijacked! We've got this lunatic retired pilot in the cockpit and he's suicidal — he's trying to kill us! It's like 9/11 again!"

"Stop this! Give me that gun!" Jack said. At this point, Jack felt that he had to try something drastic to stop Peter, he couldn't let his panic-crazed co-pilot continue. He also realized that he had to implement Ray's plan as quickly as he could because the dual engine runaway might occur at any time — it had happened before with no warning, and it certainly seemed possible that it could happen again. Jack had released his seatbelt a few moments earlier, and with Peter's attention being diverted by the absurd, irrational radio call that he was making, Jack thought that he saw the opportunity that he needed. The captain lunged across the short distance between himself and the co-pilot.

The enormous, smothering sound of one gunshot went off in the cockpit, followed a few seconds later by a second gunshot as all three men in the cockpit struggled for control of the pistol.

The jetliner itself, with the autopilot selected off and with no one handling the flight controls, began to maneuver on its own. Linda tried to release her own seatbelt and to push her way around the struggling men in order to get to the aircraft's flight controls. The captain's control column, she could now see, was less than a dozen inches from her outstretched arms — but she could not reach it. By now, she could feel the aerodynamic G forces begin to build up as the airliner launched itself into another wild ride. "Out of control!" she shouted.

In a handful of seconds, the Consolidated 768 jet had begun an uncommanded roll to the left. Soon after that, the rolling motion transformed itself into a nose-down, high speed dive. At a rate that was increasing with every passing moment, Trans-Continental Flight 3 was headed straight down toward the glistening surface of the cold Atlantic Ocean that was seven miles below.

Chapter Eleven

Tina was entering the first class section when she heard the two moderately loud explosions in quick succession from the front of the airplane — sounds that she had never heard in all her years of flying. She had finished briefing the other flight attendants and had made the PA announcement to the passengers that the captain had asked for, and by the time she had walked back to the first class section, even the coach cabin had been returned to some semblance of order. The two explosions froze her where she stood in the middle of the left aisle of the first class cabin. Before Tina could formulate any additional thoughts on the meaning of those sudden noises, she could feel the airplane dropping out from beneath her as it began another sudden pitch-over. "Oh my god!" She tried to maintain her balance but couldn't and found herself falling forward and to the side as her body slammed into a seat back.

"Got you! Here."

Tina was being pulled to her right, and when she turned she could see that it was Doctor Frankel. He had caught her arm and had pulled her into seat 3C, the seat to the left of his. "Don't let go!" Tina shouted to him as she felt the airliner pitching down more rapidly and her body become nearly weightless. Without him holding onto her, she could have been slammed up into the ceiling and then tossed around the cabin like a rag doll.

"Won't." Lee Frankel had both his arms around her as he pulled her further into the seat. He saw that until she could get her legs in front of her there was no way to get the seatbelt on, but he also saw that he should be able to keep her where she was — as long as the motions from the airplane didn't get much worse. "Move your legs," he said. "Around. Grab the seatbelt."

"Okay." Their faces were near to each other and once again Tina was surprised at how calm he sounded and how calm he appeared. She knew that she must look very frightened, which indeed she was. This close to him, she starred directly at the doctor to help herself remain in control – if she looked around the cabin, she thought that she might completely freak out. Tina knew that she needed to keep herself focused, to stay calm, if she had any chance to ward off the mounting fear that was building up nearly faster than she could keep it at bay.

"Keep moving. This direction. Push down," the doctor instructed her.

"Okay," Tina said again The single thought of staying focused on the task of getting strapped into the seat was helping her channel her emotions. She kept her eyes locked on the doctor's face: he had very expressive eyes, and his long, thin features were balanced by a trimmed mustache and a short goatee. Tina knew that she needed to keep focused on the details directly in front of her, that she had to keep her mind on anything but what was happening to the airliner. The doctor's hair was mostly grey, with some streaks of black...

"Keep moving," the doctor repeated. "Push."

"Yes." Tina could feel that her self-control was barely hanging on – this was, by an enormous margin, the worst in-flight situation she had ever experienced in her entire airline career. Finally, she managed to get her legs in front of her and her body settled into the seat. "I'm okay," she finally said, in a hollow and trembling voice that seemed not her own.

"Right." Lee kept his arms locked around the flight attendant. "Seatbelt."

"Got it." She grabbed the seatbelt and snapped it securely, then pulled it tight. By now, the airliner seemed to be pointed nearly straight down, and she could see that everything inside the cabin that hadn't been restrained was being tossed around. Small articles were everywhere. Firmly secured in her seat, Tina felt that she could finally take a glance around the cabin. There were continual screams from the cabin behind her, and she could hear hysterical crying from the woman in the seat to her immediate left.

"Got to level the ship out," Lee said. "Soon." Even though she had gotten her seatbelt on, Lee continued to hold onto her. Tina was holding tightly onto him.

"Yes," Tina answered. It was all that she could think of to say. Tina knew that if the pilots didn't regain control of the airplane soon, the airliner would either disintegrate in flight or dive straight into the Atlantic Ocean.

◇

In the cockpit of Trans-Continental Flight 3, the situation had become critical within a few seconds after the two gunshots from Peter's .40 caliber pistol had gone off. "Linda, grab the wheel!" Ray shouted as he attempted to maneuver the inert bodies of the two other pilots who were laying sprawled across the co-pilot's seat and into the co-pilot's flight controls.

"Can't budge it!" Linda had, a moment earlier, managed to get herself far enough forward and to her left in spite of the increasing G forces that were mounting on them as the airliner continued its dive. She now had a firm grip on the captain's control wheel in her left hand, while her right hand had a firm lock on the center control pedestal so she could maintain her balance. But even with her left hand on the wheel, Linda couldn't get the control column to move aft.

"Pull back! Quickly!" Ray said.

"Locked!" Linda answered. She was, she knew, on the verge of nearly giving in to panic herself. "Locked!" Linda said again, although she knew that there were no sorts of control locks built into the airliner's hydraulically-boosted system. They had locked flight controls, yet it wasn't possible. Instead of giving into panic, she concentrated on what had to be done. Linda knew that the controls couldn't be completely locked, that it was something else. Finally, by applying more physical strength than she thought she possessed, Linda did manage to get the column to come aft an inch or two. "Won't come back...jammed..."

Ray ignored the warning bells and flashing lights that were flooding the cockpit as he looked around and focused on what was causing the flight controls to jam: the inert weight of Peter's lower body was caught between the first officer's flight chair where he was slumped and the base of the control column where it rose out of the cockpit floor. "Peter's body! Against the column! Hold the wheel, I'll pull him out!"

"Right," she answered, nearly out of breath. Linda was pulling back with all her strength, but she had to be ready to immediately slacken up when the obstruction was removed or the airliner would be yanked from too much nose-down to too much nose-up. A sudden maneuver like that might pull the wings off. "Ready!"

"Okay." When the struggle for the gun had begun, Jack had almost managed to wrestle the pistol away from the panic-crazed co-pilot. Instead, it had suddenly gone off and Jack fell heavily forward and against Peter. At that moment, Ray grabbed for the pistol himself and, locking hands with Peter as the two of them continued with the struggle, Ray's advantage of standing while Peter was sprawled backward in his flight chair with the weight of Jack's body against him gave Ray a fighting chance against the younger man.

Ray gained the advantage and had almost pulled the weapon away from the co-pilot when, again, the gun went off with that second unintentional shot. This time, the barrel of the weapon had been pointed backward and was aimed at Peter himself when the co-pilot inadvertently pulled against the trigger during the on-going struggle. When Peter slumped down, the lower portion of his body had slid into the small open space between the co-pilot's flight chair and the control column directly in front of it. "Get ready," Ray said as he pushed Jack's body aside and grabbed hold of the unconscious Peter by his shoulders. "Now!"

"Free!" Linda had managed to time the maneuver perfectly and the airliner had the mildest bump in its flight path as it began to transition from an exaggerated condition of nose-down to something like a normal flight attitude.

"Easy, now," Ray said as he pulled Peter's body to the rear of the cockpit and laid him on the flight deck floor. "Level out. Push the power to a low cruise setting"

"Right." Linda was straddled across the captain's flight chair with much of her body laying prone against the center pedestal where the radio controls were. She could see that the ship's airspeed was being reduced into a normal range again, and that the altimeter — which read 28,000 feet — was settling down. "Leveling out. I need help."

"Hang on. A few seconds." Ray had come forward again and was removing Jack's inert body from where he had pushed it aside to get to Peter. The captain's white shirt, face and hands were covered with blood, but Ray thought that he could feel Jack breathing. Maybe. He laid Jack's body beside Peter's, then rushed toward the captain's flight chair. He reached over Linda and grabbed the control wheel. "Got it. Let go."

103

As Linda let go of the control wheel and pulled herself backward, Ray stepped around her and slid into the captain's flight chair. "Okay," he announced. "I've got it. We're steady. We've got to get medical help for both of them," he said as he gestured over his shoulder at the bodies of the two pilots laying on the floor at the rear of the cockpit. "Right now."

"Yes." But Linda's mind was filled with other, more immediate thoughts. Peter's last words echoed in her thoughts as she clearly remembered what he had said, that Ray was trying to commit suicide, that his wife had committed suicide, that he hated the airline. Linda reached for the gun where it had fallen on the floor. She knew that Peter had panicked and she knew that he wasn't being rational with his shouting and accusations, but still....

Linda picked up the pistol. She held the gun with both of her hands on its grip and pointed it in the general direction of Ray. Was there any possibility that Peter could have been right? "What are you doing?" Linda asked Ray, in a voice as firm and steady as she could make it. "What are you planning?"

"I..." Ray glanced away from the flight panel and back toward her. Linda was standing alongside the second officer's seat with the pistol in her hand. Her hands were trembling, but the pistol was pointed more or less at him. "Put that damn gun down," he said. "Don't go crazy like him," Ray said as he gestured toward where Peter lay.

"Answer the question. What are you intending to do?" Linda asked. She kept the pistol leveled and she swung its barrel directly toward Ray. "Answer me." She had to be sure; things were happening too fast for her to keep up with them, for her to reason them out.

"Those two men are going to bleed to death if you don't do something, if you don't get help up here."

"Answer the question. I'm in charge," Linda said, although it sounded bizarre even to her. Technically and officially, first officers and second officers were totally qualified to take over the ship and do everything that a captain could do. Realistically — especially for newer people like herself — it was an apprenticeship. She knew enough to be able to steer the airliner, but she couldn't kid herself at this critical time — she certainly didn't have the experience to *command* it. Still, it was

104

her official responsibility, and she wasn't absolutely sure that Peter – in spite of his ranting – wasn't on to something. "I want to know what you intend to do. Then I'll decide if I'll keep you here."

"Yes, you are in charge." Ray looked at her, at the pistol, then back at the flight panel. "But I've got the experience. I've got a very strong feeling about our situation. If you'll remember, Jack agreed."

"Not really. It was still being discussed." Linda saw that the pistol was trembling in her hands, even though she was trying to hold it steady.

"Right," Ray answered. "You don't have the experience to make this unorthodox decision. I'm making it for you. And I'm making it for myself, Jack and for the other two hundred-plus back there." Ray gestured over his shoulder toward the closed and locked cockpit door that lead to the cabin. "I'm shutting down one of the engines — the left engine—in thirty seconds." He was going with his gut reaction and his instincts, which were that shutting down one of the engines needed to be done.

"No." Linda took a half step forward and pushed the black pistol further in front of her. She had only fired a handgun a few times in her life, but she knew that all she had to do was point it and then pull against the trigger. "This thing has lots of bullets left. Don't make me shoot you."

"It'll only take one shot to stop me, you won't need lots of bullets." Ray looked at the panel clock, then at her. There was no time to talk, no time left to think. He *had* to do it. "Twenty seconds. That's what it will take to stop me from shutting down the left engine. You'll have to shoot me."

"I'm warning you." Linda raised the gun slightly. She could feel the pressure of the gun's trigger against her finger. "Keep your hands away from the fuel shutoffs."

"In fifteen seconds I'm shutting off the left engine. We don't need two running engines to get this crippled airliner to the Azores. There's a good chance that we're going to need an engine in reserve if the current operating engine runs away on its own. It's possible. That's where this nightmare started, with an impossible scenario, at least according to the damn book. Both engines locked together and ran away, which all of you said was impossible. So we might need to do something that's not in the book. That's what we need to stay alive."

"Let's talk about it." Linda was wavering; what he said was making sense, but could she take that much of a chance? Could Peter have been right?

"No time." Ray reached for the left engine's fuel shutoff lever on the center pedestal.

"Stop!"

"Three, two, one." Without looking at her, Ray pushed the left engine's fuel shutoff lever fully down. An instant later the engine gauges on the left side began to unwind to verify that it had been shut down, and a number of red warning lights began to blink. He quickly made the control adjustments necessary for operating on one engine.

Linda blinked a few times, then lowered the pistol. Finally, she laid the gun on the empty observer's flight chair behind the captain's seat — the seat that Ray had previously occupied. She had, she realized, made her decision not consciously, but subconsciously. It had been based not on the man's words or the details of the flight, but strictly on her feelings. Now, in every way that mattered, Ray Clarke was in the captain's flight chair.

Linda had always felt that she was a good pilot and a careful pilot, but she also knew that what they needed right now was not just a good pilot. What they needed right now was a great pilot, a great *captain*. Ray was apparently going on his gut feelings about their nightmarish situation, and now she was going to do exactly the same. She knew that Peter had been irrational – in a complete panic – and in her heart she also felt that Ray Clarke had the best chance of getting them out of this. He was their only chance. "I'm going to get help. For them," Linda said as she pointed to the bodies of the two pilots laying on the floor. She turned around, stepped aft, unlocked the cockpit door and headed into the cabin.

"Tell the people in the cabin we're headed for the Azores," Ray said as Linda left the cockpit. Gently, he banked the big jet in order to follow the electronic magenta line that was on their navigation screen as he flew across the featureless Atlantic Ocean, toward their best hope of salvation. Flying on one engine and at a reduced airspeed, Ray knew that the Azores would be a slightly more than one flight hour away. That is, if nothing else happened to them.

Chapter Twelve

Ray was flying the Consolidated airliner with his left hand on the captain's control column and his right hand on the power lever for the right engine — the only operating engine that they had at the moment. Ray was continuing to steer the flight along a direct course line to the airport in the Azores, as Jack had been doing when all hell had broken out in the cockpit after the co-pilot panicked and became irrational.

From behind him, Ray could hear activity. He glanced over his shoulder. Although it had been hardly more than a minute since Linda left the cockpit, she had returned with two of the flight attendants and with one male passenger. Without turning around, Ray could hear the three of them as they began the process of removing the two unconscious pilots from the flight deck. From the snippets of conversation that drifted to him, the male passenger the flight attendants had brought forward was some sort of doctor or medical person, and he was instructing the flight attendants on how to maneuver the two wounded pilots and what he would need to deal with them.

Ray wanted to know more about their conditions — particularly Jack's — but he was far too caught up in the tasks at hand in keeping the airliner established in its single-engine flight operation to spare any attention in their direction. He would check on Jack and the co-pilot later; for now, he needed to make certain that the cockpit tasks had been dealt with. He flipped on the autopilot switch, then retrieved the emergency checklist from its holder on the glare shield.

Ray knew that he needed to go slowly and methodically, and if he did it would all come back to him. Although it had been two years since he had looked at those procedures, he had done them so often in the past — usually for training, but once in a while during a real event — that he could get through the list quickly and accurately. Ray paused several times while he was working with the checklists, to be sure that he wasn't rushing. Doing the wrong thing could be worse than doing nothing and what they didn't need now was for him to compound their problems by making a stupid blunder.

In a few minutes Ray had finished. He returned the emergency checklist to its holder, knowing that everything that needed to be done had, in fact, been accomplished properly. That was step one. Ray exhaled slowly, then looked carefully around the cockpit.

Trans-Continental Flight 3 was in the customary single engine configuration, and the flight computers were making the prediction that — at their newly reduced airspeed and cruising altitude — they would reach the airport in the Azores in one hour and fourteen minutes. Ray allowed himself the luxury of a several more deep breaths before he proceeded with the next steps. He knew that rushing when you didn't need to was the biggest single cause of cockpit errors, that it was always important to take your time. They had lots of time left for him to get ready for the landing.

<>

Linda had come from the cockpit and into the cabin a few minutes earlier. She had told Tina that Jack and Peter had both been accidentally shot by Peter's anti-hijacking gun during the final portion of that last wild ride. Tina rushed into the first class cabin to get the man she knew had been listed on the manifest as a doctor, the man who had helped her when she had been caught in the aisle during that second wild ride.

"Medical emergency," was what Tina had said to him and, without another word, the man from seat 3D got up and followed her forward. Tina had the presence of mind to announce in a loud voice to the others in the first class cabin that the two additional pilots they had onboard were fine and that the ship was under control. There would be more news coming from the cockpit soon.

Tina, assisted by the off-duty flight attendant Fred Lyle, and with the help of Linda and the doctor, went to the cockpit and carried back the unconscious bodies of the captain and co-pilot. There was enough floor space between the first class galley and the beginning of the first class seating to lay both men in that area.

Dr. Lee Frankel knelt down between the two unconscious pilots. He looked at Tina. "I hate to ask such an obvious question, but how in god's name could a gun inadvertently go off in the cockpit?"

"Don't know," Tina answered.

"Maybe we should find out."

"I was here in the cabin when it happened. Linda should know."

"Well?" The doctor glanced up at the lady pilot for a moment, then turned back to the two unconscious pilots on the floor. He began to tentatively probe around their wounds.

"It was...an accident," Linda answered. She knew that she was offering a feeble explanation, but there was no need to go into what had happened. Nothing good would come of it. "I'll explain later." There would be more than enough time for that sort of thing when they got on the ground in the Azores.

Lee glanced up. "An accident. Good to hear. I had guessed that it wasn't a recreation of the OK Corral at 35,000 feet." He glanced at the flight attendant who had summoned him and who was, evidently, in charge of the cabin. "I'll need a knife to cut away this clothing," Lee said. He had decided that the older of the two unconscious men, whom he assumed from the four gold stripes on the shoulder epaulets of his blood-soaked shirt was the aircraft's captain, needed the quickest attention. "And a bucket of water, and towels. Get out whatever first aid kits you have, it may have things I can use."

"We have a medical practitioner's kit onboard. Fred has gotten it, and he's opening it right now. I'm afraid we're not allowed to have sharp knives in the galley anymore," Tina said.

"Isn't that like our constrained-view government," Lee said. "They fiddle with their bureaucratic theories of potential assailants and knife-less flights while Rome and this airplane continue to burn."

"Excuse me?" Tina didn't follow him, although it did seem as if he were talking more to himself than to her. "There's no fire. None that I know of." She looked over at Linda, who nodded in agreement.

"I know," Lee answered. "A metaphor. A bad one." For the thousandth time he told himself to stop thinking out loud — that it usually threw people off. He turned to the unconscious captain and began to rip the man's shirt away with his bare hands. "Forget the knife," Lee said while he kept his full attention on the unconscious captain. "Don't need it. I don't want to get in trouble with the government over a security issue. I can see enough of the entry and exit wounds by pulling his shirt away."

"The practitioner's kit is open. There's a scissor in it." Tina took the scissor from Fred and handed it to the doctor. "Here."

"That'll work fine." Lee glanced up at her, nodded, then returned to his patient. "Now, I'll need towels and warm water. Eventually, we'll need blankets."

Tina turned to Fred, who was standing nearer to the galley than her. "Fill up an empty bucket with warm water, then grab a handful of those towels from the overhead bin. See if you can find anything else that might be useful. After that, round up blankets and pillows."

"Okay." Fred turned around, grabbed a bucket and began to fill it with water from the hot water tap.

"How is he?" Tina asked as she turned back to the doctor. The doctor had completely cut away the captain's shirt on the side where the blood was coming from.

"Too early to tell. Not doing real well, that's for certain."

"Keep us informed," Linda said. "Let us know if there's anything we should radio to the medical people ahead of time. We should be in the Azores in an hour," repeating what she had told them a short while earlier. She was anxious to see what the pilot's conditions were, but she was also anxious to get back to the cockpit. "Got to help Ray." Linda turned and walked directly to the cockpit, closing the door behind her.

<><

"How's it going?" Linda was climbing into the co-pilot's seat as she asked the question. "Problems?"

"No." Ray glanced at her. "I ran through the engine-out checklist. Everything is done. Go over it yourself, to be sure I didn't miss anything."

"Right." Linda took the printed checklist out of its glare shield holder and began to recheck each of the items. A minute later she announced, "like you said, it's done." She looked at the co-pilot's flight panel. "We're down to 19,000 feet. The indicated airspeed is lower, too. Two hundred sixty knots. Why?" As soon as she asked the question, she hoped that it hadn't sounded like a challenge. She had already committed herself – hell, she had committed everyone onboard – to whatever this retired pilot decided was best, there was no turning back now.

"I let them drift down." Ray glanced over at the center instrument panel where the fuel gauges were. "Fuel isn't a concern, so our altitude and airspeed doesn't matter either. I don't want to ask too much of our only operating engine. Going lower and slower won't make any difference."

"Right." Linda paused. "The right engine working normally?"

"Seems to be. Haven't seen a quiver."

Linda paused, then asked, "How do you explain this." She waved her hand in front of the engine gauges.

"Can't. I can only guess that the failure has something to do with the two engines getting locked together. Maybe that's why the right engine's running normally now, when there's no second engine coupled to it to screw it up. I once had a situation like that with electric propellers on a Convair 240 when I was doing contract co-pilot work before I got the airline job."

"What kind of airplane?"

"Never mind." For a moment Ray had forgotten how young she was and that she wouldn't have knowledge of a piston engine airliner built in the 50's – airplanes like that were ancient history even when he started flying. Ray took another deep breath; he had allowed himself to relax, and, because of that, he knew that he was thinking clearly and beginning to plan ahead, not simply reacting to each developing situation. That was a good sign. The bad sign was that he didn't know for sure what was going to happen next, if anything. Regardless, though, it was now time for him to get on with the next logical steps.

"Have you contacted air traffic control?" Linda asked

"Not yet." That was the next thing Ray intended to do, although it was not something high on his priority list. If he was talking on the radio, he knew that he wasn't listening to the airplane or watching the instruments as carefully as he should be. He had seen that sort of thing thousands of times at the airline. And he had seen it with Katie, too. It was, he knew, something that Katie was inclined to do, to talk on the radio when she

112

should have been doing something else. Ray shivered and forcibly pushed that memory aside. "Too busy for the radio," Ray said tersely to Linda. "You do it."

"All right."

Ray watched Linda as she reached for the microphone on the co-pilot's side panel. Like most modern pilots, he knew that she, too, wanted to establish that radio link with the outside world as soon as possible, as if those men and women sitting in those control rooms thousands of miles away could have some beneficial input to their current situation. To Ray, giving a radio report was far down the list of what needed to be done.

Ray knew that establishing a radio link with the ground was basically a sham, a potential temporary psychological boost for the pilots, but nothing more. More often than not, it would become a distraction. In his mind's eye he could see Katie reaching for the microphone instead of the flight controls when things started to go bad for her. He had preached to her hundreds of times not to, but now was not the time to think about that. He, more than ever, needed to forget Katie, to let it go.

Ray began to concentrate on what he was doing at the moment and what still needed to be done. Nothing else mattered. He glanced out his side window. The only reality for them for the next hour-and-a-quarter was the cold North Atlantic water below and the promise of useable terrain beyond the horizon that he could land the airliner on. "When you get hold of them, tell them that we're proceeding directly to the airport at Lajes. Give them our current position and our ETA. I don't think we made our 30 degree west position report, so they're probably wondering where the hell we are. "

"Right."

"And also tell them that we'll need immediate medical attention as soon as we land." Ray gestured over his shoulder, toward the cabin door. "How are they?"

"Both unconscious when I left. The man dealing with them is a doctor."

"What I figured."

"He seems competent," Linda said, "and it looked like he was doing everything he could. They're both still alive. The doctor said that Peter's wound didn't look serious, but that Captain Schofield's condition seemed worse. He'll let us know if there's any medical information we need to pass on before the landing."

◇

"I don't suppose there's another doctor onboard, is there?" Lee asked as he continued to work on the captain's gunshot wound.

"When I sent Annette back a few minutes ago to try to keep things calm in coach, I told her to ask around," Tina answered. "She'll make a PA announcement very soon, asking for any trained medical people to identify themselves. But I don't think there are." Tina watched the doctor as he continued to wipe away the blood, evidently looking for exactly where it might be coming from. He seemed tentative, although perhaps he was just being thorough.   Then another idea hit her. "You're not some doctor of English or history or something like that, are you?" Tina asked.

Lee tilted his head toward her, and her question had made him smile. "No, but you're very perceptive. I'm not far from it. I'm a practicing psychiatrist. The good news is that I do have an MD degree, and I have dealt directly with this type of thing in my distant past." He wiped away more blood and found what he was looking for. "Okay, this is what I was looking for," Lee said as he began working on the captain's left side, near to his stomach. "This is what appears to be the entry wound, and it certainly is where most of the blood has come from. We've got it mostly stopped with direct pressure. We can bandage this area tight."

"Did the bullet do any…big damage?" Tina asked.

"No way to tell. But, if I had to guess, I'd say no based on the clean and relatively straight exit wound. That's another good sign." Lee pointed to a smaller spot on the captain's side, not very far from the entry wound.   By now, he was even surprising himself at how many of the medical techniques from those early years were coming back to him; he knew that half the battle would be in not second-guessing himself. He knew that's what Viktor would have said.   "These ballistic trauma cases are difficult to diagnose," Lee said to the flight attendant, "especially in these conditions. My guess is that we're dealing more with the effects of blood loss and hydrostatic shock."

114

"How about the co-pilot?" Tina asked as she pointed to Peter. He was laying a few feet away, and even from where she stood he didn't look as bad off as the captain did.

"Also blood loss and certainly shock, but his wound is through the fleshy part of his shoulder. I wouldn't suspect anything crucial has been injured – hell, there's nothing crucial up there. As long as we can keep the bleeding..." Lee suddenly stopped talking, because he heard and felt a dramatic change in the airliner's flight condition.

<>

The enormous surge in both vibration and engine power came at Trans-Continental Flight 3 at once, in one powerful sweeping motion, like an express train roaring headlong through a local station in the dead of night. The run to full power and beyond had instantly transformed their tranquil flight status into a complete and utter nightmare once again.

"Christ!" Ray immediately disengaged the autopilot and grabbed the control wheel with his left hand. His right hand slammed the operating engine's throttle fully aft to its flight idle setting, but he didn't need to look at the engine gauges to see that, once again, the engine had gone into an unbridled runaway condition.

"Going beyond full power!" Linda shouted out.

"Pull the engine control circuit breakers! All of them!" Ray shouted as he wrestled with the airliner and did the only thing that he could — he pulled on the control wheel and allowed the airliner to once again begin a steep climb. Having only one running engine hadn't made the slightest difference in whatever was wrong – horribly wrong – that created these runaways. But with only one engine running this time, and with their beginning altitude lower, there was no immediate danger of running out of performance parameters if they kept the nose pointed increasingly upward. "Linda, hurry! Pull the engine control circuit breakers!" he repeated. The idea of pulling engine circuit breakers had entered his mind a short while ago, but he had been reluctant to change anything about their condition since their single running engine seemed to be doing fine. Now, he regretted not having pulled those circuit breakers.

Linda dropped the microphone, unbuckled her seatbelt and jumped out of the co-pilot's flight chair as she began to maneuver herself toward the countless rows of circuit breakers that lined the cockpit ceiling and the aft flight deck sidewall. "Which ones?"

"Don't know! All of them!" Ray didn't know what else they could do, and a quick glance toward the center instrument panel confirmed what his gut instincts were telling him; that the right engine — their only operating engine — was surging far above the published limits and that there was no way it could go on like this indefinitely. It was now obvious that his guess that the runaways had something to do with both engines being locked together was dead wrong; what other things had he also guessed wrong? The way the right engine was running away it would fail internally very soon. Then, they would be without any engines. "Hurry!"

◇

The noises from the airplane were increasing with every passing instant, and Lee knew in his heart that they were about to experience the same incredible problems that they'd experienced too many times already. "Starting again!" Lee shouted as he laid down against the captain's body to hold the unconscious pilot steady so his gunshot wound wouldn't reopen. "Grab onto something!"

Tina wrapped her arms around the edge of the bulkhead as the airliner pitched its nose upward again. Her mind immediately locked onto a single thought, that Ray was the only one who could help them, who would be able to save them. Tina felt the aircraft continue to pitch its nose higher and higher.

"Going straight up!" Lee said. For an instant, he marveled at how detached he felt from this calamitous event, as if it weren't happening to him, as if it were some sort of movie he was watching rather than being an integral part of it. It was, he knew, like the descriptions of those prisoners in Auschwitz, Treblinka and Buchenwald that he had read about and, eventually, spoken with. *Detachment*. That's what he had labeled it, and now Lee Frankel was living through the same sensations, living inside his own research project. If they somehow survived

116

this, he would understand – he would *feel* – for the first time what those prison camp inmates had been trying to explain to him these past few years.

"Yes...we're climbing. Straight up. Too much engine noise. Something really bad is happening. God help us." Tina held on to the airplane sidewall and waited for this nightmare to end. To finally end, one way or the other. Tina closed her eyes; in her mind's eye, she could see Ray in the cockpit, struggling with the airliner's flight controls.

<>

Linda had begun yanking out handfuls of circuit breakers from the panel locations that she remembered were most directly related to the engines and their electronic control circuits. With each one that she pulled, she prayed that the right engine would suddenly snap itself back to flight idle as the engines had earlier. But there was no change. With the increasing G forces and the pitched deck angle she began losing her balance, but she managed to remain upright.

Then, with the biggest surge and shudder yet, and with an audible but surprisingly muted and dull explosion, the right engine on the airliner tore itself apart internally; it completely failed.

"No power!" Ray shouted as he pitched the airliner nose-down to make up for the instant lack of flight thrust. He glanced at the captain's altimeter and saw that they had reached an apogee of 23,400 feet for this particular wild ride to hell. They had, in one instant, become nothing more than a 150 ton glider that was headed downhill at a rate in excess of 2,000 feet per minute. They could fly, but downhill only — and in ten minutes they would reach the surface of the Atlantic Ocean.

Linda jumped into the co-pilot's seat immediately after their only running engine had failed, and after she rebuckled her seatbelt she grabbed for the co-pilot's microphone. "Mayday...Mayday...Trans-Continental Flight 3...Out of control...Clarke has taken over..." she hollered into the microphone as she held onto it with both hands. Her mind was a whirl of conflicting thoughts and impulses, and she didn't know what to do next. There was nothing left to do, except hold onto the microphone and...

"Stop that! Put that down! Start helping me!" Ray shouted. He could feel the loss of control of the ship's pressurization system as he felt the discomforting popping in his ears, but that was the least of their problems and, besides, they would be descending into thicker air nearly as quickly as the internal cabin pressure would be bleeding off from the lack of any running engines.

Linda dropped the microphone and turned to face Ray. "Do what? How? What can we do?"

"The left engine. In reserve. Restart it. Do an airstart."

"Damn." Under this incredible pressure, Linda had momentarily forgotten that Ray had *voluntarily* shut down the left engine to keep it in reserve — which was an unheard-of procedure. But, by doing so, the left engine should be useable. If they could get it restarted. "Keep the airspeed where it needs to be. I'll get the ignitors on, then the fuel," she responded, pulling up the short air start drill from her memory.

For an instant Linda rehearsed the drill carefully in her mind since getting a shutdown engine to properly relight during an unpowered descent required that the airplane be at the proper forward speed for its particular altitude, then ignition would be introduced and, finally, the fuel. The sequence had to be right...and so did...lots of other factors...Linda reached up for the left engine ignitor switches on the overhead control panel.

"Holding the airspeed," Ray said. "Go ahead. Now."

"Okay." Linda pushed the ignition switches to the on position. But the monitor lights beside the engine ignition switches remained extinguished. That pair of lights for each engine would indicate when the engine ignitors for that side were receiving proper power . "No ignitors!" she shouted.

"Cycle them! Hurry!" Ray held their airspeed constant by maintaining the proper degree of nose down pitch. "Nineteen thousand feet," he announced, mostly to himself as he watched the unwinding altimeter. They had eight more minutes. At the most.

Linda took the ignition switches to the off position for a count of one, two, three, then cycled them back to the on position again. "Still nothing," she announced as she looked up at the unlit bulbs in disbelief. Those bulbs turning bright meant the difference between getting the left engine running again or not. In living or dying.

"What's happening?"

"Nothing. I don't understand." Inexplicably, there was no ignition. Linda took her eyes off the overhead control panel and looked at Ray in the captain's flight chair. She was absolutely perplexed. "Nothing." Linda could see that Ray was carefully flying the airliner, holding the airspeed exactly where the book said that it needed to be. But all the proper airspeed control in the world would make no difference if she couldn't get the ignition for the left engine to turn on. "Don't know what else to do," she said, in a voice almost too low to hear. Without ignition to the left engine to relight it, and with the right engine already destroyed, they would have no available engine power. They'd have no chance at all, they were going to die.

Chapter Thirteen

In the captain's seat of Trans-Continental Flight 3, Ray was dividing his attention between keeping the ship's airspeed where it needed to be if they had any hope of doing an inflight restart of the left engine and glancing around the cockpit to find a clue as to why the engine ignition systems wouldn't turn on. He resisted the impulse to look out the cockpit window – all that would show him was where their lives would end. Any hope for them would come from the ignition switches and the readings on the instrument gauges.

They were down to 15,000 feet in their unpowered descent, which, he knew, meant that at this accelerated airspeed and at the rate they were gliding down, they had hardly more than six minutes until they hit the surface of the Atlantic Ocean. Yet with only minutes until total disaster, his mind remained a blank; he had run out of options and ideas.

Linda, in the co-pilot's seat, looked over the inert engine instruments once more, then decided that the chance of getting the left engine to run was hopeless. She picked up the public address system handset at the rear of the center console. "Ray, should I tell the cabin to prepare to ditch?" she asked. Doing something – anything – was better than waiting, even something as futile as preparing for this North Atlantic ocean ditching.

Ray glanced at her. Reluctantly, he finally replied, "Yes." He didn't know what else to say since he hadn't come up with a single additional way to get the ignitors to turn on. The odds of them — any of them — surviving a mid-Atlantic ditching were slim to none, and the odds of any survivors being rescued before they died of exposure were even less. "Slowing the airspeed. More time before we hit the water." Even though he knew it was hopeless, Ray's piloting instincts kept him at the controls. He would fly the airliner until there was no more airplane left for him to fly. They had five more minutes. Ray gently pulled on the control wheel in order to transform their airspeed into a lowered descent rate. "Giving them time to get the cabin prepared," he said, although that remark sounded nearly insane. Prepared for what? Prepared to die.

"Right." Linda held the PA handset up to her mouth and pressed the button. "Cabin Attendants! Attention! Prepare the aircraft for ditching in five minutes! I say again, immediately prepare the aircraft for ditching. Ditching in five minutes!" Linda allowed her finger to slide off the handset button. She had tried to sound calm, but she knew that she wasn't and she knew that her voice reflected that. She could hardly believe that she had made that announcement and said those words. Ditching. It was a horrible, horrible dream. Then another gang of thoughts raced through her mind, pushing everything else out, as she began to focus more on herself, focusing on the harsh truth that she would never see her mother again. Or her father. That she'd never see her sister. All of them would, she knew, be devastated. Karen would be devastated.

"Tell the cabin we'll give them a one minute warning," Ray said to her.

"Okay," she answered distractedly, getting her thoughts back in focus as she fumbled for the PA handset.

Ray scanned the instrument panel. The engine gauges were stone-dead, but the flight instruments were showing him the readings he was looking for. The ship's airspeed was steady at 180 knots, and the rate of descent had momentarily decreased to under 1,500 feet per minute. The altitude was down to 10,400 feet as the altimeter continued to unwind.

He had gained a minute or, at the most, a minute-and-a-half of additional life expectancy for them by slowing the aircraft and decreasing their rate of descent, but by doing so he had also given up any chance of getting their only useable engine to accomplish a successful air start and begin producing power again. They were committed now. The book called for at least 220 knots as the absolute minimum to attempt an air start and he was voluntarily giving up that option. But then Ray suddenly realized that the speed recommendation was from the Boeing 767 pilot's handbook. He had never seen the Consolidated 768 version of those procedures. "Are the relight speeds and procedures for the 768 the same as they were on the 767?" Ray quickly asked her. Maybe he wasn't going fast enough – or too fast.

"Yes," Linda answered. She had picked up the PA handset but hadn't pressed the button as yet. "Exactly the same."

121

"You sure?" His heart fell again; it was hard to believe that there were any more disappointments left, not with the surface of the North Atlantic only four minutes below them. Somehow, he had managed to find another one.

"Positive." Linda pressed the PA handset button to make the additional announcement. "Cabin attendants, we will give a one-minute warning before impact! I say again, a one-minute warning for bracing!" She let go of the handset button and pushed the PA microphone into its cradle, then looked at Ray. "I'll get our life jackets," she said. She grabbed two life jackets from their holders and began to put hers on. "Help you with yours."

"Okay." But Ray wasn't thinking about the life jackets, his mind was on the ignition system of the jetliner and he was trying to figure out this incredible puzzle as to why they weren't working for them. Could their failure somehow be related to whatever was causing these massive engine runaways, whatever was causing this sort of impossible electronic short-circuiting that had somehow...or was it that the new ignition indicator lights that had failed, or there was some subtle difference in the 768 version, or...hundreds of technical snippets were running through Ray's head, but none of them gave him a clue as to what the problem might be.

"Should I shut down the main battery switches before we hit the water?" Linda asked. She had given up on the relight attempt, but she was still looking for something useful to do, some way that she could add something positive to those final minutes of their flight. Thinking about useful flying procedures was far preferable to looking out the window and watching the waves getting larger. If she sat quietly and looked out the window, Linda wondered if she might panic as Peter had done. Her churning insides told her that it was certainly a possibility, that she needed to stay busy. "Here." Linda had gotten her life jacket on and was picking up Ray's life jacket to help him put it on.

But Ray wasn't thinking about his life jacket, he was thinking about what she had asked him about shutting down the battery switches. Ray took his eyes off the flight instruments and glanced at the overhead panel where the system operating switches were. *Batteries...circuits...breakers...* Those words kept rolling through his mind, and, suddenly, a crystal clear thought hit him like a bomb: *circuit breakers.* In one instant he had gone from totally clueless to completely understanding their situation. "Damn! Linda, quick, get up! Those circuit breakers you pulled, push them in! All of them!"

In their desperate attempt to stop the right engine from continuing its runaway that eventually led to its total destruction, they had yanked out all the engine circuit breakers, an unorthodox procedure. That was why, in this stress-filled situation, neither one of them had focused on what they had done only minutes before. They had pulled out all the circuit breakers. Neither one of them had seen the connection between their current situation and their previous attempts to solve the earlier problem. The ignition circuits were undoubtedly getting their power from along the same routing as the other engine electronic circuits. "Quickly!" Ray said.

"Yes!" Linda understood. She jumped from her seat and reached for the countless rows of circuit breakers that she had manually disengaged in that last-ditch emergency effort to save the right engine. It was only minutes before but, now, it seemed hours ago. "They're in!"

"Hit the ignitors!"

"Right." From her standing position between the two pilot's seats, Linda reached forward and flipped the ignition switches to their Flight positions. Instantly, the pair of indicator lights adjacent to them turned on. "Yes! Ignition!" she shouted. "Should I turn on the…"

"No." Ray saw her hand go to the fuel valve for the left engine. "Not yet. Airspeed." He knew that he needed to get the airspeed back up, to at least 220 knots. He had given their precious airspeed away when he abandoned any hope of getting a relight, when he was getting them ready for the ditching. "Wait."

"Right." Linda stood motionless behind the center console, her right hand on the fuel lever of the left engine, the only engine they had left, the only chance they had. Ray had to get back the airspeed they had given up. He absolutely had to. "Tell me when."

Ray pushed forward on the captain's control column, which increased the airspeed as they pointed themselves downhill at a steeper angle. But doing so also rapidly increased their rate of descent. They were passing through 7,000 feet, but the rate of descent was approaching 3,000 feet per minute in their dive to gain airspeed. "Wait...wait..." Ray watched the airspeed indicator as it continued to rise. "Now!" he said as soon as the number got to the book figure of 220 knots.

Both of them turned their attention to the center instrument panel where the engine temperature gauges were. That would show the first sign of a successful relight. Nothing happened. The needle on the left engine temperature gauge remained locked on the bottom of its scale.

"The book says that it can take up to thirty seconds," Linda volunteered nervously, her eyes riveted to the instruments.

"I know." But Ray also knew something else, too — that a particular technical book he had once read had said much more. It had said that the use of higher airspeeds will provide a far better chance of a successful relight in nearly all high-bypass engines. Maybe this was a greater factor in the Consolidated 768 version of the airplane. Maybe. He had to try.

Ray glanced at the altimeter: they were now down to 5,100 feet. They had, once again, become downhill skiers — but this time, they were running out of mountain. "Shut off the fuel lever!"

"What?!" Linda couldn't believe what he was saying. "Shut it off?!"

"Yes! The left fuel lever — shut it off! Right now!" Ray pushed aggressively forward on the captain's control wheel. "Need a reset!" Out of the corner of his eye, he could see that she had immediately complied, although Ray knew that she didn't understand what he was about to try. "More airspeed!" is all he had time to say as he tried to figure how much of a last-ditch attempt they had left. 4,600 feet. Rate of descent was slightly over 3,000 feet per minute. Airspeed was now 245 knots and climbing.

"Running out of altitude," Linda said in a frightened, trembling voice. She could no longer keep her eyes averted – she looked outside at the surface of the Atlantic Ocean below, and it was coming up quickly. She had never been this low over the ocean before, and she could easily see the patterns of large swells from this low of an altitude. *An angry sea,* was the expression that popped into her head. It was a deadly, angry sea.

"Get ready." Ray had decided to gamble on one more attempt. He would trade their precious altitude for airspeed and try to get the ship to at least 260 knots of forward speed. If there was no relight by 500 feet, he would abandon the attempt, flatten out their flight path and let the airliner settle onto the ocean surface. It would, at best, be a hopeless situation for them if the engine didn't relight. "Left engine fuel lever on! Now!"

Linda moved the left engine's fuel lever to its on position, and her eyes locked onto the left engine temperature gauge on the center instrument panel. Five seconds, six seconds, seven seconds...she knew that with every passing moment, the odds of getting that engine running again were diminishing. She had heard that sometimes these engines wouldn't do an inflight restart for God knows what reason, and there was always the chance that the left engine had been internally damaged from the previous runaways. Regardless of the reason, they were almost out of altitude, but she wouldn't allow herself to look outside.

"Two thousand feet," Linda said. She starred intently at the left engine temperature gauge. "Still nothing...nothing...wait..." Suddenly, she pointed at the temperature gauge on the instrument panel. "Yes...look!"

Ray saw it, too. The needle had begun to rise. Slowly. Very slowly. It was creeping up from the bottom of the scale. He needed to keep the airspeed where it was, but he was also almost out of altitude. The altimeter quickly wound down through 1,500 feet, while their rate of descent was holding steady at 3,000 feet per minute. There was 30 seconds left, no more. In half a minute they would hit the water.

"Ray — slow the descent!" Linda shouted. She had finally looked up from the instrument panel and saw the ocean directly in front of them with the ship's nose pointed down at a steep angle. The view was startling — no, far beyond startling, it was terrifying. From this close, Linda could see the waves themselves, and the cross-currents and the white caps. It was a moderately rough sea – a deadly, angry sea – and they would have no chance whatsoever on this ditching attempt if he didn't pick up the ship's nose very soon. "Flatten out the descent!"

"No!" 900 feet. The left engine was spooling up, but it had a long way to go before it would produce useable power. Ray decided, at that instant, that it would be all or nothing for them.

"Keeping the airspeed up! Without that engine, we don't stand a chance!"

Linda was frozen by the sight outside the cockpit window: the churning Atlantic Ocean now only a few hundred feet below them. For an instant, she thought that Ray was going to dive the airliner straight into the water, as if he'd rather have them die instantly rather than go through the hopeless agony of this futile ditching attempt. But, at the very last moment, he began to tug on the captain's control wheel and began to level the airliner out.

"Steady..." A few seconds ticked by. Finally, Ray said, "Push up the left throttle! Now! All the way!"

They were hardly more than a hundred feet above the surface of the water but, for a few seconds at least, Ray had leveled the airliner by trading their extra airspeed in an aerodynamic exchange to stop their downward travel. But the airspeed was bleeding off quickly, far too quickly. And without engine power...

"Here comes the power!" Linda shouted. Her eyes were back inside, locked on the engine gauges.

Ray could literally feel the push of the power from the big engine on the left wing as it began to get them going forward again. "Steady..." he said, mostly to himself. It was, he knew, a race of pure momentum — that the increasing engine power had to stop the airspeed's previous deceleration trend and turn it into an accelerating motion instead. That would take time, and enough time to do this enormous swing of momentum might not be available. "Steady..." he said a second time, the sound of his own voice helping to keep him as calm as possible, as focused as possible.

Linda glanced at the airspeed indicator. 190 knots. 185 knots. 180 knots. She knew that the airliner would stall and fall out of the sky if the airspeed went much lower. "One seventy-five," she announced, her eyes fixed rigidly to the airspeed indicator on the captain's flight panel. She did not want to look outside at the surface of the ocean again. She wouldn't, no matter what. She knew that life or death was directly in front of her, in those numbers. "One seventy-three."

Ray was threading an aerodynamic tightrope; he had no altitude left, and no airspeed cushion either. Their only chance was that the left engine would accelerate quickly enough to hold their airspeed. If not, the ship would stall and fall into the ocean. They would die, most likely immediately on impact with the waves when the airliner disintegrated.

"One seventy-three," Linda said again. The airspeed needle seemed to be stuck at that number for an eternity. "One seventy-three," she repeated a third time. Then she said, "One seventy-five! Oh, my God! One eighty! One eighty-five! One ninety!"

Cautiously, Ray gently maneuvered the captain's control wheel so that the airliner began a gradual climb to give them more distance from the tumultuous waters of the Atlantic Ocean below. While he was doing it, he pushed everything else – his conscious thoughts, his emotions – aside. He was flying the airliner on pure instinct and feel.

"Two hundred knots," Linda announced. "We made it! God Almighty, we made it!"

When the altitude reached 500 feet and the airspeed reached 220 knots, Ray reached up with his right hand. Without a word, he shut down the aircraft's master electrical switches on the aircraft's overhead instrument panel. Instantly, every light, every instrument, every radio, every piece of modern high-tech equipment in the entire airliner went completely dark.

Book Four

There is no question in my mind that management decisions and actions, or more frequently, indecisions and inactions, cause accidents.
—John Lauber, National Transportation Safety Board

This is a nasty, rotten business.
—Robert L. Crandall, CEO & President, American Airlines

Chapter Fourteen

Martin Luffman sat at his desk at the rear of the Trans-Continental Airlines dispatch office with a stack of routine expense reports spread out in front of him. He took a cursory glance at the report on the top of the stack, initialed his approval at the corner, then laid the stack down. Marty swivelled in his chair and glanced out the large window that separated his private office from the dispatch area where the current duty shift personnel were working with the midday flights.

It was the busiest time of the day for the airline. In the expansive, windowless room on the third floor of the airline's Operations Center adjacent to their three large maintenance hangars at JFK International Airport, only a handful of the twenty-two computerized dispatch stations were not currently occupied. So far, it had been a completely routine day for flight operations, and a routine day of personnel issues with only one dispatcher on sick call and one other dispatcher away to a technical conference.

Marty looked up and down the rows of dispatchers sitting at their consoles, some of them typing at keyboards, others sitting back and looking through their paperwork, a few others on the telephone. If anyone from the Executive Offices in Manhattan had elected to take the trip to the airport and walk in at that moment, the picture of the dispatch center was exactly what Marty would want them to see — low key, professional, and unquestionably competent.

No one in upper management had ever hinted that the Dispatch Department, under his leadership, was anything less — which was exactly what Marty was counting on. When he became the Director of Dispatch two years ago he had shaped up this portion of the airline by letting a few select heads roll; it was the sort of display that the new President seemed to particularly like. His departmental moves were not popular with the rank and file, but those changes had payed off with fast and very positive improvements. Marty had done the job he had promised the new President he would do.

Marty turned in his chair and looked at the few empty dispatcher desks on the far left of the room. Those empty desks were the International departure stations, and they would be fully staffed with dispatch personnel a few hours from now as the airline's standard preparations for the nightly assault on Europe began. By 4:00pm, that side of the room would be humming. Yes, indeed, everything was running like clockwork, running precisely as it should.

Marty was about to turn and get back to his expense reports when he noticed that Dave Wilder, the shift supervisor, was moving rapidly across the open area that separated the communications room at the right front of the dispatch facility from his office. Marty swivelled to face the glass door, knowing full well that Dave would be wound up over something. Wilder was a good supervisor, but he always let himself get agitated over whatever the latest problem might be – problems that ranged from a jammed pencil sharpener to a glitching computer.

The door burst open and Wilder rushed in, waving a sheet of paper. "Marty, a real emergency…!"

"Calm down, Dave."

"Flight 3! From Rome!"

"Dave, I know where Flight 3 comes from." Marty smiled indulgently. "Now, calm yourself down. Tell it to me slowly and carefully. What's today's problem with our Flight 3 from Rome? Did the interline baggage misconnect again?"

Wilder stared down at Marty's round, cherub face with that annoying smirk plastered across it. What Wilder had a sudden urge to do was to pick that little 5 foot 6 inch Napoleon up by his shirt lapels and smash him against the office wall. Instead, Wilder stood where he was and took a deep breath. Finally, he spoke. "Flight 3. A hijacking."

"A what?!" Marty stood up; he could see a bevy of activity across the dispatch area as, apparently, the word was rapidly spreading throughout the department. "Is it confirmed? How do we know?" Marty began to move toward the open door.

"The information is sketchy." Wilder was following the director out of the room and toward the dispatch position that handled Flight 3. "But it's specific. Two separate radio messages. They were transmitted on the usual high frequency air traffic control channel for that sector of the Atlantic."

"Two messages?"

"Yes. Twelve minutes apart. The transcripts have been emailed to us, and we'll have the actual voice recordings of those transmissions in a short while, also via email." Wilder pointed in front of them, toward dispatch desk number 17. "The text of those messages are up on Wally's monitor."

"Right." Marty took the last few strides to where Wally Poel's dispatch station was, and, apparently where every other dispatcher on duty had decided to congregate. "Hey, folks," Marty announced to the assembled crowd, "we've got other flights to work out there so let's get back to it. We'll keep you informed of everything that we know about the Flight 3 situation as more information comes in." Marty waited a moment until the dispatchers had dispersed toward their assigned stations, then he turned and looked at Wally Poel.

Poel was the dispatcher who had picked up the monitoring of Flight 3 when the morning shift had taken over from the late night crew. "Wally," Marty asked, "was everything normal until we got these radio messages relayed to us?" he said.

"Absolutely." Poel fidgeted nervously in his seat. "The flight was strictly routine through 20 West. In every way. We never did get another position report after that, although their 30 West report was due several minutes ago." Poel squirmed, then added, "But it's not particularly late, even now. Then we got those two radio messages from Shanwick and confirmed by Santa Maria."

"So, we never had any reason to suspect that something was going on up there, right?" Marty wanted to be certain that there would not be a hint of a screw up in his department. In one way, he hated the fact that covering his ass – having the proper and correct dispatch paperwork on file – had become his main mission in life. On the other hand, that was the reality in the modern corporate world where proper form had become more important than substance. Complying with the endless laws and rules of the government and the airline had become his *raison d'être*, as the French station manager had once pointed out to him.

131

"Yes, that's right. We had absolutely no reason to suspect a single thing." Wally Poel had been a dispatcher for a long time — in fact, he was the most senior dispatcher on duty today — and he knew exactly what Marty was getting at, and he damn well knew what Marty wanted to hear. "Everything on our end is air tight. Whatever happened out there, we didn't contribute anything negative to the event from our end. Our hands are totally clean."

"You certain?"

"Yes," Poel said emphatically. "Bet my career on it." Which Poel knew was true: betting his career was exactly what he was doing.

"Okay." Marty looked down at Poel's computer screen. "Are these the transcripts of the radio messages?"

"That's what they're telling us. Like I said, they've indicated that these messages were picked up simultaneously by both the Shanwick and Santa Maria receivers. Both locations have them recorded."

"Okay." Marty leaned closer to the computer screen to read the two text messages:

Message Number 1, recorded at 1827 UTC / 12:27pm EST:

Mayday, Trans-Continental Flight 3 is being hijacked. We've got this lunatic retired pilot in the cockpit and he's suicidal — he's trying to kill us. It's like 9/11 again.

Message Number 2, recorded at 1839 UTC / 12:39pm EST:

Mayday...Mayday...Trans-Continental Flight 3...Out of control...Clarke has taken over...

Marty took a half step backward from the computer screen at desk 17 in disbelief. He certainly couldn't have predicted what the two radio messages might have been, but nothing like these. Marty looked at Wally Poel, then at Dave Wilder in stunned silence. He turned back to the dispatcher's computer screen. After a brief time, Marty spoke. "This is incredible," he said in a low voice. He shook his head slowly. *Retired pilot...suicide...9/11.* Finally he added, "Heaven help them." At that moment, that was the only additional thing that Marty could think of to say.

◇

Captain George Fisher was sitting behind his desk, with Al and the magazine reporter Jennifer sitting across from him, when the telephone rang. The three of them, along with Maynard, had spent an early and long lunch hour in the employee cafeteria and had quite a good time of it.

What ostensibly began as a general background interview for Jennifer's magazine article on the retirement of Albert DeWitt had somehow developed into a never ending array of airline stories, each one better than the last. Some of Jennifer's questions – particularly those about Kyle, the Board of Directors and recent policy shifts at the airline – were verifying to George what he suspected her real intentions might be, but he decided to wait and see what would develop.

After lunch, Maynard left the group to run errands in the building while Jennifer and Al joined George in his office. They were laughing about a story from the old days when George reached for the ringing telephone.

The call came on an internal company line. "Hello, Marty." The call was from the Director of Dispatch and George listened in silence for a few moments, his facial expression turning cold. Finally, he spoke. "Be right down. Get every detail of that flight assembled on your desk. See if there are any new details coming in from Shanwick or Santa Maria." George hung up, then turned to the other two. "Got a problem. A real problem."

Al knew George well enough that there was no question that this would be something big — he could see it on the man's face. "I'll help if I can."

"I'll take you up on that." George rose from his chair and motioned for Al to follow him. "As I remember from the management briefing last week, the new Director of Public Relations doesn't arrive at his office until next Monday."

"That's right." Al rose from his chair and followed George.

133

"We're going to need immediate public relations coverage." George paused. "It's a hijacking."

"A hijacking. Damn. Which flight?"

"Three. From Rome."

Al pulled his new pocket watch out and glanced at it. It was not quite 1:00 pm, so if Flight 3 had left on schedule, then they were still four hours out of New York. "The flight is over the Atlantic, if they departed on time."

"Yes. They did depart Rome on time. That's where the flight currently is, or so I've been told. We'll know more in a few minutes." George walked out the office door and toward the elevator that would take him to the Dispatch floor.

"What about me?" Jennifer asked. Normally, she wouldn't ask an open-ended question like that – it was the quickest way to get the wrong answer – but she had put herself in George Fisher's hands and needed his direct approval to continue. Sink or swim, she had already committed herself to George Fisher. Jennifer walked a few steps behind the two men, her notepad out. She knew that this would probably be the end of the line for her. There was no question that Henry was going to be pissed, really pissed, when she told him how close they had been to pulling this off. It was damn bad luck for them.

George stopped, turned and looked at her for a long moment. He was wrestling with alternatives, considering his options. Normally, at this point, he would have told a member of the press to leave the building. But these times weren't normal, not by a long shot. *Fuck Brandon Kyle.* Finally, George spoke. "I would guess that fate has intervened on your behalf," he said.

"In what way?" Jennifer asked. She had no idea what he might say next.

"You said that you wanted more than fluff, that you wanted the real story for your article."

"Yes. That's what I said." Jennifer paused. "It's important. For the reasons I said before." Her instincts told her to take the chance. Right now. "And even more reasons than that." It was time to let it all out, not to hold back. "For more reasons than I mentioned earlier. For very important reasons that I'm absolutely certain you'll agree with."

"So, you're telling me that there's more to this than you've said so far. At this point, that would have been my guess." George nodded toward her. *Fuck Brandon Kyle. Fuck his Puzzle Palace buddies.* "Okay, you stick with us. As far as I see, there's no reason that you shouldn't. You're already authorized to be here." George pressed the elevator call button. "Now, instead of talking about it, you can watch Al at work. That'll be good for your article, wouldn't you say?"

"Yes, it would."

"And it would be good – very good, I would imagine – for those other reasons that I'm certain you'll want to explain to us in the very near future," George added as he glanced over his shoulder toward where she stood at the rear of the elevator.

"Absolutely," Jennifer answered. "You have my word. I'll explain everything."

"Good enough for me," George answered. "How about you, Al?"

"Yes." Al turned toward and slowly stepped in her direction until their faces were hardly more than inches apart. Then, standing that near, he spoke in a low but calm and friendly voice. "I had this feeling," Al said, "from nearly the beginning that there was more to this than a retirement interview. Hell, you're too sharp a lady to squander your time on old stories from old men. Am I right?"

"...Well...I..."

Al didn't wait for her stammered reply. Instead, he said, "So far, you've only been showing us the face cards." He paused for an instant, smiled, then added, "I look forward to seeing what sort of cards you might be holding in the hole."

"...I..." Jennifer was stunned. They knew. They had known all along. Both of them.

"Not right now." Al took a step back, then held up one finger on one hand. "Soon, but not right now," he repeated. "Our problems with Flight 3 need to come first. You can tell us more when we have more time to listen."

When the elevator door opened, George wordlessly led the way down the corridor with Al and Jennifer walking in silence a few feet behind him.

◇

Marty was on a self-imposed tight rope since the news about Flight 3 had been brought to him. His first concern was the safety of Flight 3, but after that Marty needed to see that everything connected with his department was absolutely perfect since their actions would be analyzed and scrutinized endlessly. As George had asked on the phone, Marty was using the time to get the Flight 3 data assembled on his desk. Then, after he arrived, George Fisher would be the man in charge and Marty could breath a little easier – as long as none of his dispatchers had stepped on their dicks. Any discoveries that the dispatch department screwed up would find themselves in Marty's lap.

Marty had gotten a printout of the Trans-Atlantic flight planning paperwork, and Wilder assured him that the crew list and passenger manifest would be brought within five minutes. Wally Poel brought in printed sheets of the pertinent weather, and, while this was being assembled, Marty opened the company's emergency procedures handbook and was carefully checking the official list of who had to be notified and in what order. He was reading through that checklist when his office door opened and George walked in, with two others walking in behind him.

"Marty, we'll use your office as the command post," Fisher announced as soon as he stepped inside.

"Right. I assumed we would." Marty looked at the other two who had walked in with Fisher: Al DeWitt, plus an attractive young lady who was standing next to him holding a notepad in her hand. "Al, I'm surprised to see you. I heard you retired yesterday."

"I did. I was doing a magazine interview. George asked me to help with this Flight 3 situation." Al stepped aside and gestured toward Jennifer. "This is Miss Lane, from *Public Relations World Magazine*. We were finishing the interview in George's office when you called. Since she has official approval to be here, she'll follow me while I handle whatever public relations aspects this Flight 3 situation calls for."

Marty stood silently for a moment, then turned to George. He hated to make a scene in front of the lady, but.... "Do you think we should have a...press representative... here while we're still getting our...bearings? I mean, we don't know what happened, and where any of this might be..."

George, who had been scanning the copy of Flight 3's paperwork, picked up another pile of papers from Marty's desk. "Brandon Kyle knows that Miss Lane is here today. He's provided her with an interview this morning," George said as he glanced at Marty. "So, let's get off that subject and down to operational particulars. Any new word on Flight 3's situation?"

"Nothing." Marty gestured toward the paperwork in Fisher's hand and at the pile of papers on the table at the far side of the room. "I'm getting a copy of everything. Everything that might be relevant. I've learned that Flight 3 is not answering radio calls on the usual frequencies, and they are not responding to our electronic paging messages sent by either HF or satellite. They are, for the moment at least, out of communications."

"Really?" Jennifer took a half step forward. Now that she was officially accepted, there was no reason not to ask questions. With this turn of events, this is going to be one hell of a piece for *Business World Media*. Maybe even a series. Henry will shit when he hears that I was standing right here, right in the middle of their dispatch headquarters while it was happening. "Are they still flying okay?" Jennifer asked.

"We have no idea." Marty didn't like answering questions from this lady reporter, but if both George and Brandon Kyle had authorized it, then...

"No idea? How about, like, radar or something?" Jennifer glanced at Al, then at Marty. "Surely you can tell that the airliner is flying normally and that the airplane is headed this way, can't you?"

"No," George answered. He had finished scanning through Flight 3's computer paperwork and laid the large stack down on Marty's desk. "Contrary to what the public thinks, there is no radar coverage over the ocean. We only know a flight's location when the pilots tell us. They transmit their position via radio or satellite messaging. If we can't communicate with them, we can only guess where they might be and what their situation is."

"Really?" Jennifer made a note on her pad. "That's frightening."

"And so is this." Marty took a single sheet of paper from the far corner of his desk, another piece of the puzzle in this incredible turn of events and, so far, the most shocking portion of it. "Here is the complete transcript of those last two radio messages that I told you about, the last known messages sent out by Flight 3. What I didn't say on the telephone were the particulars in the messages. I wanted you to read them for yourself." Marty handed that single sheet of paper to George.

George read the paper silently, not showing any emotion. Finally, he said, "This is unbelievable." *Retired pilot...Clarke.* The Clarke name had jumped out at him, but George dismissed it. No way, it had to be a coincidence. George decided that the name was a common one – after all, Trans-Continental had several pilots named Clarke over the years, some long retired, some still active. Hell, this message could refer to a pilot who had flown for a different airline, or maybe a retired military pilot by that name. It could be any number of people. George handed the paper to Al before turning to Marty. "Where is the crew sheet, and the passenger manifest?"

Before Marty could answer, the office door opened and Dave Wilder walked in carrying another stack of papers. "Here are the names — the flight crew and passengers. There are two non-revenue passengers onboard. One is an active flight attendant, Fred Lyle. The other is a retired pilot, just as the radio messages indicated. He retired from Trans-Continental two years ago. Captain Ray Clarke."

George paused for several seconds, then spoke again. "That's impossible." He reached over and took back the single sheet of paper from Al, the paper that was the transcript of the two final radio messages that had been sent by Flight 3. George's eyes scanned the printed words again, words that he could hardly believe the first time he had read them, words that contained a familiar name that he had also dismissed as an impossibility. But now.... *Hijacking...lunatic retired pilot...out of control...Clarke has taken over...* "This is absolutely out of the question," George announced in a loud and firm voice to everyone in the room. "Absolutely impossible."

Chapter Fifteen

Brandon Kyle sat further back in his office leather recliner and glanced out the corner window from his Manhattan suite. Although the particular view wasn't the best vista of the New York skyline that he'd ever seen, it wasn't a bad one — and it was certainly a large improvement over those horrible airport views from his old office at Trans-Continental's Airport Executive Center. How anyone enjoyed watching airplanes wander around on the tarmac was a mystery to him.

The intercom on his desk buzzed and Kyle leaned forward and pressed the receiving button. "Yes?"

"I have a call from Vice President of Flight, Captain George Fisher," Kyle's secretary announced. "He says that it's quite urgent. He needs to talk to you immediately."

"Thank you, Nancy," Brandon Kyle said. With his plan to sell off the airline's assets and dissolve the company about to see the light of day, he didn't really give a damn about whatever operational problems might come up at this point. Insignificant drivel. Still, he had to play his part until the announcements were officially made. "Hello, George? Brandon here. What can I do for you?"

"Afraid we've got a problem," George said. "A big problem. Flight 3 from Rome has sent two radio messages. It's been hijacked."

"Hijacked?" Kyle sat upright. *Crap.* This might be real trouble for them. "What are the details? Where is the aircraft now?"

"Don't know." George went on to explain the details about the sudden loss of communications — both voice radio and the satellite text messages — and the overdue position report at the mid-ocean point, 30 degrees west.

"Do you think the airplane has gone down?" Kyle asked.

"No way to know for sure, but my feeling is no, that Flight 3 is still airborne," George answered. "There's more to it than that. Let me read to you the text transcripts of the two short radio messages that were sent from the aircraft and recorded by air traffic control."

Kyle sat in silence and listened carefully as he took in the enormity of what the two short radio messages were telling him. *Hijacking...lunatic retired pilot in the cockpit...suicide...9/11 again...out of control...Clarke has taken over...* "This is incredible," Kyle said. He sat silently for several more seconds. The fact that there was a retired company employee involved might add real complications, and one thing they didn't need on the verge of the upcoming corporate announcements were any unnecessary complications. Finally, he added, "What can we do at this point?"

"Very little. We will, of course, be following our emergency notification handbook to the letter. Since this is a potential hijacking, we also need to notify the Federal security people, the TSA."

"Fine. Make the notifications that we're required to make. Be certain that we don't omit anyone or any agency that is on the list. If there's even a remote possibility that we're supposed to notify some agency or department, make certain that it's done promptly and logged in with names, numbers and times. We've got to be certain that we are doing everything the law requires."

"Of course."

Kyle's thoughts were moving forward rapidly as he mentally scanned the situation for the possibilities that needed to be dealt with, the possibilities that could be trouble, the possibilities that could be turned to their advantage. His first priority was that all of this news had to be considered within the scope of the corporate breakup that he and his special team were about to embark on. "I noticed that you called the situation a 'potential hijacking'. Why did you use a phrase like that when we have radio evidence that one of our past employees has apparently gone off the deep end and is doing something that might be suicidal?"

George suspected that this sort of response would come from Kyle as soon as he heard himself use that 'potential' phrase. Kyle was a bastard, but he was sharp. George took a deep breath, then said, "Because I don't believe it."

"Don't believe what? That the flight has been hijacked?"

"I don't know what to believe. Not yet." George was at a loss for the words to explain himself, but he knew that none of this added up. "The messages were brief and panicky, and sent under stressful conditions. Also, I haven't heard the actual recordings as yet — I'm told they should be getting to us shortly. So far, we've only seen the written transcripts. The actual recordings of the spoken words will tell us a great deal more, they always do in these situations. And on top of that, I know Ray Clarke. Personally and quite well. He was with this company for a long time, and he was always an outstanding pilot in every way. He flew co-pilot for me years ago, back in the early eighties. I know the man. He's is absolutely incapable of doing what these radio messages are implying."

"Implying?!" Kyle had allowed himself to raise his voice slightly, which he normally never did. His voice immediately returned to its usual flat pitch, the one that his wife called his Boardroom Demeanor. "Doesn't sound to me that you're being quite rational, George. Perhaps you've known this man too well or too closely to be objective."

"Well, I don't think that I'm..."

"No, Captain, you hear me out. There are no implications in those radio messages, it is an outright statement of fact: that one of our former employees has commandeered one of our airliners and he is either suicidal or bent on some elaborate hijacking scheme or God knows what. Regardless, I absolutely insist that you not say a single word in support of this crazy ex-employee. Do I make myself clear?"

"Yes."

"I'll get our chief legal officer involved in a few minutes, and he'll make the necessary decisions with regards to what is best to protect the corporate assets from liability." Kyle knew that protecting the corporate assets had to be his first order of business or else his plan to dissolve the company and sell off the pieces could be measurably diminished. Or even totally squashed.

"What about the welfare of the passengers and crew?" George said. "We need to think of them first."

"Of course. Do whatever is necessary to get us more information, and in getting a current position of the aircraft if a search and rescue effort is called for."

"I will." But George, like all long-haul over water pilots who cared to think about it, knew that the only search and rescue effort necessary for going down in the middle of the Atlantic

141

Ocean in the wintertime was to remember one line: bend over and kiss your ass goodbye. Anything else would be, as Brandon Kyle was apt to say, ineffectual. "I'll go ahead with our notifications to the Federal agencies involved, the FAA, the TSA and, hell, even the FBI."

Kyle was beginning to get a better handle on the developing situation, and a new thought entered his mind. "No, I don't want you to make those notifications. Except for the call to the FAA which your department can take care of, my office will be in charge of the necessary notifications and the liaison with the law enforcement branches such as the FBI and the TSA. I'll have William Wesson take command of that." If he couldn't control the news itself, at least he could control the dissemination of that information to the government agencies – the agencies that would become key players afterward. Kyle instinctively knew that he needed to stay in firm control of that loop.

"Fine with me, if that's how you want to do it," George said. "Gives us more time to concentrate on flight details."

"We'll set up a direct line here at corporate, in the board room, for the coordination efforts. You carry on the technical work on your end, and we'll take care of the legal and governmental logistics at our end. Put a complete blackout on everything until you get a direct approval from me, and, of course, keep us informed of the current situation."

"We will," George said. "I'll call with an update as soon as I have more."

"Right." Kyle hung up the telephone, buzzed his secretary and told her to get William Wesson to come into his office immediately. Brandon Kyle was beginning to get an idea that — like all bad situations — there might be some benefit to be culled from this unexpected turn of events if he played his cards right.

◇

William Wesson had been back from lunch a short while and had opened the first legal brief on today's review stack when the call came in from Nancy, Brandon Kyle's secretary. She had not said what the problem was, but she had made it perfectly clear that Wesson was to hot-foot it down to Kyle's office as quickly as possible. Wesson got up, headed down the corridor and soon entered Kyle's outer office.

"Go right in," Nancy said as she pointed to the closed door that led to his private corner office. "He's expecting you."

"Thank you." Wesson opened the door and stepped into the room. Brandon Kyle was at his desk and he motioned for Wesson to come forward and sit in one of the chairs.

Kyle rocked slightly back in his swivel chair, then said, "George Fisher called. We were notified a few minutes ago that Flight 3 from Rome has been hijacked."

"Oh, my God." Wesson sat more upright and leaned closer to Kyle's desk. "Where is Flight 3 now? Where are they headed?"

Kyle shook his head. "Nobody knows. Not for certain. Matter of fact, Fisher and his group don't have firm evidence that Flight 3 is still in the air. He suspects the flight is airborne, but he can't tell me why."

"Then how do we know that Flight 3 has been hijacked? How do we know that it hasn't disappeared or crashed for some other reason?"

"Two radio messages." Kyle began to read the contents of the two recorded radio messages from his notes and then added that Flight 3 was, at that moment, out of communications and that its current position and status were unknown. "Set up the corporate boardroom as our executive command center. Fisher will do the technical work from the dispatch department, and I've ordered him to report directly to you with whatever information he comes up with. I need you to stay on top of everything and not to let any information out that might somehow compromise us in the near future. I don't have to remind you that in the near future we are set to announce the shutdown and sale of the airline."

"I understand." Wesson stood up. "Our focus needs to be on the short term. Even with a disgruntled ex-employee involved, we're not any worse off because the company will be long dissolved before any judge or jury would decide that we should have seen this coming. You can't sue a company that doesn't exist. It's another reason for the hold-outs on the board to go along with us."

"An excellent point, William." Kyle then explained to Wesson the need for him to contact the government agencies listed in the Emergency Handbook except for the FAA, which Fisher would take care of. Kyle paused, then added, "Remember what the Lockerbie accident did to Pan American – everyone agrees that they should have shut down Pan Am right then and there. At that point, at least they would have had something worth selling. We need to view this situation in much the same way."

"Yes. You're right." Wesson turned and headed for the door. "I'll have the boardroom set up shortly," he added as he left the room.

Kyle watched Wesson leave, then stepped back to his desk to make a few additional notes. While he didn't wish the passengers and crew of Flight 3 any harm, their fate was certainly out of his hands and, hence, not something that he needed to spend any time on. His focus would be on a purely corporate point of view based on the financial plans they had already developed. Brandon Kyle, as his father was fond of saying, had bigger fish to fry.

Chapter Sixteen

It took only a few minutes for William Wesson to get the corporate boardroom opened and outfitted for its role as the emergency management center for Flight 3's hijacking situation. As Brandon Kyle had indicated, Wesson would concentrate on establishing contact with all the government entities excepting the FAA, which he had left to George Fisher.

Starting out with the Transportation Security Agency in Washington, Wesson called them on the emergencies-only number listed in the airline handbook. For the first two minutes on the line, Wesson navigated the customary sea of electronic voices that told him which keypad button to press to file which type of report. Finally, Wesson connected with a human being.

"Tell me your name again, please."

"Rebecca Heyburn."

"Thank you." Wesson logged the exact time — 1:41 pm — and her name, then quickly went on to explain that one of their flights was having a problem that would, they felt, involve the TSA. Finally, he made it absolutely clear that he would speak only with the Director or the equivalent before he would pass on more. It was, he knew, what Kyle expected of him. Wesson also made it clear that timing was crucial and that any delay could be critical.

Wesson waited. Kyle always wanted to go all the way to the top, to the highest ranking person in each agency or organization – that was Kyle's method of doing business with any organization, private or government, and Wesson had no intention of doing anything less. Those were his marching orders. Finally, there was a click on the telephone.

"Hello, Mr. Wesson?"

"Yes?"

"This is the Assistant Deputy Administrator of the TSA, Steven Chew. I understand that you don't want to work with us in the customary manner, or leave details with my people," he said. There was no small level of irritation in his voice. In fact, the man was fuming. "So, here I am. I am the highest ranking official in the agency today because the Administrator and Assistant

Administrator are out of the building at the moment, attending the Presidential inauguration."

"Good. I..."

"Perhaps you hadn't heard," Chew said, interrupting Wesson, "but today a good number of people who live and work in this city are celebrating the inauguration of our new President-elect William Taylor. Actually, looking at the wall clock, I see now that he is the official President of the United States. I can only hope that I'm suitable for you and your information since I'm the highest ranking person available. Otherwise, I can't help you."

"Yes, Mr. Chew. You are certainly suitable."

"Now, what is so sensitive and so crucial that I am the only one in the entire TSA organization who can assist you with whatever is this mysterious problem that one of your flights is having?"

◇

Assistant Deputy Administrator of the Transportation Security Administration, Steven Chew, holding the telephone to his ear, looked westward toward the suburbs of Alexandria, Virginia from his sixth floor office. To his right he could see an airliner as it navigated along the Potomac River. Soon, it would disappear behind the corner of the building as it made its final turn for a landing on the south runway of Washington's Reagan National Airport. The Washington skyline was on the other side of the TSA building, where his two bosses had their offices.

Chew expected that this telephone call from Trans-Continental Airlines Vice President William Wesson was another complaint about something the agency had done badly toward one of the airline's VIP passengers or its executives. He had gotten calls like this before, and they started the same way with some airline big shot demanding to speak to the Director of the Agency and only to the Director. It was the sort of calls that his bosses shoveled down to him even when they were in their offices, so having to handle this wasn't an unexpected interruption to his day – it was the type of crap he dealt with too often.

Now that Wesson of Trans-Continental had him on the line, Chew was resigned to hearing about the so-called incident that involved today's Flight 3 from Rome. It was, Wesson was telling him, en route to New York and scheduled to land at JFK before 5:00pm. Then Wesson used the words that got Chew to sit straighter in his chair. "A hijacking?" Chew repeated, hardly believing what he had heard.

"Yes. A hijacking."

"Are you certain?"

"As I said," Wesson explained, "that's what the radio message — actually, the two radio messages — have indicated."

"Are you in communications with the pilot? Where are the hijackers intending to take it?" Chew asked. As he spoke, he buzzed his secretary. "Hold on Wesson." Chew leaned toward the interoffice intercom. "Barbara, get hold of the Security and the Operations Sections and tell them to come to my office immediately. I've gotten information on a hijacking that is, at this very moment, in progress."

"I'll call them immediately Mr. Chew."

"Very good." Chew turned back to the telephone. "Mr. Wesson, go on. Give me the details you have," Chew said, not knowing what else to do. This sort of call – an actual hijacking *while it was in progress* – was not the sort of call that the TSA had ever gotten before, and he wasn't certain how to handle it.

Wesson took a deep breath, then said, "I can't really answer your questions, not at the moment. This Flight 3 business is more complicated than you'd imagine. The only indications we have of the current situation are two intercepted radio messages. Other than that, we don't know a single thing — we don't even know for certain if the airplane is in the air. Let me read the transcripts of the two messages."

Chew sat in absolute amazement at the words that he was now hearing on the telephone. While the story from Wesson about what was happening to Trans-Continental Flight 3 from Rome was shocking, two phrases in the messages that he was hearing were particularly attention-getting: *suicidal* and *It's like 9/11 again.*

As Chew had often said at the public meetings where he spoke, this large and powerful government agency had been created out of the smoke and flames rising from the wreckage of the crumbling World Trade Center Twin Towers in 2001. Since then, most of what the TSA did was administrative, and it was always after-the-fact. But now, it appeared, the TSA would need to react to a developing situation that was similar to the tragedy that initially created the agency. "I know you said you don't have firm evidence," Chew said. "But where do you think this hijacked airliner might be headed? I've got to tell my people something."

Wesson said, "New York. That would be my best guess."

◇

Marty had ordered his people to pull every bit of information pertaining to today's operation of Flight 3. Dave Wilder, the Shift Supervisor, and Wally Poel, the Dispatcher assigned to Flight 3, had come into Marty's office with paperwork about the flight that the company computers were generating.

Marty was glad that Al DeWitt and that lady magazine reporter had left his office — they had gone downstairs to George's office to find Maynard and to get general background information on Flight 3. There was something about that lady reporter that made Marty uncomfortable and he hoped that she and Al would stay downstairs — he didn't need the distractions of a public relations person or a representative of the press to complicate the developing situation.

Marty looked up from his desk as Poel walked in. The dispatcher was carrying another stack of paperwork. He handed it over. "What's this?" Marty asked.

"A readout of the satellite messages that were sent to and from the flight since its departure from Rome," Poel answered. "Probably nothing that matters in this stuff, but you did ask for everything."

"Yes, I did." Actually, it wasn't Marty who had asked that every bit of data that included or touched on the operation of Flight 3 be scrutinized, it was George. Marty glanced at George, who had finished with a telephone call and was headed across the room again.

"Anything new?" George asked as he came up to Marty's desk. "What's in that stack?" he asked.

148

"Printouts of the automatic satellite communications to and from Flight 3. The final weight and balance data. The departure time, the liftoff time. The usual stuff. Strictly routine."

"Might as well look at everything," George said, "since we're grasping at straws. If we don't hear directly from the flight, we're at an absolute dead end. I don't know what else we can do."

Marty glanced up from the papers on his desk. "We can ask for a search and rescue effort. Probably out of the Azores, since that would be the quickest access to their last known location."

George looked at the wall clock: 2:10 pm. "The last positively known location was logged well over three hours ago, at 20 degrees West. Even if we make the assumption that the flight was still on-course when the first radio message was sent and that they were nearly at 30 degrees West, that assumption is more than two hours old. I just got off the phone with Maynard. He had run several plotting chart arcs to see what sort of search areas we might be dealing with."

"Yes?"

"Maynard gave me two ballpark possibilities. If we assume that the flight stayed on-course with a maximum variation of 15 degrees of track to either side, and we assume that they maintained something near their normal cruise airspeed, then the potential search and rescue area would be a pie-shaped slice of the North Atlantic Ocean that is nearly 600 miles long and almost 300 miles across at its fat end."

"That's an enormous amount of ocean," Marty said.

"And that's nothing compared with the assumption that the flight could have turned in any direction. Using that possibility as the criteria, the search area becomes a circle with a 600 miles radius centered at 30 degrees West. My geometry isn't what it used to be, but I believe the potential search area with that assumption comes out to something over one million square miles."

Marty nodded in agreement. "If they turned, there's no chance of locating them."

"Right," George said. "If they've gone down, we both know that there's no chance of finding them alive even if they've flown exactly on the course line and managed to get the airplane onto the ocean's surface without totally destroying it when they hit the water. If they've wandered off the direct course line, then there's no chance of finding a single piece of the wreckage."

"I have to agree with you," Marty said. He knew, for a fact, that a good number of airliners over the years had disappeared forever on some trans-oceanic flight.

"So that's why we need to operate on the assumption that the flight is in the air. Any other assumption is a dead end." George tapped his finger on the stack of papers on Marty's desk. "Maybe there's some clue in this pile that will help us narrow the possibilities, but unless we find something definitive, then all we can do is keep praying that they're airborne and headed this way."

"I see your point."

"Right." George sighed, then turned around and began to walk toward the far side of the room. "Now, we wait," he said to no one in particular as he headed back to his chair and the telephone so he could make more calls.

Marty understood the parameters that George had spelled out, and he felt, in his heart, that these efforts on their part were a useless gesture. More than likely the flight had gone down, and more than likely they would never find a hint of wreckage to determine in which hundreds of square miles the airliner had initially hit the water. Marty had poured himself a cup of coffee before George had come over; he reached for his coffee mug and took another sip. It had turned cold. He put down the coffee mug and flipped through the latest stack of papers that Poel had brought in a few minutes before.

It was on the fourth page of that pile of computer printouts that Marty spotted something. It was a two line entry, generated automatically by the computer equipment that operated their satellite communications setup. "George, come here," Marty called out as he waved for George to head toward his desk. "Look at this. It might mean nothing, but it is slightly out of the ordinary."

George came up and leaned over Marty. "What?"

"Here. Look at the time of the request and the reply. A couple of hours before the first emergency radio message."

George followed Marty's pointing hand and read the computer generated printout that he was referring to. It was buried in a list of the requests for information that had been sent by the flight, and the automatic computer responses to them. One readout, in particular, had their attention.

1524 UTC: KDCA WX RQST

1525 UTC: KDCA METAR 1452Z, 34011G20KT 10SM FEW045 OVC250 M02/M13

"They requested the Washington, DC current weather," George said. "Could that — or Dulles — be their alternate airport?"

"Don't think so. Wait." Marty ruffled through a stack of papers on the other side of the desk, until he located the Flight 3 flight plan. "No. Newark was their filed alternate, the weather in New York was clear enough for the dispatcher to go with that."

"Yet I see that they asked for the Washington, DC current weather not long before everything began coming apart for them." George was thinking out loud. Finally, he shook his head. "Could this mean something? Maybe, maybe not. It could mean nothing beyond a cockpit crew member becoming bored and playing with the satellite link." George had, himself, written memos asking the pilots not to make irrelevant requests of the satellite system since each message cost money to the airline. But, he knew, most of the pilots continued to do it anyway, at least on occasion.

"It might mean something today. Something significant." Marty reached into his trash can and pulled out a copy of today's morning newspaper. "Here. This could be the tie-in," he said as he pointed to the headline:

William Allan Taylor to be sworn in as the President of the United States.

Below that was another sub-headline, that read:

Inaugural Parade until 6:00 pm, new President Watches from White House Stand.

Chapter Seventeen

Marty sat at his desk without saying a word. Pacing nervously in front of him was George Fisher, who was carefully listing the reasons why the Flight 3 crew might have requested the Washington, DC weather, even though that airport was not in today's flight plan. But even to George, the reasons sounded pretty lame — especially considering that the Washington weather request had come only a few hours before the first hijacking message from the distressed crew.

Marty shook his head. "George, I wish I could agree with you. But the timing of this weather request, even more than the request itself, has tremendous significance."

"Why's that?" George stopped pacing and looked at Marty. "You're guessing."

"Yes. So are you." Marty rocked forward in his chair. "But my guess is based on something concrete."

"Which is?"

"The radio messages from the flight. They are indisputable."

"Probably." George paused, then added, "but we still haven't heard the actual recordings. I've worked on enough accident investigations to learn that these written transcripts can convey a different impression than what you get when you hear the actual voices. The voices have inflection and emotion, the printed words don't."

Marty was going to argue that point – it was a big stretch, to say the least – but at that moment he saw that Dave Wilder was headed at a rapid pace toward his office with one of the communications room portable hard drives in his hand. There was only one reason that he would be bringing that piece of computer transcription gear with him. "We'll know very soon if there's any difference between the spoken and the written word."

"What?"

Marty pointed at the private office's glass door as Wilder opened it.

"Here's the recorded transcript of the two radio messages from Flight 3," Wilder announced as he headed for the computer on Marty's desk. "They were downloaded to us a couple of minutes ago by Shanwick." Wilder quickly plugged the hard drive into Marty's computer, then, utilizing the keyboard, he accessed the voice files and activated them.

The other two men gathered behind the computer screen and the three of them listened carefully to the words that were coming from the small speakers on either side of the computer. The first voice was a male's. He was shouting and sounded nearly hysterical:

Mayday, Trans-Continental Flight 3 is being hijacked! We've got this lunatic retired pilot in the cockpit and he's suicidal — he's trying to kill us! It's like 9/11 again!

After a pause of a few seconds, the second of the two radio messages began to play. This time, the voice was female and while it was unquestionably full of emotion, it sounded slightly more measured than the first message had been:

Mayday...Mayday...Trans-Continental Flight 3! Out of Control! Clarke has taken over...!

Wilder hit some keystrokes that allowed the audio messages to be played two more times before any of them said anything. Finally, George gestured for Wilder to stop the computer. The room turned silent for several long seconds before George turned to face Marty. He said, "Guess you're right. It's hard to believe, but the words and the tone of those voices don't lie." George shook his head in frustration and disbelief.

"We need to pass this information on to Kyle." Marty looked at the computer, then at George. "While we were listening to the voices, I was trying to put myself in their position, trying to fill in the time line for the things that happened that we know about. While it's a guess on my part, I'd say that Ray Clarke was either invited or forced his way to the cockpit a few hours before the first transmission..."

"He was invited," George said. "Ray and Jack were old friends." George knew that Jack Schofield and his wife had attended Katie's funeral because George had been there, also, on that sad day. "There's no doubt that Jack would have invited him to the cockpit at some point during the flight."

"That's against the security rules," Marty said.

"Right," George answered with disdain. He was so tired of the fucking endless rules, with more being heaped on them every damn day. In this case, he knew that bending those sorts of hard-ass security regulations were the sorts of things that Jack Schofield would certainly do. That, and much more.

"Well, I guess that was the beginning of their problems," Marty said.

"Maybe." George always liked the Jack Schofields of the world. Although he was obliged to put on a pretense that it was an unspeakable crime against good airmanship to violate any of the current regulations that were on the books, George would conveniently turn a blind eye toward that growing list of technical infractions that he considered downright silly to start with. Like forbidding a long-career captain from visiting the cockpit when his old friend was in command. But, apparently, George's convictions had been proven dead wrong, and Ray Clarke had somehow gone off the deep end and had come up with this elaborate and suicidal plan...

"So," Marty continued, "here's what I think might've happened. Clarke knew that he was going to be invited to the cockpit, so he waited. He got the flight crew to pull up the weather that he wanted to see, then he waited a few hours until just before he would be expected to leave the cockpit. At that point, he got control of the airliner. Naturally, I don't know how he did that part, but he could have used the cockpit crash axe as a weapon."

"I can do better than that," Wilder said. He took a sheet of paper out of his pocket. "I had gotten this list out of the computer a few seconds before the Shanwick audio recordings were downloaded to us, so I brought it along. Here," Wilder said as he offered it to Marty who glanced at the sheet for a moment and then handed it to George.

"Okay. That fills in another blank," Marty said. "The co-pilot, Peter Fenton, was an armed flight officer, part of the TSA's FFDO program. Perhaps that was the weapon that Clarke used to commandeer the airliner — he asked Fenton to look at his pistol, then Clarke turned it against the flight crew."

"I suppose that's possible." But George knew that it was not likely because he knew enough about Fenton to doubt if the ever-rigid First Officer on Flight 3 would have allowed a non-authorized cockpit visitor like Ray Clarke to even get a glimpse of his TSA-issued weapon, never mind to actually touch it. Over the past years, Fenton had called his office with this or that complaint about some particular infraction or evidence of non-compliance to their endless list of rules and procedures.

Fenton was, to put it as Maynard Lyman had once phrased it, a real wart on the butt of the airline. But maybe, this time, Fenton was right. Dead right. "It doesn't matter if he got hold of that gun, or even if he didn't. These voice messages confirm that Ray Clarke has apparently hijacked the airliner," George reluctantly admitted. "But we still don't know what his actual intentions are."

"George, we might." Marty patted his hand against the folded newspaper that was laying on a corner of his desk. "As the radio message had said, Clarke's intention is to duplicate the 9/11 thing. He must have blurted something out to the crew during the initial moments of the takeover, and that's when one of the male pilots grabbed the microphone to make that first transmission. My guess is that the female member of the cockpit crew — I see from the crew list that her name is Linda Erickson — grabbed the microphone for one last transmission while Clarke was forcing her and the rest of the cockpit crew off the flight deck. Or worse."

After a few seconds of thought, George said, "Marty, you're certainly right about one thing. This is nothing beyond pure speculation, absolute guesswork on your part."

"Perhaps. But it's based on the evidence we have. Nothing I'm saying — nothing I'm guessing at — contradicts that. Based on what I've seen and heard, I'd have to say that Ray Clarke is intending to fly that airliner to Washington, DC and, thanks to the clear weather that he's verified from the weather request he sent for before the hijacking, he'll have no problem with the final moments of his plan."

"And what is your current guess for what this so-called ultimate plan is supposed to be?" George asked, although he already knew what the obvious answer would be. He desperately wanted to dismiss this speculation, but the problem was he couldn't think of any way to refute it, no goddamn way at all.

"With no clouds to speak of and unrestricted visibility in Washington, DC area, Clarke will be able to navigate the airliner visually using the Potomac River. He'll be able to easily locate and then crash the airliner into the middle of the Presidential Inaugural Parade — perhaps even into the President's viewing stand."

At that point, George didn't say anything in response; he shook his head slowly. The only thought going through his mind was how absolutely impossible all of this was. But he didn't know what to say, or how to phrase any of his doubts. Impossible or not, the evidence against any other explanation had become overwhelming, and even George had to admit to that.

"That being the case," Marty said as he put his hand on the telephone and looked up at George. "we need to let Kyle and Wesson know, right now, so that they can alert the Federal authorities."

George stood motionless for several seconds. Finally, in a low voice, he replied, "Okay." George nodded toward the telephone. "You make the call to Kyle and Wesson, tell them what you think. As far as I see, at this point we have no other choice." George turned away from the desk and walked back to the chair on the far side of the room. He sat down to think about what would be the next thing for them to do, what their next course of action should be. But, instead of that, his mind kept going back to what his original thought had been: that all of this was absolutely, completely fucking impossible.

◇

When the telephone call from the Trans-Continental dispatch office was put through to the corporate headquarters board room in Manhattan, Brandon Kyle took the call himself. He listened carefully to the news and the explanations coming from the Director of Dispatch, Martin Luffman. Kyle asked several questions, took a few notes, then hung up.

Kyle turned to Wesson. "That was Luffman in Dispatch. More developments."

"Yes?"

Kyle provided Wesson with the details of his conversation — the satellite weather request for Washington, DC, the connection between the retired pilot and Flight 3's actual captain, and the opinions of what might have occurred onboard and how it fit too well into the timing and the content of the two emergency transmissions from the airliner. All of that, plus the presence of the TSA-supplied handgun on the flight deck. Finally, Kyle told Wesson about the theory of where this suicidal flight might be headed — to the Presidential Inauguration.

"Christ Almighty. That would be...catastrophic," Wesson said. "In every way possible. Even if this ex-employee of ours doesn't get the President himself with his suicide attack, he could wipe out hundreds — even thousands — of people." Wesson paused, then added, "The fallout would be immediate, and it would potentially be..." Wesson paused again, before finally adding, "astronomical."

"Shit." Kyle sat down in one of the upholstered boardroom chairs, took a deep breath, then turned back to Wesson. "This is a hell of a thing." Kyle shook his head. "And the timing couldn't be worse for us."

"I agree."

"If this lunatic pilot crashes our airliner into the Presidential Inauguration, then by the close of business today we would have been handed an absolutely unmanageable nightmare."

"Right."

"Can you imagine the World Trade Center disaster being caused not by Muslim fanatics, by foreign terrorists, but by someone who worked for the airline itself? Can you imagine the corporate *culpability*," Kyle said, emphasizing dramatically that last word, "if it were the airline itself — nothing but one airline and some of its employees — that caused all of that?"

"It would be certain – and immediate – corporate suicide. This company would effectively have been infected with the Black Plague."

"Exactly." Kyle got up from his chair, paced slowly around the room, then walked back to face Wesson. "With a manageable disaster, a few of those holdouts on the Board would find it easier to go along with the breakup and sale of the airline.

But if this disaster becomes too large to contain," Kyle continued, "then we wouldn't have a damned thing left to sell."

Wesson nodded. "Unfortunately, I agree. There would be absolutely no buyers for the odd pieces of Trans-Continental Airlines that weren't being tied up in litigation if this madman crashes into the Presidential Inauguration. Trans-Continental Airlines would cease to exist as a saleable entity at the moment of impact. Our insurance coverage wouldn't approach being enough."

"Yes." The two men stood in silence for several seconds, before Kyle added, "get me George Fisher on the telephone."

"Okay."

In less than a minute George Fisher was on the line and the telephone was handed back to Kyle. "George, we need to get accurate flight figures. I need to know that Flight 3 has enough fuel onboard to get to Washington, DC if that could be this retired pilot's plan. I also need to know what its estimated time of arrival would be, and what the arrival time would be for New York, if he elected to go there."

"Already worked that up, wait..." George said as he consulted his paperwork. "Here. They have enough fuel to reach Washington, DC with nearly one hour of fuel to spare. This is based on the flight maintaining its normal cruise airspeed and altitude. If they go to a lower altitude, they'd have less fuel on arrival although the arrival time should be basically the same. If they increase speed to maximum cruise, they'll arrive a few minutes earlier but they would use a good portion of their reserve fuel. For that reason, increasing speed didn't seem like a sensible choice."

"Really? You don't think that this pilot might try that?" Kyle asked. "Getting to Washington as soon as possible would seem a logical goal. How many minutes would a higher speed take from the arrival time?"

George didn't say anything for a moment while he consulted his figures. Finally, he replied, "In the neighborhood of ten minutes, depending on how soon he went to that higher airspeed. But, like I said, that would cut down his available fuel reserves — he'd have less options for any last minute maneuvering or changes in plans."

"I see."

"This late in the flight," George continued, "the aircraft's normal cruise speed seemed to be the best compromise. All of us here agree on that."

"I understand," Kyle answered.

"Based on normal cruise altitude and speed, and considering the forecast winds," George continued, "the estimated arrival time for New York is 4:22 pm Eastern Standard Time, which is a half hour ahead of the published schedule — the headwinds were lighter today than average for this time of year. The estimated arrival time for Washington, DC would be 4:59 pm Eastern Standard Time, assuming that they are headed directly to Washington from their last known position over the North Atlantic."

"Okay, I've got the picture." Kyle looked at the wall clock. "It's 2:40 pm, so we've got less than two hours until a potential New York arrival, and slightly over two more hours from now if the Washington scenario materializes. Do you agree with those times?"

"Yes."

"And from what you said earlier, the airliner would run out of fuel by approximately 6:00 pm — is that correct?"

"The exact figure generated by the flight plan computer is 6:03 pm Eastern Standard Time," George answered. "That is, of course, based on those assumptions of speed and cruise altitude."

"Yes, yes, of course," Kyle said. There was a slight irritation in his otherwise-flat verbal demeanor – he didn't like technical details or any unnecessary variables added. "What's the time of sunset at both locations?"

"Hold on, I have that right here," George said. "I've looked it up since we also thought that darkness might become a factor. Obviously, any sort of...need to do visual flying, a need to locate specific things on the ground...would be far more difficult in darkness."

"I imagine it would be," Kyle responded.

"Right. It turns out that official sunset is a little after the estimated arrival time for the flight at either of the locations."

"Really?" Kyle said. "That's even more evidence of how carefully this retired pilot selected this plan."

"Maybe." George was going to point out the obvious, that all of the Trans-Continental westbound flights from Europe arrived in New York well before sunset — in fact, the Rome flight was one of the last scheduled arrivals — so that information was irrelevant. But he didn't bother to put up an argument because he knew it would be a waste of time. "For a New York arrival, sunset would be at 4:58 pm."

"How about for Washington?" Kyle asked, putting the final missing portions of the puzzle into place.

"At Washington, sunset tonight will occur at 5:14 pm. Also remember that the official sunset time is when the sun first cuts below the horizon line," George added. "The sky will remain reasonably illuminated for nearly thirty minutes afterward — especially considering today's lack of any cloud cover at both places."

"Okay, I understand. Keep us informed of new details." Kyle hung up the telephone and turned back to Wesson. "What about the personnel file on this retired pilot? What did you find?"

Wesson tapped his hand against a file laying on the boardroom desk. "There's not much of significance in it, other than the impression that this pilot was sometimes inclined to not follow company procedures completely. Other than that, his employee record paints him as quite competent."

"The trait of not following the rules certainly fits squarely with what we're thinking he's doing today," Kyle said. "Here we have a pilot who periodically believes that the airline's rules don't apply to him. I would imagine that any psychologist would have a field day with that."

Wesson said. "There's also one other entry in the file that's worth making note of — the death of Clarke's wife who was also a company employee. Katherine Clarke was a flight attendant. She was killed a little over three years ago."

"Killed?"

"Yes. An airplane accident — a light airplane that she and her husband owned. She was an amateur pilot and she was flying it alone when it crashed and killed her. Like I said, that was over three years ago."

"An airplane accident?" Kyle mulled that over in his mind, then said, "Which means that he retired barely a year and a half after his wife's death occurred in an *airplane accident.*"

"That's right."

160

"And he left the airline and his flying job as quickly as he could after that particular incident, after that devastating personal incident." Kyle nodded to himself.

"Yes," Wesson agreed. "That sums it up."

"What I'm thinking now is that this information could help the TSA in coming to a decision," Kyle said.

"A decision?"

Kyle paused, then said, "Remember, we would much rather have Flight 3 go down over the ocean than to run the risk of that airliner successfully making it to the Presidential inaugural. Putting aside the question about the flight itself for a moment, our upcoming plans for the airline require nothing more than a *manageable* disaster, certainly not an unmanageable one. That's a necessity, no matter how grim the truth might sound."

"Of course, but..."

"William, we've got to do whatever is necessary to keep this disaster manageable," Kyle said.

Chapter Eighteen

Assistant Deputy Administrator Steven Chew had the resources of the TSA's portion of the Department of Homeland Security in full swing by the time he received the second telephone call from Trans-Continental Airlines. Wesson passed on the latest data that had been gathered about Flight 3 — the flight's estimated arrival time at New York, and the fact that Washington, DC and the Presidential Inauguration was also a strong possibility as the hijacked flight's target.

When Wesson had finished, he handed the telephone over to the airline's President, Brandon Kyle. After a brief introduction, Kyle began to explain what his people had come up with.

"Yet you don't know for certain that this airplane is still flying," Chew said. "Or, for that matter, if the hijacker has control of it. Is that correct?"

"Yes and no," Kyle answered. "We aren't certain if it's flying. Frankly, I don't think we can be sure of anything until it either shows up at New York or Washington, or comes up on its fuel exhaustion time."

"Which is?"

"6:03 pm, Eastern Standard," Kyle answered quickly. "After that, we can assume that the airliner has crashed somewhere in the North Atlantic after this hijacking attempt began. My people tell me that, more than likely, we'd never know more since it's doubtful that we could locate any of the wreckage before it disappeared into the ocean."

"I'm more concerned with the immediate threat." Chew looked at his wall clock. It was 2:56 pm. This was, in one way, becoming something of an opportunity for the TSA – a way to get some good press on the heals of the negative fallout from the ongoing security enhancements the agency was continuing to make. "The potential jeopardy from this hijacked airliner begins in less than two hours from now and ends in three-plus hours. Is that correct?"

"Yes," Kyle said. "If the airliner is flying, the hijacker must have control of it. If he didn't, our own pilots would be back in communications with us."

"Makes sense."

"But I can tell you this," Kyle continued, "that there is very little doubt on this end about this retired pilot's intentions."

"Really? Why?"

"I'm no psychologist," Kyle said, "but a company psychologist would adamantly say that this retired pilot — Ray Clarke — shows the classic symptoms of a post-trauma mental breakdown based on the death of his wife in an airplane accident a few years ago. His own personnel records that show many incidents of his growing behavior disorders."

"Behavior disorders?" Chew knew that having more information of substance would be an important element in their upcoming decision and the resulting action.

"Yes. As the professional psychologist would indicate, this man — whose current mental state contains elements of rage against authority figures, might be expected to strike out at the highest authority figure that he is capable of venting rage at," Kyle said. "Hence, our very strong assumption that, while New York City would be an attractive target, Washington, DC and the Presidential Inauguration Parade would be even more so."

"I see," Chew said as he made of note of what had been told him. He knew that the TSA was getting everything it needed to make a decision in accordance with their rules and guidelines. In fact, they nearly had enough already.

"For more background," Kyle added, "in those last months before his premature retirement, Clarke was thought to have become increasingly hostile toward designated authority of any sort, and constantly rebelled against authority that was directed toward him."

"What did you mean by 'premature retirement'?" Chew asked.

"Clarke retired very early for an airline pilot, if you get my drift."

"So, in effect, he was fired?" Chew asked.

"I'm not at liberty to say," Kyle answered, "because of the privacy laws and the labor statutes. We'd be happy to turn over everything we have on this man when the proper legal documents are filed through a court of law."

"We don't have time for that," Chew said emphatically. "What I need to know *right now* is whether you feel that the man who has been identified as the hijacker of your airliner has not only the *ability* but also a *high degree of probability* to crash this airliner into either New York City or the Presidential Inauguration." Chew knew that positive answers to those questions would be the final keynote triggers for implementing the TSA's resources. With those positive answers in hand, nothing that he was about to do could be questioned later on.

Kyle paused for a moment, glanced at Wesson, then said, "Absolutely. There is no doubt in the minds of our people that this man could easily target either of those cities. Our dispatch department has worked out the fuel and flight time scenarios, and they fit perfectly. Remember, this man was a qualified captain at this airline for many years, and the last airplane he flew was basically the same type and on exactly the same route that he commandeered it on today. The aircraft today is a Consolidated 768, which, as you might be aware, is an updated conversion of the Boeing 767 — the aircraft that our hijacker flew for Trans-Continental."

"Also," Kyle continued, "there is no doubt in the minds of those of us who have seen his personnel file — and there would be no doubt in the mind of any airline's psychologist — that retired Captain Ray Clarke is a loose cannon that is currently aimed at one of those two cities."

"Your people feel certain that Washington would be his primary target." Chew asked, although the answer seemed obvious. Still, he wanted – no, he *needed* – to have the airline people telling him, not vice-versa. Those were the TSA rules.

"Yes, for the reasons I just mentioned," Kyle said. "In fact, our overwhelming opinion here is that the only thing that could stop Ray Clarke from striking one of those cities is that he's already crashed the airliner into the sea."

"Okay, we'll take it from this point," Chew answered abruptly, knowing that he had gotten more than enough. It was a go. "We have an established protocol for dealing with this sort of event. I'll require additional hard data so that we can proceed in accordance with our rules and procedures, which are very strict.

I'll need your technical and records departments to email directly to us in, let's say no more than the next fifteen minutes, various categories of hard data that we'll require."

"What things?" Kyle asked.

"The complete passenger manifest and the crew manifest, along with the Passport numbers and the name of the issuing country for everyone onboard. A copy of the actual flight plan, including the originating fuel load. Most importantly, we need the exact type and description of the aircraft involved, including a complete physical description. For that, several photographs that will clearly display the exterior paint scheme on that particular aircraft would be best. Finally, we require the *exact* registration number that is displayed on the exterior of the airframe of that aircraft, and any other tell-tale signs that might help to positively identify it by another aircraft flying in formation with the subject aircraft, and at a distance of no greater than approximately one hundred feet."

"I understand," Kyle said.

"Your people should call the same emergency handbook telephone number that they called before. The answering operator will be standing by for this information, and they will guide your people on how to send these emails and any other issues." Chew stopped for a moment, then added, "You can personally call me if you get any other information you think is relevant."

"Of course."

"We have the full authority under law," Chew said, "to use our assets in whatever way we deem as necessary." Chew paused, then added, "We not only have the power of the law and the power of the courts, but we also have the full force and capabilities of the military."

◇

After Steven Chew hung up the telephone from his conversation with the President of Trans-Continental Airlines, he called the various department heads within the building to alert them that hard data would be arriving from the airline at any moment. He told each of them that the TSA would, in coordination with the Air Force and Navy, immediately put 'Operation Full-Shield' into effect. It would be the first time that this secret protocol had been used. The irony was that it was being called for by the TSA itself, and not simply being reported to TSA after the fact. As Chew had often wished, the TSA – under his command – was finally becoming proactive.

With those telephone calls behind him, Chew attempted to call two other numbers — the same two cell phone numbers that he had attempted to contact several times in the past hour. But what no one in the government had the foresight to realize when this emergency communications network had been setup was that with the city flooded with people attending the Presidential Inauguration — the media estimates the crowd to be over *three million,* and far more than any previous Presidential Inauguration — every cell phone tower and wireless link in the area would be enormously overloaded and incapable of letting most new calls go through. It wasn't the TSA wireless channels themselves that were bogged down to a standstill, it was the electronic switching networks that routed those signals. There was no way on earth that Chew could get in contact with either of his two bosses at the TSA, at least for awhile.

At first, this bothered Chew. But then, he realized that he had been handed a golden opportunity to take over this ship of state and steer it clear of this imminent danger. He was doing everything strictly by the book, and he had already received more than enough justification for his upcoming actions. Chew sat back in his chair and thought about it for a few moments, then reached for the telephone and dialed the TSA's military advisor, Rear Admiral Oliver Starke.

Starke answered his telephone on the first ring.

"Ollie, this is Steven Chew. I expect that you've already been brought into the loop on this Trans-Continental Airlines hijacking, am I right?"

"Yes. I was notified of the latest elements a few minutes ago. What's the current status?" Starke asked.

"We're going directly into 'Operation Full-Shield'. We have no choice, especially now that I've heard enough to know that we are well into that 'high degree of probability' category."

"Then we're ready on this end." Starke paused, then asked, "have you spoken with the Director?"

"No. There's no way to get hold of either him or the Deputy Director because of the cell phone overload and that enormous crowd out there. I'll make the call on this situation."

"Oh?"

"Yes. I've got the authority and I've already gotten enough firm data logged in for us to go ahead."

"Fine with me," Starke answered, "except that you know I'll need that encrypted authorization email from you containing the required referencing of the flight data from the procedures protocol, plus the exact phrasing of the required 'high degree of probability' statement above your electronic signature. Then I can make my notifications through the Pentagon and through NORAD, and we can get the final arrangements enacted. I understand that the target remains one of two: either New York or Washington, is that correct?"

"Yes," Chew answered. "Although our best guess leans the odds far more in favor of Washington."

"Figures, considering what today is."

"Right. We've got," Chew said as he glanced up at his clock, "about one hour and fifteen minutes before a potential New York arrival, and one hour and fifty minutes if Washington is the actual target. Are you absolutely certain we've got enough time so there's no chance of a problem on our end?"

"Hell," Starke shot back, "you and I could go to lunch first, and we'd still have enough time to set it up when we got back. 'Operation Full-Shield' has been tested and massaged in every way possible, and it's spring loaded to the on-position — that is, as soon as I get that finalizing email authorization from you."

Chew leaned toward his computer keyboard. "It's almost finished — you'll have it in sixty seconds."

"Then in less than five minutes the radar walls will be fully entrenched, including the over-the-horizon stuff from the Navy, and all of it coordinated through the Pentagon War Room," Starke said. "Doesn't matter if your hijacker is flying super-high or low enough to touch the top of the waves, I can guarantee you he will be locked into our sights well before he's within thirty minutes of the Continental coast line. There's absolutely no way past that radar wall."

"Good. And the..." Chew paused, "...attack protocol."

167

"Strictly by the book. Multiple fighter coverage in the possible quadrants, with every fighter carrying a full complement of air to air missiles — any one of which would easily accomplish the assignment."

"The rendezvous and the identification protocols?" Chew asked, although he already well understood the strict scenario that 'Operation Full-Shield' worked under. He also knew that he needed to ask the right questions since all these conversations were being recorded. As Chew well understood, to prevent any chance of a mistake of any sort, no ground to air missiles were allowed, and the subject aircraft had to be positively identified by *two* separate intercept aircraft, both flying in a close formation. Only then would one of the fighters be authorized to maneuver to a position directly aft of the target aircraft and begin the sequence to release its first missile. Chew shivered when he thought about the moment of release for that first missile – as the protocol documents had indicated, only one missile would be needed to take a given target down. Chew realized that he was taking down an airliner full of innocent men, women and children, but he had no choice. No choice at all.

"Also strictly by the book," Starke continued, "a positive VID — visual identification — by *both* aircraft, with NORAD keeping command and control, and, of course, full liaison from the Pentagon." Starke paused, then added, "As you know, the intention is to have the target splashed at a point that is no less than fifteen minutes of flight time from any US coastline."

"You're comfortable that everything we need is in motion," Chew said as he finished typing the encrypted message to the TSA military advisor that would authorize the downing of this specific target, this target of 'high probability'. Steven Chew pressed the send key on his computer keyboard. "The final authorizing message has been sent."

"I've got the email," Starke answered a moment later. He, too, was well aware that these internal phone calls were being recorded and that his words would be reviewed afterward by everyone from Pentagon brass to the President himself. "I wished to God we could help those innocent people who've been caught up in this nightmare, but we need to guarantee that Trans-Continental Flight 3 is prevented from repeating our 9/11 nightmare. That airliner — which has effectively become an enemy's guided missile – can't be allowed to reach our shores. What we're doing is exactly what we need to do."

Book Five

A pilot's business is with the wind, with the stars, with night, with sand, with the sea. He strives to outwit the forces of nature.
—Antoine de Sainte-Exupery, *Wind, Sand and Stars*

What is chiefly needed is skill rather than machinery.
—Wilbur Wright, 1902

Chapter Nineteen

Wednesday, January 20th
Latitude 41N, Longitude 47W; 480 miles southeast of
Newfoundland, Canada
3:15 pm, Eastern Standard Time

"Ray, what are you thinking?" Linda asked as she continued to hand-fly the airliner from the co-pilot's flight station. She was working at keeping the airliner straight and level and pointed properly with none of the normal flight instruments functioning. Doing that was not an easy task.

Ray opened his eyes and looked at her. "Not much," he answered.

"Doubt that."

"Okay, I lied." Ray forced a smile as he sat further upright in the captain's flight chair, ending the short rest break he had given himself fifteen minutes earlier. Linda had been correct — his mind had been churning over the myriad of details of the past two-plus hours of the flight, and he felt more worn out after his break than he had been before he had allowed himself to turn the airliner over to her and close his eyes. Ray exhaled slowly, then said, "Reviewing things."

"Like what?"

"Like the decisions I've made."

"Bad choice. You're second-guessing." Linda had allowed the airliner to drift a couple of degrees off heading; she quickly pushed the jetliner slightly left again. It turned out that flying a big airliner without any working flight instruments was damn hard. Harder than she thought.

Ray said, "It seems like we've been doing this for ten years."

Linda glanced at her wristwatch. "It's two hours and twenty-four minutes since the engine spooled up. To me, it seems like twenty years ago." Linda paused, then added, "I don't know how you managed to stay focused. I could hardly keep my eyes on the airspeed indicator with the ocean out there."

"I was too scared to look." Ray allowed himself another small smile, then glanced out the captain's side window. He estimated their current flight altitude to be approximately 800 feet. The ocean was even more of a churning, boiling mass of frothy grey water than it had been earlier.

It was just as forecast. The increase in the heaviness of the sea made sense, and it was something that he had actually been anticipating since the weather forecasts and the en route weather maps showed that the storm system in Canada would be reaching this far south. That was the good news, since the forecast winds that he was calculating the magnetic heading adjustments for should be basically correct. Yet he also knew that those forecast winds better be close to being correct or they were screwed. Royally.

Ray pushed that thought out of his mind. The aircraft rocked gently back and forth and, occasionally, a moderate ripple of turbulence rolled through the airframe, but otherwise the ride itself had remained mostly steady. "I can take the flight controls again," Ray said as he reached for the captain's control wheel.

"No. You relax, I'm doing fine," Linda answered. "Let me earn my pay. Hey, it just occurred to me that I'm getting paid for this flight and you're not."

"Right. But you're not getting paid enough."

"You can say that again."

Ray dropped his hands into his lap, and he sat further back in the captain's flight chair. They were in a lull period, with the big decisions behind them and the eventual outcome too far away to see. From the reports they had gotten from the cabin, conditions had quieted down to a reasonable level from the full chaos they had been earlier. In addition, the medical reports on the injured captain and first officer were encouraging; Peter, in particular, seemed to be coming back around as the effects of the drugs from the medical practitioner's kit were wearing off. Ray needed to have another discussion with that doctor about Peter's physical condition, and about Peter's mental condition, too.

"Ray, let's talk about the things you were thinking about," Linda finally said. After watching him for awhile, Linda felt that this needed to be brought into the open — the last thing they needed now was for Ray to begin doubting his earlier decisions. Linda knew how much their ultimate chance of success — of survival — would increase if Ray wasn't questioning things he'd already done. Besides, talking over the situation was better than sitting in silence and brooding. "Maybe a review of what we've done will help us think clearly about what needs to be accomplished."

"Suit yourself. But talking won't change a damn thing. We're committed," Ray answered bluntly. He knew that he had made a thousand decisions, some small, some huge – but each and every one of them had taken this stricken airliner further along the line that he'd selected. On more than one occasion he thought that maybe he should have done something differently, but it was too late now. Right or wrong, he had made commitments they would have to live – or die – with.

"A review won't hurt," Linda said. And she also wanted to get Ray out of his own head. That wouldn't hurt, either. She glanced at the standby compass in the middle of the center windshield, to be certain that she was holding their calculated magnetic heading as precisely as possible. That old-fashioned wet compass in front of her, plus the bare-bones emergency altimeter and its companion airspeed indicator were the only instruments working inside the airliner since Ray had disabled everything electrical immediately after their recovery at wave height. There was nothing else onboard that was functional – not a single light, not a single radio, not a single instrument. "Let's talk about shutting down the electrical system."

"Ancient history," Ray said. "More of a reaction than a thought-out procedure." He glanced at the switches on the panel above his head. It had been his ingrained pilot's instinct to get rid of what he now guessed was the core of their major problem, the source behind those incredible engine runaways. His first priority was to get rid of all the power sources to the engine computers, and since he didn't know how to isolate them electrically, Ray shut down the entire electrical system. That was the only way he could be damn certain that those malfunctioning computers didn't get another single volt from any of various electrical circuits in the airplane. If the computers did get powered up and another engine runaway began, they'd be doomed.

Ray knew that Boeings would be flyable without any electricity, and from what everyone had told him about the

173

Consolidated 768 conversions, the basic Boeing was underneath the modern wizardry. By shutting off the electrical power, Ray had hoped that they would go from a 768 back to a 767.

And, basically, they had. The 768 without any electricity acted like the old 767. Without that electrical power they were prevented from doing any of the other normal tasks, but that was a small price to pay to keep a functioning engine that didn't have the potential for going nuts. The fact that they had no navigation abilities and no communications abilities were facts that they would – and could – live with. With the flick of his wrist, Ray had turned this modern computer-driven and computer-dependent airline jet back to the roots of aviation and, in many ways, back to something akin to the *Spirit of St. Louis*. For Flight 3 to make it back to dry land, Ray would have to become Lucky Lindy.

"A good reaction to shut everything down," Linda said. She was giving his past decisions her full support because she figured that he could use it. "Can't run the risk of having the left engine running away."

"Goes without saying."

"So, with no electricity we have no problems."

Ray glanced out the cockpit side window at the ocean waves below. He was relaxed enough to indulge himself with a small measure of sarcasm. "Oh, really? No more problems? That's good to hear."

"None with that engine, that's my guess," Linda said, keeping the conversation moving along as she intended. "Since we don't know what caused those runaways — not for sure — then, by taking away the ship's electrical power we do away with any chance of another computer-generated runaway. Good call on your part."

"Or so it seems so far," Ray answered.

Linda ignored his negative remark; she was going to sound positive and she wanted him to be positive, too. "That puts the electrical question to bed. Like you said, that decision is history. Can't run the risk of turning the ship's power on, even for a short while."

"That was my thinking. Still is."

"Absolutely," Linda said. "I agree." She decided to take this time to catalog her feelings, her reasoning, her expectations. It was good for them to talk; it was good for *her* to talk. "The fuel for the operating engine will gravity feed from the wing tanks as long as we stay in a reasonable flight attitude. The pressurization system is unnecessary flying this low, and the cabin temperature control valves will remain locked at their last settings, so the temperature and airflow through the cabin will remain the same. We've got one running engine, two wings and a tail. That's all we need."

"Yes." Ray nodded; he already knew this, but he was glad to see that she knew it, too, and could appreciate the nuances. She was a knowledgeable pilot. Ray had always felt that those pilots who didn't bother to learn the ins and outs of their airplanes as thoroughly as possible – Linda obviously had – were basically just along for the ride.

"And we can live without the radios." Linda glanced down at the radio sets on the center console. With the electricity off, that collection of expensive radios and electronic navigation gear had become nothing but dead weight, unnecessary ballast. "There's nothing that anyone can tell us on the radio that matters. We're on our own, even if we could transmit and receive voice messages."

"That's always been the case." Ray also noticed that Linda could hand-fly the airliner properly, which was something of a lost art with many of the modern pilots. She was using all the flight controls, including the rudder pedals. That was good.

"The ship's in a stable condition," Linda continued. "We've eliminated the factors that could have caused the runaways. Now, all we've got to do is locate the North American coastline. After that, all we've got to do is find a suitable airport or big and empty stretch of beach."

"Right. That's all." Ray blanched at the enormity of the piloting tasks still facing them.

"Yes." Linda gestured toward the archaic wet compass that hung in the center of the windshield. "Hold our calculated heading. That's it. North America is too big to miss. Once we find land, there are lots of airports. Lots of beaches."

"That's true," Ray answered, although he knew that there was more to it than that. First, they had to remain out of any clouds or even a heavy, obscuring rain since, without any electricity in the ship, they had absolutely no blind flying instruments. They had turned the aviation clock back a hundred years and the only way to keep this modern widebody jet straight and level was to look out the window and keep the wings and nose in proper relationship to the horizon. If they couldn't see enough of the horizon line to remain relatively level, the airliner would quickly assume some absurd flight attitude and then spin into the sea. Then there was the question of the forecast winds, which they had used to calculate the magnetic heading they were steering. North America was too damn big to completely miss, but exactly where they would intercept that enormous coastline was another matter.

"We've got our current situation nailed down," Linda said. "Do you agree?"

"Sure." Although Ray also knew that it could turn out to be like the nails in a coffin.

"Let's talk about that turn to the west," she said. Linda knew that his decision to turn the struggling ship away from its approximate heading toward the Azores — the nearest land mass at the time — and pick a heading to intercept North America was the toughest one. Ray had made that decision a few seconds after turning off the ship's electricity.

"A calculated risk." Ray answered.

"I can see that now." Initially, Linda had protested loudly against turning the airplane away from the heading toward the Azores — turning away from a chain of Islands that were hardly more than 400 miles away and steering instead toward a land mass that was a thousand-plus miles in the distance. The thought of not heading directly for whatever was the nearest land was an incredibly frightening idea. It was something that Linda didn't have enough courage to make.

Ray shook his head. "That decision was based on guesswork, flying habits and my overview of the weather. You had every right to object. Maybe the Azores would have worked out, but..."

"No buts, not now, not at this point," Linda answered. She couldn't let him get down on himself. For that matter, neither one of them could afford to have any doubts, there was no room for that. "Okay, so I screamed my head off," Linda said. "Now I'm glad you ignored me. Now I understand."

"Good."

Ray had explained to her that if they didn't hit exactly onto the tiny Azore Islands — using nothing beyond a standby magnetic compass and beginning from a starting point on the charts they weren't sure of — that they would fly past the Islands and wind up ditching in the ocean somewhere to the south. "I wasn't thinking clearly," Linda said, "when I objected to the turn to the west."

"I wasn't thinking clearly either. I was reacting. Jack had shown me the weather map with clear skies to New York. That's when I noticed the expected low cloud cover to the south of our route, between our course and the Azores. The weather in the Azores is supposed to be a low overcast with rain showers. That was in the back of my mind, too."

"It was a good reaction to turn west."

"Hopefully." Ray paused while he ran through those thoughts again. By flying southeast toward the Azores they were trying to find a needle in a haystack. They were already committed to flying low and they had absolutely no navigation aids beyond a basic magnetic heading to steer by. At a low altitude they could miss the Islands by a handful of miles and they'd never see a hint of them. The weather was a factor, too, since they had no ability to fly inside the clouds or even heavy rain – they needed clear skies to keep the airplane upright. Besides, North America was too big to be missed, while the tiny Azores Islands could be flown past without getting the Islands in sight. Even if they could stay clear of clouds on that course line, which was doubtful. "If we missed the Azores, we'd never know how close we came."

"Exactly. North America is impossible to miss," Linda Erickson said. "You convinced me. Like I said, good choice. Holding that heading toward the Azores was an emotional response, and I didn't consider the weather. I was too frightened to think clearly, I wanted to head directly for the nearest patch of dry land and not something that was nearly three times further away. It was wishful thinking."

"Right." Ray knew that both of them had to feel confidence in their decisions or they'd be stacking the deck against themselves – a deck that was already stacked pretty damn high. "Anyone onboard who says they aren't scared doesn't understand our situation. The only difference for us is that we've

177

got to keep our thoughts and actions separate from our emotions. There's no room for wishful thinking, not for the rest of this flight." Ray grabbed the captain's control wheel and gestured for Linda to sit back. "Got it, take a break," he said as he began to concentrate on holding the exact magnetic heading that would eventually take them to somewhere along the North American coastline.

In the back of his mind, Ray knew, in spite of what he had said, that he, too, was now engaged in a great deal of wishful thinking. At the altitude they were flying, the jet airliner was consuming more fuel than it normally did. They were getting far less miles to the gallon because of their reduced forward speed. Would they have enough fuel to reach any portion of the North American coastline? Without electricity, there was not only no way to communicate or navigate, there was also no way to check the fuel levels in the tanks, no way to know for sure one way or the other.

Jack had put on extra fuel at Rome, but would it be enough to take them all the way to the North American coastline at this altitude and airspeed? Ray had tried to do preliminary figuring in his head, but there were too many unknowns for him to make an educated guess. Finally, he gave up trying. Barring any other unforseen problem, their only functioning engine would continue running until they sucked the last gallon of fuel out of the wing tanks. Then the engine would quit. Would they reach land first? It was impossible to guess.

At this point, all he could do was hope. Ray fully realized that he was now engaging in that one trait that he had tried to steadfastly avoid when he was an active airline pilot, the one trait that he had said was the fastest way to get himself and everyone onboard killed: wishful thinking. But he had no other option, so he was going with it. Wishful thinking, plus lots of additional prayers thrown in.

◇

Tina was allowing herself a few minutes of rest in seat 1C of the first class cabin. Earlier, she had asked the man who had originally been assigned to 1D to take any of the other empty seats in so that the doctor could sit beside her. By being seated in the middle of the first row of the first class cabin, they were only a few feet away from the two pilots who had been laid out on the floor of the galley. With the curtains pulled away, both pilots were easily visible, and each of the unconscious men had a bright yellow life jacket propped beneath their heads. "I didn't realize how incredibly tired I was until I sat down," Tina said. "Makes me wonder if I'll be able to get up again."

"You'll have no trouble getting up when there's a need," Lee answered. He looked away from Tina and toward the two pilots laying on the galley floor. "The captain seems stable. If I took a guess, I'd say he'll eventually pull through."

"That's great."

"Yes." Lee paused, then added, "That's a pure guess on my part since I don't have x-ray fingers and my clinical equipment is limited to a stethoscope, a blood pressure monitor and a thermometer. But his vital signs are getting stronger and there are no apparent secondary symptoms. The odds are good that nothing of ultimate consequence was hit by that bullet."

"Wonderful." Tina had wondered how on earth *two* accidental gunshots could have gone off in the cockpit, one right after the other. She had broached the subject with Ray on one of her trips to the cockpit and, reluctantly, Ray told her the story about Peter's panic attack and how he had suddenly decided that Ray was hijacking the airliner. It was a bizarre story, to say the very least, and when she returned to the cabin she talked to the doctor – the psychiatrist – about it. He had listened carefully, then said that he would explain the significance of it to her later, when they had more time. "How about explaining to me what the co-pilot's panic was about?" she asked. "We've got time now."

"Yes, we've got time." Lee Frankel sat back in his chair, folded his hands together and took a deep breath. Frankel also knew that he shouldn't be negative or maudlin. He needed to do exactly the opposite. Right now. Here was his chance. "Okay, I'm going to share my suspicions and my guesses, but only because you asked. Even more importantly, I'm going to answer only because you are obviously a person of great authority here in the passenger cabin, a force of sheer willpower to be reckoned with." Lee made an exaggerated gesture, waving one hand around the cabin of the airliner.

179

"Are you joking?" Tina asked. She wasn't sure if he was being serious or not since what he said seemed so out of character from what she'd seen of him so far. "You must be."

"Certainly not." Lee smiled broadly to show that, yes, of course, he was just kidding. He was trying to keep it lighthearted whenever he could, as Viktor would have recommended. "This section of the aircraft is your exclusive domain. That's obvious, and I can see that you rule this area with an iron hand. Since you're officially in charge of everything going on back here, I feel a professional obligation, not to mention a legal mandate, to answer any and all of your questions. Putting it another way, you raised the question so I'll spill the beans." While he continued to joke with her, Lee also found that he had relaxed enough to allow his own private thoughts to effortlessly roll through his mind. Lee knew that he wanted to talk to her, too, that he wanted to hear her questions...and he wanted to hear her answers.

Tina laughed. "I thought you were joking. Now it sounds like you're setting me up." She smiled back at him. He didn't seem like some stuck-up doctor, he seemed very real, very easy to know. "What's the punch line? Am I going to get a bill for this?"

"No. I won't bill you. I'll bill the airline." Lee was impressed with her class and style, her sincerity and quickness. "Okay, I'll explain what I've guessed from what I've been told. Told by you and told to me by Ray. You've got to understand that my conclusions could be wrong, or some of what you folks have told me could be off-base. Because of that, there's no guarantee that what I'm telling you is particularly correct."

"A Doctor shouldn't care about being correct. That's why it's called a practice."

"Right you are." Lee laughed again, then took a few seconds to look at her. She was strikingly beautiful. She was quick witted and intelligent. And she instinctively understood the need to make light-hearted conversation between them – Viktor would have been proud of her. "Here's my take on the information I've gotten so far."

"I'm all ears."

Lee began by explaining the evolution and makeup of the human brain. He began by telling her that we think of our brain as a single functioning unit when, in fact, it contains distinct

180

modules that run simultaneously and in parallel – all of this was once hardly more than theory, but has since been conclusively proven with modern diagnostic equipment. Lee went on to explain that each of these modules has its own purpose. Sometimes those modules compete and sometimes they cooperate, but the ultimate result is a mental experience that usually seems unified and seamless.

"I know what you mean by 'usually'. Every now and then I can feel those mental separations," Tina said. "You know, when your insides are being pulled in two different directions." Tina was making a subtle reference about her relationship with Ray. Now that she thought about it, having his insides pulled apart is also how Ray described his own feelings toward her. For the first time she realized how true the existence of those mental separations were, no question about it.

"You're absolutely right," Lee answered. She was very perceptive. "To keep my analogy basic, humans have a cogent, reasoning system inside their heads, plus an automatic system. The emotion of fear resides in the automatic portion, and it is outside the control of your conscious thoughts. A reaction of extreme fear – like the episode you described from the co-pilot's symptoms – will shut down the prefrontal cortex where the conscious mind resides and total control will then shift to the automatic areas. Another part of the mind that will shut down with extreme fear is memory, which is why victims of intense trauma often cannot remember what happened to them even though they were completely conscious the entire time."

"Really?" Tina sat back and thought over what he had said. "Interesting."

"Most of us think so." Lee grinned. "Mostly because it's about us. We love to talk about ourselves and we love to hear about ourselves."

"Can't argue with you there." Tina was impressed with how Lee could talk about complicated things so...plainly. It was a real gift. She paused, then added, "so, fear is bad because it takes over. It takes control of us."

"Sometimes." Lee paused. "Okay, I'll ask you a question. Are you afraid right now?" He gestured with his hand around the cabin again. "Because of our situation."

"Hell, yes. Scared to death, although I'm not supposed to let the passengers know. Don't tell anyone."

"You're doing a great job of hiding it, but that's not the point. If you weren't afraid considering our situation, you'd be a reckless fool," Lee answered. "The modules of the brain were built to work together, to balance and counteract each other."

"Then what happened to the co-pilot? Why didn't it happen to Ray, too, or Linda, or to Jack? According to what Ray told me, they were frightened but functioning. Peter completely panicked. Why?"

"You must be working on your doctorate. If you can understand those sorts of subtleties, you could easily get one."

"Maybe someday, but not today." Tina smiled at him warmly, then touched him on the arm. "You're evading my question. Am I right, doctor?"

"Yes." Lee smiled; she was absolutely charming. "People are different in their balance between conscious tools that they've created inside their heads and the automatic responses that balance them. From what you – and Ray – have told me about this co-pilot, his entire world revolved around procedures and rigidly learned techniques. When the airliner did things that were outside the domain of those areas – far outside, as it turns out – he was suddenly, completely and hopelessly lost. The only thing left to him at that moment was the automatic response, a response which shut down everything rational in him."

"Why did he accuse Ray of being a hijacker?" That, of all the things she had heard, was the most bizarre, the most insane. It was ludicrous and even laughable, if the entire situation hadn't become such a never-ending nightmare for them.

"I'm guessing here, of course, but Peter was grasping at straws, at snippets of knowledge and memory that were rushing disjointedly through his mind. He was a drowning man grabbing a life preserver, the only life preserver he could find. He needed to make sense of the enormously threatening world around him and to find some way – some explanation – that he could function with to begin getting himself out of that life-threatening situation. He needed to find a cause behind this building traumatic condition that he could comprehend and, more importantly, that he could deal with by using the tools he had available. His procedures and learned techniques had completely deserted him, so he turned to something that he had available. With his officially-issued government handgun and his official title as the onboard guardian against hijackings, Peter's mind created a make-believe condition that was now within his grasp to deal with."

"Wow."

"That was exactly my reaction the first time someone explained this stuff to me," Lee said. "Wow."

Tina laughed and wrapped her fingers around his arm again. "You have a wonderful way of getting your message across. I understood everything you've told me."

"My patients should be that lucky." Lee indulged himself by looking directly at her face; she was, indeed, very beautiful – although Lee knew that their dire situation would cause him to search out positive traits such as beauty, meaning and direction. Being human, he would amplify them. Was that what he was doing? Was he seeing in Tina – a woman he hardly knew, a woman he had spent barely more than a few hours with – only what he wanted and needed to see? Could those reasons be why she appeared so incredibly gorgeous, so intelligent, so sensitive, so alluring to him? Lee knew that he needed to stop being so damned clinical, to enjoy the moment. No, it wasn't an illusion, Lee decided. She was all those things. Maybe even more. "Any more questions?"

"Only one. How long does this panic condition last? If Peter comes around, will he wake up normal or wake up panicked?

"Another good question." Which was, Lee knew, precisely what he was expecting from her. "I can tell you definitively that there's no way to tell."

"And you charge people for answers like that?"

Lee laughed again; with her around, he was almost forgetting how critical their situation was. "Only the insurance companies, I assure you. And Medicare, too – they can afford it."

"No wonder the government is going bankrupt."

"That's a problem above my pay grade," he answered. "Now, back to the question about Peter. Since his physical problems were mostly from shock and blood loss, it's a matter of time until the sedative I gave him wears off and he comes around again," Lee said.

"Do you think he'll be able to rejoin the pilots when he wakes up, that he'll be able to go to the cockpit to help them?" Tina asked. She paused for a moment, then added, "I guess I'm really asking if that would be a good idea."

Lee gave her a soft smile without saying anything for several seconds. Finally, he spoke. "At this point, do you think that they need him?" Lee asked. "After all, this retired pilot, Ray Clarke — a man whom you have obviously known quite well in the past — seems to be handling the situation as well as anyone could. My initial feeling was that the ship was in very capable hands, and after talking to Clarke an hour ago, I'm absolutely convinced of it. And you know what they say about too many cooks and spoiling the broth."

Tina didn't know what to say in reply; by design or not, this man had hit a nerve. As she was all too aware, Ray Clarke was certainly a man that she had known quite well in the past. After several seconds of silence, Tina finally answered. "I thought I knew Ray once. I see now that I was wrong. Completely wrong."

"Perhaps." Lee reached over the small table between the first class seats and laid his left hand on the top of hers . "And perhaps not." He paused, then added, "In matters of the heart – matters that are packed with emotions – our first inclinations are often the most truthful." He had spoken in a detached, off-hand manner, but the emotions stirring inside him were the opposite. He knew that he had to be careful here, he was on shaky ground. What he was doing was, in fact, meddling. Lee pushed his professional cautions aside and found himself saying everything that he initially intended, even though he knew that he shouldn't. "Our lives have potholes in them, and those potholes cause lots of twists and turns in our ride. You've got to let yourself take those twists and turns in stride. Accept them, don't fight them. Keep your head up because sometimes you can find exactly what you're looking for when you least expect it, when you thought you weren't looking."

Tina didn't know quite what to say in response. "...I guess...I have been...fighting..." Tina thought for a moment that maybe Ray had said something to this doctor during one of his visits to the cockpit, but she immediately dismissed that as not being Ray's style. Of all people, Ray wouldn't say a word. Tina glanced down at Lee's hand, which was resting on hers. She was very aware of his touch. Even though he was basically a stranger, she did not want him to remove his hand. Finally, she turned slightly in her chair to face him fully and said, "That reminds me of something. Something that I've been wanting to tell you."

"Certainly." Lee slowly moved his hand from hers and moved himself around in his chair, so he was facing her squarely. "Feel free."

"I can't get out of my mind those first words I heard from you. Do you remember what you said to me back then and when it was that you said it?" she asked.

"Not clearly," he answered, "although it was in that first bout of those engine runaways. You were caught here in the cabin, next to my seat, when the airplane began to pitch up. I do remember how, immediately after getting yourself into a seat, you looked at me and shouted for me to buckle my seatbelt. Even while you were being surprised by that alarming turn of events, you kept yourself focused on your job. That's very commendable."

"Thank you." Tina smiled at him; she had thought of him as a good looking man from the first moment that she had seen him, but now that she had spent considerable time working with Lee she realized that much of that attractiveness was in his eyes. They were alive, alert, soft in appearance yet quite determined. It was his eyes that set him apart from most other people. He had a strong presence about him, too, yet there was also an unquestionable aura of calmness in him. "Like I was saying, the first words that you said were about our flight situation and, a few seconds after that, about the beginning of the recovery. The words themselves didn't catch my attention as much as your tone did. You remained absolutely calm throughout that incredible event, as if you knew what the final outcome would be. How was that possible?"

Lee laughed. "Well, I can tell you up front that I'm a psychiatrist, not a psychic. I had no idea what was going to happen next. If my memory serves me correctly, I said something about our situation not being so good. That was quite an understatement."

"That was the understatement of the entire flight," Tina said. "I'd give you a prize for saying such a brilliant, insightful thing, if I had a prize to give you."

"You've already given me that prize," Lee said. He exhaled slowly, letting his thoughts wash over him. Lee cleared his throat, then said, "Tina, you've been working alongside me for hours now. For me, that's been one hell of an unexpected prize during this nightmare. As far as I'm concerned, having you next to me has made a major difference – it's been the only positive moments in a completely negative situation."

"Thank you." Tina looked at him directly for a few seconds, thinking of how she should respond. Finally, she said, "I suspect that you're smart enough to know that I've been feeling the same way."

"I'm smart enough not to have mentioned this if I didn't already think so, or at least hoped so." He laughed self-consciously, surprising himself that he felt slightly uncomfortable at the moment, slightly awkward. Like he often told his patients, most of life's major decisions were about the risk-to-reward tradeoffs we elect to make, and for an instant he was wondering which side of the ledger this personal conversation with this mesmerizing woman was taking him. Lee pushed that distracting feeling aside and pressed on in the direction that he had set in motion. "Some of us do like a healthy dose of reality now and then. But none of us like a harsh, cold, indifferent reality. Not if we have a choice."

"Another great answer. Who, exactly, do you get to write your material?"

Lee touched his hand to hers, then leaned further back in his chair and allowed his hand to slide away. "When it's time for me to say something of consequence, I usually quote other people. They do my material, or, at least, a great deal of it."

"Lee, you have a fabulous way with words," Tina said. "I'm probably not the first to tell you that."

"Words are the basic tools of psychiatry. They can function as either scalpels or bandages. Sometimes they can become complete blood transfusions." He paused, then added, "If you're not careful, they can become a sledge hammer."

186

For an instant, Tina realized how incredibly bizarre this scene had become. Here she was, chatting casually with a charming and witty man while the airliner they were in was barely cruising above the waves of the Atlantic Ocean as they struggled westward with only one of the ship's engines running and the electricity shut down. As if that wasn't enough, the captain and co-pilot of the flight were trying to recuperate from gunshot wounds and were laying unconscious on the floor of the first class galley while retired Captain Ray Clarke — a man she loved who she couldn't get out of her mind — was doing the flying of the airplane. Totally, completely bizarre.

"Well, I can see that my analogies about psychiatry have gotten you to think about something else," Lee said with a self-conscious grin.

"Yes, they did," Tina answered. "I was thinking about how bizarre this entire situation is," Tina said.

"Good choice of words," Lee answered.

"Yes." She allowed her hand to gesture toward her yellow life jacket on the seat beside her, the two unconscious pilots on the galley floor, then around the rest of the airplane's cabin. "Look around. The passengers and crew are either wearing life jackets or have them nearby, and we're flying so low you can count the individual waves. According to our flight crew, they're not certain where we are and they have no firm idea when we might make landfall or where that landfall might be. Frankly, I'm afraid to ask either of them if they think our only running engine will keep operating. This entire flight has become more than surreal to me. As far as I'm concerned, it's become absolutely, totally nuts. Hopefully, that's not offensive to a practicing psychiatrist."

"No offense taken. Matter of fact, I agree with you. This flight *has* gone nuts — like a great deal of the other elements in human lives often do. The *nuts* part of our lives is where the cutting edge can be."

"How? What do you mean?"

Lee pulled his wallet out of his pocket, pulled out a piece of folded paper and handed the paper to her. At this point he was going to go the entire route with her, there was no reason not to. "This is something special I'd like you to read. Before you do, let me explain a few things."

187

"Sure." Tina took the paper from his hand but didn't unfold it yet, just as he had asked. Instead, she found herself watching him, watching his eyes.

"A very famous psychiatrist passed away a number of years ago. He was an Austrian named Viktor Frankl."

"A relative of yours?"

"Not at all. Our names are not even spelled the same," Lee answered. "But he turned out to be more important to me than any relative could have been. Perhaps it was pure curiosity that our names were so similar that got me interested in him. Perhaps it was pure serendipity, or even a mystical connection that's outside our human perception. Regardless, his writings are what got me involved in medicine and directly into psychiatry."

"Did you ever meet him?" Tina asked.

"No, although I did attend several of his final lectures. Believe it or not, I might have been able to meet him personally at one point late in his life, but I was afraid to – his stuff meant so damn much to me – so I passed up the chance."

"Really? You don't impress me as having any fears."

"I've got plenty of fears. For example, I'm afraid right now that we might not live through this. You've had a similar fear — in fact, you mentioned fear a few minutes ago," Lee added. "But being afraid doesn't require us to turn our thoughts and our actions over to that fear. In fact, it means exactly the opposite."

"I don't follow you," Tina said.

Lee leaned closer to Tina and lowered his voice slightly. "Viktor Frankl was a doctor in Austria in 1942 when he and his entire family — they were Jewish — were arrested by the Nazis and sent to concentration camps. Frankl spent the next three years in Auschwitz, Dachau and other places, finally being liberated at the end of the war. The rest of his family — father, mother, wife, brother — were killed in those camps."

"Oh."

"While a prisoner, Frankl helped many of the other prisoners to cope with the nightmares of their situation. After the war, he wrote 'Mans Search for Meaning' in which he described how he and other prisoners found meaning in their lives and thus, were able to summon the will to survive. That book of his on psychotherapy sold over ten million copies in twenty-four languages, and Frankl later published another thirty-one books on that and related subjects. That small document that I've given you," Lee said as he pointed to the folded paper in Tina's hand, "is one of his most brilliant summations. I carry a copy of it with me at all times." He glanced at the paper she was holding; even though he clearly understood, analytically, why it was so personally important to share this part of him with her *right here and right now*, he didn't give a damn about the reasons and the justifications. He was going to do it.

Tina nodded, unfolded the paper and read it.

What was really needed was a fundamental change in our attitude toward life. We had to learn ourselves, and, furthermore, we had to teach the despairing men, that it did not really matter what we expected from life, but rather what life expected from us. We needed to stop asking ourselves about the meaning of life, and instead to think of ourselves as those who were being questioned by life — daily and hourly. Our answer must consist not in talk and meditation, but in right action and in right conduct. Life ultimately means taking the responsibility to find the right answer to its problems and to fulfill the tasks which it constantly sets for each individual.

"Incredible." Tina looked up at Lee. "I've never read anything like this." She paused, looked down at the paper in her hands, then back at him. Her hands were actually trembling; she had noticed the trembling when she glanced down, and she also noticed that Lee saw it, too. She knew that the raw emotion that displayed itself through her trembling hands was a combination of two things: the words on that paper, and the fact that Lee wanted to share those words, those ideas with *her*. That was, she knew, exactly where those emotions were coming from. Finally, Tina found enough focus and enough energy to speak again. "Lee...this is...very, very powerful." She hesitated for another moment while she searched for better words. Finally, she added, "It's truly incredible. Beyond incredible. I can't think of any other words to describe it. " Tina knew that she wanted to say more, but she also knew that she couldn't phrase her feelings properly so she said nothing else.

"I had a hunch you'd appreciate it." Lee sat silently for a moment, clearly considering what he was going to say next. It was unusual for him, but his thoughts were not focused. Yet the lack of focus was not in any way something he could label as being negative. His thoughts were mellow and diffused; they were there – and yet, they were not there at the same time. Finally, Lee spoke. "There's one more thing I need to tell you, so that you have a complete understanding of what I'm doing these days. I've been doing follow-up work on what Viktor Frankl had started so brilliantly."

"Follow-up?"

"Yes," Lee said, hesitantly. He didn't know how much more of this he would or should get into. After a short pause, he continued. "I've made a number of trips to Europe and other places around the world to interview the last of the concentration camp survivors as part of my own writing on the subject, to give testimony as to what ultimately happened to those who managed to survive those calamitous events and go on to live long lives. I wanted to document what might be called the end, the final chapter, of that particular human story."

"That's an astonishing idea." Tina folded the paper, laid it on the small table between the seats. As Lee reached for the paper, she placed her hand softly on top of his. "You are an amazing man," she said, knowing that the words themselves were inadequate but maybe he would hear the feelings that were behind them. She really wanted him to. "Really. You are." Tina paused, then added, "I meant every single thing that I said."

"Me, too." They looked at each other in a long silence before Lee glanced toward the first class galley, then turned to her. He cleared his throat, then said, "Well, I hope that our co-pilot thinks I'm half as amazing as a medical doctor as, apparently, you think I've been as a collector and compiler of other people's intellectual work, and a man who usually quotes others."

"I can tell that you've done more than compile and quote."

Lee smiled warmly at Tina. "Perhaps a little." He then said to her, "Here's an idea. Let's see if we can do something that goes beyond our conversation, as enjoyable – hell, as personally significant – as that conversation has been to me."

190

"Like what?" Tina asked. An enjoyable conversation? Yes, it really had been. Had it been significant? Yes, very much.

Lee pointed at the first class galley area. "I noticed that Peter has finally begun to wake up. Let's go see what he has to say, how he feels and, maybe, see what he remembers from what happened in the cockpit a few hours ago."

Chapter Twenty

The sight out the cockpit windshield was an unusual one, even with someone with as much flying experience as Ray. In the past ten minutes, the cloud cover had grown considerably and Ray could see that the ragged bases of the clouds were hardly more than a few thousand feet above their own flight altitude, which was hardly more than a couple of thousand feet above the surface of the ocean. "I'm surprised we're getting this much weather this far south," Ray said as he glanced over at the co-pilot.

Linda, sitting in the co-pilot's seat, was looking at the weather forecast maps and the printed reports that she had spread across the center console between the two pilot stations. That flight planning material was old news since it was a printed copy of what was available when they left Rome. But, still... "Assuming we're flying the track we think we are, according to the paperwork we shouldn't be seeing any of these clouds — certainly nothing as thick as what we're running into." Linda glanced out the window at the cloud deck above them, then at Ray. "What do you think?"

"Either the crosswind gradient from the south is heavier than forecast and we've drifted further to the north, or the weather itself has taken a turn to the south." Ray looked out his side window at the sea below. The surface conditions were unmistakably rougher and there was no question now that, because of the height of those frothy waves and the big cross swells, their chance of a successful ditching in the open ocean had gone from minuscule to non-existent. But the bad part was that the weather around them was unquestionably turning sour, and the charts they had onboard showed that none of that was supposed to be happening. Something had definitely changed – changed for the worst.

"I wouldn't want to put this thing down on that water surface," Linda said as she saw what Ray was looking at. She, too, knew that their only chance of survival depended on the airliner's single functioning engine continuing to work as well as it had been. "But we're not going down," Linda added. She didn't want him getting negative, and she didn't want to get negative herself. "The engine is working fine."

"Yeah, from what we can tell." Ray pointed at the airliner's center instrument panel where, normally, the engine data was displayed. The electronic screen remained completely black, as it had been since Ray shut down the ship's electrical circuits nearly three hours earlier. Any developing engine trends were hidden behind the blanked-out gauges; all they knew for certain was that the left engine was running, and it was producing enough power to keep them airborne. That was it. "Truth is, we don't have a single damn clue what's going on in that engine."

"Don't need to know. Running fine," Linda said again, more to convince herself than Ray. "Just fine."

"Yeah." Ray glanced at the blank instrument panel again, but then turned away. There was no need for him to create imaginary problems, and for damn sure they already had enough real ones to deal with. "Having that display doesn't mean a thing. Not really. Nothing we could do even if we had the readings."

"Right." Linda wouldn't allow herself to even *think* of anything negative at this point, but what Ray said was the cold, hard truth. Linda shrugged. "Nothing we could do about less than perfect engine trends," she said as she looked at the blanked-out instrument panel in front of them, then at Ray. "Out of options in that department."

"Out of options in most departments." Yet Ray knew that there were a few choices that could be made, some of which he was hoping he wouldn't need to deal with. Reluctantly, he knew that he did need to deal with them right now. "Here's our situation and our options," Ray said. "Tell me if you see things differently."

"Okay." Linda let out a deep breath, then sat back in her flight chair as the airliner bobbed and rocked in the low level turbulence that had increased during the past quarter hour. "Don't see any options at this point."

"We have two, which are the only two factors we can influence. Heading and altitude. Talk about heading."

"Oh. Right." Linda glanced at the magnetic compass in front of them, that archaic instrument that basically hadn't changed since Christopher Columbus left Spain for the New

World. For navigation, that's what they were down to: a calculated line drawn on a plotting chart, a guess for wind correction thrown in, and a magnetic heading that was supposed to run them into the North American coastline. Very archaic.

"We calculated a steering heading of 285 degrees, and that heading should remain constant from this point considering the slight change in magnetic variation in this area and further west."

"That's what we decided earlier," Linda answered.

"We've taken a few degrees off that heading to compensate for the southerly wind flow," Ray continued, "but I'm wondering if that was enough. Maybe we're flying further north than we expected, and we're running closer to that Canadian low."

"Possible." Linda looked out the windshield, then at Ray. "So is the chance that the Canadian low has drifted south or gotten larger. Maybe it's affecting more area than forecast." Linda paused again. "For the life of me, I don't know how to tell which scenario is closer to the truth." Linda had wanted to keep talking because it calmed her, but this conversation was getting her more nervous, not less. The last thing she wanted now were more options – which meant more choices to be made. Maybe the wrong ones.

"No way to tell about the wind and weather," Ray answered. "But the only certainty is that we're not too far *south* of our intended track. You agree?"

"I see your point. Yes, I agree."

"That's a mistake we need to avoid. The further south we go, the longer it'll take to intercept the coastline." Ray shook his head then said out loud the one word that he absolutely dreaded to think about. "Fuel. We have no way of knowing how much we're burning, and how much is left. Even with Jack's extra 6,000 pounds."

Linda nodded. "True." She pointed to an aircraft operations manual sitting opened. "I've tried to come up with something from the performance charts. The longer I work at it, the more I realize how many pure guesses are going into my calculations." Linda shook her head. "What I'm going to give you is probably meaningless. I finished rechecking my numbers a few minutes ago."

194

"Right." Ray paused. He didn't know if he wanted to hear this number, this rough guess. Ultimately, they would need to keep the left engine running until they landed or they ran the fuel tanks dry. Finally, Ray said, "Your number is a pure guess, that's okay. We've been guessing about lots of things. What'd you come up with?"

"6:39 pm, Eastern Standard Time." Linda glanced at her wristwatch. "It's 3:36, so, from what I can tell, we've got a few minutes over three hours of fuel left."

"Nine hundred miles of range," Ray said. "Maybe a little more."

"Correct."

"I saw you working on the plotting chart." Ray pointed with his right hand at the large North Atlantic plotting map spread across the center console between them. "You worked backward from our last verified position and came up with a ballpark idea of how much further to the coastline, right?"

"Yes."

"And?"

"And, like I said, very preliminary, very much based on a great number of unknowns."

"Linda, I know that," Ray said with some irritation. "Just say the damn number. Trying to sugar coat it for me won't make it any easier."

Linda hesitated, then finally said, "My guess agrees with yours. Nine hundred miles to the coast. Maybe a little more."

"Going to be close," Ray said. "Too goddamn close, but we already knew that."

"Yes, we did," Linda agreed.

Ray glanced at the chart for a moment, then at her. "If we're real lucky — really lucky — we'll stumble onto the Eastern tip of Long Island. That'll shorten the distance. There are big airports at that end of Long Island where I could put us down."

"Right." Linda glanced out the windshield and her eyes got a little wider. "Ray, the cloud cover is getting lower." She pointed to the right front. "Looks like rain or snow showers in that quadrant. Damn."

"See it. I'll give it wide berth." Ray gently banked the airliner to its left, taking five degrees off the calculated magnetic heading they'd been holding. "Can't go further south. Don't have enough fuel for a tour of the North Atlantic."

"That's for sure." For some reason, she was more nervous now than she had been earlier. "This is not good," she said. "Not good at all."

"Right." Ray peered at the indistinct horizon ahead of them. He estimated that, at the moment, their forward visibility was down to five miles. At the most. That much forward visibility provided enough of a visual reference to keep the airliner straight and level. But if they stumbled into a heavy rain or snow shower, the visibility would go down to one mile or even less, and the chance of him being able to keep them upright would be much less. "Trading off altitude to maintain good surface contact," Ray said while he pushed forward on the control wheel to allow the airliner to slowly drift downhill.

Linda squirmed in her flight chair. She didn't want them flying any nearer to the surface of the ocean, but she knew that feeling was illogical since no amount of altitude would make a difference if the left engine quit. "How much lower?" she asked.

"Not sure." Ray divided his attention between looking out the forward windshield and then glancing to his left, straight at the churning sea. "Low-level scud running is not something I've done, not under these circumstances."

"I've never done any of it," Linda said.

"It was called contact flying. Not done anymore," Ray said, the sound of his voice helping to keep him focused.

"Tell me about it," Linda said. She, too, wanted him to keep talking. Anything was better than sitting in silence and waiting. Waiting for the flight visibility to get better – or to get worse.

"Done lots in the old days," Ray said. His attention was riveted on what little he could see out the windshield. The visibility was getting worse.

"Did you do it?"

"Some." Ray's lips were dry. He ran his tongue across them while he thought about what the old-timers had said. Most of their tree-top flying was in slower piston-powered DC-3s, Convairs and DC-6s, and they always had a full compliment of basic blind flying instruments on the panel. The more Ray thought about it, the more he realized that the differences between that and what he was doing now were enormous.

"Okay, you've done this. What airplanes did you use?" Linda asked. She needed to keep the two of them talking.

"Lockheed Electra turboprops," Ray answered. "I flew them the first two years. Some captains on the Electra went low and slow when they could." But Ray knew that what those men were trying to do, by using roads, rivers and terrain features, was to *find* something on the ground that they were hunting for — the end of a runway, or a low valley in a set of hills that would lead to a runway. They weren't worried about keeping the airplane upright, like Ray was trying to do. They were flying low so they could accurately see where they were headed; he was flying lower so he would be able to tell up from down. But in many ways, the basics were the same. "Going lower," Ray announced.

Linda didn't answer. The flight visibility was decreasing steadily, and once again she had to accept the fact that they now had a new and dire problem to face. In many ways, it was as frightening as the engine runaways had been. Linda glanced at the emergency altimeter on the captain's flight panel — that, and the companion emergency airspeed indicator, were the only instruments they had other than the old-style magnetic compass. "Fourteen hundred feet," she announced. "Not accurate. No altimeter setting."

Ray ignored her. He was trying to remember what the old timers said to him — was it Edwin Johnson, John Bushing, Maynard Lyman or Richard Burdick's words that he was remembering? Or was it all of them who agreed that it was best to get as low as you could when you did this contact stuff? They had told him other things, too, other tricks that he was now remembering: *Get a solid reference altitude.* "Going down. To the wave tops. When I get there, reset the altimeter to read zero."

"What?"

"Reset the altimeter to zero," Ray said loudly, his voice raised while he kept his eyes fixed on what he could see of the ocean below. The forward visibility had reduced markedly in the past handful of seconds, and the view straight ahead and to either side was ominous. Ray knew that the patches of light and dark and the streaks of vertical motion in the sky meant that the visibility would be reducing even more in the very near future.

"Ray, I don't understand," Linda said. "What about the altimeter?"

"Reset the damn altimeter! Reset it to zero when I tell you!" Ray said firmly. He glanced at the emergency altimeter: it read 800 feet, but they probably weren't flying at half of that altitude above the waves. Probably less. Faced with no choice — he knew that losing contact with the ground meant an inevitable upset in their flight attitude and certain death — Ray pushed the airliner as low as he dared. "Get ready!" Ray announced as he continued to fly the airliner lower.

Linda now understood what he wanted. She reached across the center console for the altimeter adjustment knob and rotated it downward. "Ready!" she announced. "Waiting for your command!" She was, to her relief, doing something positive again.

"Standby." Ray continued down, to what he estimated was hardly more than a hundred feet above the churning waves. Since they had no barometric setting for the emergency altimeter, he would use the ocean itself to provide a base in case he lost visual contact. It was exactly what Captain Johnson had done with a Lockheed Electra flying low over Lake Erie thirty-plus years ago while Ray sat in the co-pilot's seat. "Now! Reset to zero!"

"Reset to zero!" Linda repeated. She adjusted the altimeter so that it read zero feet. The view out the windshield was startling: the tossing waves, the heavy clouds, the shafts of rain and snow in vertical sheets that surrounded them on all sides. They were not above the waves, the sensation was that the airliner was actually riding *on* the waves. "Keep the wings level!" Linda said nervously, knowing that it was nothing more than a stupid comment being pushed out by her fear.

"Yes," Ray answered distractedly. He was completely focused on the job of hand-flying the airliner at an altitude that was barely above the reach of the waves. He couldn't spare a tiny fragment of his attention on anything else.

"Oh, God. I'm losing visual contact with the water," Linda said in a frightened voice. She was peering hard over the side, but the rain and snow and clouds were beginning to obscure her view, beginning to have the water and the sky meld into oneness, into an amorphous mass. "Nothing."

"Me, too. Losing it," Ray said. He turned from his side window and toward the emergency altimeter. With his attention focused out the side window, the airplane drifted upward slightly: they were now at an indicated altitude of slightly more than one hundred feet. He pushed the airliner down to a zero indicated altitude.

"Careful!" Linda shouted as she saw what he was doing.

"No choice! Need to stay visual!" Having an accurate readout of their height above the surface of the ocean had helped for those few seconds when he lost visual contact with water, but having nothing but an altimeter to go by was a trick that wouldn't work very long. More than anything, he needed to keep the airliner steady. After a handful of seconds with no visual reference, the airplane would develop an undetected pitch-up or roll, and soon after that they would simply fall into the sea. "Linda, see anything?" Ray asked nervously. His own voice echoed in his ears and seemed distant to him.

"Yes. Maybe. Not sure," Linda answered, her face pressed against the co-pilot's side window, her eyes searching for the surface of the water below. "Dear God, please..." Linda said in a low voice. After a few more moments, she said in a louder voice, "...maybe..."

Ray glanced at the altimeter, which was now reading zero, then out his side window. He looked straight down. Perhaps he was seeing the surface of the water beneath them and they were basically flying straight and level, and perhaps it was nothing but an illusion and they were pitching and turning. He couldn't tell, not for sure. "Anything? Anything at all?" Ray asked again. Clearly, he was desperate but he fought off any impulse to do anything but what his pilot instincts told him to do. Do what was necessary, nothing more. He had to hold the ship steady. Straight and level.

"Yes...a little...keep the wings level!" Linda answered, this time in a trembling voice. Was that the surface of the ocean she was seeing directly beneath them, or was it a layer of mist or an optical illusion. She couldn't tell. "Keep the wings level!" she said once more, then sat in silence while an unspoken plea, a fervent prayer filled her thoughts. *God Almighty, keep the wings level...please, God, keep the wings level...*

Chapter Twenty-One

Tina had felt the slight change in the aircraft's pitch and the reduction in engine power. She was kneeling on the floor beside where Peter was laying in the first class galley. Tina rose to her feet, stepped into the cabin and looked out the window. The aircraft was rocking more than it had been. "We're descending," she announced in a non-committal voice. "Slowly."

Lee had also gotten up and come to where she was looking out the cabin window. He stood beside her in silence a few moments, then said, "Yes, we're definitely lower. I see more details in the waves. What do you think?"

"The engine is running, I can feel it," Tina said. She knew damn well that at this altitude, they'd already be in the water if it wasn't. As she spoke, she could feel the engine power increase. "Power is picking up. A controlled maneuver." Tina pointed to the view through the window. "Ray is taking us beneath these building clouds, or around a rain shower. Like he said he might."

"Makes sense." Lee nodded, then stepped back into the galley area so he could return to his patient.

"Where...am I?" Peter asked. He was beginning to get his thoughts into focus. Peter was laying on the galley floor with a blanket wrapped around him, but he had propped himself up and had his back against the galley wall. "Who are you? Where are we?" Peter asked hesitantly. Laying on the floor of the galley initially made no sense to him. Finally, fragments of his disjointed memory began to come back. "What's the..." Peter paused, then fumbled for the proper word. "...Situation," he said. "The cockpit situation."

Lee replied, "I'm a doctor. I've been treating you." Lee looked carefully at his patient before he said more. He knew that he had to feel him out and go slow. "The cockpit situation is fine," he said. "We're over the Atlantic, but expect landfall soon. Everything will be fine. You lay here and relax, you've been through quite an ordeal."

Peter glanced at the inert body of Jack Schofield, who was laying on the galley floor beside him. For an instant Peter couldn't understand why the captain was laying there, but then he remembered what had happened to him, to all of them. It had been a hijacking. He and Jack had struggled with that retired pilot Clarke when that lunatic tried to take Peter's gun away. "How's the captain?" Peter asked.

"He'll be fine," Lee answered. "He's unconscious because of the sedative, but his vital signs are very good. It's a matter of time before he wakes up, like you did."

"I understand." Peter could see that Jack was breathing steadily. While he watched, Jack's left hand — which was laying across his body and outside the blanket they had covered him in — moved in a slight trembling motion. Other than that, Jack was absolutely still. "Who's doing the flying?" Peter asked, his memory and thoughts blurry but increasingly coming into focus.

Lee knew what the proper answer would be, at least as far as this co-pilot was concerned. "Linda Erickson," he answered. Lee intended to feed him information, but not too much. Above all, he knew that he had to go slow.

"Thank God." Peter closed his eyes and allowed his body to slump lower from where he sat against the galley wall. Fragments of memories were coming back to him, some of them quite vividly. After a few deep breaths, Peter opened his eyes and looked at the doctor. "How did you get that crazy man out of there?" Peter asked, gesturing toward the closed cockpit door. "Can't remember."

"Who?" Lee asked. The doctor was, as he often did in professional situations, playing for time so his patient would fully commit to whatever their next line of reasoning might be. It was now obvious to Lee that the co-pilot was still deeply in the grips of it, and would be best to just wait and see. While he waited for a response from Peter, a small rift of turbulence rocked the ship. Lee steadied himself with one hand against the floor while he continued to kneel beside the injured co-pilot.

Peter was initially puzzled by the doctor's question. Finally, he understood what he must have meant. "You know — that retired pilot. Clarke. Ray Clarke. The crazy man."

"Oh, yes." Lee would simply let him talk, without feeding it or pushing it.

Peter sat further upright. "Clarke was suicidal. Hijacking the flight. Linda must've told you. Jack and I were trying to stop him from hijacking the airplane."

"Linda's been too busy to say much." Lee answered softly. "She's flying the airplane."

"Oh. Right. Of course." Peter paused, took a deep breath, then said. "Yes, she would be busy. Even with the autopilot, it's a big airplane to fly by yourself."

Lee smiled reassuringly. "Yes, it is," he agreed. It was definitely time to reassure him. Lee added, "We assume that when you get your strength back, you'd be able to tell us more about what happened in the cockpit."

"Right. I will." Peter closed his eyes again while he took several more deep breaths. Finally, he opened his eyes. "I'll get my strength back soon." He paused, took more deep breaths, then said, "I'll go back to the cockpit. I'll help Linda. Relieve her. Take over."

"No rush. You need to regain your strength. Everything is okay with the airplane and Linda is doing fine. The ship is flying fine." Lee continued to watch the co-pilot carefully. There was now no doubt that the co-pilot was still hallucinating, and Lee's clinical experiences told him that the young man could go either way from that point. Making him comfortable – both physically and mentally – was all they could do for the moment. "Let me assure you that you'll fully recover from your injury."

"Thank you." Peter began to rub the temples of his head — he had developed a throbbing headache and was very weak. He looked at the man kneeling beside him – this friendly doctor who was helping him — and nodded. "Okay." Peter found the strength to say something else before he laid his head down and closed his eyes. "Good you got Clarke out of there. His plan was to kill us."

◇

Ray thought for sure that he had lost the airplane on two separate occasions during the five minute span when they were barely skimming above the ocean waves. The flight visibility had gotten so low he couldn't estimate it, they were flying in an impenetrable grey mist.

"Look!" Linda shouted from the co-pilot's seat. She pointed straight ahead.

"What?!"

202

Linda paused. For a moment she thought she was mistaken. The dim glow of a lighter shade of the grey sky that surrounded them was an illusion, a figment of her imagination, the result of her wishful thinking. "I...don't know..."

"Yes!" Ray could see it, too, out of the corner of his eye. The sky was getting lighter and brighter to their left front. He allowed himself to glance in that direction for an instant. "Yes!...We're breaking out!" Ray shouted with a laugh.

As if his voice had commanded it, the airliner punched through a wall of cloud and mist and into the bright late afternoon sunlight. The sunlight had gotten so bright so quickly that it caused Ray's eyes to water. "Through it!" he shouted. Ray let out a deep sigh, then added, "That was close. Too damn close."

"Thank God." Linda knew it wasn't her wishful thinking that had brought out the sunlight; she knew it had been her prayer. "Look at that wall of clouds! Look at that bank!" Linda said as she pointed. As if it were a sheer wall of rock instead of condensed water vapor, a solid mass of thick clouds were mounded in a straight line to their right front and stretching ahead as far as they could see.

"Climbing to a thousand feet," Ray announced as he gently played with the captain's control wheel and allowed the airliner to slowly pitch upward. He took a deep breath and glanced around the cockpit. The late afternoon sun straight ahead was flooding the cockpit with bright, beautiful light. Ray turned. "Almost the end for us."

"I know."

"But it wasn't." Ray was buoyed up by their success at getting through that line of weather – a broad area of nearly-zero visibility conditions that, even with hindsight, he wondered how they managed to accomplish it. But they had. Ray studied the line of clouds. They extended from the very top of the ocean to far above any altitude that they could fly. "If our track had been more to the right, we'd be in the water right now."

"Yes."

"Lucky." Ray glanced at the magnetic compass, then banked the airliner slightly north. Once again, they were back on the magnetic heading that would take them to a safe haven in North America. "This heading works. The cloud bank veers further away in the distance. We can do everything we need to — hold the magnetic heading and stay out of clouds."

Linda was smiling; she looked at the clouds, then at Ray. "Hard to ask for more than that." She felt as if an enormous hurtle was behind them. They had come through yet another impossible situation, and they were alive. She glanced around the cockpit, taking in the details that the sunlight was illuminating. Perhaps, Linda thought, it was the presence of that sunshine — the warmth, the clarity that it added — that had lifted her spirits. For the first time since their nightmare had begun, she was beginning to feel positive and optimistic. It wasn't an act to keep Ray's spirits up, either. Linda thought that, maybe, they would be able to live through this.

"This is wonderful, but I'd like two more things," Ray said. His thoughts were getting back on track, just as the airplane had.

"What?" Linda asked.

"The most obvious first. That the engine keeps running. That's primary." Ray gently laid his right hand on the throttle of their only functioning engine. He did that for no other reason than to feel the small vibration that were feeding back through the throttle's mechanical linkage, the original linkage that Boeing had installed in the 767. Thank God Consolidated hadn't taken those mechanical connections out when they added those high-tech computer controls to the engine fuel metering systems.

The continuous flow of raw power being produced by the airliner's left engine was their only hope of survival, and by laying his hand on that throttle, Ray could feel those tell-tale pulses of power in his fingertips. He had done that sort of thing throughout his flying career, and it had always been reassuring. It was particularly, incredibly reassuring today.

"Yes, primary," Linda agreed. "Absolutely primary." She glanced down at Ray's hand laying on the left engine's throttle and she understood what he was doing and what he was sensing. "Running fine. It'll take us to the coast. I can just *feel* that the engine's going to stay with us. "

"No argument from me," Ray said as he nodded in agreement. Then he added, "My second wish is that, somehow, we could figure our actual position."

"Is our exact position so important?" Linda asked. "We pretty well know our approximate position."

"Approximate is okay, but if we could establish our exact position, then our calculations would be that much more accurate. If we could somehow do that, we'd have turned the odds in our favor. We could take out all the accumulated error of the past few hours and get ourselves pointed directly toward the nearest land."

"Oh. I see what you mean," Linda answered.

"Right." Ray shook his head, then sat quietly while he gently worked with the aircraft's flight controls. Now, he was sorry that he brought up the position business to her because there was no possible way to get an accurate fix. No damn way at all. It was wishful thinking, nothing more.

◇

When the airliner passed from the darkness of the rain, snow and clouds that had enveloped them for what had seemed an eternity and suddenly exited into brilliant sunlight, there was a spontaneous eruption of cheers, shouts of joy, laughter and applauding throughout the cabin. Without any announcement from the crew as to what this change in their flight condition meant, everyone onboard was reacting positively to it.

Even though nearly none of the passengers or flight attendants understood the technical advantages — the technical *necessities* — for the airliner to be away from clouds until they found land again, they had, on a purely emotional level, understood what this fabulous transformation had meant. Their lives had gone from darkness and despair. Now, they were basking in the bright sunlight.

"I understand why everyone reacted positively to the sunlight," Lee said. "And I'd be lying to you if I didn't admit that I feel the same way. It's human nature to associate sunlight with life. Humans are not nocturnal creatures. Now, because the sun is shining, there's an increased level of hope in all of us."

"I can feel it, too," Tina said. She sat down in seat 1C again, and the doctor joined her. "I assume this is a good thing," she added. "Right?"

"For awhile." Lee leaned closer to her, then took her hand in his. "You and I know from talking to Ray that he needed sunlight — or, to be more accurate, no heavy clouds — to keep the airliner upright. We know how important this change was. The rest of them," Lee said, gesturing toward the cabin with his free hand, "are reacting with a more natural, more basic response. The trouble with that comes when their conscious minds try to deal rationally with their emotional reactions. If they think about it very long, they'll convince themselves that the sunlight ultimately doesn't mean much."

"Oh." Tina glanced around the cabin at some of the faces, then looked at Lee. "Maybe we should explain to them what Ray told us — how important it is that we have a clear sky to fly in."

Lee smiled, then squeezed her hand. "Good suggestion, Tina. But only if you're trying to promote panic and hysteria at the sight of the next cloud on the horizon." Lee laughed, then added, "That would be a case of providing too much information to people who have no experience and no training to handle it. When we put ourselves in the hands of experts — doctors, lawyers, Indian Chiefs and assorted modern techno-experts — they have become defacto gods to us. Another component of human behavior is the core belief that it's best not question the gods too often or too closely."

"Really?"

"Sort of." The two of them laughed together for a few seconds. It was, Lee knew, so therapeutic to be able to be able to find something to laugh about, especially now. Even he had been astonished at the stories from those concentration camp survivors who told him that they, too, had occasionally found things to laugh about during those years that they were living that Nazi nightmare. It was like Viktor had said, those who didn't laugh at least occasionally were the ones who wouldn't survive. "All we can do is wait," Lee added, "which is the hardest part. Wait to see if we will live. Wait to see if we've been selected to die." He winced slightly when he realized that he had been so blunt – perhaps too blunt – with her. "Tina, sorry. I shouldn't have phrased it that way. But it's the truth."

"I can handle the truth," Tina answered.

"Good. Most of us can't."

Tina looked directly at him, then asked, "Is that what the people from the concentration camps told you? That waiting to see was the hardest part?"

"Yes." Lee sat in silence for a moment, obviously in thought. Finally, he added, "That, and much more."

The two of them sat quietly while Lee continued to hold her hand. Finally, Tina pointed toward the men laying on the galley floor and asked, "Is it normal for Peter to fall back to sleep so soon?"

Lee nodded. "Yes. I gave him the verbal assurances that he wanted, so any buildup of anxiety was diverted. He'll drift in and out of a natural sleep for awhile, before he finally wakes up. By then, it's possible that he'll allow himself to deal more rationally with the subject."

"Do you think so?"

"Stranger things have happened."

"What else is possible?"

"Frankly, most anything. Remember, Peter's had a huge personal trauma and his extreme fear took total control of him. His mind has come up with an elaborate cover story to help him deal with that trauma. Like I said, that sort of thing is well within the boundaries of natural human behavior."

"There's nothing we need to do about Peter?" Tina asked.

"Not that I can see. I could give him more sedative, but I don't see any purpose." Lee mulled over that thought for a moment. He could have given him more sedative, and something about that idea was appealing. But since Peter hadn't seemed like a threat to himself or anyone else, there was no justifiable reason not to let him come slowly back to the real world at his own pace. Like he figured earlier, it was best to just wait and see. "We'll keep an eye on Peter, although we can't allow him back into the cockpit. More than likely he will slowly come back to his senses."

"I understand." Tina nodded her head, then said, "If I'm allowed to ask, I'm also wondering what else Ray might have told you?"

"That's a loaded question if I ever heard one." Lee leaned toward her, smiled softly, then said, "I think what you're actually asking me is why Ray Clarke doesn't love you while you're still in love with him? Am I right?"

207

"Lee, stop that." Tina attempted to get up from her seat but Lee reached up and grabbed her arm. After a moment, she sat down. He continued to hold onto her arm. "There's no need to get that personal," Tina said. "None of my relationship with Ray is your business. Not a damn bit of it." She was surprised at her outburst, but she couldn't hold it back.

"It's time for you to stop that crap." Lee pulled her slightly closer and spoke in a harsh whisper that only she could hear. "We're a thousand feet above the goddamn Atlantic Ocean in a crippled airliner. We could both be fish food in two minutes. You know that's true, and so do I. Please, no pretenses and posturing. We don't have time. We haven't used any of that crap so far, let's not start now." Lee kept looking at her and waiting. He knew that he had to give her time, and, with that, she would come around. Maybe.

Tina didn't answer. Instead, she looked at Lee for a long moment. Finally, she nodded in agreement.

"Good." Lee said, "I don't pretend to understand your relationship with Ray Clarke, I only know what I've seen — that you're in love with him and he does not reciprocate. If you stop to think about it, that sort of thing is not that unusual. On a scale of one to ten in personal tragedies, I'd have to objectively give it somewhere around a one-point-five. Maybe a two-point-three if you knew him for a long time."

"I did."

"Great. So take your two-point-three — hell, I'll give you a two-point-five if you'd prefer — and sit there feeling sorry for yourself. That's a good, healthy way to move forward in life." Lee paused, then added, "I'm being spiteful, cutting and sarcastic, just in case you hadn't noticed."

Tina's initial reaction was, once again, to stand up and walk away. Instead, she sat there. At that moment, she wasn't so much *thinking* as *feeling*. "Okay, Lee. You want reality, so here it is. I loved Ray. I think I still do. Since you're interested – and you've already told me how much people enjoy talking about themselves – let me tell you about Ray Clarke, me, Katie and the things that happened to the three of us."

"Go ahead. Got lots of time," Lee answered in a calm and measured voice. He knew that it would be a personal struggle for him, but if he could somehow find a way to stay absolutely

208

neutral for the next few minutes then maybe he'd be able to give her the help she was asking for. Maybe.

Tina began explaining their history. Slowly and carefully, she worked her way through the years, through Katie's death, through the subsequent flights with Ray and that trip to Paris. Then Ray's refusal to see her any more and his early retirement not long after that. Finally, she spoke about everything that happened between the two of them after Ray boarded the flight in Rome, and she talked at length about Ray's unjustifiable guilt over Katie's death.

When she finished, Lee sat quietly for some time before he turned and faced her directly. "I shouldn't be commenting on any of this for one very good and very professional reason. As you've already guessed, I'm finding myself emotionally wrapped up in you."

"Lee, I..."

"No. Wait. Don't be worried because you're going to get your money's worth. I'm going to suspend my professional ethics for the duration of this flight. For that matter, I'm going to suspend my normal fee." Lee forced a smile in her direction, although his insides were churning. He knew damn well that he shouldn't be doing this, that he'd become an idiot, a deaf and dumb psychiatrist. But he owed her his best shot. "Tina, I'm only doing this because you can use guidance right here and now. Frankly, from what I can tell, there aren't too many other places for you to get reasonable advice at this particular moment. And I've offered to work for free."

Tina laughed; again, Lee had managed to lighten their conversation at the right moment. She could do the same for him, too. "That's true, doctor. You've got a captive and – I'll admit – willing audience. It's either you or one of the flight attendants, and I don't think they're particularly qualified." Tina was watching his eyes for a moment, then smiled at him. "And your price is right. So go ahead. Tell me where I've screwed this damn thing up."

"You haven't. Your love for Ray is one thing, his response to that love is quite another. The two elements in this equation have no connection to each other – that's the important part for you to understand. You haven't screwed anything up."

"Why? How?"

"To be blunt, you're asking a prisoner who is desperately trying to escape from a concentration camp to voluntarily walk back into it."

"I see." Tina nodded several times. She then said, "Lee, some people might be insulted by that analogy. It's damn blunt and certainly unflattering."

"Some people, but not you. I know you better. Or at least I think so. I hope so."

"So I represent a concentration camp to Ray..?"

"You represent an enormous manifestation of his guilt, whether it's justified or not. He can't possibly allow himself to love you while he feels that huge mountain of guilt over his wife's death. He didn't protect her, and he feels that he should have. From what you've told me, those are obvious conclusions."

"Will he love me if and when his guilt ever ends?" Tina asked.

Lee's immediate urge was to tell her no, no way, never, absolutely not. Instead, he said, "Yes." Lee sat in silence for several moments. "Probably," he added. That was the most damning comment Lee could make against Ray Clarke, even though every ounce inside him wanted Tina to walk away from the man. Walk away from Ray. Walk over to him. But he couldn't steer her, she had to steer herself. He knew that, and he suspected that she did, too.

The two of them sat in silence for a good while. Finally, Tina asked, "Is something like Ray's guilt – which is absolutely unjustified as any of the airplane experts would tell you – a curable thing. Will it fade with time, or is there any way that someone – maybe you, or maybe someone else – can help him get rid of it? Obviously, I can't."

"You're right. You can't." Lee sat back in his seat. He looked over at her. "If it were the emotional state that we label as shame, it would be difficult to deal with. Guilt is another thing."

"There's a difference?"

"The difference between shame and guilt is the difference between heaven and earth." Lee paused to allow his words to sit with her for a moment, then continued. "Shame is directly about the sense of self. It is a painful and ugly feeling that has negative

210

implications on behavior, and it often produces a general sense of seething, bitter, resentful anger."

"And Guilt?" Tina asked.

"With guilt, the sense of self is not central. Only the thing that matters was what was done or overlooked. In a guilt experience, there is often a nagging preoccupation of thinking about it over and over, of continuous wishing that it could be undone, that time could be reversed."

"Yes." Tina needed to say no more; clearly, Lee understood.

"Guilt is a repairable situation. On the other hand, shame often is not – or at least not so easily." With that, Lee sat back in his chair. He had attempted to sound uninvolved and nonchalant, but he knew that he hadn't, not to himself at least. "So, as you have already figured, if and when Ray is able to finally throw that guilt away, then he would more than likely be capable of loving you." With his professional diagnosis now complete, Lee then decided it would be acceptable to add a few extra words. Words of his own. "You are, after all, a rather loveable creature. If Ray doesn't see it, I'm here to tell you that I certainly do."

Again, they sat in silence for quite some time. Finally, Tina spoke. "Lee, are you married?"

"No." Lee answered immediately. For the first time, he had absolutely no clue as to where she might be going with her question. "Never been. As that old and worn-out cliche says, I've been married to my work."

Tina leaned toward him. "Tell me — I'm just curious, of course — would a person like you who is so damned intelligent and so enormously understanding of what basic human nature is about, would that sort of person ever bother to have their own relationship, would ever bother to marry a real person? I mean a female type of person."

Lee laughed. "Well, I can tell you candidly that the female of the species is the only category that my personal inclinations would consider for a marriage partner." He decided to press her more, to see if his intuition about her change in direction was on-target. "What I also think I'm hearing is that you might be proposing to me right here and now. Am I right?"

Tina grinned. "Proposals inside a crippled airliner flying a thousand feet above the Atlantic Ocean have no validity in any court of law. I read that somewhere."

"In that case, I formally accept your proposal of marriage." Lee leaned forward and kissed her on the forehead. He knew damn well what she was doing and, for that matter, what in God's name he was doing. Both of them were play-acting out a skit – play-acting roles – that contained the elements that they both desperately needed at that moment: an exchange of human tenderness and the sense of a potential future. They both needed that much, at the very least, to keep the reality of their current situation at bay. But Lee also knew that — all the fancy psychological bullshit aside — he was incredibly buoyed up at that moment because of this unexpected bridge of human contact between the two of them. He did, in fact, really like her and felt very close to her. More amazingly, she seemed to feel the same way toward him.

"Lee, I..."

"Sorry, but you'll have to excuse me," Lee said as he got up from the chair beside her. "I need to be let into the cockpit. I need to talk to Captain Clarke about this Peter Fenton thing, and about his guilt – you've already given me that assignment – and I also need to talk to him about this other lame-brain thought that I had a few minutes ago."

Tina rose from her chair, stepped up to Lee and put her hands on his shoulders. "No cockpit access for you until I hear more about your lame-brain thoughts. You're not allowed to have any secrets from your inflight wife, especially when she's the senior cabin attendant and is someone with great power and authority here in the cabin."

"Okay," he said. Lee leaned forward, kissed her on the forehead again, then said, "Here's my lame-brain idea," he whispered. "I've got this satellite telephone that I use for sending text messages from Europe in my carry-on baggage..."

"Satellite telephone!" Tina stepped back. "We could call..."

"Wait!" Lee held his hand up, then added, "It won't work inside an airliner, period. I know that for a fact. There's no chance, so don't get excited. But, while I was sitting here I was wondering — guessing, really, since I don't pretend to understand the technical aspects — if there was any way we could connect this battery operated portable satellite telephone to one of the airliner's outside antennas so that we could get a position readout and, if we're really lucky, send some text messages."

"Position readout?" Tina reached up, put her hands back on his shoulders and pulled him slightly closer to her. "What do you mean?"

"Didn't I tell you," Lee answered as he more than willingly allowed himself to close the distance between the two of them, "When this damn satellite telephone is working properly — which isn't all that often, mind you — it has this special feature that I had always considered as absolutely useless. It displays a readout of your current latitude and longitude."

Chapter Twenty-Two

After Tina unlocked the cockpit door, Lee stepped onto the flight deck of the jetliner with his carry-on bag. Tina followed into the cockpit, then closed and locked the door.

"Hello again," Lee announced in a loud voice to make his presence known to the two pilots. He could see that Ray was flying the airplane, and that Linda was looking through paperwork that was laying on the center console.

"What can we do for you, Doctor," Ray said over his shoulder as he continued to fly the airliner.

"Probably wasting your time," Lee said as he stepped forward to a spot directly behind the center console, "but I've had an idea. Might not amount to anything, but I thought I should check with you."

"Linda, take over so I can talk to the Doctor," Ray said.

"Sure." Linda grabbed the co-pilot's control wheel. "Got it."

"Hold our heading," Ray said. He turned to face Lee. Behind him, Tina was standing quietly and listening. Ray was uncomfortable having Tina around, but he knew that the feeling was childish and irrelevant so he forced himself to ignore it. "Let's hear your idea, Doctor. We find ourselves low on ideas and high on available time to listen."

Lee reached into his bag. "Got this older model satellite telephone with me," he said as he pulled the black telephone out and showed it to Ray.

"Satellite telephone?" Ray took the unit from Lee. It was seven or eight inches tall, and three or four inches wide, with a keyboard and a display screen. It looked like a modern cell phone that had been hopped up on steroids. "I'll be damned. Will this work? Can we get it connected?"

"No," Lee answered immediately. "Let me explain."

"Go ahead," Ray answered with a sigh; he had, for an instant, hoped that they had stumbled onto a miracle, but it was probably nothing beyond another disappointment. He was getting used to them. "Tell me more." Ray had no personal experience with portable satellite telephones, although he

214

understood the general theory behind them. From what he had heard, small satellite phones were expensive, erratic and undependable.

"This is a older unit. I got it at a discount price since the company's announcement about their satellite problems," Lee said.

Ray continued to hold the unit, but his attention was on the doctor.

"If my memory is correct, their press release said something about satellite anomalies for these sets and some sort of temporary limitations, particularly on the voice services."

Anomalies. There it was again, that modern techno word. Ray nearly laughed when he heard the doctor say it – it reminded him of what Jack had said about anomalies earlier in the flight, that Peter liked to call them anomalies because he couldn't explain them, either. To Ray, that discussion seemed like years, not hours ago. So many incredible things had happened to them that, in a very real sense, they weren't able to accurately explain. *Anomalies.*

"Anyway," Lee continued, "I bought this unit strictly for sending data messages into my Internet account from various interviews throughout Europe and other places in the world. I can sometimes receive emails from my office through it, although that feature isn't as dependable as sending outgoing messages. That's been my experience. Making a voice telephone call is nearly impossible. As the press release stated, it'll remain that way until the company gets their satellites permanently fixed. That's supposed to happen sometime soon, I hear."

"So, you're thinking we might be able to send out an email…"

"Sorry, but I have to say no again," Lee answered. "I wish it could be that easy."

"Me too." Ray turned the unit over. There was a long telescoping antenna on the back side that could be extended out.

"I know for a fact that the satellite phone won't work inside the airplane. It needs to clearly see the satellite — or, more accurately, any one of the dozens of communications satellites since this unit uses a particular low-earth orbit system with multiple satellites passing by. Don't get the idea that I understand the technical aspects of this," Lee continued. "What I'm quoting is what I read in the user's manual."

"You're absolutely sure that it won't work inside the airplane?" Ray asked. "If there's a chance, we should try."

"A waste of time, I'm absolutely certain. I've tried it in the past," Lee said. "To be doubly sure, we tried it a short while ago. Before Tina and I came up." He nodded toward Tina. "It was her idea to give it one more try, by a window seat."

"Yes," Tina said. She took a half step forward and stood alongside Lee. "We waited ten minutes, but got no connection with a satellite. I figured we should at least try it once more before coming up. We extended the telephone's antenna and held it flush against the cabin window, but it made no difference."

"The cabin windows are thick," Ray said. "Multiple panes of glass and clear plastic." He looked at the satellite phone once more, then handed it to Lee. "If this electronic contraption won't work, what's your idea?"

"I was wondering — it was a thought that came to me a short while ago — if it was possible to attach one of the airliner's outside antennas to it?" Lee pointed to where the telescoping antenna was attached to the rear of the handset. "Maybe we could plug one of your ship's radio antenna cables into it."

"Let me see it again." Ray took the unit from Lee and looked it over, more carefully this time. Like most modern electronics, it looked like its plastic case had been poured in one mold. "This built-in antenna is integral with the unit. I don't see how we could remove it." Ray turned the unit on its side. "Here's a plug for a connection. It might be for an external antenna, but it takes a special adapter."

"Now that you've mentioned it, I recall seeing something about an adapter and a car antenna in the accessory list," Lee said. "But it's nothing that I have. Sorry."

"Besides, a unit this exotic would require a particular style or type of antenna — not just any antenna, even if we could trace a lead wire from one of the airplane radios. I couldn't even guess what that antenna requirement might be. This is purely academic anyway, since we surely don't have the proper size fittings to make it work." Ray handed the telephone to Lee.

"It's a shame, too, because I was saving the best part for last. If we could get this thing to lock onto a satellite, we could get our exact latitude and longitude from it. It's a feature that I always thought was pretty useless, but then I remembered what you told me earlier about needing one good position fix to get the landfall navigation right."

"Latitude and longitude?" Ray shook his head in disgust. "Damn. One good position fix would make a hell of a difference in our landfall chances."

"We're not going to get any latitude-longitude readouts if we can't get linked to a satellite." Lee put his hand on Ray's shoulder. "We're not going to do that unless we take the ceiling off the airplane." Lee paused, then added, "Sorry to have wasted your time. It was just a thought." He closed the telephone's antenna and began to put it into his carry-on bag.

"It was a good thought," Ray said. *Latitude and longitude. Damn.* "But it's impossible to connect it to the airplane's antenna system." While Ray would have tried about anything to get a solid position fix, he also knew that if they scattered their attention on hopeless solutions, they might miss something that they should have seen. He had to balance reality against desire – there would be no operating on wishful thinking, no matter how beneficial that wish might be.

"Good thought, Lee," Tina said. "Good try. What we need is a volunteer to climb outside on the airplane's roof and strap the telephone out there. Then the phone would see those satellites as they passed above." Tina laid her hand on Lee's shoulder. "You up for outdoor activity?" she asked, trying to keep the conversation light again. She, too, was disappointed. Nothing was going right for them. "We'd appreciate it."

"Might prove a bit breezy," Lee said. "Captain, how fast are we going?" he asked Ray.

"Three hundred knots."

"Yes, too breezy for walking on the roof." Lee began to turn toward the cockpit door.

"Wait..." Ray held up his hand. "What Tina said gave me an idea." He glanced at her, then at the doctor. "Let me see the telephone again."

Lee took the telephone out of his bag. He handed it to Ray.

Ray took the telephone and extended its antenna. He glanced around the cockpit roof line, confirming what he already knew from spending thousands of hours sitting inside this small metal and glass enclosure. The windows were large and they conformed to the shape of the cockpit itself — which was rounded toward the top. It might just work.

"What are you thinking?" Lee asked. But by following Ray's eyes, he was able to figure it out for himself. "Oh, I get it. The cockpit roof line curves inward, and so do these big rear windows. That's lots different than the cabin windows." Lee pointed over Linda's shoulder toward the co-pilot's side window. "We might have enough view of the satellites if we hold the telephone antenna as far into that window as we can get it."

"I can do better than that," Ray said. "I can bank the airplane and fly in a circle so that the bank angle plus the window angle will give us an almost direct view of the sky." Ray turned in his flight chair. "Linda, I've got it."

"You've got it, skipper," Linda answered as she relinquished the flight controls. "I can hold the phone against the window," she said. "It's worth trying."

"Right." Ray began to mentally calculate the amount of bank he would need in order to get the required angle. "Okay, let's get the telephone powered on and we'll..."

"Wait." Lee put up his hand. "I know you're focused on getting that latitude and longitude readout, but since we need to connect to the satellite to get it, why don't we use that connection time to send a quick email."

"Email? How?"

"Through my laptop computer. It plugs into the phone. Do it all the time."

"Where's the laptop?" Ray asked.

"Here." Lee reached into his carry-on bag and took out a small laptop computer. "Give me a message and the email address to send it to."

"Okay. Let me think," Ray said.

"Take your time. I've got to power up this thing," Lee said. While he opened up the laptop computer and attached the data cable between it and the satellite telephone, he continued talking to Ray. "We need to send an email so that, if nothing else, the world will know what's happened to us," Lee said while he worked with the satellite phone and the laptop computer. "The email needs to be short, so that it doesn't get hung up if we only have the satellite connection briefly. I've had that happen in the past when I tried to send complex documents." Lee then added, "Be certain that whatever email address you pick is being continuously monitored. We can't have our message sit in someone's junk mail file for a week."

"Right." Ray turned to his co-pilot. "Linda, take the ship. I'll write out a short message that we can type into the computer and send it while we're retrieving our latitude and longitude from the telephone. We can send that message to the Trans-Continental Dispatch office — I know their email address, assuming it hasn't changed in the past two years."

"No, it hasn't," Linda volunteered. "The same." The fact that they were doing something positive was wonderful.

"You write the email address clearly and precisely, and also the message you want to send," Lee said. "I'll type it in. I should have this thing up and running and connected to the telephone in a couple of minutes." While he worked at the laptop keyboard and then waited for the telephone to boot up, Lee thought back to what he had heard in his interviews with many of the concentration camp survivors — that not being able to get any message out of those camps to let others know what had happened to them was an additional, incredible burden to their overall torment. The idea of disappearing without a trace had been, they said, an on-going part of their torture at the hands of the Nazis. For the first time since he had heard those observations and opinions, Lee understood what they meant.

◇

When Peter woke up from his sleep, he knew immediately that he was — as the doctor had predicted — feeling better. He still ached in places, his shoulder was sore as hell from the gunshot wound, and had that same headache he had felt before, although it, too, seemed to be letting up some.

Slowly and cautiously, Peter rose to his feet. Captain Schofield was laying on the floor in the first class galley with a blanket over him and a life jacket beneath his head for a pillow, and Peter could see the regular rhythms of his breathing. If that doctor was correct, Jack would eventually be fine, too.

Peter could feel the light rocking motions of the airplane beneath him as he carefully worked himself into the first class cabin. Although he was feeling better, he could tell that he was too weak to take command of the airplane anytime soon. Besides, according to the doctor, Linda was doing fine. All Peter needed at this point was to gain enough strength to be in the cockpit for the landing. She could do the actual landing and he would monitor the situation and give advice.

Although Peter didn't know what time it was — he had taken his wristwatch off before he was going on his cabin break because he found that he slept better without having it on — it felt late in the day. For an instant he wondered how far from the Azores they were. For that matter, maybe Linda had elected to turn back to Europe since that would have been the next closest alternate airports. He would ask that question soon enough, as soon as he ran into one of the crew members.

A few of the passengers in the first class cabin glanced in his direction as he walked slowly down the aisle, but there was no one sitting close enough to say anything directly to him. Peter continued walking for a couple more rows, then decided to sit. He was, he could tell, very weak, lots weaker than he thought. Peter eased himself into aisle seat 3D.

Even this small amount of effort on his part had been exhausting to Peter, and he wondered if perhaps it wouldn't be best if Linda handled the upcoming Azores — or European — landing on her own. She was a competent pilot and Peter knew that he wouldn't be much help, considering his condition. The airplane was relatively automatic in its operation when the autopilot was used to it fullest, and Linda knew what she was doing. Peter closed his eyes and sat back in that comfortable first class chair.

"Are you all right?"

Peter opened his eyes. He had, apparently, fallen asleep as soon as he sat down. Standing over him was Annette Riley, the other first class cabin attendant. "Yes," Peter said hesitantly. He propped himself up in the cushioned first class chair. "Better. Thank you."

"Good." Annette glanced around the cabin, then at him. "You look worn out. I did hear that the doctor said you'd be fine once you'd gotten enough rest."

"Right," Peter said with a weak smile. "Not back to normal. Not yet. Lose my strength quickly. Need more time."

"There's no reason for you to get up. Everything's under control. We've got a while to go anyway, so you might as well sit here and relax."

"How much longer until..." Peter touched his empty wrist. Now, he wished he hadn't taken his watch off. "...until we get to..."

"The last word I heard was another two and a half hours." Annette looked at her own watch. "It's a few minutes after 4:00, so the arrival time should be 6:30."

What Annette said to him got Peter's full attention. He sat further upright in his chair. The time of the day didn't make any sense, but it ultimately didn't mean much since he didn't know what time zone they were in or what time zone she was talking about. But the additional flight time was a complete impossibility, a red flag. "Two and a half hours? To the Azores? Or Europe?"

"Azores?" Annette looked at him, puzzled. Finally, she said, "Oh, I forgot how long you've been asleep. You hadn't heard. We're not going to the Azores or to Europe. That arrival estimate is for New York."

"New York?" Peter shook his head. None of this made any sense, and his throbbing headache wasn't helping him to understand any faster. "Linda is taking us to New York? Why?"

"Bad weather. That's my understanding. New York has clear skies and forecast to stay that way," Annette answered.

"Oh." Peter was still unsure. The thoughts in his head were muddled, but he thought that he distinctly remembered that the weather in the Azores was supposed to be basically okay, a little cloudy but well above their alternate airport requirements. The Azores would be the obvious choice, unless... "Maybe the weather's changed," he said to Annette as he tried to come up with an explanation that made sense. They were going all the way to New York? Why?

"Yes. Maybe. You don't have to worry, because I'm sure that any decision that Linda and Ray came up with..."

At the sound of that name, Peter found enough strength to jump straight up from his seat. "Ray!" Peter shouted. "Impossible!"

221

"No," was the only response that Annette could think of. She took a few steps back in complete surprise — she certainly wasn't expecting that sort of reaction from him. She could see that several of the passengers in the first class cabin had also gotten to their feet and were looking directly at him. "Peter, please keep your voice down," Annette said. "Everything is going to be all right. Linda Erickson and Ray Clarke are flying the airplane. We're headed straight for New York."

"This is insane!" Peter shouted. His voice was quivering and his hands had begun to shake. "Don't you understand?! Don't you know what's happened!? Don't you know who he is!?"

"What? Who?"

It had come back to him vividly, and Peter could now see in his mind's eye everything that happened in the cockpit during that attempted takeover; Peter was living the nightmare over again. "Ray Clarke is the hijacker who shot both me and the captain!" He said in a voice loud enough for everyone within several rows to easily overhear. "He's taking us straight to New York for one reason — so he can crash this airplane into one of those buildings! It's 9/11 all over again!"

◇

When Lee said that he was ready, Ray began to roll the airliner into a moderately steep turn to the left. "Soon as you get that message away and our position downloaded," Ray said, "tell me. Can't spend time off our heading." Ray concentrated on maneuvering the airliner through the circle that they would fly.

"Okay." Lee peered at the display screen of the satellite telephone as he waited for the tell-tale indicators to inform him that a satellite signal had been found and that the unit was locked on. Soon after that — sometimes sooner, sometimes later — the full connection would be made and the data exchange would occur. "Nothing yet."

"Everything set up correctly?" Ray asked. He had his full attention on flying the airliner by maintaining as precise an angle of the upper windshield post against the horizon line as he could. Ray didn't know how important it was to keep the satellite antenna at a steady angle — probably not important at all, as long as he didn't allow the aircraft's metal roof line to cut off the view of the satellite — but he wasn't taking chances. They would only have one shot at this, so he would stack the deck in their favor as much as he could. Ray kept the ship in a steady bank that didn't vary by more than a few degrees.

"Might be getting something now," Lee said as he continued to watch the display screen with its signal meters. "Yes...something..." Lee could feel Tina's hand on his shoulder. She was holding him steady and he could feel her fingers wrapped tightly on him. "...something..." Lee repeated.

"Can't keep doing this," Ray said. "Fuel," he added as he watched the horizon line. Using the far edge of distant clouds as a visual reference, he knew that they had already completed one full circle and that they were into the second. He had to set a limit on the time – and fuel – they would spend on this experiment. "Three turns and that's it. All we can make," Ray said. Even that might be too many. "Don't have fuel to make more." Ray's gut feeling was that they couldn't spare hardly any of their precious fuel on this maneuver, but he couldn't bring himself to not try at least a few turns. He desperately wanted that position fix. But the time for this indulgence was nearly up. More than ever, this was not the time to indulge in wishful thinking.

"Definitely have an initial satellite signal capture," Lee said, working hard at keeping his voice steady. "Low strength, but useable. This thing has worked with less signal strength." Lee stopped himself from saying more — that he had also seen this attempted connection be unsuccessful with even more indicated signal strength, for God knows what reason. "Keep the turn steady."

Ray finished the second turn, the nose of the airliner cutting past the visual reference of the distant clouds. "Final turn," Ray emphatically announced. "Absolutely the last." The issue about their fuel state was looming too large to ignore it any longer. He couldn't ignore reality. "Don't have the fuel. Rolling out on our westbound heading. "

"Steady," is what Lee said in response.

They were silent while the airliner continued its steep left bank, now more than half way through what Ray had determined would be their last off-heading moment. "Twenty more seconds.

Rolling out," Ray said as he began to pick up that distant clouds in his peripheral vision. "Fifteen seconds."

"Ray, keep the ship turning," Lee replied. "Almost there. I can feel it. Trust me on this."

"No. Rolling out. Now."

"Captain, keep turning!" Lee said in a loud, forceful voice. "Please…this connection makes all the difference, you said so yourself." He paused, then added, "Ray, we've got to do what's necessary. You know that better than me. We need this."

"No." As he approached the visual line he'd used to determine the beginning and end of each circle — this would be the end of their third full turn — Ray made a slight motion with his hand on the captain's control wheel to put the airliner in its upright position. But as quickly as he began that rolling motion, Ray reversed it. Instead of rolling out, Ray kept the airliner set in its steeply banked circle to the left to begin turn number four.

Nobody in the cockpit said a word.

They were not half way around that fourth circle when Lee finally shouted, "Connected! Got it! Got our current position and our email is away! Roll out any time, we're finished! Got what we need!"

Tina, who was holding Lee's shoulder, spun him around toward her. "You did it! Damn! That was fabulous!"

"It certainly worked out fine." Lee smiled broadly at her.

"It sure as hell did." Tina grabbed hold of Lee's head with both of her hands, pulled his face toward hers and kissed him.

Book Six

For what then counts and matters is to bear witness to the uniquely human potential at its best, which is to transform a tragedy into a personal triumph, to turn one's predicament into a human achievement.
—Viktor Frankl, Psychiatrist

If the only tool you have is a hammer, you tend to see every problem as a nail.
—Abraham Maslow, Psychologist

Chapter Twenty-Three

Wednesday, January 20th
John F. Kennedy International Airport, New York
4:16 pm Eastern Standard Time

For the past two hours the dispatch office of Trans-Continental Airlines had been a buzz of activity, but Marty knew that none of that activity had borne fruit. They were no more knowledgeable about the whereabouts — hell, even the continued existence — of Flight 3 than they had been when the first notifications of the hijacking had come in. It seemed like days since this tragedy had begun, but it had been less than four hours since that first Mayday message had been sent by the flight. "If New York is the target, they should be approaching the coastline."

"Right." George glanced at the wall clock: 4:17 pm. The flight computers had predicted a New York landfall at 4:22 pm, but that figure was, of course, pure conjecture. It was based on the ship continuing to fly its normal airspeed and altitude — which were ironic assumptions since nothing about this flight had been normal since it began crossing the Atlantic. "The military would have them on radar already if they were anywhere near New York. Like they said, they would let us know as soon as the flight was located so we could try one final message to them on the company data link."

"Right." Marty added. "So we can tell them one more time what we've told them a hundred times — that those fighters on their wing will shoot them down if the hijacker doesn't give up."

"They must feel that the sight of those armed intercept aircraft might jog Ray back to his senses." Even while he was saying those things, George knew that in his heart he didn't believe a single word of it. Getting Ray back to his senses? Could he actually be a hijacker? It was a crazy idea. It was impossible to imagine.

"Standard procedure." Marty fidgeted in his chair. "They don't want anyone saying that they didn't try everything before they blew that passenger plane out of the sky."

"Marty, the conversation we're having is academic because Flight 3 is obviously not within radar coverage of New York," George said. "If it were, the military would've let us know. While I don't know this for a fact, I'll bet the military radar goes out damn far."

"Yeah." Marty didn't know what else to say. William Wesson had called an hour ago to let them know that the TSA and the military were implementing an anti-hijacking plan that would guarantee the safety of the two potential target cities, New York and Washington. While Wesson hadn't spelled out what the procedure was beyond indicating 'armed interception', it didn't take much imagination to figure what the possibilities could be. "Can't believe that Flight 3 is airborne," Marty added, "Can't believe that Clarke would be crazy enough to ignore the messages we've sent. Messages on the company data link, and messages the military's been sending on the common radio frequencies. We've made it clear that the flight will be shot down if it approaches the coastline without first establishing radio communications and turning control of the ship over to the regular pilots."

But what if the regular pilots weren't alive? What then? George pushed that scenario out of his mind; it was based on Ray being a crazed hijacker and that, George knew in his heart, was absolutely fucking impossible.

Slowly, George got up and paced back and forth in front of Marty's desk. Finally, he stopped, leaned forward and spoke. "Hell, I can't believe *any* of this. Not a single bit of the story that we've pieced together makes sense. Not to me." George added in a low voice, "I'd stake my life on the fact that Ray Clarke is neither crazy nor suicidal. Maynard says the same thing. None of these things could have happened the way we think. There's got to be another explanation."

"Like what?" Marty asked.

"Because I can't piece one together doesn't mean that it's out of the question."

"George, I'd like to believe that, too," Marty said. "I really would. But I can't. I can't come up with the remotest possibility of another explanation, not after hearing those two radio messages. Our corporate hierarchy in Manhattan has signed onto this explanation. So, apparently, have the TSA, the FBI, the

227

Air Force and the Navy. I'd argue with them, if I could think of a single set of circumstances that would fit the facts."

"Me, too." George exhaled deeply, then sat himself back down again. "I got sick to my stomach when we got that call from Wesson ordering us to not do anything that could later be construed in a court of law as supportive of this hijacker. Can you imagine how someone, at a time like this, could be focused on crap like that?"

"Yes. By being lawyers, politicians and judges. They live in a world of their own. Our fault because we've turned the entire damn country over to them."

George glanced at the wall clock. 4:20 pm. Flight 3 should have been on final approach to JFK Airport in New York by now, and, obviously, they weren't. "The military hasn't located our airliner in the vicinity of New York so one of those three possibilities for the flight is behind us."

Marty nodded. "Seems that way." He paused. "That leaves Washington, or..."

"Or they're in the water. Probably for a long time. It's an enormous ocean out there, we'll never know for certain where they went down." As George finished speaking, he heard the door open behind him and he turned to see Dave Wilder standing in the doorway with a paper in his hand.

"Unbelievable!" Wilder stepped forward and took the message directly to George. "Came into our Internet mailbox a couple of minutes ago. An email message from Flight 3! From over the Atlantic!"

"What!?" George jumped up, grabbed the paper from Wilder and read it.

TO: *Trans-Continental Dispatch*
FROM: *DR R Frankel*
SUBJECT: *Flight 3*
MESSAGE: *Headed for New York after double engine runaway, suspect automatic engine system lockup. Right engine destroyed, all electrical power now selected off. Flying magnetic heading 285 degrees, 1,000 feet above ocean @ 290 knots airspeed. Fuel remaining and fuel endurance unknown. This message sent via portable satellite telephone, unable to send additional messages. Estimate NY area arrival time at*

approximately 6:40 pm EST. Alert military to provide escort to nearest available airport for a visual approach as soon as possible. Situation critical. Ray Clarke.

When George finished the message, he handed it to Marty, who was now standing beside him. George turned to Wilder. Was this too good to be true? Was it possible? "Are you sure this message is real? How'd we get it? Who the hell is this Frankel on the sender line?"

"My thoughts, too," Wilder said. "Since it came in on the Internet link, that means anybody in the world could have sent it. Maybe the word has gotten out about the situation of Flight 3 and this is from some crackpot. Nothing but a bad prank."

"Prank?" George said. "Hell, no. It's exactly what we need. It's one piece of the puzzle. A goddamn big piece. We've got to find the other pieces. Quickly, too."

"Well, I guess it's possible that it's a prank," Wilder said, "but I agree with you. Don't think so. How could anyone know Ray Clarke was onboard? I checked the passenger manifest. The flight does have a Dr. Lee Frankel listed in first class. It must be his satellite telephone that they've used — it's the only explanation for an Internet message from over the Atlantic. For my money, this message must be real," Wilder added.

"Right." Marty pointed to the printed Internet message in his hand. "Clarke says that he wants the military to send an escort. What he doesn't know is that the Air Force and the Navy are out there and waiting. They're waiting for him so they can shoot him down."

◇

Brandon Kyle was in the Trans-Continental Airlines conference room in Manhattan when the direct telephone line from the dispatch office rang. He picked up the telephone and, in short order, understood what George Fisher was telling him. "Yes, that Internet message is quite startling. Fax a copy to us and we'll take it from here. I'll call back in a few minutes." Kyle hung up the telephone, then turned to his legal advisor. "A message from Flight 3."

"From the flight itself?" Wesson was momentarily stunned, then his mind quickly whirled with possibilities. "Has the hijacker come up with demands?" he asked.

"Not hardly." Kyle paused, then said, "George Fisher is faxing a copy of what's come into the dispatch office via the Internet. Should be on our machine by now." Kyle pointed to the door that led to the adjacent room where the fax machine was located. "He told me what it said. See for yourself."

When Wesson returned a few minutes later, he said, "An amazing turn of events." He read the message in his hand again, then looked at Kyle. "Apparently it's been some sort of airplane problem from the start. One of our new Consolidated 768 conversions. We need to immediately let the TSA know that…"

"Wait." Kyle held up his hand. "Let's not change directions too quickly. Not until we're certain. There's a great deal at stake here for us." Rushing off in a new direction without checking the facts and the possible permutations was not good business. In this instance, it would be reckless, foolhardy and potentially financially disastrous.

"I don't understand," Wesson said. "It says right here that they've had a mechanical problem. It says that they have no electricity, so that must be why they haven't spoken to…"

"Maybe." Kyle stood up. "And maybe not. What everyone is conveniently forgetting are those initial hijacking messages. How do you explain those? How do those two separate hijacking messages, sent by two different members of the flight crew, comport with what has suddenly come into the dispatch office from over the Internet?"

Wesson paused for a moment in thought, then shook his head. "Good point. Can't explain it," he answered. "Now that you mention it, none of this adds up. Doesn't make sense, not after the hijacking messages."

"It does if this message is a fake," Kyle said. He had reached that conclusion as Wesson stepped back into the room with the fax. Kyle took the copy of that Internet message from Wesson's hand. "It occurred to me that anyone could have sent this. Anyone in the world. Perhaps our hijacker has an accomplice, someone in Europe or even in the United States."

"I see." Could it be true? In a strange way, it fit with what they knew.

230

"Let's play the 'what-if' game," Kyle said. "Let's see if we can come up with some reason why the hijacker would benefit from us being in receipt of this message."

"Okay." Wesson paused. "He would certainly expect us to stop any defensive measures. He would expect the military to begin an all-out search off the New York coastline so they could guide the stricken flight to the nearest airport. If it's a ruse, that means that he wants the military to concentrate on the particular area he's given us — New York."

"Exactly." Kyle nodded. "My guess would be that it's the area where he has no intention of going. Which means that he's going somewhere else. He sent this message to throw us off track."

"Washington?"

"Correct." Kyle nodded as he waved the message in his hand. "I see this Internet message as backup plan to be certain that he's not intercepted on his way to Washington. Either he somehow sent this message from the aircraft, or, more probably, it was prearranged to be sent either by a willing accomplice or by some automatic electronic system."

"Yes, that could be easily arranged," Wesson said. "This could be nothing but an automatic Internet message that was prearranged to be sent at a particular time. I believe that there's software readily available that can easily do that sort of thing. That way, he didn't need an accomplice — which makes more sense."

"Right."

"Still, we need more to go on than guess work," Wesson added. "I'm not comfortable with that. There are lives at stake...this is...incredibly risky." Wesson fidgeted with his tie, which suddenly seemed too tight.

"Of course we need more." Kyle had made a career out of going with his own thinking and his own hunches, but he was also willing to listen. For awhile. "There's too much at stake here for us to take chances. There's too much at stake for everyone, including us and all our business plans."

"We're talking about a great many innocent lives in that airliner," Wesson said nervously. "Got to be absolutely, positively sure."

"Naturally. But we're talking about even more innocent lives on the ground in Washington, if it comes to that," Kyle added. "We've also got to protect the corporate assets – that's what we get paid to do. Can't run unnecessary risks with them."

Wesson looked at the printed Internet message one last time, then laid it on the table and looked at Kyle. Wesson was incredibly uncomfortable about this. "We've got to do what's right," he finally said. "Unless we come up with an iron-clad reason not to believe this message, its existence has trumped everything we've said so far and all our speculations. I recommend — I *strongly* recommend — that unless there is a valid reason to believe that this message is a hoax, that we immediately turn it over to the TSA. We can't withhold this new information, and I would expect that this message would remove the flight from their *high probability* category."

After a few moments of silence, Kyle replied. "Fair enough," he finally said. "If this message is true, then the corporate assets are not in jeopardy.*"*

"Then it's okay to call the TSA with this?" Wesson asked.

"In a minute." Kyle mulled over his thoughts again – there was too much, financially, on the line. The other side of the coin was that if this message was false and the hijacked airliner then made it through to the Presidential Inaugural, their plan for selling the airline was absolutely and completely destroyed – no matter who made the final decision not to stop this crazed pilot. Kyle knew that he needed unequivocal proof of the validity of this email message, either one way or the other. He also had to play it safe, to leave no possibility that the corporate assets could be in jeopardy.

"Mister Kyle, we've got to act," Wesson said. "Right now."

"As soon as we check one more thing."

"Which is?"

"Need to check if there's any technical reason why this email might be false. If we could show that it was, then nothing has changed," Kyle said. "If the message is a hoax, then we let the government deal with what we both agree would be the greater risk — the hijacking and its end result for us."

"Check on the email?" Wesson asked. "How?"

232

"Only one way. Give the dispatch department a few minutes to see if everything in the message adds up. If it does, then we take the message to the TSA and tell them we believe it. And it won't affect our future plans in the slightest, regardless of whether the flight ultimately crashes or not. But if this message doesn't check out, then we have enough reason to believe that it's a hoax."

"Logical." Wesson nodded, then reached for the telephone to call Luffman at the dispatch department. "If the dispatch department gives us a concrete reason to not believe this message, then we'll have solid ground for our actions — or, more accurately, our inactions. If this message is a ruse and the attack on Washington is the hijacker's primary goal, then the military must shoot them down. We can't allow any doubt to creep into anyone's mind on that issue, or our potential liability for a Washington attack is incalculable. Our work this past year would be wasted, and our financial planning and the preliminary arrangements would have been for nothing."

◇

When the telephone rang in the dispatch office, George Fisher picked it up. He was expecting to hear from Kyle that the TSA had been advised and that the armed military search-and-destroy mission had been called off and a pure intercept mission was in its place. Instead, it was Wesson on the phone and he told him that they needed additional information. He wanted to speak with Martin Luffman. George handed the telephone over.

Marty picked up the receiver. "Luffman here," he said, then began to listen carefully. Finally, Marty spoke. "Yes, I did have some of the same feelings, although, to be honest, I didn't think of that Internet angle. Not with the name of the sender being the same as a name on the passenger manifest. I see your point, about how it could be a carefully crafted ruse," Marty said in response, using Wesson's exact words. "Could have been Clarke himself who developed the Internet message, finalizing it by picking a suitable name when he saw the passenger manifest at Rome. Or, it could have been an accomplice. Those are good points." Marty didn't know what to think, but he wasn't going to disagree with Wesson and Kyle unless he had some concrete reason to. What they were now saying did, in fact, make sense.

George, sitting beside Marty, was stunned to hear the way the conversation was going. He couldn't imagine what the hell they were up to now. "Marty, this is insane — tell him that he's got to call the TSA and..."

"Wait." Marty held up his hand toward George, then turned his attention back to the telephone and the notes on his pad. "What initially struck me," Marty said into the telephone, "was how the Internet message was out of wack with our computer fuel endurance estimates. My gut feeling was that the flight didn't have enough fuel onboard to meet the time requirements dictated in the Internet message. Got a dispatcher checking that angle right now."

George was going to grab the telephone from Marty and protest what Wesson was saying when he spotted Wally Poel walking toward the office. He would, George knew, have those fuel and time figures that Marty had asked for.

"Here they are," Poel said as he walked briskly into the room and walked directly to George. "None of it adds up." Poel tapped the paperwork in his hand. "If what he says in the message is their actual flight profile — flying on one engine at one thousand feet above the water at just under 300 knots — they'll run the fuel tanks bone-dry at least a full hour before they could reach New York. Don't have to tell you how much fuel they'll consume by flying that low."

"You don't," George said. By flying at only 1,000 feet, the airliner would be guzzling fuel at an enormous rate. All of them knew that, but George had hoped that the increase in fuel consumption would be offset by the standard fuel reserves the airplane carried on their trans-oceanic flights and that they'd have enough to reach land. Apparently not. "A full hour. Sonovabitch."

"Yes," Poel said, "If not more." He glanced at the papers in his hand, then at the men in front of him. "They'd be at least three hundred-plus miles out to sea when they run out of fuel. There's no way that any competent pilot wouldn't know that from the aircraft handbook and the flow charts they have with them, even without any of the gauges working like the Internet message says. He may not know exactly when the engine was

234

going to flame out from lack of fuel, but he would know *approximately*."

George slowly shook his head in disgust without saying another word. One full hour, probably more. Damn. He knew that he had to refute Wesson right now, but he was at a loss as to what to say, which direction to turn.

Marty sat in stunned silence for another long moment; he, too, had felt that Flight 3 might make it safely to New York. Finally, he cleared his throat and began to speak again into the telephone, giving the new fuel endurance details to Wesson. After another pause on his end of the telephone conversation, Marty added a few more words, then placed the telephone handset back in its cradle. He turned to George.

"Hell of a note," George said. He shook his head.

"Yeah." Marty pointed toward the files on his desk. "Wish it wasn't true, but I could just *feel* that this message wasn't right," he said. "Wally has confirmed it with the flight planning computer, so Wesson says they're reluctant to say anything to the TSA in support of a message that's potentially fraudulent. He gave me more crap about corporate liability and the appearance of supporting the hijacker. What he did say was that he would pass on the information to the TSA that an Internet message had been received, but that the allegations in it —those were his exact words — were unsupported by the facts."

"But some of those facts…"

"No, George," Marty said, interrupting George. "If the message was true, Flight 3 will run out of fuel hundreds of miles before it reaches the US coastline. More than likely, the message was meant to throw us off, like Wesson is saying. He also reminded me of the two radioed hijacking messages that were sent hours ago and the fact that the regular flight crew is not even mentioned in this short email. As reluctant as I am to agree, this message does appear to be a trick. It leaves out more than it says."

"What do Wesson and Kyle expect us to do?" George asked as he stood up and allowed his eyes to travel slowly around the crowded dispatch room on the other side of the glass doors.

"Expects us to wait for word," Marty said as he, too, stood up and looked out at the faces of the dispatchers who were staring back at them. Marty turned away from them and back to

George. "Word from the military that they've either found the wreckage where our flight ran out of fuel and ditched into the Atlantic, or..."

"Or?"

"Or word that the military has finally intercepted the aircraft. Word that they've shot it down."

Chapter Twenty-Four

The grey US Air Force KC-135 tanker continued on its steady westbound heading while Lt. Col. Jack Clary nudged the flight controls of his F-15C jet fighter. Within a few seconds he had cleared the tanker and had turned his aircraft around to an eastbound heading so he could rejoin Shield 22 in formation flight. "Shield Two-One is clear. On the way, Sonny," Clary announced on the tactical frequency their two ship element had been assigned.

"Right. Waiting for ya'," came the immediate reply from Major Sonny Bellman in his own F-15C. "Holding steady on 090."

"Gotcha," Clary transmitted as he glanced at the radar display screen in front of him. Bellman's F-15C was clearly visible on the electronics in his cockpit. "There in a jiff. On your left."

"Roger."

Clary looked out the Plexiglas bubble of his single seat fighter and into the clear skies between him and Shield 22, his wingman on this mission. Sonny had been his wingman on many missions over the past years and the two of them had spent countless hours together in the base ready room during their rotations on alert status. Their professional relationship had turned into a close personal friendship. "Sonny, got a visual. Alongside in less than a minute."

"Understand."

When the two F-15C fighters from the Massachusetts Air National Guard had departed Barnes Air National Guard Base in Westfield, Massachusetts thirty minutes earlier, the weather had been overcast with the threat of snow. The two aircraft element topped the overcast shortly after takeoff, but once they had passed Cape Cod on their direct routing to their assigned combat air patrol area, the clouds below them disappeared. They were now operating in clear skies and excellent visibilities. "Shield 21, on the left," Clary announced on the tactical frequency. "Sliding in."

"Okay," came Bellman's reply. "Got ya'." Normally, they'd have more personal chatter going on between them on their tactical channel — Bellman and Clary had been doing these tactical formations for a long time and it was purely second nature to both of them. But these Air National Guard Officers were well aware that every word of every transmission of every aircraft sent out on Operation Full Shield that afternoon would be recorded, analyzed and fully critiqued. This was, as both men clearly understood, not a training mission. You needed to watch everything you said, and certainly everything you did — or, for that matter, what you might not do. Both men were conducting themselves accordingly. This was as real as it gets, they needed to stay sharp.

Clary manipulated the flight controls of his F-15C. Finally, he pulled alongside Bellman in a wide, loose formation. Clary watched as his wingman wordlessly took up his proper in-flight position, slightly below and behind his own aircraft. With their air to air refueling done and their two-ship element where it belonged, Clary pressed the transmit button on his control stick again. "Homeplate, Shield 21 flight is on station."

"Roger, Shield 21 flight," came the radioed response from the combat control center. "Understand refueling completed. On station."

Even though everyone's voice was calm and cool — like every training mission they'd ever been on — Clary could detect a hint of tension in everyone's voice, even his own. He needed to stay loose and he considered saying something to Bellman and had his finger poised above the transmit button to make a comment about keeping tension down but decided against it. There was no need for extra or unnecessary transmissions today — not with what was facing them.

Instead, Clary glanced around his ship. The F-15C Eagle was a fighter pilot's dream — amazingly agile, with a phenomenal rate of climb and equipped with the best combat radar in the world. The big combat ship — it was 64 feet long and had weighed almost 68,000 pounds at takeoff — loped along at a fuel conserving speed. For today's mission they were carrying external fuel tanks so they wouldn't need to rejoin the KC-135 as often, but they had elected to refuel when they had the opportunity. According to everyone's radar, the target aircraft was no where in their sector at the moment, so they used the time to maintain their combat readiness.

Clary glanced down at his radar display. Nothing. No targets whatsoever. Other inbound airline flights coming into this area had been diverted off this route to reduce any chance of a mistake or a conflict. There was nothing at all on the radar, and that was good.

The APG-70 radar onboard the F-15Cs was effective for a hundred miles in front of them, maybe a little more. For today, they would use it in its most basic mode — strictly for joining up on the airliner after they'd been directed toward it by the controllers at Homeplate. Then, he and Major Bellman would be following the strict protocol for Operation Full Shield.

Clary shook his head. For the first time in his long military career, Clary found himself on a mission that he would rather not be part of. There was no combat aspect to this assignment — it was a slaughterhouse mission once they positively identified the airliner in question. Shooting down a hijacked airliner was, he knew, a vital job and he would — if the task fell to them — accomplish that mission. But it was not something he was relishing, to put it mildly. He knew that Sonny felt the same way.

No discussion was needed during their preflight briefing as to who would be taking which of the two assigned tasks: Sonny would participate in the required positive identification drill then position his aircraft to follow the target to its splash point. Clary's assignment was to fire the AIM-9 Sidewinder that would accomplish the kill, since he was the ranking officer and the flight leader. That was the way it had to be.

Clary glanced at the brand-new fancy pilot's watch wrapped to his left wrist. 4:40 pm. Libby had given him that wristwatch that very morning when they were having breakfast before he left for the base. Once the alert began, Clary barely had enough time to telephone her before he and Sonny left the briefing room. He needed to tell her that their dinner plans were postponed because of this emergency scramble, but he didn't get to talk to her directly; instead, he got their answering machine. He left a short message, and also told her that she should call Dianne. It was just as good that Libby wasn't at home. Jack didn't have the time – or the inclination – to explain.

The initial briefing had said that the airliner — Trans-Continental Flight 3 from Rome, Italy — had been hijacked and that there was a high degree of probability that the hijacker was intending to crash the airliner into either New York City or the Washington, DC area. The ship itself was a Consolidated 768 — which was one of the new and upgraded conversions of one of the older Boeing 767 widebody airliners. The registration number of that particular aircraft had been reported as N731TC, and that number was clearly painted on each side of the rear fuselage near the tail. It should be easy enough for both him and Sonny to see and verify that number, as the Operation Full Shield rules of engagement required.

The estimated arrival time for New York for Trans-Continental Flight 3 had been given as 4:22 pm Eastern Standard Time, but when the airliner hadn't showed up on any of the radar screens when that time came and went, it was decided that their element should take the opportunity to refuel so they'd be ready for whatever might happen next. According to Homeplate, the hijacked airliner hadn't been found yet — even though military radars from the Air Force and Navy had been searching continuously. The military photo satellites were being re-tasked to the region, but there was no word whether they had been repositioned and whether they had spotted anything. At the moment, the position of the terrorist-controlled airliner was unknown, and it was a fucking big ocean out there.

Clary scanned the expansive emptiness ahead of him. It was no wonder they haven't found the airliner as yet, but he also knew for certain that they would. Clary looked at his radar and navigation displays, then transmitted, "Sonny, time to circle the wagons."

"Roger. When you're ready, Jack."

"Here we go." Clary made a slight movement with his wrist and the F-15C began a left turn that kept them inside the twenty mile racetrack pattern that was their on-station patrol area. Clary knew that there were other two-flight elements up and down the coastline doing exactly the same thing. If this hijacked airliner was airborne and headed this way, when it crossed into any of the assigned combat operations areas it would be shot down.

"He's not just late," Bellman transmitted. "He's damn late. Wondering if the second scenario isn't today's player," he added.

"Could be." Their briefing had included the fact that the airliner had been totally out of contact with everyone for some time, so it was possible that they had gone down at sea. That part wouldn't involve them, since fighter aircraft were not good search and rescue machines. Besides, Clary knew that crashing into the Atlantic Ocean in January meant that there would only be a search, there would be no chance of any rescue. "We'll know. Soon enough."

"Right. Unless he flies into another sector, don't expect a recall until the subject's fuel endurance is exhausted," Bellman transmitted. "Be here awhile." That portion of the preflight briefing had been open-ended, since no one knew how long this threat might be valid. There were conflicting ideas about the airliner's fuel endurance.

There had been no evidence of involvement of other aircraft, but one thing for certain was that the United States military wasn't going to run the risk of a 9/11 repeat. For that reason, the new protocol was being strictly adhered to.

Clary saw from his electronic flight screen that they were approaching the western boundary of their assigned combat operations area. He began to turn the F-15C left again, and he could see that Shield 22 was following in formation. With nothing for the two of them to do but wait, Clary began to think about the original 9/11 attack, and how different their air defense posture was today.

No one could blame the 102nd out of Otis for what had happened that horrific morning of September 11, 2001. Two F-15Cs on alert status were ready for takeoff before the first airliner hit the World Trade Center, but there had been communications problems and they were held on the ground until six minutes after the first World Trade Tower had been hit. The fighters were launched at that time, but they were sent south of Long Island because of confusion as what to do with them. Basically, nobody knew what the hell was going on.

By then, the second airliner was approaching the Manhattan area. That airliner flew into the south tower of the Trade Center while the two fighters from the 102nd remained south of Long Island. Finally, ten minutes later, the two F-15C fighters were cleared from their holding area and they flew to Manhattan where they established a combat air patrol over the area. But it was too late when the two F-15Cs finally got overhead. Far too late.

The irony of it was that the 102nd at Otis had been scheduled to be deactivated as a fighter Wing when 9/11 occurred. The aircraft from that Wing and a good number of its personnel were eventually transferred to the 104th Fighter Wing at Barnes. Those transfers were completed years ago. Now, the 104th was the last line of defense against this most recent threat on New York City. After all these years, the defenders included some of the same personnel and some of the same airplanes.

For a few minutes the two F-15C fighters flew in radio silence. Finally, Bellman pressed his transmit button. "Jack, we should keep fuel reserves up. Refueling more often. Then we can go with contingencies." Bellman paused for a moment, then added, "Refuel when there's no inbound target."

Clary knew his friend well, and he understood that Sonny wasn't any happier about this assignment than he was. But Clary also knew that his friend was a professional, so he'd be able to push his emotions aside and think through their strategy – like he was doing now. "Good idea," Clary transmitted back. "Refuel every 30 minutes. Keep the tanker guys on their toes, keep our tanks full."

"Right." But Bellman knew that, if they were both lucky, the airliner had gone down and they would be spared the job of being the executioners of a plane packed with innocent passengers. There was no doubt that this was one shit assignment. "They've crashed or they're headed for Washington. With the inaugural today, Washington is the target."

"Makes sense," Clary answered. He knew that both he and Sonny were hoping that the hijacked airliner didn't show up in their sector; no one wanted to be the one to carry out the actual mission of shooting down this airliner, no matter how necessary it might be. They would do it, but they sure as hell didn't want to.

"Yeah, Washington makes sense." If the hijacked airliner was headed for Washington, the intercept would be handled by elements from other bases that were disbursed further south of their current position. In fact, the latest information being passed along was that Washington was the most likely target and that it was being defended accordingly.

"Homeplate, Shield Two-One," Clary transmitted. "Advise the tanker that Shield Two-One and Shield Two-Two will refuel in 20 minutes. We'll maintain that cycle of refueling — thirty minute intervals — until recall."

"Will do, Shield Two-One."

Clary sat back in his flight chair as much as the tight confines of the F-15C would allow. For the next few minutes he sat in silence, thinking about their options — and thinking about other things, too. If they were very lucky today, he and Sonny would be recalled to Barnes and they could pick up the wives and go to that dinner that Libby had arranged for the four of them. Tonight's dinner was, in fact, something special: today was Lt. Col. Jack Clary's 40th birthday.

Chapter Twenty-Five

The clock on the wall of the office at the rear of the Trans-Continental Airlines Dispatch office said 4:42 pm, Eastern Standard Time. That meant that it was exactly twenty minutes past Flight 3's estimated time of arrival at JFK Airport in New York, and that fact was seriously bothering Marty. "To be on the safe side," Marty said to the man to his right as he scanned through a pile of printouts, "I need you to feed the flight data into the computer again."

"Again?" Wally Poel asked. "It'll give the same answers."

"Maybe." Marty knew, as the Director of Dispatch, he would be held responsible by Brandon Kyle if Poel or any of the other dispatchers working on Flight 3 had made some sort of error — a misplaced digit, a bad keystroke, whatever — and the information that he personally gave to Brandon Kyle, the FAA and the TSA turned out to be wrong. "Need to be certain that what we've said is true," he said. What he didn't say was that it would be his ass if the dispatch department had made a mistake.

"A waste of time. I was careful the first time and the answer the computer gave made perfect sense," Poel answered. "Hell, it came out *exactly* the same — to the minute, matter of fact — to what the flight itself was indicating as its New York arrival before the hijacking began. How much validation do we need?" Poel patted the pile of printouts on the desk. He was a meticulous man by nature and for this assignment he had taken extra care.

Marty shook his head. "I know, but..." He paused because, up until that point, he hadn't had the time or the inclination to share much information with the working dispatchers — he had only gotten information from them, and then given it to others like Kyle, Wesson and the TSA. It was time to tell everyone what he knew. "The TSA called. Said that the flight isn't anywhere near the New York area and that it hasn't shown up on the radar screens that are monitoring the ocean approaches to Washington."

"The Washington ETA is computed to be 4:59," Poel said as he glanced at his paperwork, then at the wall clock. "Fifteen minutes from now."

"Which means they should be in radar contact." Marty shrugged; he was saying the obvious, but saying it out loud to someone else was easier than thinking about it. "Assuming normal cruise speed, fifteen minutes equates to no more than 150 miles. Probably less. The TSA said that the military radar would see them 250 to 300 miles out no matter what their altitude or course was."

"Understand," Poel answered. "That means the flight has already gone down." He paused a few moments, then added, "There's no other answer, unless Ray Clarke found some way to put that ship into hover mode outside the military radar coverage zone."

"Huh?" Marty looked at Poel — there was something in the man's comment that had rung a bell, a faint bell, in Marty's thoughts. "Hover mode?" he asked. It was something about that particular phrase that had caught his attention. *Hover mode.* To Marty, that expression meant something.

"A stupid phrase," Poel said. "Sorry. He's not in a helicopter." Poel picked up the pile of paperwork and asked Marty, "Want me to rework the fuel figures and the ETAs, even though the information we have says that the flight has, most likely, gone down?"

"Well..." Marty couldn't get that one stupid, nonsensical, annoying phrase from Poel out of his mind. *Hover mode.* Damn it, he knew that it meant something to him, but Marty couldn't remember what. *Hover mode.* "Forget it. No reason to recalculate the figures, they made perfect sense the first time. They're correct."

"Academic, too, wouldn't you say?" Poel added as he began to gather the rest of the paperwork off Marty's desk. "At this point."

"Academic." Marty paused, then reached for a stack of his own paperwork so it wouldn't get mixed in with Poel's. Once it was official that the flight had gone down — really, the only feasible explanation — there would be reports to write and a comprehensive file to be developed that would show how the dispatch department had...*Hover mode.*

All at once, the memory of where Marty had first heard that stupid expression flooded over him — it had been a joke in the ground school training class he had attended last year, a euphemism for a type of cruise-and-fuel chart that they had in the official books but never used. Long Rang Cruise Charts. Below that heading was the subtitle: For Maximum Fuel Endurance. That page of charted figures was printed in the flight manuals. "Damn!"

"What?!" Poel said.

"Long range cruise — we didn't run that scenario!" Marty said as he reached across his desk for a closed book and began to rifle through it. "High altitude and slow speed, for maximum fuel endurance," Marty said as he found the page he was looking for.

"I..." Poel was dumbfounded for a moment, until he realized that he, too, hadn't thought about that possibility. "We focused on how quickly the flight could get here. We never thought..."

"Right." Marty pointed to the printed chart in front of him. "Even a rough figuring shows that they'd have lots of fuel left and lots of distance to go if Ray Clarke had stayed high but slowed the ship to best fuel endurance speed after he took over. Maybe his plan was to trick everyone into thinking they'd already crashed at sea — that they'd run out of fuel — and then he could sneak across the coastline with the air defenses down."

"Yeah. Maybe." Poel shook his head. He had no idea about any of that, but he did know what had to be done next. He quickly headed toward the door. "I'll have those new scenario figures for you in a couple of minutes," Poel said as he left the private office and headed for his dispatch station and flight computer.

"Hurry." Marty knew that he had made a mistake by overlooking that one possible scenario, but he had also been the one to catch that oversight. Maybe that would make the difference. He made the mistake, but he had also found the mistake. While it was possible that Flight 3 had crashed into the ocean, it was also possible that Ray Clarke had been flying at high altitude but low airspeed to maximize his fuel endurance so he could eventually sneak into either the New York or Washington areas after everyone thought he had run out of fuel.

Marty reached for the telephone on his desk so he could call Brandon Kyle and tell him what he had discovered.

◇

"So, let me clearly understand this," Brandon Kyle said into the telephone. There was an icy edge to his voice as he responded to what Martin Luffman had told him. "What you are saying now is that, somehow, you and your dispatchers simply overlooked the possibility that this hijacker could remain at high altitude, slow the ship and thereby get a large increase of both the fuel range and the fuel endurance when compared to normal operating speeds." Kyle paused, glanced up at Wesson, then spoke into the telephone again. "Is that right?"

"Yes Sir," Marty answered nervously. "But let me explain why we…"

"You'll have more than sufficient opportunity," Kyle said as he interrupted Luffman, "to explain yourself later. I'm certain of that." As far as Kyle was concerned, he was dealing with idiots.

"Please," Marty responded. "Let me explain right now. The TSA and the FAA could use this information."

"All right," Kyle said. "Be brief."

Marty knew that Kyle wouldn't give him much time to get his point across, so he spoke rapidly. "There was no reason to think about this particular operational option since everyone assumed, logically, that the hijacker would want to get here as quickly as possible. We had even figured in the sunset and that he would want to make his attack before darkness. Do you remember?" Marty asked. "You brought that up yourself."

"Go on," Kyle said without committing one way or the other — he had no intention of being quoted on a subject until he knew for certain which way the cards would fall.

"Right. Well, we kept thinking along those lines," Marty continued, "and didn't come up with the idea of using those long-range cruise settings so the airplane could stay airborne longer. Those are airspeed and fuel flow settings that we never use in airline operation."

247

"And why is that?" Kyle asked. He always disliked these technical discussions, but for once he needed to understand the nuances involved.

"It would add to both sides of the ledger," Marty said. "It does decrease the total fuel used, but it increases the flight time."

"You'll need to explain yourself more thoroughly — I don't follow you on this," Kyle responded, even though he hated this sort of crap. "Go on."

Marty relaxed slightly because, for the moment at least, he had Kyle's attention. Maybe he would hold onto his job. "High performance is bought with the use of energy. It's like with your car, you can get better gas mileage if you drive it slower."

"Continue," Kyle said. It was like pulling fucking teeth, and he'd been through this drill many times in the past with these technocrats. They were all alike, they either gave you too much information, or not enough. "And get right to the point."

"Yessir, I will. With jet airliners, there's the additional factor that they are most efficient at their highest operational altitude. It has to do with their true airspeed being greater even though the engine fuel flow..."

"Don't get too technical," Kyle said, trying to control his growing anger while he was being forced to listen to these endless details. If he didn't need this information so badly, Kyle would have already hung up the damn phone. "Provide me with a quick overview of the concept. That's all I'll need."

"Understand. Okay." Marty took a deep breath, then continued. "We never use these long-range settings because, even though we'd save fuel, the airplane would be going as slow as the old piston airliners. It would take forever to get a flight across the Atlantic."

"Now I understand. Go on."

"So that's why none of us thought that the hijacker might use them."

"And why do you suddenly think that the hijacker might be using them now?" Kyle asked.

"Because if he isn't, then they've already ditched in the Atlantic. The TSA technical people have told us that the military radar hasn't found them yet, and they can see out from the coastline for hundreds of miles. So we know for a fact that Flight

3 hasn't gotten to the New York area as expected, and we also know for a fact that it won't be getting to Washington at 4:59 pm either since the flight is not in radar contact. That means only two things: that either they are airborne — flying at high altitude with low fuel flows to maximize fuel endurance — or that they've already crashed. Nothing else adds up."

"I see." Kyle paused on his end, then said, "And what about that single Internet message? Does this mean that you've still discounted that? The one about them flying very low — at a thousand feet above the water, with only one engine running. How does that Internet message fit with your new thinking on what the hijacker might be doing?"

"Nothing has changed on that Internet message," Marty answered quickly. "It's still an impossibility."

"I know you told me earlier, but tell me again. Why?" Kyle needed to keep this technical data straight in his mind so he could make a proper decision.

"Because if the aircraft is, in fact, flying that low," Marty said as he worked hard to keep the frustration out of his voice while he once again explained what he considered obvious, "they will be getting so many less miles to the gallon. That means that they will run the fuel tanks bone dry at least three hundred miles before reaching land, probably even more. Those fuel figures are absolutely indisputable, and any competent pilot would know it — especially someone as competent as Ray Clarke."

"I see." Kyle paused, then said, "So, the original fuel exhaustion time of approximately six pm…"

"6:03 pm, Eastern Standard Time," Marty said.

"…is not necessarily valid, depending on what speed the hijacker is flying the airliner and at what altitude he's flying," Kyle said. "What's the new time for Flight 3 to run completely out of fuel?"

"That number was just handed to me," Marty said. "7:10 pm, Eastern Standard Time. That would be the absolute end of their fuel endurance if the hijacker kept the airplane high but slowed to their best economy airspeed as soon as the hijacking began."

"And why would this hijacker want to do that?" Kyle asked. The good news here was that the dispatchers were, apparently, finally covering every option.

"We're guessing of course," Marty said, "but our thinking here is that perhaps he's trying to fool us into believing that he's run out of fuel and gone down. Maybe then the air defenses along the coastline would be lowered. Then he might have a better chance of making a successful attack before the fighters could be regrouped."

"I see," Kyle said. He knew that if the airliner did somehow manage to get through, it would screw up everything. Big time.

"You see now why the TSA and the military need to be notified immediately? So that the fighter coverage isn't removed early," Marty said. While he didn't want to believe that one of their retired pilots had hijacked the airliner, the facts prevented him from thinking otherwise.

"Yes," Kyle looked down at the notes he'd been making. "I see that." He paused, then asked, "What are the revised estimates for arrival at New York and Washington? Have you come up with them yet?"

"Yes," Marty answered. "Based on that configuration, Flight 3 would arrive at New York at 6:13 pm, or arrive at the Washington, DC area at 6:52 pm. It's a few minutes before 5:00 pm now, so the Flight 3 hijacking has to end, one way or the other, in a little over two more hours. Probably less."

"Okay," Kyle said. "I'll make the TSA and the military aware of these new figures. I'm certain that they'll act accordingly." He hung up the telephone, then sat back in his recliner and closed his eyes. Kyle's head was throbbing and he knew that he needed to sit quietly before he could make that final telephone call to the TSA. After a few moments Kyle opened his eyes, then reached for the telephone. This Flight 3 situation had turned into a hell of a mess for them; what they needed at this point was for that hijacking son-of-a-bitch to crash the airliner straight into the fucking ocean and be done with it.

Chapter Twenty-Six

It was a few minutes before 5:00 pm when George left the dispatch area and walked quickly down to his office. It had been Maynard's suggestion, through a short telephone call to the dispatch room, that the two of them get together to privately discuss what their options might be.

George knew that their options were few, and getting less with each passing moment. If Flight 3 hadn't gone down already — and there was strong evidence that they might have — then George knew that the military had their orders to shoot them down as soon as the airliner was located.

George moved down the long corridor rapidly, his left hand wrapped tightly around the latest paperwork that he had taken from the dispatch office — paperwork that showed what the absolute fuel endurance of the flight would be if the airliner was flying high but at a slow airspeed. That was the latest variation on the hijacking theme, and the final explanation as to why the airliner hadn't shown up — the choice on Ray Clarke's part to go with a long-range cruise configuration so that he might reach his target area later than expected and, thus, fool the military.

What bullshit. As a theory, George knew that it was pure rubbish because the military wasn't going to pull combat air patrols and issue stand down orders because some guesswork arrival time for this alleged terrorist threat had come and gone. George realized that and, for that matter, so would Ray Clarke. But it was a waste of time trying to explain those nuances to people who were determined to make this puzzle fit together the way they expected, even if they had to trim the pieces with a big carving knife.

This is impossible. It's nuts. Those were the only thoughts in George's mind when he went over the latest details that had been handed to him. The idea that Ray had hijacked the airliner was as wrong as wrong could be, but George didn't have a single piece of evidence to refute it.

George opened the door to his office. Standing in the far corner of the outer room was Al and Jennifer. Maynard was sitting on the corner of his desk, explaining something to them. He stopped talking, slid off the desk and walked up to George.

"Don't have much time," Maynard said.

"You're telling me." George waved the paperwork in his hand. "More hijacking scenarios from Luffman's group." He glanced down at his paperwork, then back at Maynard. "Their latest guess is that Ray has kept the flight at a high altitude but slowed to long range cruise speed. That would, of course, add both flight time and fuel endurance."

"Right. But why in god's name would he do that?"

"To fool the military into thinking they've gone down, based on the normal fuel exhaustion time."

"And?" Maynard knew there had to be more to it than that, since nothing George had said had made a damn bit of sense.

"And then Ray could sneak past the military interceptors because they wouldn't be looking for him."

"Christ! That's...." Maynard stumbled for the right words, until he finally said, "...damn stupid!" He shook his head. "The military's not that dumb!"

"Of course not."

Maynard shook his head again, then said, "We can dismiss that craziness easy enough, but frankly, I can't think of another direction to turn in."

Al stepped forward, to where the two men stood. "I find this entire hijacking theory too absurd to believe, and I don't even know this retired pilot. There's something we're overlooking. Need to get back to the basics to find it."

Jennifer, who had been sitting next to the desk and taking notes, stood up. She closed the short distance across the room. "For what it's worth," she said as she approached the three men, "as an outsider I agree. This hijacking idea is based on only one thing — those two short and emotional radio transmissions. Their other reasoning is a fabrication combined with wild-ass guesswork. That's the way I see it. If there's something I can do, I'll be willing to help."

"By the way," Al said, "Jennifer has filled us in on the real reason she's here," Al nodded toward Jennifer, then looked at George. "You'll be interested to know that Brandon Kyle and his friends on the Board are going to shut the airline down in a

252

few weeks. They're going to dissolve the company and sell off the pieces."

"What?!" George could hardly believe what he had heard. Yet, considering what he knew about Kyle, he found himself believing it easily.

"True," Jennifer said. "The major article I'm here to do is a top secret assignment – an exposé for *Business World Media* on what's going to happen to this airline."

"Bastards! I knew, sure as hell, they were up to something!" George was fuming; if Brandon Kyle were standing here, he'd choke that rotten weasel with his designer tie and shove his gold Rolex up his ass.

Jennifer shook her head. "I was trying to get my initial piece completed by tomorrow so that we could run it on our nightly TV show. Then we'd run it again on our Internet magazine several times this week." Jennifer stopped for a moment, then continued. "I'm sorry to be the one to tell you this."

George found himself taking a half step backward, as if he could somehow distance himself from this information by stepping away from it. A thousand different thoughts ran through his mind. *Shut the airline down...Kyle...those bastards...this just isn't....* He looked at Jennifer again. "I figured there was something in the wind from their behavior. The company's been losing money for the last few years, so I thought it was either a hostile merger or maybe a substantial downsizing. Nothing like this. Nothing this irrevocable."

"Yes. Shut it down. Completely. As soon as he does that, they'll sell off the assets. That part is prearranged. The airline would be gone before any serious opposition could be mounted."

"Where'd you get this information?" George began to get his thoughts focused. "Certainly not from Kyle and his people."

Jennifer shook her head. "An insider on the Trans-Continental Board. There's at least one member of that Board – maybe more – who are extremely opposed to this. This one man – I don't know his name, only my boss knows who he is – has been leaking the news. But this man can't come out publicly because of the confidentiality rules that the Board operates under. If he did, that would make him personally liable for a lawsuit."

"Damn." It was all that George could think to say. That sonovabitch. He turned back to Jennifer. "Maybe we can do something about this. Maybe there's time to head it off. Tomorrow. After the Flight 3 problem is behind us." George knew that the Flight 3 situation would be long behind them by tomorrow, one way or the other. "You willing to help us try to save the airline?"

"Absolutely," Jennifer answered without hesitation. There was a story angle here, too, so she wasn't cutting herself out – and she saw that it would be a far more powerful news piece if she approached the topic from that angle. This place was an *institution*, for chrissake, like Pan Am and Braniff and Eastern had been. So, it was coming down to another modern installment of corporate and upper management profits versus long-term survival; survival of an institution steeped in history and service, and staffed by thousands of loyal employees. That was the point of view she would use, and it would be a real winner. On top of that, it might actually do some good. "I'll help any way I can. Tell me what to do."

"Tomorrow," George answered. "Our focus needs to be on Flight 3."

"Back to Flight 3," Al said as he stepped forward. "I've had a thought. Maybe we have too much overview and we need to attack each part of the problem on its own."

"How?" George asked.

"Break the information into bit-sized pieces," Al said. "Start with the argument that the Internet message we got from Flight 3 is a hoax because the dispatch department says it's aerodynamically impossible. I don't understand the technical aspects, but it seems to me that their only issue revolves around fuel range. Is it possible that the dispatchers have made a mistake about that and, somehow, Flight 3 could be flying low and yet still has enough fuel to reach land?"

"Off the top of my head, no. Let's think about it," George answered. "Maybe if we ran our own…"

"The opening part of that Internet message is more intriguing to me," Maynard said. He reached for a piece of paper on the desk and then held it out so all of them could read it. "Here's an area no one has given enough thought to." He pointed at the sentence that began the message:

Headed for New York after double engine runaway, suspect automatic engine system lockup. Right engine destroyed, all electrical power now selected off.

"Now," Maynard said, "according to current thinking, Ray Clarke sent — or had sent by someone else or by an automated system — this Internet message to fool us into thinking that he was flying a disabled airplane low and slow."

"What would be the advantage of that?" Jennifer asked.

Maynard shook his head. "None. Which is why I know that the message must be true. There was no sense in a hijacker sending this message."

Al had been reading the message over Maynard's shoulder. "The proponents of the hijacking theory would say that Clarke wanted the military interceptors to be looking low while the hijacked airliner was flying up high. That way, the flight could slip by the fighter airplanes and…"

"Pure horseshit." George tapped the message in Maynard's hand. "This isn't 1941 with Japanese Zeroes sneaking into Pearl Harbor. This is nearly seven decades later, and military radar can count the angels on a head of a pin from a few hundred miles away, and it wouldn't matter what altitude you wanted those angels to fly. Any modern pilot would know that. Ray Clarke would sure as hell know that. But, evidently, not those morons in the Puzzle Palace."

"So, again, this points to the Internet message being real." Al looked at the others. "I don't know anything about military procedures, but if we could convince them that this Internet message was telling the truth, then they'd escort the airliner to a landing rather than shoot it down."

The four of them stood silently for half a minute until George said, "Follow me, I have an idea." He led them into his inner office and to his desk where he sat down behind the company computer. After several keystrokes he was into the internal maintenance records of the airline. A few keystrokes later, the latest maintenance records for the aircraft in question — N731TC — popped onto the screen. "Here…look," he said as he pointed to the last entry.

The others huddled behind him, looking down at the computer screen. "Rome's transit check," Maynard said as he read the words in front of him. "Cleared a few minor write-ups, mostly cabin items. Then…"

"Then they changed the electronic software in each of the engine EEECs." George looked at the others. "That's quite a coincidence since that operational software is changed every three months at the most. It's what controls the automatic engine systems on the 768 and what the Internet message says might have been at fault in the engine runaways. This may be the connection we need."

"Well…" Al cleared his throat. "As inclined as I am to agree with you, I'm not sure that words like 'might' and 'may' are going to carry enough weight to change anyone's mind except ours."

"Because our minds don't need changing," Jennifer said. She laid her hand on Al's shoulder; as strange as it seemed, at some level she was actually worried that Al DeWitt – a man she'd never met until that very morning – would be upset at her for turning his retirement interview into something else. *Honest, sincere, mature, gracious.* By now, Jennifer absolutely knew that her first impressions of this man had been completely accurate. No matter what, she promised herself that she would do that promised retirement article on Al, and that it would be a good one. And she would do whatever else she could to save the airline.

"All the others are convinced," Al said as he casually patted Jennifer's hand, then turned to George. "They're convinced of the opposite. What we need is hard evidence. Something irrefutable."

"Only going to get one shot at this," George added. He pointed to the other stack of papers that he had laid on his desk that contained the flight's fuel endurance figures, then looked at Maynard. "What do you think?"

Maynard stroked his chin a couple of times, then said, "I assume that our point would be that this new software has somehow screwed up both of the EEEC units — that's pretty far-fetched."

"But not impossible. It's a goddamn computer, they screw up all the time," George answered.

"You're right. It's not impossible." Maynard paused for a few moments as he studied the computer screen in front of him. "When it comes to computers, nothing is impossible." He paused again, then finally added, "Then why haven't any of the other 768s we've got flying out there experienced the same problem? Bad software in a computer is like serving poisoned food to your dinner guests — everyone that eats it is going to get sick. It's cause and effect."

George was studying the computer screen at the same time as Maynard. He was about to turn away from the screen when he spotted it. "Look. Right here."

"Where?" Maynard followed George's hand and looked closely at the computer entry that he was pointing at. "Okay. I see."

"What is it?" Al asked. He knew how to read many of the company computer screens, but the maintenance records files were one area that he had never bothered to learn.

"The code on the software change shows that it's not effective until 12:01 am *January 21st*."

"That's not for another seven hours!" Jennifer said. "Could putting it in early make it.... "

"No," George said quickly. He turned around to face the three of them. "Putting it in one day early wouldn't make any difference, excepting that now — because of the Rome mechanic reading the date wrong — Flight 3's airplane is probably the only ship flying with this new update."

"We're on a roll. Good evidence, but not iron-clad," Al cautioned. "The link between the software update and the reported double engine runaway hasn't been proven. In a sense, we're guessing that there's been a connection — like they're guessing about everything else."

"I'll take the guesswork out," Maynard said as he moved toward the door. "There's a 768 on the ramp beside the hangar. It's not going out until tomorrow morning, which means it'll have that software change in it."

"Great." George nodded. "Give it a good run," he said. "That should tell us something — one way or the other. Call me on my cell phone if you find anything we can use."

"Right." Maynard headed for the door, then stopped and turned. "Maintenance has control of that aircraft. We could get around that, but it would take paperwork and signatures. That would take time."

"Don't have time," George answered. "I'll override standard procedures and authorize it with a phone call downstairs to the supervisor." George reached for the telephone.

"Wait. Got a better idea, one that won't tip our hand. There's no need letting anyone know what we're doing until we find something concrete. Remember, Kyle and his friends are going to shut the airline down and begin selling everything in the near future – god knows what his reaction to this would be if he somehow hears what we're doing. Maybe he *wants* the flight to crash, or they'll try to stop us with more of that crap about liability and the appearance of aiding the hijacker."

"Wouldn't put anything past that bastard," George said. "What's your idea?"

Maynard looked at Al and Jennifer. "You folks come with me — we're headed out on our pre-approved public relations event and to complete our tour of the facilities. While we're there, we'll get into that particular airplane on the ramp for our final interview and photo session."

"Might work, except I don't have the magazine's camera," Jennifer said.

"Use your cell phone. The maintenance guy won't know the difference. That's how he takes his own pictures." Maynard led the way as the three of them walked briskly down the corridor that would take them to the elevator and, eventually, to the maintenance ramp.

"Be quick about it," George called out after them as they disappeared down the corridor. He turned and glanced at the wall clock. It was now 5:11 pm, which meant that Flight 3 — *if* they were still flying — would be totally out of fuel in a little over a half hour, *if* that Internet message from Ray about flying barely over the ocean on one engine was true and *if* the dispatcher's fuel figures were correct. That would put the airliner into the cold Atlantic waters at least 300 miles from the nearest shoreline. They'd be dead in five minutes, if not sooner.

George went to his desk and began to randomly pour through the flight's paperwork. With Maynard working the airplane angle, George needed to discover some way to prove that the fuel figures from the dispatch department were wrong.

258

With that sort of evidence, he might be able to convince the military to back off on their plan of attack.

◇

Steven Chew sat at the desk at his office in the TSA headquarters in Washington, DC and stared out the window. There was nothing there that held his interest; instead, his mind was focused on whether or not he should continue his attempts to contact either the agency's Director or Deputy Director.

Chew had laid his hand on the telephone once again. He had attempted to contact either of his two bosses at the TSA any number of times since this Trans-Continental Airlines Flight 3 hijacking alert had begun and, so far, he had been unsuccessful. The communications problem was, without a question, a matter of overload. With over three million additional visitors in Washington today for the Presidential Inauguration, every cell tower and wireless link in the city had been enormously overwhelmed. *You've tried enough times. No one can fault you for taking control.*

Chew allowed his hand to slide off the telephone receiver. He would make no more calls. He glanced at the wall clock. It was 5:15 pm, Eastern Standard Time, which meant that hijacked Flight 3 — if it were still airborne and hadn't gone down at sea — had nearly two hours of fuel onboard. That was the latest revised fuel endurance figure that had come from the airline. Chew understood this was based on the possibility that this hijacker had gone to some extreme operational techniques — low speed at high altitude — to make it happen. If the hijacker hadn't, then they'd be out of fuel much sooner.

Chew sat back in his chair. He knew that he had to be dead-on or his career would be over. Everything was making sense and he knew that the bases had been covered, but something was bothering him — something that he couldn't put his finger on. Those calls from the airline president, Brandon Kyle, had all but assured him that they had absolutely no choice: that the retired pilot who had hijacked their airliner had a long and easily documented history that led up to his actions today. The criteria for a high degree of probability had been more than satisfied and Chew was confident that either of his bosses in the

259

TSA would be doing exactly the same thing as far as this threat to national security was concerned. Instead of attempting to call his bosses again, Chew reach for the telephone and dialed the number of the TSA's military advisor.

"Ollie, this is Steven. What's the radar status?" he asked.

"The same. No contact yet," Rear Admiral Oliver Starke replied. "Even with the airline's new fuel exhaustion figures, I'm wondering if he's not already down."

"Certainly could be," Chew answered. "But the airline president, a man named Brandon Kyle, tells me that his people are certain that this airline pilot/hijacker would be clever enough to do these sorts of things."

"Maybe." Starke paused, then added, "If he's trying to be clever, then he doesn't know much about the military. We're certainly not going to alter our operational and defensive posture based on some airline's guess about fuel exhaustion."

"Understand." Chew paused, then added, "I agree."

"That false Internet message about being at 1,000 feet on one engine so he'll be able to sneak past us by flying high is plain stupidity. As I said before," Starke continued, "our radar wall will locate him no matter what his altitude or course line might be. Guaranteed."

"Makes me wonder where he could be," Chew said, "since the radar hasn't found him yet."

"Either already in the drink," Starke answered, "which is becoming more likely with every passing minute, or this latest flight profile is the real one. Based on this last data from the airline, and considering an ultimate fuel exhaustion time of a few minutes after 7:00 pm, that means that he's still a hundred or more miles outside our coastal radar wall. If that's the case, he'll show up on the radar screens within the next 20 minutes."

"Fine." Chew glanced out the window. It was past sunset time in Washington, which meant that the sky would be barely light enough for visual operations for the next half hour. After that, the hunt for this terrorist-controlled airliner would become a nighttime operation, which had its own set of parameters and difficulties. "How long after fuel exhaustion time will you maintain the air patrols?"

"At least two hours," Starke answered. "We'll have a good number of alert-status aircraft ready for an immediate launch for a good while after that."

"That'll cover it."

"Absolutely." Starke then added, "I'll let you know immediately when we spot the hijacked airliner on radar."

"Okay." Chew sat in silence for a moment, then finally asked, "Ollie, what's your gut feeling on this?" Normally, he wouldn't phrase an open-ended question like that to a high ranking military officer, but something was bothering Chew about this operation, he couldn't put his finger on it. Also, Chew felt that he knew Starke well enough to ask since the two of them had gone to dinner together several times.

"They're already down. That's why we haven't seen or heard from them," Starke replied. "If they're not, then I know for certain what will happen next. In the neighborhood of 30 minutes after that first radar contact, they'll be in the ocean."

Chapter Twenty-Seven

The damn fuel figures for Trans-Continental Flight 3 were correct, and George sure as hell knew it. He had gone over every single line on the paperwork countless times, and there was absolutely nothing out of order on their flight plan and nothing out of the ordinary, for that matter. The simple fact of it was that Flight 3 would — if Ray's Internet message had been correct — run out of fuel far, far short of any land mass they could reach.

George threw his pencil down on the stack of computer paperwork on his desk and sat back in his chair. There was no doubt in his mind that Ray would have realized what their true situation was. Even though his Internet message had said that the fuel situation was unknown, even eyeball figuring by an experienced pilot like Clarke would show that they weren't even on the playing field. It would be the equivalent of taking your car out of the garage in New York and expecting to drive all the way to Miami without getting gas. What this meant to George was that he had to be missing something. But what?

George glanced at the stack of paperwork again. Over to one side was a sheet with the names of the cockpit crew for Flight 3. Captain Jack Schofield; First Officer Peter Fenton; Second Officer Linda Erickson. George didn't know Erickson at all, he knew Fenton only slightly and mostly by his negative and uptight reputation, and he knew Jack Schofield quite well.

The thought of those trips over the years with Jack Schofield as his co-pilot made George smile. Jack had been a very good co-pilot and had, as far as George was concerned, turned into an excellent captain. He was apt to sometimes take a joke too far, and he was inclined to ignore the rules when the situation seemed like they should be ignored. But he always did a great job for the airline, kept everything safe and sound, and provided lots of operational margins whenever…

"Damn!" The thought hit George all at once. He grabbed for the top page of the Trans-Atlantic flight plan for Flight 3 and scanned the column of figures until he saw the one he was looking for: *Extra Fuel.* That was the fuel they were carrying which was above and beyond the fuel that they needed to satisfy the rules. It was only 1,000 pounds today, which translated into hardly more than ten minutes of flight time beyond the normal contingencies.

There was no way in hell that Jack Schofield wouldn't add extra fuel. And George knew how he would add it, too — the way that George would, or Maynard, or Ray, or any of the other guys from the old school. The mantra was loud and clear: that they'd rather be overweight for takeoff than out of fuel at landing. Naturally, this extra and unaccounted fuel was officially illegal, and George had to officially frown at it. It was one of those infractions of their ever-increasing rule book that he didn't want to know about — if the ship's captain wanted extra fuel for the wife and kids, then put it on the airplane and let's not split hairs.

But it wasn't shown on any of the paperwork since that extra weight would've restricted the available payload for these long-haul maximum weight flights. That meant some of the passengers or cargo needed to be left behind. That would raise a red flag in the operations department and there would be inquiries and potential trouble. So, if the captain really wanted extra fuel, he would tell the man fueling the airplane to add it. Jack would've done that. For sure. The fuel man pumped it onboard, the airline paid for it — but it didn't show up on any of the official weight and balance paperwork. George had done it himself, many times. They all had. But George had been stuck at this fucking desk for so damn long that he had temporarily forgotten how the real world worked. Now, he suddenly and clearly understood why Ray didn't think that the airliner was definitely going to run out of fuel – he had more onboard at departure time than any of them had thought. The question was, how much?

George reached for the computer keyboard and punched in an entry. Within seconds the information he was looking for was on the display screen: the home telephone number of the Trans-Continental station manager in Rome. George picked up his telephone and dialed the number. After an interminable wait, the telephone on the other end of the Atlantic Ocean finally began to ring.

"Allo?" came a groggy voice on the other end.

George glanced at his wall clock; it was 5:20 pm in New York, which meant that it was not far from midnight in Rome. "Aldo Valenti?"

"Si...Yes."

"This is Trans-Continental Vice President of Flight Operations George Fisher from New York. Sorry to call you at home this late, but this is an emergency."

"Si...yes...go ahead...I am listening..."

◇

Aldo Valenti, the Trans-Continental Airlines station manager at Rome, jumped out of bed, said a few brief words to his wife then rushed into the living room of his apartment. His head whirled with ideas on the best — and fastest — way to get the information that Captain Fisher said was urgently needed. For a moment, Valenti considered rushing to the airport, but the driving time alone would take nearly 30 minutes. This had to be done by the telephone, and it had to be accomplished immediately.

Valenti picked up his personal telephone directory and found the number that he needed. He placed the call and in less than a minute Valenti was speaking to the contract fueling services supervisor at Fiumicino, Giulio Cannavaro. After a hurried explanation and a brief pause, Cannavaro came back on the line with the news that he had the fueling records in his hand: Flight 3 — ship number N731TC — had been fueled with a total of 86,400 pounds of fuel earlier that day.

But that wasn't the information that Valenti was asking for — what he needed to know was the name of the man who did that fueling, and his home telephone number, because he needed to talk directly to him. As Valenti explained, what they needed to know *right now* was not how much fuel had been *added* in Rome, but how much total fuel the aircraft had onboard when it taxied from the ramp. That crucial number would be the fuel that had been added, plus whatever was remaining onboard when the aircraft landed at Rome. That was the exact total fuel figure that Captain Fisher said he absolutely needed to know, and he needed that figure to be verified by an actual witness to the fueling and not by any paperwork or calculations. That seemed like a very

264

strange request, but Valenti certainly wasn't going to argue with a Vice President.

"Well..." Cannavaro held the telephone to his ear and hesitated for a moment about giving out a telephone number because the rules were specific that no personal information was to be released, especially over the telephone. "We are not supposed to..."

"Please. For me," Valenti said.

Cannavaro knew the Trans-Continental station manager well — the man had always been generous with him and the other fueling supervisors at Christmas time — and, right now, he sounded sincere and very desperate. "Okay. Because it is your request." He scanned down his list. "The man who fueled that aircraft was Adriano Scajola. He lives in Fregene, which is not far from the airport."

"Yes...I know. What is that telephone number?" Valenti asked.

Cannavaro carefully recited the number from the personnel listing.

"*Grazie*," Valenti answered as he jotted the number down.

"Prego," Cannavaro said. He hung up.

Valenti immediately dialed the number he had been given and soon he was speaking to the wife of Adriano Scajola. She was awake, watching TV. After Valenti explained who he was and what he needed, Angela Scajola explained that Adriano was not at home — he was at a friend's apartment, playing cards. It was what he and his friends did on most every Wednesday night.

When Valenti asked for Adriano's cell phone number, she said that it would do no good because he had left his cell phone at home: the men had a rule among themselves that no cell phones were allowed at the card game. But she did know the street address of where the game was being held — would that be useful?

Valenti copied down the street address, thanked her, then hung up. He stood motionless for several seconds, not knowing what to do next. It was an even further drive from his home to Fregene, and Captain Fisher had stressed how important it was to get him this fueling information within the next fifteen minutes. In a flash, Valenti realized that what he needed was a police escort or, better yet, the police themselves.

Valenti went back to his telephone directory and found the next number that he needed. He knew that his friend Claudio Borraccia, who was an *Ispettore Superiore* of the *Polizia di Stato* would be at his desk at the airport from 4:00 pm today until midnight, since Valenti had spoken to him before he left the airport for home this afternoon. Valenti dialed the number.

In short order, Valenti was speaking with his friend Claudio Borraccia. Once the situation had been explained, Borraccia told Valenti to hold on while he contacted one of his patrol cars that he knew was in the Fregene area. One minute later, a blue and white Alfa Romeo from the *Polizia di Stato* was en route to that street address in Fregene, an address off the Via Agropoli.

Valenti made small talk with his friend while they waited for the officer to report back. It took five full minutes — it seemed like an hour to Valenti — but, finally, the patrol car officer had Adriano Scajola on the telephone connection to the police department at the airport. Valenti passed on to Borraccia the question that he needed Scajola to answer.

Valenti knew that this man was their only hope – if he could remember. Each man driving a tanker truck at the airport usually fueled up to a dozen airplanes each day, so it was possible that he might not be able to recall. As Captain Fisher had explained, the information he needed must come from an actual witness to the fueling of Flight 3, it could not come from any calculations or paperwork. That meant that it had to come from this man and this man only. Scajola was the only person in Rome who knew for certain what the actual departure fuel load for Flight 3 was.

After several exchanges back and forth, *Ispettore Superiore* Borraccia got back on the telephone with his friend Aldo Valenti. "Okay...this took additional time because I had to assure Scajola repeatedly that he was in absolutely no trouble. Until I did that, his memory was very foggy."

"Yes? And then..."

"And then he could suddenly remember quite clearly, so I will quote Scajola directly. He said that he knows exactly which aircraft you are asking about since he often gets this request for extra fuel from this particular *comandante*. He is a very nice man, always laughing, full of jokes..."

"Yes, yes...go on..."

"So, when this *comandante* asks for five thousand pounds of extra fuel, Scajola is more than happy to pump it onboard. Scajola reminds me that there is nothing in this for him, that the company is being paid for the fuel, and that he is just being nice."

"The man who did the fueling says that he put five thousand pounds additional fuel onboard Trans-Continental Flight 3?" Valenti said. He needed to immediately send an email to Fisher's Internet address with this information, and he would then back that email up with a telephone call to Fisher's cell phone number. "*Grazie,* Claudio," Valenti said. "*Molto grazie*...now, I'll hang up to..."

"Wait," Borraccia said to his friend. "Let me finish." *Ispecttore Superiore* Claudia Borraccia cleared his throat, then continued. "Scajola said that because he likes that particular *comandante* so well that he did not add just the five thousand pounds."

"No?"

"Scajola tells me that since this *comandante* is always such a friendly man and always so full of jokes, he puts an extra thousand pounds into the fuel tanks as a little gift for him. He is absolutely positive that the aircraft left the ramp at Rome with six thousand pounds more fuel than was called for on the original paperwork."

◇

It took Maynard a great deal longer than he wanted to locate the maintenance supervisor on duty at the main hangar. Finally, they located Teddy Visnoski at the hydraulic shop where he was reading the riot act to some mechanic about something the guy did or didn't do.

Finally, Maynard got Visnoski's attention long enough to explain that they needed quick transportation out to that airplane on the far ramp for publicity photos, they were running out of time and needed to get out there right now, they didn't have the time for the normal paperwork. What they needed, Maynard said, was one of their bigger aircraft for interior shots, and one that was parked as far away as possible from the glare of the big hangar floodlights. The only aircraft out there at that moment that fit that description was a Consolidated 768, ship N744TC.

"Well…" Visnoski paused for a moment while he thought things over. Normally, for any non-standard use of one of their aircraft he'd need to get the Aircraft Utilization form filled out and authorized by one of the bigshots in the maintenance office. Those were the rules. But Maynard was a legend at Trans-Continental and Visnoski knew that pissing off a legend wouldn't be the smartest thing, and he had already pissed off enough people for one day. And if he did let it go, then Maynard would owe him one. "Okay," he said, "Go ahead. Don't tell anyone you didn't fill out the forms – they'll cook my ass if you do."

Maynard smiled. "Thanks. Don't worry about it, Teddy. The only ass I ever drop into the cooker is my own."

"Yeah. I hope so." Visnoski pulled a small two-way radio out of his pocket. "I'll call the mechanic with the airstair truck. He'll be at the northwest corner of the hangar in two minutes."

"Thanks." Maynard turned and led Al and Jennifer across the crowded hangar floor and toward where the mechanic with the airstair truck would be meeting them. Everything was good so far. By the time the three of them reached the far corner of the hangar where the access door led to the outside, the mechanic with the airstair truck had pulled up. The three of them climbed in the truck's double cab, with Maynard up front with the mechanic who was driving. "Need to get inside," Maynard said to the mechanic before he could say anything. "Get us to the front entrance door of that 768, then pull back across the ramp. I'll probably need to start an engine and maybe swing the nose around…"

"Engine run? Visnoski didn't say anything about…"

"For the pictures, so we can change the background outside the cockpit window," Maynard said before the mechanic could say more. "Visnoski knows that we might need to, and I'm not even sure that we will." Maynard just kept talking while he pointed at the aircraft, which was looming up as they drove toward it on the dark ramp. "Yes, the left forward door. After we get inside, you drive to the hangar corner. I'll call you on the radio, on the company frequency, when I need you to come back to get us. Your radio working?"

"Yeah." The mechanic patted the radio set on the truck console. "On the company frequency. You can also talk to Visnoski if you want, there's a radio set in the supervisor's office."

"Good." Maynard sat silently as he watched the mechanic maneuver the truck alongside the left front of the airliner. Finally, he positioned the extended airstair ramp snugly against the aircraft's entrance door. "Okay," Maynard said, "we can open and close the airplane door ourselves. Once I get the door closed, you drive back to the hangar and wait. I should be calling you on the radio in a half hour to pick us up."

"Sure thing." This assignment had turned into a comfortable way to spend the next half hour, and maybe even more time than that. It was lots better than having Visnoski hovering over you. "Take your time," the mechanic said. "Let me know if you need anything, I'll be listening on the radio. Good luck."

"Right." The three of them scurried out of the truck cab and quickly up the airstairs. Maynard worked the external lever on the entrance door and it swung open. "Get in," he said. "To the cockpit." The three of them walked into the darkened cabin of the 768 airliner while Maynard swung the big door closed. He pushed the lever down, which shut the door tightly.

Good luck, were the mechanic's last words to them, and those words echoed in Maynard's thoughts. He walked toward the darkened cockpit, realizing how appropriate those last words from the mechanic had been. What was needed right now, for all of them, was some good luck. Hopefully, they'd be able to transfer that good luck to everybody onboard Flight 3 — if Flight 3 was in the air and not already at the bottom of the ocean.

Chapter Twenty-Eight

It did not take Maynard long to get the Consolidated 768 that was parked on the airline's maintenance ramp fully powered and operational. He slid into the captain's seat of the airliner, while Al climbed into the co-pilot's flight chair and Jennifer sat in the middle cockpit seat aft of the two pilot stations.

When Maynard flipped on the ship's electrical master switch, a good number of panel lights of various colors — red, blue, white, green, amber — appeared, along with general illumination inside the darkened cockpit. A minute after that, the auxiliary power unit in the aircraft's tail — a small turbine engine connected to a large capacity alternator — came to life.

"Okay, we're ready for engine start," Maynard announced. "I want to get us up and running on both engines and taxied to the blast fence before Teddy figures out that this is not a photo session."

"What's a blast fence?" Jennifer asked.

"Over there, you can barely see it in the darkness," Maynard answered. He gestured toward their right-front before his hands got busy with the task of getting both of the airliner's big turbojet engines running. He needed to get the airplane moving, right now.

"I know about blast fences," Al said. He turned in his flight chair to face Jennifer. "A giant set of Venetian blinds made of steel. They direct the jet blast from our engines up and out of the way, so we don't knock down everything behind us."

"Yeah." Maynard's experienced hands worked quickly as he got both of the jetliner's engines running, then the other necessary systems online. The sounds of the running engines were filling the cockpit with a steady background noise, and the power and vibration from them could be felt in the airframe. "We're going to produce a mini hurricane behind us, so we'll need a blast fence to direct that airflow up instead of straight across the airport. Don't want to blow over baggage carts and maintenance trucks."

"I understand." Jennifer took out her pad and began writing a note. After a moment, she looked at Al. "Aren't you going to miss this? I never much thought about airlines beyond trying to buy cheap tickets. This place is like its own universe. You've been living in this universe your whole life. You've got to miss it."

"Don't miss it yet," Al answered. "Haven't had a chance. Check with me in a few months."

Jennifer reached forward and laid her hand on his shoulder. "I certainly will. You can bet on it." Jennifer now knew for certain that her first assessment of Al DeWitt – honest, sincere, mature, gracious – had been dead-on accurate. It was almost a cliche` to say it, but Al was the epitome of a great guy – Jennifer could *feel* it. She let her hand slide off his shoulder and turned back to Maynard, who was beginning to push the ship's throttles forward. As he did, she could see the airplane begin to slowly move across the blacktop ramp. "Can't stop us now."

"Yes, they can." Maynard had his eyes on the airstair truck at the corner of the hangar building; if Visnoski jumped into it and sped across the ramp, he could block their exit. But Maynard didn't think he would, because he knew that ultimately Teddy really didn't give a shit. "Few more seconds," Maynard announced, mostly to himself. He steered the airliner with the captain's tiller wheel on the side console and maneuvered toward the blast fence. "Once we're on that narrow taxiway, no one in the hangar can stop us." Maynard was taxiing the jetliner more rapidly than usual, to be sure that no one in a ground vehicle would be able to get in front of them.

"Made it," Al announced as the 768 entered the short stretch of narrow pavement that led to where the blast fence had been built on a wider portion of the maintenance ramp.

"Yes." Maynard began to pull the throttles back and apply wheel braking. As he did, he felt a tingling in his arms and down both legs. *Damn it. Not now. Give me more time.* It was a sensation that he knew too well from his past; it was the same sensation that he had felt before each of his heart attacks. *Give me time. Please, God, give me time. I'm not going to turn away from this. Not now.*

Somehow, Maynard managed to get the airliner turned at the blast fence and then get the parking brake set. With the airplane stopped, he sat back in the captain's flight chair and took several deep breaths.

271

Al had been looking out the windshield to his right, along with Jennifer, as they watched to see if anyone from the hangar had followed them. They hadn't. "No one from the hangar is…" Al stopped in mid sentence because he could now see what was happening. "Maynard…are you all right? Maynard…"

Maynard was leaning back in the captain's flight chair with his eyes closed. Slowly he opened his eyes, and even more slowly he made himself sit upright again. "Give me a minute," was all he could muster the energy to say, the words coming out softly at the very tail end of a shallow breath.

"What is it?" Jennifer asked. She had one hand on the man's shoulder to steady him, the other hand against his forehead. She could feel the cold sweat pouring out of him. "A heart attack, isn't it?" she asked. "Al told me you've had heart attacks."

Maynard didn't answer; instead, he nodded slowly. He knew damn well what it was, a heart attack. Again. Christ Almighty. He knew it, and they did, too. Finally, he spoke. "Give me…a minute," he said to her. *God, please…give me more time…* Maynard was trying desperately to rally himself, but he wasn't certain if he could. Yet he had to.

"Jennifer, the oxygen mask. To his left." Al had been in many cockpits over the years. When some of the old timers knew he was onboard they'd invite him to the cockpit and would, en route, put him in the co-pilot's seat. On occasion, the captain would give a short briefing on how to use the crew oxygen mask if something happened while he was riding up front. "Put that mask against his face, then push that red lever on the panel to the constant flow position — it's labeled. I'll get someone on the radio to come out and…"

"No." Maynard grabbed the oxygen mask from Jennifer's hand, pushed it against his face and took several deep breaths. He then pulled the mask away. "No radio. We've got to run this engine test." He knew that was what he had to do. Maynard took a few more breaths from the oxygen mask, then dropped the mask in his lap. "Feeling better," he said weakly.

"You sure as hell don't look better. We shouldn't take the chance. Get you to a hospital," Al said.

"Need to do this first." Maynard managed a small smile. "I said I'd bet my life that Ray Clarke didn't hijack that flight.

Don't interfere in my bet with the gods." With that, Maynard reached forward and pushed the twin throttles of the jetliner to a high power setting — a high enough power setting to see if the fuel controllers would lock up with each other and begin the double runaway, as Ray's Internet message had said they did. He would run the test just like he planned.

The Consolidated 768 began to rock and sway as the high level of engine power attempted to push the aircraft forward in spite of its hydraulically locked wheel brakes. The aircraft didn't move, but the entire airframe was vibrating — bouncing, actually — as the thrust of the two powerful engines fought against the friction of the locked wheels laying on the pavement.

"Al, anything happens, you throttle back, then shut down these two fuel levers," Maynard said as he gestured toward the controls he wanted them to use. Maynard felt as if he could pass out at any moment. Maynard picked up the oxygen mask from his lap, took more deep breaths, then put the mask down again. His vision was beginning to darken and close in on him, as if he were looking through a continually narrowing tube. But he could see well enough to tell that there was suddenly a great deal of activity around the Trans-Continental hangar — the high power runup at the blast fence when there wasn't supposed to be a runup had gotten everyone's attention. They were coming outside and, a few of them, were cautiously moving across the ramp in their direction.

"Maynard, nothing's happening," Al said. He gestured toward the blur of cockpit gauges. None of what those instruments were saying made sense to him, yet there was no doubt that both of the engines were continuing to run flawlessly, continuously, powerfully. Anybody could tell that. "Maynard, nothing's happening — shut it down! Get you to the hospital!"

"Hell, no!" Maynard shouted as forcefully as he could. *God...please...can't hang on...much longer...let it happen...right now...*

And it did. That last thought, that final prayer, had hardly been completely formed in Maynard's mind when both engines on the 768 suddenly began to roar louder as the corrupted software inside the electronic control circuits began to pour in far too much fuel for what the powerplants had been designed for.

"Runaway!" Maynard shouted, this time loud and clear. He snapped back both of the ship's throttles, but the double runaway continued unabated. "No control! Double runaway!" At that point, the increased levels of thrust were beginning to pry the airframe loose from its locked brakes and, within seconds, the ship would have busted free and tore headlong across the ramp and directly into the massive maintenance hangar.

But Maynard was conscious and knew exactly what needed to be done. With the last ounce of strength he could muster, he grabbed both fuel control levers on the center pedestal and shut them down. The two engines immediately went from beyond full power to absolutely zero output. The airliner rocked backward one final time, then became completely still. Within seconds of engine shutdown, the airliner was sitting motionless on the ramp in front of the blast fence.

Maynard looked at the two people sitting in the cockpit beside him. "Al, call George. A double runaway…has been…confirmed…" With those last words, Maynard slowly slumped forward and fell unconscious in the captain's flight chair of the Trans-Continental Airlines Consolidated 768 jetliner.

◇

George was pacing around his office when his cell phone, which was sitting on his desk, rang. He grabbed it and answered, expecting that it would be the station manager in Rome. Instead, it was Jennifer. She had news from the ramp: the double runaway had, in fact, been confirmed. "Okay," he said, "Got it." Ray was right.

"Wait. There's more." Jennifer then told him that Maynard was unconscious with, apparently, another heart attack. She also added that Al had used the company radio to call for help and that the maintenance people were onboard the airliner giving him first aid. The ambulance was on its way.

George was momentarily stunned by that news, but he realized that there was nothing he could do about it, that Maynard was being attended to. "You and Al stay with him. Call me on my cell phone with updates."

"Will do." Jennifer hung up.

274

George took a deep breath, then sat at his computer and began to type an emergency message to be broadcast to all stations and all departments:

FROM: VICE PRESIDENT OF FLIGHT OPERATIONS
ATTENTION ALL PERSONNEL. ALL CONSOLIDATED 768 AIRCRAFT ARE GROUNDED IMMEDIATELY, WITH NO EXCEPTIONS WHATSOEVER. ANY CONSOLIDATED 768 AIRCRAFT THAT ARE CURRENTLY AIRBORNE MUST BE DIVERTED IMMEDIATELY TO THE NEAREST SUITABLE AIRPORT. ONCE ALL AIRCRAFT ARE ON THE GROUND, THEY MUST NOT — REPEAT, NOT — HAVE ANY MAINTENANCE DONE ON THEM. IN ADDITION, NO CONSOLIDATED 768 AIRCRAFT ENGINES ARE ALLOWED TO BE RUN FOR ANY REASON WHATSOEVER — IF THE AIRCRAFT MUST BE REPOSITIONED, IT MUST BE TOWED.
MORE DETAILS WILL FOLLOW AS SOON AS POSSIBLE.
SIGNED:
CAPTAIN GEORGE FISHER

Now that he had done what was necessary to protect the other passengers and crews who were flying onboard their Consolidated 768s — in theory, the double runaway wasn't a possibility until the new software update was installed, but there was no sense taking any chances — George could turn his full attention to Flight 3. He punched the computer keys to get out of that screen and to his email inbox.

There it was, a message from Aldo Valenti, the Rome station manager. George clicked on the message and it displayed on his computer screen.

TO: Captain George Fisher
FROM: Aldo Valenti, Rome Station Manager
SUBJECT: Flight 3 fuel
The man who fueled the aircraft says that he remembers the flight very well. He says that the comandante had personally requested 5,000 pounds of additional fuel be added above the flight plan paperwork, but because he is much fond of this comandante that he does, in fact, add even more fuel to make a total of 6,000

275

pounds extra fuel that is not shown on the flight paperwork. Of this the man is quite certain. Although I did not speak with him directly — the police spoke with him — all agree he seemed quite sincere and I have no doubt that Flight 3 departed Rome with 6,000 pounds extra fuel.

Will attempt to repeat this message via Trans-Atlantic telephone as soon as possible.

After reading the message, George hit the reply button on his computer and began to type:

I have received the message, understand that 6,000 pounds of extra fuel beyond the paperwork was put on Flight 3. Thank you, there is no need to telephone.

Once he hit the send key on his computer, George printed out a copy of that message and shoved it in his pocket. He thought about what his options were and which of them would be his best move. With Jack Schofield having put an additional 6,000 pounds of fuel on the airliner — that was quite a lot, but thank god that he had — George didn't need the dispatch department to help him with the fuel endurance figures.

The dispatchers had already documented that if Ray's Internet message was true, then the flight would have run the tanks dry at least 300 miles from New York. With that as the known starting point, George could easily figure the difference in his head. Since that airliner — flying at low altitude on one engine — would go a little over one hour on 6,000 pounds of fuel, and since they were probably flying at approximately 300 miles an hour, then they would have enough fuel to make it to New York. Barely. Maybe. That is, if they hadn't used too much fuel during those runaway engine episodes that Ray indicated in his Internet message. There was no way to tell for sure. The fuel situation would be really close.

George also knew that with the ship's electrical power shut down, that meant that Ray was hand-flying that airliner with absolutely no instruments beyond the emergency airspeed indicator, emergency altimeter and the basic magnetic compass. That meant that he had no way to fly in the clouds, or, for that

276

matter, to fly in heavy rain or snow where he couldn't see the ground.

George had already checked the weather along the New England coastline. The low off Nova Scotia was pumping a great deal of moisture — low clouds, rain, snow — far inland and as far west as Cape Cod and beyond. The fact of it was that the New York City area was the nearest place that had everything Ray needed: a big airport, and clear skies. Clarke had to make it to New York, or else...

George shook his head; the die had been cast, Ray was bringing that ship all the way to New York. George now knew why. Ray would either make it or he wouldn't, there was nothing that anyone on the ground could do about that. But there was something that George could do about the other problem that Flight 3 would be facing.

George had the ammunition he needed: the hard facts on the airliner's fuel situation and the confirmation of engine runaways. Now, he had to take his best shot with those facts. George's copy of the airline's emergency handbook was on the corner of his desk — he yanked it open and found the hotline number for the TSA.

George would deal with Brandon Kyle and those Puzzle Palace bastards tomorrow. For the moment, he was now confident that he now had more than enough evidence to convince everyone that a military attack on Flight 3 would be a horrible mistake.

George began to dial the TSA's emergency hotline number but, as he did, another thought flashed through his mind. It was possible that, even armed with this new information, it might be too late to stop the military attack on Flight 3. George would know in a few minutes.

<>

"Maynard, can you hear me," Al DeWitt said. He leaned over the man being strapped into the ambulance gurney which had been wheeled up from the front service door and positioned aft of the cockpit. Al and two of the airline mechanics had lifted Maynard from the captain's seat of the Consolidated 768 and carried him back to where he was now being strapped in for the ride down the hydraulic lift platform and into the waiting ambulance. "Maynard," Al repeated. "Can you hear me?"

"Yeah." Maynard opened his eyes, pushed the oxygen mask off his mouth and looked up at the people hovering over him. "Got that message to George, right?"

"Sure as hell did," Al said. "Now, we're going to take care of you. Get you to the hospital."

"Don't want you to come," Maynard answered in a low voice. The two medical technicians were finishing strapping him in and he would be moving toward the service door and the ambulance in a few seconds. Maynard glanced slightly to his left. "Just the pretty lady here, she can keep me company," Maynard said as he took hold of Jennifer's hand. "Not you, Al. Need you to stay. You're our witness to the engine runaways. Might be necessary. Might need a real witness, just in case..." Maynard's words trailed off and he closed his eyes again.

"Okay, we're moving out." One of the medical technicians slid the oxygen mask back onto Maynard's face as the other began to push the gurney toward the service door and the hydraulic platform that was positioned outside.

"Jennifer, he could be right," Al said. "Having a witness to the double engine runaway might become important. You go with Maynard, I'll stay here and call George."

"Okay. I'll get back to you with details. I've got your cell phone number." Jennifer followed the gurney out to the platform and rode down with it.

Al watched from the airliner's open service door as they got into the ambulance and the doors were shut. It sped across the expansive ramp with lights and siren on, then quickly disappeared around the corner of the hangar. Al took out his cell phone and dialed George's number, which was answered on the first ring.

After reporting that Maynard had been put into the ambulance and was en route to the hospital, Al told George that he had stayed behind to be a witness to the double engine runaway if it was necessary – it had been Maynard's idea. That's why Al was still at the hangar.

"A good idea," George said. "Although maybe we won't need it. The TSA emergency operator took the information from me without any problems, or at least that's how it seemed."

"What information did you give them?"

"That the Internet message that we got at dispatch has been positively validated and that Flight 3 might – just might – have enough fuel to reach New York. The operator said that he'd immediately pass that information on to the man who was making the final decisions on Flight 3. Hopefully, that's enough. But it's still good that I've got you here to back me up, you know how government agencies are, they might call me back."

"Can the TSA stop the military attack in time?"

"I have no idea." George said. "All we can do is hope and pray." He paused, then added, "Since having you available as a witness to the double engine runaway might become a player, keep your cell line open. But what I need you to do right now is to get over to the International Arrivals area. They tell me that there's some level of panic going on in the area of our service desk."

"Panic?"

"Yes. The people who are waiting for the passengers. Someone's managed to convince them that Flight 3 had already gone down at sea. I need you to handle that."

"I'll do my best." Al hung up his cell phone, ran down the portable stairs that had been pushed up to the airplane, and sprinted over to where Teddy Visnoski was standing with a gang of the mechanics from the hangar. "Ted, have someone get me to the terminal building, George Fisher's orders. Real trouble going on over there."

"Shit, there's real trouble everywhere," Visnoski said. He pointed toward a maintenance truck in the distance and the two men began walking briskly toward it. "I just got this ALL-STATIONS emergency message from Fisher that grounds all the 768's. What the hell's going on tonight, anyway?" Visnoski gestured for Al to get into the truck while he issued orders to the driver. "Good luck," Visnoski shouted as the truck lurched away from the ramp and sped onto a dark service road that would lead to the International Arrivals building.

"This is one hell of a night, huh?" the mechanic driving the truck said as he steered down the winding service road.

"You're telling me. And I don't even work here any more."

"What?!"

"Forget it." Al pulled out his new watch and glanced at it. Based on the fragmented information that they had, all this would be coming to an end in less than an hour. Al was thinking about the possibilities of what he might say to a group of hysterical friends and relatives when the maintenance truck jolted to a halt at the entrance to the Trans-Continental service desk at the International Arrivals Building. Al jumped out and ran into the building.

There was a big mob surrounding the service counter, and people were pushing and shoving and screaming and crying. There were a few airport policemen on the scene, but they were standing to the side, not knowing quite what to do.

There must have been 50 or 60 people in the crowd, and their focus was on the people at or near the airline service desk. One man, in particular, had gotten onto a baggage scale and was addressing the crowd, apparently stirring them up even more. Al went directly toward him. "Sir! Sir!" Al shouted loudly, his voice carrying over the man's shouts. "Listen to me, I'm from the airline! I've come from the Operations Center! I've got news for you – an update!" Al didn't know where he was going with this, but he knew that he had to do something. Clearly, the three airline employees behind the counter – one young man and two young women – were way over their heads in this situation.

"You could stop this fucking lying to us!" the man shouted as he turned away from the employees at the service counter and toward Al. "That's all your goddamn people have done for the past two hours, and now we know better!"

"Calm down, Sir. I've got the information," Al said in loud but measured voice that carried over the crowd.

"The flight has already gone down, hasn't it! Gone down in the ocean!" The man's face was a cross between anger and anguish.

"No," Al answered firmly. "Absolutely not."

"Then where the hell are they? Why are they so late? Why doesn't anyone know *anything*, for chrissake!"

"Because there has been a problem, but it's just about over." Instantly, Al regretted his choice of words – *over* was not a good selection – so he quickly added, "Flight 3 is expected to be here shortly."

"Bullshit. I'm a pilot and I know that there's something bad going on out there."

"What airline are you with?" Al asked. He needed to divert the man's attention and, more importantly, to calm the entire situation down.

The man paused. "None," he finally answered. "A private pilot. But I know how this shit works. None of the communications are working. None of the inflight telephones are working because my father *always* calls when they're two hours out! Why hasn't he called?"

"Okay, let me explain." Al took a few steps forward and stepped onto the baggage scale beside the man so he could address the assembled crowd more easily. Everyone in the group quieted down. "You're correct in that the flight has had a problem. But it's a manageable problem. Even in our operations center we had difficulty learning the details because it had affected inflight communications. But we now have the information."

"Why are they so late?" someone else from the crowd asked. "They should have been here almost two hours ago! That's what the arrivals board said!" There was a rising murmur from the crowd.

Al raised his hands and the crowd fell silent again. "Okay, here's what we know. The flight had a problem with one of their engines over the Atlantic, and they had to shut it down." There was a hushed undertone at that announcement, but it quickly petered out as they focused again on the man speaking to them. "The flight is going much slower now because of that engine problem. It's too complicated to explain, but the same problem also affected their ability to communicate, so that's why there have been so few updates."

"Is everyone onboard safe?" a woman in the back asked.

"Absolutely," Al answered. "All that has happened to Flight 3 is that it's late because of an engine problem and there are no telephones available for the passengers to use. Matter of fact, the pilots have only been able to communicate to us periodically. We need to be patient a little longer."

"When will they land?" a man to the side asked.

"45 minutes," Al answered as he looked directly at the man. "Forty-five more minutes," he repeated. Al DeWitt, as was his nature, was being as honest as he possibly could. To the best of his calculations and by what he had been previously told by George and the others in the dispatch office, the Trans-Continental Flight 3 saga would terminate within the next 45 minutes. It would terminate one way or the other, but there was no need to share that additional information – that the outcome for Flight 3 could be anything from very good to very bad – with the friends and relatives who were waiting. All of them would learn the end result soon enough.

◇

Clary had finished his aerial refueling from the KC-135 tanker for the third time since this combat air patrol mission had begun. As they had discussed, both he and Bellman in the other F-15C fighter would be topping off their fuel tanks as often as possible so that — if and when they were needed — they'd have a full complement of fuel. So far, there was nothing coming into their sector, which was good news. "On your left, Sonny," Clary transmitted as the two aircraft did their standard drill of resuming formation flight after refueling.

"Roger. Steady," Bellman replied.

It was dark, with a lingering hint of sunshine directly behind them in the western sky. As he got near the other aircraft in his two aircraft element, Clary nudged the flight controls of his F-15C to put himself in the lead position in their combat air patrol circuit.

This time, Bellman slid his jet into a loose trail position behind Clary's fighter without saying a word on the transmitter. They had been in their combat air patrol area for what seemed like endless hours of nothing but orbiting in the clear skies above the Atlantic Ocean. At this point in the mission, neither man had much to say to the other — each knew quite well what the other man was doing, and they also knew what the other man was thinking.

Finally, Clary spoke on their tactical frequency — mostly to break the tedium of those endless racetrack patterns they'd been assigned to fly. "Sonny, look at the time. We're supposed to pick up you and Dianne for my birthday dinner. Hope you'll be ready."

"Your memory's bad, skipper. Always ready." Bellman was glad to have this personal interlude, it was a good way to break the tension. "You're the one who's usually late." He paused, then added, "Happy birthday, Jack. Many more."

"Thanks." Clary looked down at the radar screen in front of him. There was no target showing, although he knew that the first sighting would come from the NORAD systems that were scanning far ahead of that area. NORAD would see the target first, then provide a general steer to get them started. The onboard radar in their fighters would pick up the target in the neighborhood of 100 miles. Clary was about to bank his fighter into another turn to begin another of their endless patrol patterns when his radio headset came alive.

"Shield 21 and flight, this is Homeplate."

"Homeplate, Shield 21. Go ahead," Clary answered.

"We have radar contact on the suspected target aircraft. Their bearing zero-nine-six, distance two hundred forty miles. Target's altitude is currently five thousand feet, target's speed is two hundred ninety knots. You are a go for Operation Full Shield."

Ah, shit. "Roger, Homeplate," Clary responded as he sat upright in his flight chair and began to work the flight controls of his fighter jet. "We are leaving our patrol area on a heading of zero-nine-six. Advise us when we've closed the distance to 100 miles." *Damn, damn, damn.*

"Roger, Shield 21. Will do."

"And confirm that we are a go for Operation Full Shield," Clary said. He knew that he had heard them correctly, but he wanted – no, he needed – them to say it again.

"Roger, that is correct Shield 21. You are authorized a go for Operation Full Shield. We will advise when you have closed the distance to one hundred miles."

A go for Operation Full Shield were not the words that Clary wanted to hear. He nudged the F-15C throttles to give them more speed, but that wasn't hardly the issue today. With the target flying directly toward them at nearly 300 knots and their own fighters heading east at 500 knots, it would take only 10 minutes until they had the target airliner locked on their own radar, and only another eight minutes before they intercepted them for the beginning of Operation Full Shield.

"Want to check the floods?" Bellman transmitted. He, too, was working hard at keeping his mind focused on their mission. "Need them soon enough."

"Sure thing. Hit it," Clary answered. As part of the upgrades necessary for Operation Full Shield, both fighters had been equipped with powerful floodlights on each side of their fuselage so they could illuminate the target aircraft at night, as the engagement rules required. Unless both pilots could make a positive visual identification of the target aircraft by type of aircraft and specific registration number, they could not continue with the mission. Clary could see that the floods on both sides of his aircraft were working normally. "My lights checked," he transmitted.

"Mine, too," Bellman answered. He paused, then added, "At the hundred mile mark in seven minutes."

"Right." But as much as he tried to strictly keep his mind on business and to concentrate on the radar screen in front of him and on his flight instruments, Clary couldn't get one particular phrase out of his mind — a phrase that his friend had said a few minutes ago. With the situation facing them as they hurtled through the night sky toward the hijacked airliner, that phrase had become particularly disquieting to him. *Happy birthday, Jack. Many more.* Because of him, Jack knew that the people onboard that airliner wouldn't be having any more birthdays.

Book Seven

There's a big difference between a pilot and an aviator.
One is a technician, the other is an artist.
—Elrey Borge Jeppesen

Anyone can hold the helm when the sea is calm.
—Publilius Syrus

Chapter Twenty-Nine

As the sun got lower in the western sky, Ray began to think about how he would keep the airliner upright once the sky got completely black. Their visible line of reference that he was using to keep them level would, soon enough, be disappearing into the growing darkness. Would it be a problem? Probably not, he decided – as long as he could see *something* that told him up from down. The stars would do.

Linda, sitting in Flight 3's co-pilot seat, leaned forward and looked carefully out the windshield. "We'll lose the glow on the horizon in a few minutes," she said.

"Yes." Ray shifted in the captain's flight chair. "Gotten real accustomed to that solid horizon line," Ray said. "Got spoiled," he added with a short laugh as he glanced in her direction. Ray had hoped that the moon would be somewhere above the horizon line before full darkness set in on them, but now he could see that it wouldn't be. "No moon," he announced as he scanned the darkening sky. "Hoping for one." Evidently, moon rise wouldn't occur for awhile yet. "Don't need it."

"No, we don't. A clear sky above. All the way to New York," Linda said as she gestured in the direction the airliner was flying. "Good cap of stars. That's enough."

"Right," Ray said. He sure as hell hoped so. To be on the safe side, and because there were no clouds to be dealt with, he had allowed the airliner to drift upward for the past half hour. When they reached an altitude of 5,000 feet, Ray leveled the ship. He wanted more margin between him and the ocean surface, in case he had a problem keeping the airliner straight and level in the growing darkness. But now, with the first stars showing up, he could see that he wouldn't.

"Flashlights are checked. They work," Linda said, as she gestured toward where she had the three crew flashlights laying on the floor aft of the center console, plus a small penlight in her hand. "Everything's going fine," she said, as much to herself as to Ray. "Should see coastline lights soon." Linda noticed that the inside of the cockpit was growing darker with each passing moment; Ray had already become hardly more than a dark silhouette against the captain's side window.

Ray sat further back in his flight chair as he continued to steer the airliner on its westerly heading. "Lucky there's no overcast. If there was, in a few minutes we'd be inside an ink bottle with the cap screwed on tight." At that point, Ray heard a sound behind him. He turned.

Linda had heard the sound also. She aimed a flashlight in that direction and turned it on. "Hello," she called out when she saw that it was Lee Frankel who was entering the flight deck. She turned the flashlight off. "What can we do for you, Doctor?"

"Need to chat with Ray a few minutes," Lee said. He stepped forward. "Could I slide into your seat so he wouldn't have to turn around?"

"Absolutely. I could use a minute to stretch my legs, use the bathroom, get a glass of water." Linda turned to Ray. "Okay with you?"

"Sure," Ray answered with a wave of his free hand.

Lee stepped backward to give her room to get out of the co-pilot's seat. As she brushed by him in the darkness, he leaned over and whispered to her, "Give me ten minutes before you return. Need to talk to him. Privately."

Linda was surprised, but she didn't express it. Instead, she announced in a louder voice, "Ray, if you don't mind I'll take a few extra minutes to stretch. I'm really stiff from sitting so long."

"Suit yourself."

"Be sure to lock the cockpit door when you leave," Lee said. "Don't let Peter up here when you come back, no matter what he says."

"Really? Is he acting...crazy again?" Linda asked.

"Let's not take chances." Lee turned to Ray. "You agree, Captain?"

"Got his gun put away, but I don't need the distraction. I agree."

"See you soon," Linda said. She opened the cockpit door slightly, let herself out, then locked it again.

Lee maneuvered slowly in the dark cockpit and carefully slid into the empty co-pilot's seat. The cockpit was almost pitch-black so he couldn't make out many of the details. But it was obvious that being up here was a totally different experience than riding in the cabin. "Quite a view you've got."

"Never been in a cockpit before?" Ray asked.

"Not in flight."

"A different world."

"Obviously." Lee paused for a moment, then said, "Need to tell you about Peter. He's causing trouble in the cabin. I should've given him more sedative when I could, but I had no idea that he'd stayed so wrapped up in those delusions. He's telling everyone that you're going to crash us into the buildings of Manhattan."

"Did he mention which buildings?" Ray asked. "So that I'd know."

Lee laughed. "Good to see you're keeping a sense of humor. A good sign." Lee knew that as a mental barometer, keeping a sense of humor was a fabulous sign. "I came up to talk about two things. First is Peter Fenton."

"Figured that." Ray glanced at him in the dark cockpit. "Go ahead."

Lee said that Peter was absolutely certain that both he and Jack had been shot by Ray during a struggle to get control of the ship away from the flight crew. Peter was, Lee continued, causing problems in the cabin by telling that story to anyone who'll listen.

"Hope you're defending me," Ray said.

"I'm telling everybody that Peter is in a state of shock and suffering from delusions. I'm reminding them that I'm a doctor, so I'm not taking a wild-ass guess here."

"And?"

"And some of them are buying it, some of them are not. That's to be expected."

"Why?"

"Because their scared. Beyond scared. Peter is letting all sorts of boogeymen out of the closet, at least for those who are susceptible to that sort of suggestion."

"For chrissake, keep him out of the cockpit, okay? I don't need another struggle with him."

"We will. You keep the door locked."

"Absolutely." Ray paused, then said, "All right, that takes care of panicked Peter, we'll keep him out of here. What was the second thing you wanted to talk about?"

"Your late wife Katie."

Ray turned toward him. "Don't want to hear it," he said abruptly. There was sudden anger in his voice. "Tina put you up to this, right?"

"Of course it was Tina who told me. She told me about your history. She explained to me about your guilt."

"Forget about it. None of that has any bearing on our situation. Go back to the cabin."

"It has plenty of bearing. I don't need you being pulled in different directions at this point. Not just for me, either. There's two hundred-plus people here who don't need you to have any distractions." Lee was keeping his voice as steady, even-tempered and authoritative as he could. "What we need – every damn one of us – is *you*. You at your absolute best. We need you with no guilt, no hang-ups, no problems. We need you totally focused on what's to come, and no distractions about what might have happened in the past. It's possible that the memory of Katie could be as distracting to you as having Peter standing right here, right now."

"You have your goddamn nerve. You don't know a damn thing about me. Tina has her nerve, too." Ray was surprised at how much anger he felt, even though he knew that he also felt great admiration for this doctor for what he'd done for them so far. But that was beside the point.

"Tina loves you and cares for you. You know that as well as I do." Lee also knew that he needed to watch his words very carefully, to keep this discussion strictly professional. More than ever. "The rest of us need you," Lee said. He then added, "Immensely. We're going to die if you are not at the absolute top of your game. Hell, even then, we might die anyway. You know that and I know that. I'm trying to add extra insurance, to improve our odds."

Ray continued to steer the airliner westward into the darkening night sky while he thought over what the doctor had said. He took a deep breath, then said, "Okay, I'm not going to mince words. I appreciate your concern, but I can assure you that I am at the very top of my game, whatever in God's name that might mean. Remember that I retired from this fucked-up job nearly two years ago, so I sure as hell might be rusty. But I'm doing the best I can, and – unlike what Peter thinks – I won't purposely try to kill you." Ray paused, then added, "I didn't ask for any of this."

Lee allowed a long and heavy silence to fill the cockpit before he spoke again. When he did begin to speak, his words came out clearly, distinctly, slowly. "Ray, it doesn't matter what we expect from life, but rather what life expects from us." Lee stopped again, this time to allow those words – those quoted words – to sink in. He then added, "Have you ever heard of the word *atonement*?"

"Yes. Some kind of religious thing."

"Sort of." Lee glanced out at the night sky in front of the airliner, then back to the dark outline of the man sitting to his left. The man who they needed so desperately and so completely. "Even though every one agrees that your wife's unfortunate death was not your fault in any way, if you have some psychological need to burden yourself with that guilt you can wipe the slate clean with an act of atonement. It's a way of making up for a particular deficit by putting something extremely positive into the ledger. It's a concept that goes back to the beginning of human thought."

"Don't follow you."

"If you think that your lack of pilot skills, insight and judgment caused your wife's death – which no one except you seems to believe – then you can balance that out by using those same skills, insights and judgments to save the rest of us." Lee rose up from the co-pilot's flight chair and stepped toward the cockpit door. "We're asking you to do that for us, if you would." He paused again. "Please," he added. With that, Lee stepped toward the cockpit door, opened it and walked into the cabin.

Ray heard the cockpit door close behind him. For the next few minutes he fiddled with the flight controls, then the engine's throttle, making tiny and unnecessary adjustments while his mind stayed basically numbed. He had been overwhelmed by the doctor's words, and by one word in particular: *Atonement.*

290

The background noise from the slipstream moving steadily past the nose section of the airliner filled the cockpit with an undertone of deep silence. Ray hadn't heard Linda coming back into the cockpit and didn't realize she was there until she was sliding into the co-pilot's seat.

"How's everything," she asked.

"Going fine." Ray cleared his throat, then took a sip of water from the bottle beside him. "How's the cabin?" he asked.

"Dark."

"Quiet?"

"Yes. That, too."

"No trouble?"

"None that I saw."

"Good."

"Right." Linda waited a few moments, then added, "Ray, tell me something."

"Sure. What?"

"It's something I've been wondering about. Stuff that Jack told me. Now that we've got time before we see the shoreline, tell me about your wife," Linda said. She continued to look in his direction, even though she could no longer see him clearly in the darkness of the cockpit. It was what the doctor had told her to ask Ray about.

"I…" For a moment, Ray was at a loss for the right words to answer her. He knew goddamn well that the doctor had put her up to this, and he was going to tell her that she should let the doctor do his own dirty work. Ray glanced in her direction, but instead of saying something, he turned away and looked out the windshield again. Finally, he spoke. "That's not something I want to talk about."

Linda reached across the center pedestal between them and touched her hand against his arm. She also knew, as the doctor had said, that the truth of the matter was that they had become so incredibly dependent on Ray. Without a doubt, if it wasn't for him they would be dead already. That, plus the other things the doctor had said to her on her way back to the cockpit. "You owe me something for not shooting you earlier," Linda said in a light, chatty tone. "If you remember, you were asking for it. I was seriously considering it."

"That so?" Ray answered. "You were so damn certain that shutting down the left engine was such a bad move?"

"No. I was going to put in for captain's pay for this portion of the flight, but now, with you in that seat, I can't." Linda smiled at him, even though she knew that he couldn't see her. "So, let's chat about something other than this airplane and this screwed-up flight." Linda paused, then added again, softly. "Tell me about your wife." Now, she had done everything she could, everything the doctor had suggested. The ball was, as they say, now in Ray's court.

Ray sat silently in the darkness for a full minute as he continued to steer the airliner. His initial reaction was to tell her to go to hell. His second reaction was to clam up. For reasons unknown to him, he chose instead a third option: he began to speak. "Katie...was a wonderful wife. We had a great life together. We were married for seven years. She was..." Ray paused, then added, "38 when she died.

"How long ago was that?"

"Four years this coming summer."

"Almost four years ago? That's a long time."

"It seems like yesterday."

"I understand," Linda answered. "Okay, then, tell me more about her — tell me more about Katie." Linda had purposely used her name as she gently pushed Ray to get more out of him.

"Well, I don't know..." Ray answered, his voice trailing off.

"Sure you do."

"Well..." Ray sat silently while a bevy of conflicting thoughts and emotions raced through him. Finally, one word began to dominate more than any of the others: *atonement*. And then there was that other thing that the doctor had said to him, that it didn't really matter what we expected from life, but rather what life expected from us. *Life expected from us*. That, in particular, had struck a chord. "Okay, maybe you're right." He glanced at Linda in the darkness. He could barely see the outline of her head against the co-pilot's side window. "I'll tell you more. But only if you promise not to shoot me."

"Okay. A deal."

There was a silence for another minute while Ray fiddled with the ship's only working throttle, making a very small adjustment. Finally, with nothing left for him to do, Ray began to talk. "Katie and I shared lots of things," he said. He felt awkward talking about Katie because he really hadn't these past years, but maybe, he felt, now was a good time, the right time. Hell, it might be the last chance he would get. "We flew trips together all over the world. We had lots of fun. We both loved those long walks we took in Paris, Munich, London. Rome, too. We saw lots of stuff that we both got a big kick out of, lots of history, lots of life…"

Ray's words trailed off at the end. He paused, cleared his throat, then began speaking again in the darkness of the cockpit. "We loved to talk about almost anything. Right from the beginning, our minds sort of clicked. Lots of times Katie could start a sentence and I could finish it, or vice-versa. You know what I mean."

"Yes, I know what you mean," Linda said. It was the first words she had spoken since Ray began saying those things that Linda could tell had not been said to very many people — perhaps to no one. Perhaps not even to himself, at least for a long while.

"We decided to try all sorts of things that we might enjoy together," Ray continued. "We took up snow skiing and tennis. We even tried some golf, although neither one of us thought much of that. Eventually, she got me to ride horses, and I got her to fly airplanes." Ray paused, then, after a few additional moments of silence, he added, "That part turned out to be a big mistake. A big mistake."

"Lots of things are mistakes in hindsight. Horses can be pretty dangerous." Linda had ignored the obvious reference he had made to airplanes. "Did you ever get bucked off?" she asked.

Her question took Ray back for a moment, but then he answered it. "I came off once. But not because of any bucking — a stupid maneuver on my part. It wasn't the horse's fault."

"Did you get right back on?" Linda asked.

"Yes."

"That would've been my guess," Linda added. "I can't imagine that you'd let an unscheduled dismount keep you on the ground very long."

"Well, I had a damn good reason for getting back on that horse when I came off. Katie and I were out trail riding and it would have been a *very* long walk back to the stable." Ray laughed openly and sincerely. "A very long walk," he repeated.

Linda reached across the center pedestal in the darkness. She found Ray's right arm and wrapped her fingers around it. "Ray, it's good to hear you laugh like that," Linda said softly. "I think you've got to do it more often."

Ray could feel her fingers pressing against his arm, holding onto him. Finally, he cleared his throat again and then said, "Does that mean you're serious about not shooting me? You've got that gun beside you."

"I've let that opportunity go." Linda slowly allowed her fingers to slide off his arm. She then sat further back in the co-pilot's flight chair and glanced out her side window at the stars above. After a full minute of watching the stars, Linda turned back to the silhouette of Ray sitting in the captain's seat. "So, here's a plan for us. Let's get this aerial tub to New York so we can get off and get a stiff drink. I think we'll deserve one."

"I think we'll deserve more than one," Ray answered. He glanced through the windshield and into the starlit sky ahead of them. He could see nothing but darkness where the horizon line had been earlier, but now he could also clearly see the canopy of stars above them spreading out in all directions. The glow from those stars would easily enable him to keep the airliner upright. In a manner of speaking, that canopy of stars would be their guidance from this point on, the guiding stars that would lead them to New York.

"Okay, then it's agreed. We'll have more than one drink when we get there," Linda said.

"Right. Two drinks is the absolute minimum, and, so far, we haven't come up with a maximum," Ray answered.

"We'll figure that out. When we get there."

"Yes. When we get there." Ray grabbed the airliner's control wheel with both hands. "Linda, shine a light on the compass," he said. "Use the small flashlight or cup your hand over the bulb on the bigger ones so I don't lose my night vision."

"Okay."

With the small flashlight shining directly on the compass and with the sky full of stars above them, he made a slight adjustment to the course line they were flying and then steadied the aircraft again. "New York, here we come," Ray announced with authority. He wanted Linda to hear those words from him — and he also wanted to hear those words himself.

◇

It was the growing darkness in the cabin that had affected them all. With Peter Fenton carrying on about how he was certain that Ray Clarke was a hijacking terrorist, the fear level among the passengers continued to rise, at least among a good portion of them. Lee had walked up and down the aisles attempting to keep everyone calm, and at first his strategy had worked well enough. He had explained to those who had specifically asked that Peter was still suffering from shock and that his memory nor his thoughts were clear. What he was saying was not to be believed.

"There's a great deal of grumbling back there," Tina said. She pointed down the aisle, to the rear of the coach cabin, although you couldn't see much in the darkness except the sweeping lines of beams of light coming from a few flashlights.

"I know." Lee nodded. "I heard it when I was back there. Some big guy named Nickerson or something like that has become a ring leader and a mouthpiece for Peter. I tried to talk to him, too, but that was impossible — he keeps shouting about the things Peter is telling him, that the only reason the electricity is off is so that no one can find us on radar and then Clarke can sneak into New York and ram the airliner into a building."

"What does our airplane's electricity have to do with the ground radar seeing us?" Tina asked.

"Who knows? Probably nothing." Lee glanced around him where he could make out the shadowy figures of some of the passengers in this section; there had been a few comments in the first class cabin when the passengers wanted to know how come the cockpit door had remained locked shut and Peter – the airliner's First Officer — hadn't been able to get back to the cockpit. "Ray was right when he said that the cockpit door needed to stay locked. I'm glad you had the foresight to take Peter's cockpit key out of his pocket while he was unconscious. There's no telling what sort of havoc Peter could have unleashed had he gotten access to the cockpit."

295

"Maybe you should try to give him more of the sedative to quiet him down. I think there's some left."

"That only works in Hollywood," Lee answered. "You know, when they run up and stick a guy with a needle and he falls down. I have enough trouble doing it properly when my patients want me to inject them."

"Oh." Tina stood silently for a moment, then said, "How did it go in the cockpit? How did Ray take your..." She looked for the proper word. "Input."

"Better than I expected. Like I said, it seems to be a problem of guilt. It's possible that he can pull himself out of it. He's a strong man, and certainly smart enough," Lee said. "This nightmare we've been trapped in," he continued, "could become a cathartic experience, if he finds the inner strength to take advantage of that opportunity."

"Cathartic. I don't know what that means," Tina replied.

"A spiritual renewal, a release of tension. Basically, he'll feel better about himself."

"Not so guilty?"

"Right." Lee was walking a thin line. He had an obligation to be as honest as possible with her, but also without saying anything that could be misleading or be misconstrued. "From the little time we've spent together, I had the feeling that Ray might be ready to move on. To finally put those old traumatic events aside. Mind you, this is just a feeling I had, based on very little evidence. More of an intuition that anything else."

"That's not the feeling that I got," Tina said.

"Ray might right be ready to move on, to move further away from his past. But he's not ready to move backward – that's going to take lots longer. If ever." Lee stopped for a brief moment, then added, "Tina, you represent the past to him. You will for quite some time." In the dim light from the flashlight behind them, he watched her eyes closely. In her eyes Lee could see what he was looking for. He could see that she was accepting it, that she was a strong person, that she was beginning to understand. Now there was no reason – professional or personal – for Lee to avoid saying the other thing on his mind. "I can see why you liked him so much." He stopped for a moment, then added softly, "I can see why you loved him so much."

"Yes, I loved him. I still have a great deal of love for him."

Lee heard the slight shift of her words. "There's a difference between having love for a person as compared to actually being in love with them. I'm sure you know that."

"I'm beginning to figure it out," Tina said. "I can see that you understand it completely. That's good."

"No, that's wrong." Lee reached up and laid his fingers gently against the side of Tina's face. "I understand the words involved. The emotion itself is as much a mystery to me as it probably seems to you."

Tina carefully placed her own hand on top of Lee's "Is this love mystery a good or bad thing?" she asked.

"Everyone gets to pick that category for themselves. By definition, it's in the eye of the beholder."

"I see." Tina allowed her hand to drop away, and so did Lee. She turned and looked around the darkened cabin again, where the light from a few scattered flashlights were playing up and down the aisles and across the faces of the people in their seats. "Everyone seems to be reasonably quiet for the moment, but I guess it doesn't matter what they think. With the door locked, Ray and Linda won't have to deal with them."

"I'm not so sure," Lee said with a frown.

"Really? Why?"

"Because of the electrical situation and the time of the day," Lee answered.

"I don't follow you," Tina said. She was standing close to him again and she now had her arm wrapped around his arm.

"Remember what happened when we were flying through the clouds and rain, barely above the wave tops?" Lee asked.

"Yes, I do. When we finally broke into the sunshine, everybody started cheering and even laughing."

"As I told you then, it's a very normal human response to associate sunshine with life, with hope." Lee pointed around the cabin, which had become a black tube with those few scattered spots of light from the flashlights being used here and there. "I imagine that you can guess what this sudden slide into darkness does to most people."

"Oh."

"Right. The opposite effect of the sunshine, it inspires doom and gloom. We've got Peter and his cohorts fueling that fire of despair," Lee said. "I'll be amazed if we don't have a major confrontation soon."

"What could they do?"

"A big enough gang of them? They could kick the cockpit door down and put Peter back in charge. He's made the promise that they subconsciously want to hear — that he'll turn the electricity back on. Lights again. He also promises that he'll call for help on the radio, something that he says Ray won't do because he's hijacked us and is intent on a mass suicide — just like 9/11. The image of that New York holocaust — which everyone onboard, hell, everyone in the world, has etched into their minds quite deeply — could easily take them over the top."

And just then, it began. Leading a march up the aisle from the rear galley was Peter Fenton, with the man named Nickerson beside him and a growing number of other people — mostly men, but some women in the group also — coming along. Several of them had flashlights, and many of the others had makeshift weapons in their hands.

Lee could see them coming forward from the movement of the flashlights. "Come with me," Lee said as he turned Tina around. He led her back several feet to the first class galley, which was only a few feet aft of the locked cockpit door. "Get into the galley," he said. "Try to protect Schofield." Lee gently nudged her in the direction of where the unconscious captain lay on the galley floor, as far into the galley area as they had been able to get him. The injured captain had opened his eyes a few times in the past half hour and had mumbled some unintelligible words, but Lee had the feeling that, while he was on the road to recovery, that the captain was light years from being able to actually function.

Tina moved into the galley as instructed, then asked, "What are you going to do."

"The only thing I know how to do," Lee said. "Talk to them. I sure as hell can't overpower them with muscle, so maybe I can do it with words."

"Good luck," Tina said as she knelt beside the unconscious captain to check on him. She turned her flashlight on for a moment, then turned it back off. "Good luck to all of us."

"You can say that again." Lee was standing with his back to the cockpit door, a few feet in front of it. He tried to appear as calm as he could, as if he were in his office dealing with this situation instead of inside of a crippled airliner flying low over the Atlantic Ocean in the darkness.

"Doctor, unlock that cockpit door," Nickerson said in a deep, forceful voice. Fenton, standing beside him, nodded in agreement. Several of the people behind them had flashlights, and they were shining them at Nickerson, at Fenton, at Lee, and on the locked cockpit door, so the scene at the cockpit door was easily visible to everyone.

"It's locked from the inside," Lee lied. He was playing for time, trying to think of some weakness to exploit or some counterpoint to erect. "The pilots up front cannot be disturbed. Everything is going well, and we will land in New York in forty minutes." Lee spoke slowly, carefully, but very confidently. When he finished, he could hear a murmur among them; it was, from what he could tell, the indication of some discord in the group. It was possible that the majority of them could be dissuaded, if only he could think of some way...

"He's going to get us to New York, all right! Then he's going to kill us!" Peter shouted. While he was carefully nursing his arm and shoulder, he had apparently regained much of his strength.

Lee raised both of his arms in a gesture calling for the crowd's attention. "Listen to me, all of you," he said in a loud voice as the beams of light played around and across his face. "I don't have the time or the knowledge – hell, I'm a doctor, not a pilot – to go through the technical reasons, but the airplane needs to stay dark until we land in order to save your lives, not to harm you."

"No, it's an excuse!" Peter shouted. In his heart, Peter knew he was right. That retired pilot had somehow engineered this nightmare for them, and this was his plan. It had to be, since that was the only explanation that made any sense to him.

"Stop," Nickerson commanded. He laid his big hand on Fenton's shoulder. "Doctor, we respect what you've done so far, but we're not going to take chances. Not with everyone's lives. The only reason that we're still talking is that this hijacking pilot has forty minutes to go before we get to New York. So, we're gonna give you a couple more minutes to talk, then we're gonna kick down that door and put this man back into the pilot's seat." Nickerson pointed at Fenton. "Do you see that uniform on him?" he said.

"Yes," Lee answered. He knew damn well where this was headed, and it was not good.

"Well, he's the designated pilot on this airplane, not the guy that's flying it right now."

"That may be true," Lee answered. "But what about the lady co-pilot, the second officer, who is up in the cockpit with the man who you are calling a hijacker?" Lee paused for effect, then asked, "What about her?"

"Don't know what I can't see," Nickerson replied. "For all I know, that other guy has killed her. Tell him to open the cockpit door and maybe we'll talk to her and maybe we'll change our minds. Maybe. That's if she's alive and she makes some sense to us."

Lee slowly nodded as if he were agreeing, but he knew that he never would. In a mob like this, there was no chance that once the cockpit door was opened that they wouldn't rip Ray out of the seat and put Peter into it. That would be, from what Ray indicated, a total disaster – and Ray's intuitions had been very accurate so far. "Okay, let's talk about what sorts of questions you'll want to ask the lady pilot."

"Well, I..." Nickerson paused. Clearly he was thinking about questions and also thinking about whether he wanted to waste any time on them. "Well, she's a designated pilot, too, but she's the *second* officer while this guy here is the *first* officer, so..."

"I see," Lee said. As he suspected, these people were reverting to officialdom, to designations, in a very real sense to the official word from the gods. They were fixated on the strict concept of designated authority figures in, apparently, a descending order of importance. They were a mob, a herd, and they were desperately seeking a *designated* leader. It was that ingrained human sense — or that ingrained human fallibility, take your pick — that made the armies of the world possible. "But what if your First Officer is not well?"

"I'm fine, dammit! I can fly this airplane fine, and after I turn the electricity on, then the autopilot can fly it!" Peter had a glazed look in his eye, but he apparently had mustered up enough strength to see this through. Getting that crazy retired pilot – a hijacker – out of the cockpit was his only concern. Dealing with hijackers was Peter's designated responsibility, he had to do his job.

"Okay, Doc, that's enough talk," Nickerson said. "We hear what you've said, but this man here, this *first* officer, seems okay to us, so you get yourself out of the way so we can get to that door. If you don't, you're not gonna like the way that I move you out of the way." Nickerson, with the beams of the flashlights still playing around him, took a half step forward.

"Wait!" Tina had pushed in beside Lee. Standing beside her, with her arms wrapped around his waist to steady him, was Captain Jack Schofield.

"What the hell is going on around here?" Jack said to the suddenly hushed crowd. The flashlights had swung over to him, his torn shirt stained with blood and his face drawn and pale, but the four gold captain's bars were riding on each shoulder. Schofield's voice was not loud, but it had a certain power, a certain *authority* to it. "Someone answer me *right now*. What the hell is going on here?"

"I..." Nickerson took a step closer. "Captain, we thought...we heard that you were out for the count. Maybe for good. We heard that the hijacker shot you."

"Baloney. It was an accident. A fucking accident. If anyone was responsible, it was this guy." Jack slowly raised one arm and pointed at Peter. "But we'll worry about that later. For now, I'm telling you people—no, I'm *ordering* you people—to get into your damn seats and strap yourselves in. There is no goddamn hijacker, the fucking engines and computers somehow screwed up. That's what happened, period. The two people in the cockpit who are flying this airplane are doing a great job, and they're doing it with my direct permission and my complete approval. I want you to sit down, strap in and get ready for the landing in New York." Jack paused, then added, "and don't listen to Peter Fenton any more."

Tina could feel that Jack was beginning to lose his strength and she was having some difficulty in holding him up. "Lee..." she whispered. "Grab him."

Without saying anything, Lee quickly moved behind Jack and helped to keep him standing straight while they waited to see what would happen next.

Nickerson blinked a few times, then turned to the crowd, the beams of light still playing off his face. "Okay, folks, the captain here is back in command. He says everything is okay and that there is no hijacking. We're going with that. Anyone don't agree, they got to deal with me." Nickerson put his hand on Peter Fenton's shoulder. "You come back and sit down next to me until the captain tells us otherwise."

Without another word, the crowd that had been intent on knocking down the cockpit door and taking over Trans-Continental Flight 3 turned themselves around and walked back to their assigned seats.

Chapter Thirty

"Shield 21, This is Homeplate. Target aircraft is one hundred miles, bearing zero-eight-seven, altitude of fifty-one-hundred feet. Target's ground speed remains constant at two hundred eighty-six knots."

"Roger, Homeplate. Standby." Clary adjusted the controls on his F-15Cs tactical radar. Within seconds of that call from Homeplate, his onboard radar picked up the airliner's display as predicted. The only way Jack could finish the job he had been sent to do was to stay totally focused on the technical aspects – that wasn't a passenger plane out there, it was strictly a target. "I have a target on my radar at that position, bearing is zero-eight-seven, distance is now ninety-seven miles."

"Roger, Shield 21. That should be the bogey we are tracking. All indications are that the target is the hijacked airliner."

"Okay, Homeplate. Shield 21 and flight are continuing with Operation Full Shield as briefed. We will call back with the positive identification protocol." Clary glanced over his right shoulder at his wingman, who was flying his F-15C slightly behind and below. "Sonny, you got him on your display?"

"That's affirmative, Jack. Good contact, numbers showing up as advertised." Bellman paused for a moment, then added, "Computer predicts intercept in seven minutes. You happy with that?"

"Maintain our closure speed, we're well within the criteria requirements." Clary wasn't in any rush to shoot down the hijacked airliner, so there was no rush in getting to the target any sooner since the mission parameters didn't require it. For the past ten minutes Jack was hoping — praying, actually — that the Trans-Continental flight crew had gotten control of that ship and Homeplate would call them to abort the current mission. Or maybe it was possible that this wasn't the right airliner.

But he knew better – it was them. Still, the real flight crew could have taken over or might do so shortly. Maybe the hijacker will come to his senses when he realizes for certain that he's been found by military fighters and that he's going to die.

He's going to die along with everyone else on board if he doesn't give up this hopeless insanity. Then, instead of shooting them down, he and Sonny would provide an escort to a safe landing. That was the birthday present Jack wanted. He wanted it more than anything that he had ever wanted in his life. Was he going to get it? It was too early to know either way, but, so far, the answer was no.

"Five minutes to intercept. How do you want to handle the pickup?" Bellman asked.

"Go a couple of miles past them, then swing into a trail position. I'll make the first positive identification on the target's left side, then slid aft. You come forward to get a positive ID on the right side. We'll transmit the hard data to Homeplate. Should take less than a couple of minutes."

"Roger, understand." Bellman paused, then added, "Four minutes to intercept."

"Roger, four minutes." Clary took a deep breath, then glanced through his canopy at the stars above them. It was a crystal clear night, and the night sky was packed with stars in every direction — there wasn't a single cloud above or below them. He knew that further to the north and especially over New England, there were heavy clouds. Clary looked at the blackness; nothing. In fact, it was impossible to tell where the sky ended and the ocean began.

"Three minutes," Bellman announced on the frequency. "Target is 40 miles. Target continues to hold steady bearing, speed and altitude."

"Roger." If this were an actual combat mission and the target ahead was an enemy fighter or bomber, they would be deep into action. In a normal combat mission, there would be an enormous amount of things happening at once. Instead, they were waiting to get alongside to do the required identification drill. If this target was Trans-Continental Airlines Flight 3, they would be released to engage the target. It would only take a minute or so to get their aircraft into the proper positions. Then, it would be a straight turkey shoot, an execution, really — and it would be Jack Clary who would be doing the shooting. He cringed.

"Two minutes," Bellman announced.

"Roger. Slow up. Don't want to go too far past." Clary worked the throttles on his F-15C, knowing that his wingman

304

was doing exactly the same to match his changes in performance. By the time the fighters had slowed to a more compatible speed for the final intercept and turn, the radar was showing that the airliner was ten miles ahead. Clary glanced up, expecting to see its lights. Nothing. He looked down at the radar, then where the airliner should be. "Sonny, no lights. Should see them by now."

"True. Maybe the hijacker's got the lights off. Maybe he thinks we can't find him that way."

"Maybe he's wrong." Clary shook his head at the idea that some hijacker thought he could sneak into America by shutting his lights off. In another couple of minutes he's going to see otherwise, and he would see it in dramatic fashion. "I think I've got a visual on an object. Eleven o'clock, two miles, slightly above us."

"Got it. Coincides with the radar position," Bellman said.

"Okay, let's get around back. Then slide up to do identifications," Clary transmitted.

"Following you, skipper."

Using the F-15C radar and some peeks out the canopy, Clary had both fighter jets into their proper positions aft of the darkened silhouette of the airliner. "Target does, in fact, have the navigation lights off," Clary said. "No strobes or beacons either."

"Don't see any cabin lights. We'll know when we pull alongside," Bellman answered. "I guess he's trying to hide."

"Guess he is." Clary paused. He took one last look at the tactical display screen on his fighter's instrument panel. They were currently 87 miles southwest of Nantucket, about 170 miles from the center of Manhattan — which everyone assumed was the hijacker's ultimate target. Clary nudged the F-15C's throttles forward. A few moments later he was in the proper formation position with the airliner: slightly above and behind the left wing of the big commercial jet. Clary could see a vague outline of the airliner against the starlight background. Satisfied that everything was going exactly as it should, he flipped on the switch for the powerful floodlight on the fighter's right side.

In an instant, the entire left side of the airliner was lit up. The floodlight from the fighter had illuminated the airliner clearly, from its forward wing root aft to its tail structure. "Homeplate, Shield 21. I have a positive identification on the target's left side. The name of Trans-Continental is painted on the fuselage as the briefing photos had indicted." Clary's heart sank. Even though there hadn't been much of a chance that this was the wrong airliner, that possibility was nearly gone. Clary allowed his eyes to move further aft, to where the aircraft's registration numbers would be painted. "Ready to copy numbers?"

"Roger, Shield 21, go ahead with the aircraft registration numbers."

"I have a positive visual identification of the following: November Seven Three One Tango Charlie," Clary transmitted. He shook his head while he waited for Homeplate to reply, although he already knew what they would be saying. *Damn, damn, damn.*

"Shield 21, this is Homeplate. We have verified that your initial identification has matched the target aircraft information. You are authorized to continue."

"Roger," Clary answered. "Sonny, sliding back," he said as he extinguished his floodlight and allowed his F-15C to back away from the darkened airliner. "Your turn."

"Here I go." Bellman made his identification run from the airliner's right side, also following the mission protocol precisely. As expected, his observations were identical to his wingman's.

"We copy your information, Shield 22. Standby," Homeplate replied after Bellman had transmitted the necessary data.

"Roger, Homeplate." Bellman paused, then transmitted, "Jack, coming back to join you." In a few moments he had positioned his fighter back to its normal wingman position. The two fighter jets were flying behind and slightly above the hijacked airliner as they continued to follow. They waited. The silence from Homeplate seemed to go on forever and Clary found himself fidgeting in the seat of his F-15C. He was trying to keep his mind a blank and, for the most part, he succeeded. Only now and then did the image of that doomed airliner push into his thoughts. It was a target, nothing but a target. Finally, he heard the tell-tale click in his headset before the transmitted words began to pour in.

"Shield 21 and flight, this is Homeplate. We have established a positive identification on the subject aircraft. I repeat, the aircraft's identification has been positively established. It has been confirmed as the hijacked aircraft. There are no radio transmissions from the subject aircraft. Subject aircraft continues to ignore our transmitted requests on all frequencies. You are released for Operation Full Shield as briefed. Authorization code is Echo-Whiskey. Report when missile is away, and report when subject aircraft has been splashed. Report precise coordinates of the target's point of impact."

Clary licked his dry lips. He knew those words from Homeplate were coming and yet, when he heard them, he could hardly believe them. Jack pressed his transmit button to answer. "Roger, Homeplate. Understand. Continuing with mission profile. Will comply. Authorization code is Delta-Delta," Clary added, using the prearranged code that would verify that the proper aircraft had been the one to respond. He slid his finger off the transmit button, then, after a few seconds, pushed it again. "Sonny, take your position. Tell me when you're ready. Commencing now, I'm drifting further in trail. As we had briefed."

"Roger, Shield 21," Bellman answered. "Shield 22 will be positioned in 30 seconds."

Clary, by slightly retarding his fighter's throttles, was allowing his F-15C to fall further behind the airliner. The target stayed rock-steady in front of him as the distance between them steadily increased. After a short while, he could no longer visually see the silhouette of that big airplane against the features of the starlit black sky and the black sea below them. He did, of course, have the target absolutely locked in with his tactical radar.

"Shield 22. In position," Bellman transmitted. Between the two of them, Sonny had the easier job of reporting the aftermath. His heart went out to his friend, who had to do something that neither of them wanted to do. Bellman had maneuvered his fighter to where he could easily follow the wreckage as it fell to the sea, and now he would wait. Wait for the explosion and the disintegration. Then he would follow the flaming wreckage down.

"Roger, Shield 22," Clary finally answered. He had paused for longer than he needed to or should have, but then he finally slid his finger back onto the transmit button. "Homeplate and copy Shield 22, this is Shield 21. Preparing for Fox Two," Clary said, using the code word for the firing of a heat-seeking missile. "I say again, Fox Two in thirty seconds."

"Roger, Shield 21. Homeplate copies Fox Two in thirty seconds."

Bellman did not answer.

Happy birthday Jack. Many more. Clary began the necessary drill for the firing sequence of one of the two AIM-9 missiles that his F-15C was carrying. He ran through it slowly, carefully, meticulously, keeping his thoughts and actions totally focused on the technical tasks in front of him, until there was only one item left to be accomplished, the one final button left to be pushed to complete Fox Two. ...*Many more...*

◇

Ray had been the first in the cockpit to spot the red navigation lights of the aircraft. They were, apparently, approaching them from the west. "Right there!" he shouted, using a free hand to point. "Two red lights," he said in a calmer voice. "They're slightly below us, I think. Hard to tell." Ray's heart was pounding, but he was working hard at keeping himself in control and his responses measured.

"Yes, I see them now!" Linda answered. Her voice, too, was excited, the words tumbling over each other. "They're moving aft. How far away?" she asked.

"Can't say. Not far. Can't be if we can see nav lights that clearly." Ray turned slightly in his flight chair. "Got to be military. Two of them. Linda, take the wheel so I can watch."

"Got it," Linda said. She concentrated on steering the airliner.

Ray twisted further in his flight chair so he could see that pair of red navigation lights as they flew past them. The lights continued beyond the airliner until he couldn't see them any more. "Disappeared." he said. "Behind us." There was disappointment in his voice, although he wasn't sure that there should be. He wasn't sure of anything.

"Did they see us?" Linda asked in a hesitant voice as she continued to steer the airliner on its westbound heading.

"Sure as hell hope so," Ray answered. "It's darker than hell out here, and we're running without a single goddamn light." He glanced at Linda in the pitch-black cockpit; he could hardly see her where she sat no more than four feet from him. It was no wonder that someone flying past could have missed them. Ray turned to his side window again. "Don't see them. Not now. Maybe I should've signaled with a flashlight."

"A flashlight wouldn't throw enough light," Linda said.

"I guess." Ray was about to take the airplane controls back from her when, suddenly, a flood of harsh white light covered the airliner's fuselage on its left side. "Look!" he shouted as he twisted around in his seat again.

"Christ!" Linda was stretching forward but all she could see was that brilliant wash of light that had been aimed at them. "What type of aircraft?"

"Can't tell. Not for certain," Ray said as he pressed against the cockpit side window. He tried to make out the aircraft type that was flooding them with a powerful broad beam light. "It's military," he said. "Got to be. A military interceptor. That's the only possibility."

"Holding a steady heading," Linda said, continuing to do what she had been.

"Yes." Ray turned around from the side window and toward Linda, who he could now see clearly because a good degree of the reflected light had gotten as far forward as the cockpit. "Got to be military. Must be inspecting us for damage. There's probably two of them out there." Ray glanced out the window for an instant, then turned to Linda. Ray's heart was pounding and he was breathing rapidly, but there was a smile on his face. "Thank God they found us."

<>

Peter Fenton was sitting at the rear of the coach cabin when a giant floodlight on the left side of the airliner suddenly illuminated. "Oh, my God!" he shouted, as he grabbed the arm of the man next to him who he knew only as Nickerson. "Look at that!"

"Yes!" Nickerson shouted with a booming voice. "They've found us!" he hollered out to everyone in the cabin.

"It's the military! The military has found us! They're gonna escort us back home!"

The emotions of everyone inside the cabin, which was flooded in that harsh white light, had gone from a palpable level of fear to an overwhelming joy in less than a heartbeat. People everywhere were yelling and screaming and jumping out of their seats and pounding on each other's shoulders and backs and hugging and laughing and crying. After less than a minute, that flood light went out — but turning it off did not extinguish the new mood in the cabin. Flight 3 had been found, and they had been saved — that was an absolute given.

Peter sat back in his chair and closed his eyes. He was as happy as any of them about the military intercept, but something else was also going on in his mind. Besides his headache, which had returned with a vengeance, he couldn't shake the memory of what Jack Schofield had said a short while earlier: that the shooting in the cockpit had been an accident, and that if any of them were responsible, it was Peter. Then he said that there was no hijacking, that it was the engines and computers that had failed.

Peter kept his eyes closed while thoughts and memories of all sorts whirled in his mind. He had been sure — absolutely, positively certain — that it had been that retired pilot who had shot at both him and the captain. He had also been absolutely sure that the retired pilot had started this by attempting to hijack the airplane. Yet the Captain had said that it was an accident, that there was no hijacking. Peter shook his head. He was beginning to remember small fragments of…something else…

Peter rubbed his fingers against his temples while he took several deep breaths. Captain Schofield had said there would be time, later, to worry about who was responsible. Peter was beginning to realize that some of the things he had been so certain of couldn't be absolutely correct, although he didn't understand why. For the first time since their nightmare over the Atlantic Ocean had begun, Peter was beginning to think, perhaps, the things that he so clearly remembered from their struggles on the flight deck were not actually the things that had happened to him, or to any of them. For some reason that he couldn't explain, his memory was jumbled and he couldn't come up with a clear picture, couldn't remember exactly what had gone on.

Lee and Tina had been sitting in two first class seats, in the darkness, when the floodlight turned on. Both of them jumped to their feet and rushed to the side windows to verify what they instantly knew: that Flight 3 had been found.

Tina wrapped her arms around Lee, buried her head into his shoulder and began to cry — tears of joy, tears of astonishment, tears of absolute relief flowing down her face.

Lee was feeling exactly the same, and he held onto her tightly while he relished that fabulous, exquisite moment. But, in another part of his mind, Lee was also seeing and hearing and feeling something else, too — he was, for the very first time, truly understanding what those concentration camp survivors had explained to him about the last days of their imprisonments and the first moments when they realized that they had, somehow, survived the most incredible ordeal imaginable.

"This is fabulous," Tina said after she finally allowed herself to step back and look up at him, although she did keep both of her hands planted firmly on his shoulders. "I didn't think I could ever feel this happy again."

"I'm glad you were wrong," Lee answered. "You haven't been wrong about much." He leaned forward and kissed her on the forehead, allowing his lips to linger against her soft skin. As he did, the floodlight on the left side of the aircraft went out. Reluctantly, Lee took a step backward. "That's to be expected. I suppose they're checking for damage, since we know that Ray can't talk to them on the radio to tell them what the problems have been."

"Right." Tina took a deep breath, then pulled Lee close to her again. She let a full minute of silence go by before she said more, letting her arms stay wrapped around his body. Finally, she looked up and spoke softly and quietly. "Now that we're getting near to New York, I realize something else."

"What?"

"I realize that our over-the-ocean marriage is almost over." She smiled, knowing that he couldn't see that smile – but hoping that maybe he could somehow feel it. "But that does raise a question. Does anyone need to file a divorce over these arrangements, or do they just end?"

"Sometimes, they just end," Lee answered after a short pause. "When the trauma does."

The two of them stood in silence for a moment, and Lee was about to say something else when an identical floodlight illuminated the right side of the airliner. "Look at that!" he said. "Isn't this great!"

"Yes. You were right about the lights, Lee. They're inspecting both sides of the ship," Tina said.

"Yes. It makes sense." Lee led Tina over to a window on the right side and they both watched that floodlight as it hovered beyond and above the airliner's wingtip. The aircraft that was carrying that powerful floodlight was absolutely invisible behind it, as if the light itself was hovering in space. After several seconds of watching that light, the two of them stepped back into the first class aisle again. A few seconds after that, the floodlight aimed at the airliner's right side went out.

The cabin was steeped in pitch darkness again — and in some ways it seemed darker now than it had been earlier because everyone's eyes had adjusted to the brilliant white light that had been flooding into the cabin for the past few minutes. Not only that, every one of them so much *wanted* to keep seeing those lights. But that was nothing but emotion; logic said that they had been found, and that they would soon be safe.

"We should be less than a half hour from New York," Tina said as she pulled Lee close to her again. "Lee, we're almost home."

"Which means that we're still over the ocean," Lee answered. *Do what you'd tell your patients to do.* "Which means that we're still married. At least for the moment."

"I guess you're right," Tina said.

"Yes, I guess I am." Lee took her head into both of his hands and gently pulled her toward him. The two of them then kissed long and hard, pulling as tight and near to each other as they could.

Chapter Thirty-One

Clary was holding the control stick of his F-15C fighter lightly in his hand, his finger poised over the final button needed to initiate the Fox Two, the firing of the AIM-9 heat-seeking missile at Trans-Continental Flight 3. Clary had the urge to close his eyes but he would not allow himself that luxury. He began to move the muscles in his right hand.

At that moment, Clary's radio headset came alive. "Shield 21, Homeplate — Abort Fox Two!"

Clary slowly and carefully slid his finger from the button while he continued to fly the F-15C. He had to take a deep breath before he could answer. Finally, he transmitted, "Homeplate, Shield 21. Understand. Fox Two aborted," he said as calmly as he could, although his hand was trembling when he had moved it away from the firing button to press the transmit button, and his voice was trembling, too. "Shield 21 wants to confirm that Fox Two has been aborted," he added, mostly because he *so much* wanted to hear those words again. They were the sweetest, finest words he had ever heard.

"That is correct," Homeplate transmitted. "Fox Two has been aborted. Authentication code is Alpha-Mike."

Clary let out another deep breath, then responded, "Roger, understand. Fox Two has been aborted." He carefully reactivated the onboard safety circuits so that the AIM-9 missiles he was carrying could not be fired inadvertently, then he transmitted, "Authentication code Golf-Yankee."

"Shield 22 also copies," Bellman transmitted from his F-15C. He, too, found that it was everything he could do to keep his voice steady. After a slight pause, Sonny added, "Happy birthday, Jack."

Clary glanced down at the radar image of the airliner in front of him, then at the sky full of stars above. He took several deep breaths, shook his head, then pressed the transmit button again. "Got what I wished for," is all he said.

"Right."

"Shield 21, this is Homeplate. We have new operational orders, ready to copy?"

"Go ahead," Clary replied.

"Operation Full Shield is on hold. Because of new information, the threat level for that aircraft has been downgraded from high likelihood to low likelihood of terrorist activities. Subject aircraft is to be provided an escort and guidance to New York JFK Airport for emergency landing on runway Four-Right. Proceed directly, the subject aircraft's fuel situation has been deemed as critical. All conflicting aircraft are being routed out of the area, and subject aircraft has been cleared to land on that runway. Approach and runway lights have been set to high. Fire and rescue crews are standing by."

"Understand, Homeplate. Will lead the aircraft directly to JFK." While he spoke, Clary pushed up his throttles and moved his fighter forward until he had a visual sighting of the airliner. Then, side-stepping slightly to the left, he took up a position above and forward of the cockpit of the airliner where he knew that the pilots would be able to see him. To make it even easier, Clary flipped on the floodlight switch so that his fighter jet was quite conspicuous against the night sky.

"Shield 21, this is Homeplate. We have additional orders, ready to copy?"

"Go ahead Homeplate," Clary said.

"Shield 21, if subject aircraft attempts to overfly JFK Airport, you are to immediately engage that aircraft and destroy it. Make every attempt to have the wreckage fall into the least populated area possible." Homeplate paused, then added, "Authentication code for the contingent Fox Two is Hotel-Uniform."

The contingent Fox Two authorization stunned Clary for a moment. Finally, he transmitted, "Shield 21. Understand the contingent Fox Two addition to the new orders. The authentication code for the contingent Fox Two is Zebra-Alpha." After thinking it over, Clary decided that Homeplate was just covering their asses and that there won't be a need for the contingent Fox Two. At least he hoped so.

"Where do you want me on the run to New York," Bellman asked after a few moments of silence between the two fighters while both men gathered their thoughts. Everything would be perfect now, if it wasn't for that contingent Fox Two. "Holding two miles in trail."

"I'll keep the lead, you hold the trail," Clary said. He glanced down at his tactical navigation screen; the end of runway 4R at JFK Airport was exactly seventy-two miles straight ahead, which, at this speed, translated into fourteen minutes. They'd keep their airspeed where it was, since that was the speed the airline pilot had selected – probably for best fuel endurance. The airliner's fuel supply, which had been calculated as critical, had to hold on for less than a quarter of an hour. What Clary had to do now was to keep everything steady and get this guy to that runway. With those things settled in his mind, he now had to take care of the next portion of his orders. "Sonny, you'll have to be ready for the contingent Fox Two from back there, won't have time to switch. Sorry."

"Understood," Bellman answered. He also felt that Homeplate was only following protocol by issuing that contingent Fox Two. Sonny pressed his transmit button again. "Jack, how in the hell am I going to find the least populated area on Long Island? It's wall to wall people until you get to Montauk Point."

"I know," Clary replied. "Pick the biggest dark area you see, it might be a park or a cemetery."

"Got a better solution, skipper," Bellman transmitted.

"What's that?" Clary asked his old friend.

"Have this guy land on four-right like he's supposed to."

◇

"Got to admit I was worried for awhile," Ray said as he continued to hand-fly the airliner from the captain's seat. Ray held his ship slightly below and behind the jet fighter that was leading them. With that aircraft's floodlights on and not aimed directly at them, it was easy to see the outline of that airplane.

"Worried? Why?" Linda asked.

"Worried about those fighters disappearing for so long. Didn't make sense to me."

"Maybe they were waiting on orders. Maybe they weren't sure where to take us," Linda said.

"Maybe." Ray shrugged; that didn't add up, but he didn't want to think about that aspect any more since he had other things on his mind. "I assume that they're taking us straight to

315

New York, but it doesn't matter which airport or which city since we don't know where the hell we are, not for sure. As long as they keep us out of the clouds, I'm going to land on the first row of runway lights I see."

"It'll be New York, if the wind forecast is any where near correct," Linda volunteered. "We've held a steady course since our position fix and the adjustment we made to our heading."

"Right." Ray paused. "Now, we've got one more decision. Need your input."

"What?"

"There's different ways to handle this approach." Ray glanced at the fighter jet; it was exactly where it needed to be. He then glanced at her outline in the darkened cockpit. "We can fly a normal altitude profile, but then we'd have to land the ship on its belly."

"Belly?" she said. "Why?"

"We have no electricity to activate the landing gear. If we turn the electric on, we might lose our engine. With no power we'd go into the drink somewhere south of whatever airport we're headed for. Drowning or freezing to death five miles from the shore isn't any better than doing the same thing at five hundred miles." Ray paused, then added, "Maybe the difference would be that they'd fish up bodies for a funeral."

"Not an appealing option," Linda said. "I imagine that the other plan would be to stay high, then put the landing gear down?"

"Yes. We need to treat this approach as if that engine — our only one — could fail at any moment, which it damn well might. I don't have to remind you about our fuel situation."

"Going to be close."

"Very." Ray stopped for a moment; he needed to go over all the possibilities, there wouldn't be time to think about them later. "If we stay high until we're south of whatever airport they've got us pointed at, we can flip on the electrical system and lower the landing gear and maybe some flaps. That'll give us a normal landing configuration. If the engine were to run away, we'd have enough altitude left to shut the runaway engine down and then glide the rest of the way."

316

"The second benefit of holding altitude," Linda added, "would be if the fuel tanks ran dry, we'd have a better glide range for getting to either that airport or the beach."

"Good thought." Again, Ray was impressed with her — as he had been throughout the flight. She understood their situation well. "We'll hold our altitude as long as we can. Can't run the risk of throwing altitude away to fly a normal glide path, it's not worth it. You agree?"

"Captain," Linda said as she reached across the center pedestal and touched his arm for emphasis. "You've been doing everything right for the past thousand-plus miles. Keep doing it."

◇

Stephanie Hilderbrandt was in the window seat of row 27, sitting in the pitch darkness of the cabin. Through the window to her right she could see the stars above them, but that was all see could see. Everything outside was a deep, impenetrable black. Stephanie closed her eyes for a moment to rest them, then opened her eyes and looked at her Blackberry smart phone.

Stephanie had turned her cell phone on hours earlier but, of course, there had been no phone coverage across the Atlantic Ocean. She knew ahead of time there wouldn't be. Instead, she had been using the phone for the past few hours for reading. One of the applications she had loaded onto it was a digital version of The Holy Bible. Stephanie continued to scroll through that Bible, finding sections to give her comfort, mouthing the words displayed on the small screen.

Maurice Hilderbrandt sat next to his wife, in the center seat of that row. "Not much longer now," he said, trying to sound reassuring as he continued to hold tightly to his wife's arm. "Fifteen or twenty minutes. At the most." He was basing that on the word that had been passed through the cabin, row by row. It was the estimate that had, evidently, been given by the pilot who was flying their airplane. Now, with the military escorting them directly to an airport, it wouldn't be much longer. Everything would work out.

"Yes, soon. Thank God in heaven." Stephanie said to her husband in a low voice. "For awhile, I surely didn't think we would make it." The light from the cell phone illuminated the

317

features of her husband's face and she looked at him. "Thank God," she said again.

"Knew we'd be all right," Maurice lied. He, too, had doubted that they would live through this – especially after that second wild ride while everything was being pitched around the cabin. He thought they would die right then and there. But they hadn't. They were going to live through this. It was God's will. Now, he was certain of it. Maurice glanced at the cell phone in his wife's hand to see which part of the Bible she was reading. That's when he noticed it, in the upper right corner of the small screen. "Christ!" Maurice grabbed the cell phone from her.

"What is it?" she asked anxiously.

"A signal," Maurice answered, more as a reaction to her question than a thought-out response. He was dumbfounded at what he was seeing: the cell phone had two bars showing! While Maurice watched, the cell phone signal indicator vacillated between one bar and two, but then went back to two full bars. It was definitely locked on. Definitely. "Got a cell signal," Maurice announced in a moderately loud voice.

"What?!" someone a few rows behind said. "Cell signal?"

"Yes! Got a cell phone signal!" Maurice said again, shouting this time, letting loose his seatbelt and rising to his feet. He then announced loudly to the entire cabin, "I've got a goddamn cell phone signal!"

Others in the cabin had heard him, and they were checking their cell phones too.

"I've got one!"

"Me, too!"

"One bar, but it's there!"

"Should we call 9-1-1!" someone from the front shouted.

"No, no," Maurice shouted back. "Call your families! We don't need 9-1-1, the military's here, we're being escorted to an airport, the government already knows! Just call your families! Your families want to know what happened to you!" Maurice pushed the cell phone back in Stephanie's hands. "Here, call Tim. On his cell phone. He's probably worried sick, waiting at the airport for us – God knows what the airline told them!"

"Yes, Tim..." Stephanie's hands were shaking, but she managed to press the buttons that would connect her with her

318

son. In the background, she could hear others in the cabin doing the same thing, calling their families and friends, telling everyone and anyone they could get hold of that they had been saved, that they were going to live through this nightmare.

One by one, the passenger's cell phones came back to life as the airliner got nearer to the shoreline – nearer to the cell phone towers – with each passing minute. Those who had cell phones were passing them on to those who didn't, once their own calls had been made. Within a handful of minutes, nearly everyone onboard had made at least one call to someone they loved and cared about to tell them that they were almost home. Almost home.

Maurice was beaming now; he felt that he had done something to help, had contributed something beneficial. He dropped into his chair and refastened his seatbelt. He could see Stephanie's outline in the glow from the phone, and he could hear the words she was speaking to their son. *Thank you, God.* Maurice closed his eyes and sat further back. They were safe. Finally, they were safe.

Chapter Thirty-Two

It was the prettiest sunrise that he had ever seen in all his years of being in the cockpit of an airliner, even though Ray knew that tonight's magical sunrise didn't in any way involve the sun. The glow that was mounding up in the sky in front of them — and had been for the past several minutes — had first begun as hardly more than a hint of grey against an otherwise black horizon. Slowly, and then more rapidly with every passing mile, the bleak horizon that they were flying toward had transformed into what they had been hoping and praying for — the first view of those millions and millions of lights of the New York City Metropolitan area.

"This is incredible. Fabulous. I was praying that we would see this again," Linda said from the co-pilot's seat.

"Me, too," Ray agreed. "There it is."

The two of them sat mesmerized for the next few moments, taking in that view on the horizon. Finally, Linda said, "The fighter is turning to the right. Slightly. My guess is that we're headed straight for JFK."

"Probably." Ray steered the Consolidated 768 to the right, to match the path that the fighter ahead and above was leading them on. "Got to get ready. At this altitude, we're not going to have much time after we see the shoreline and the airport."

"Right." Linda had taken out her instrument approach charts for JFK, even though the procedure itself would be impossible to fly since they didn't have a single working instrument or radio. But the airport diagram could be helpful, so she spread it across the center pedestal and picked up one of the flashlights to shine on it.

"Go ahead," Ray said as he watched her out of the corner of his eye. "It's light enough outside. Won't affect my vision." Ray knew JFK Airport like the back of his hand, and it certainly hadn't changed much since his retirement. Still, it wouldn't hurt to review the airport layout while they had the chance. "Turn on the flashlight. Let me look at that chart."

"I hope they only have one runway lit, the one that they'll want us to use," Linda said as she held the flashlight above the JFK airport diagram. "Less choices would be better."

"They will." Ray glanced down at the chart, then out at the military fighter in front of them. "They'll position fire trucks. They'll get other airplanes out of the way."

"Which runway do you think?" Linda asked.

Ray thought back to the New York forecast – a forecast that he had reviewed several hours ago, but it now seemed like several lifetimes ago. "The forecast wind was from the northwest, but there wasn't much — ten knots. So that means either 31 Left or 4 Right."

"Thirty-one is the longest," Linda said as she read the numbers on the chart. "Almost fifteen thousand feet. That would be my pick."

"Like you said, they'll pick the runway. I think they'll pick 4 Right," Ray answered.

"Why? It's two-thirds the length."

"In the boondocks." Ray gestured toward the chart that she was holding the flashlight on. "A good place to send an airplane in trouble. That runway is the furthest from everything — buildings, hangars, other aircraft on the taxiways. It's used for emergency landings when the crosswind is acceptable."

"Oh." Linda looked up, then excitedly pointed straight ahead. "I see the patterns of the lights themselves! I see the patches of dark and light where the inlets are cut into the shoreline! Can't be more than twenty-five miles out!"

Ray didn't respond, he was now focused on something else: the fighter ahead of them had begun a gradual descent several seconds earlier and was already a few hundred feet below their cruise altitude of 5,100. "Our fighter escort has started down. Must want us to start down, too," Ray said.

"Are you planning on staying up? Staying up until we see the runway?" Linda asked.

"That was the plan." He knew that they needed to stick to the plan, that there could be no wishful thinking.

"Right. We've got to be careful not to stay high for too long," Linda added. She would, of course, go along with whatever Ray wanted — but Linda also felt the need to point out whatever pitfalls she saw. Two heads were better than one. "Can't make it impossible to land on that first pass. If we stay high for too long, we'll have to circle the airport and come back for landing. Got the fuel situation to consider."

"I know," Ray answered tersely, although he knew that Linda was trying to be helpful. He knew that none of this would be easy, and what made it worse were that there were too many choices. Ray looked into the night sky and into that wall of lights that was getting brighter and more distinct with every passing moment, trying to recognize where they would be intercepting the shoreline and exactly where the airport might be. "Let me know as soon as you see any part of the airport — the beacon, the approach lights, the strobes."

"Okay." Linda leaned forward in her flight chair, nearly pressing her face against the glass of the co-pilot's windshield.

He had to stick with the plan and not make changes. Not unless he absolutely needed to. "Staying at this altitude until we see the runway. Then we'll start the landing drill we've practiced," Ray announced from the captain's seat. He glanced at her. "It would be a mistake to start descending sooner. Stick with what we've practiced."

◇

"Hope we didn't make a mistake," Sonny Bellman transmitted. "They're not following you down, Jack. Holding steady at 5,100 feet."

"Damn it. We're already above the glide slope for 4 Right," Clary answered. He glanced at his altimeter, then the other instruments on his F-15C panel. "Distance to touchdown is fifteen miles. He should be down to 3,000 feet," Clary said.

"I'm arming a missile, Jack," Bellman transmitted; it was not something that he wanted to do, it was something that he *needed* to do. It was a mission requirement. He paused, then transmitted, "Shield 22. Unlocking for the contingent Fox Two on subject aircraft. Aircraft is not descending into JFK runway 4 Right."

"Sonny, hold on. Give them a chance," Clary said. He let go of his transmit button and twisted around in his seat, trying to see the airliner that was above and behind him. For whatever reason — the altitude difference, the darkness, the lack of lights on the airliner, or, probably, all of the above — it was not in sight.

"Jack," Bellman said on the radio, "Your call. I'm ready for the contingent Fox Two. You give me the word." Sonny was torn both ways. He sure as hell didn't want to deep-six this airliner if there was any way out of it, but he also didn't want to screw with his friend by pressuring him for too quick a response. He and Jack would be fucked either way, not to mention how fucked the passengers on that airliner would be.

"Roger." Clary sat silently for a moment. He needed to think this out, he needed to put himself in that guy's place. Jack then transmitted, "Let me know if you see any change in their flight pattern. Anything at all."

"Nothing yet."

Clary looked at the distance readout on his instrument panel: eight miles to touchdown. But he didn't need the instruments because the long string of bright approach lights and, beyond them, even the runway itself, was becoming easily visible. "Any change?" he transmitted again.

"Negative..."

Then an idea occurred to him, and Jack immediately decided that he would go with it. "Here's the plan," Clary announced on the tactical frequency, sounding more confident than he was. "I think, maybe, that this unusual maneuvering might mean it's a fuel issue. That pilot is afraid to get low and slow until they've got the runway made. If my fuel situation was critical, that's sure as hell what I'd do. Put that contingent Fox Two on hold until they've either overflown the northern airport boundary or they've begun a turn toward Manhattan. Then, go with Fox Two. Got that, Sonny?"

"Yes Sir, skipper. Will do. Holding on the contingent Fox Two unless they blow right past JFK," Bellman answered, hoping that his friend knew what he was doing. "Remember Jack, if I wait that long I'm going to drop them into a suburban backyard, or maybe the middle of Brooklyn."

"Roger that, Sonny. But I want to give them every chance. They've come too damn far to make any rash choices," Clary transmitted.

"With you, Jack," Bellman responded. He paused for a few seconds, his finger still on the transmitter button. "Something's happening. Slowing up. Rapidly." Bellman paused, then added, "They ballooned a couple of hundred feet up, but

323

now they're descending." A few seconds later he said, "Down to 4,900 feet. Airspeed bleeding off. Two-forty. Two-twenty. Two hundred knots. 4,600 feet. Course steady on zero-four-four. They're definitely descending."

"Roger, Shield 22. Understand," Clary answered automatically while he kept his attention riveted on the two long rows of bright lights that ran along the edges of the long runway that stretched in front of him. *Land on the runway I brought you to. Don't make me into a complete idiot, not on my birthday.*

Chapter Thirty-Three

Without help from anything on the airliner's instrument panel, it was a hell of difficult job to guess at the unorthodox descent angle they needed. In this crippled airliner, the official rules and procedures were out the window — totally useless – and they had been for a long time.

Ray was relying on his experience alone to get this aircraft on the ground. It had been a long time since he practiced those skills because anything other than flying by the official rule book had been forbidden for so goddamn long. What he was attempting now was a throwback to the old days.

Ray kept his attention on the view outside the cockpit window. He was judging how much altitude and how much airspeed he should and could trade off in order to get them down onto that narrow strip of concrete. Inside him, he could feel a knot of unbridled fear welling up, and it was beginning to crowd out some of his other thoughts. Ray knew that he had to get hold of himself, to stay focused.

He had zero margins to play with because the runway he was aiming at was surrounded by one of the biggest cities in the world. There would be no second chance for them. "Linda, get ready..." Ray announced while he kept his eyes locked on the airport ahead and, in particular, that long string of bright approach lights and flashing strobes that led to the threshold of runway 4 Right. He was going to stick with the plan.

"Ready," Linda answered. As they had practiced several times, she had her left hand near the ship's master electrical switches on the overhead panel and was poised to turn them on. She was also ready, with her right hand, to lower the landing gear lever when Ray issued his command for it.

"Standby..." Ray said without taking his eyes away from the view out the cockpit window. They were over the Atlantic Ocean, but only a few miles from the first strip of land. Ray knew it was Rockaway Beach that was nearly under the airliner's nose. Beyond that first narrow strip of land, they would be flying over a couple of miles of Jamaica Bay before they reached the threshold of runway 4 Right. "Electric — now!" Ray commanded.

Linda flipped on the ship's master electrical switches, the ones that had been off for the past several hours. Immediately, the electrical relays made their connections and, within seconds, the ship's primary electrical circuits were restored. Lights in the cockpit came on, and so did warning lights of all sorts on the various instrument panels around them, and warning horns and bells, too. "We've got electric power!" Linda announced over the noise of the aural warnings as she scanned the indicators.

"I'm throttling down and..." As Ray began to reduce power for the landing, their only operating engine did exactly the opposite: it began to run itself up to even more power instead of less. "A runaway! Linda, kill it! Fuel lever!"

But before Linda could get her hand on the fuel lever in order to shut down the sudden runaway of the left engine and what they knew would be to full power and beyond, the engine — without the slightest warning — suddenly ceased to produce power altogether. "A flame out!" Linda shouted. "On its own! Didn't get the fuel lever!"

Ray didn't answer. He didn't know if the sudden failure of the left engine had been caused by an internal failure or if they had finally run out of fuel. It didn't matter. He had his attention riveted outside, on the only things that would matter to them from that point. They had become a huge glider – like the Space Shuttle coming back from orbit – except they had no instruments and no computers to help them with the descent angle, with the tradeoffs of speed for altitude, of forward energy with downward energy. He had to feel his way through this.

Ray watched carefully as they descended toward the runway. He had one ace in the hole: the landing gear; dropping it would increase the airliner's rate of descent considerably, so he had to wait until he was certain – damn certain – that dropping the landing gear wouldn't produce that extra drag too soon. If it did, they would land short. They would land in Jamaica Bay. That might be better than landing in the Atlantic Ocean, but it wouldn't be much better — especially on a cold night in January. Many of them would either die on impact or freeze to death before they were rescued. They needed to reach dry land. "Get ready!"

"Ready," Linda answered. Her mouth was dry, and she suddenly found herself desperately wanting a sip of water. She had her right hand on the gear lever that protruded out of the center of the main instrument panel and she focused on it instead. "Flaps?" she asked.

"No. Not enough hydraulics." Ray knew that the landing gear would, if necessary, free-fall from its own weight. The flaps wouldn't budge. "Read the airspeed. No less than one-eighty with no flaps," he said, repeating what they had practiced.

"Right." Linda looked at the emergency airspeed indicator near the captain's flight instrument panel — it was lit up by the normal panel lights, which had come back on when she turned on the electrical master switches. "Two hundred knots," she said. Any less than 170 and the ship would stall and fall straight down. "Steady on two hundred knots." Linda glanced out the cockpit window: they had passed the first strip of shoreline and the runway was straight ahead, about four miles. She looked at the emergency altimeter. "Altitude is thirty-four hundred feet." She paused then added, "Ray, we're high. Too high."

Ray didn't answer. Instead, he concentrated on the view out the windshield. Numbers were running through his head, the forward speed, the ship's rate of descent. He could double the descent rate by extending the landing gear. But once he did, the act was irrevocable and they would be coming down twice as fast. "Wait...wait..." *This is what life is asking from you. Stick with your gut feeling. This is what life is asking from you.*

With no flaps, the pitch angle of the airliner was far higher than normal. Linda could hardly believe her eyes as the view of the runway — hell, even the airport itself — began to disappear beneath the airplane's nose. "Ray, we're losing the airport. Oh, Christ, we're going to overshoot..."

"Gear down, now!" Ray commanded. He knew, no he *felt*, it was the right time.

Without a word, Linda pushed the landing gear lever to the down position. For a brief moment she thought that the landing gear wasn't working, that for some mechanical or electrical reason the gear wouldn't be coming down and they'd overshoot the airport and crash into the crowded streets and the buildings beyond. They'd die for sure. But then she heard and felt the landing gear coming out of the wheel wells and down to

327

its extended position. A few moments later, the three green lights on the instrument panel illuminated. "God Almighty, the gear is down! Ray, down and locked!"

Ray pushed the airliner's nose far lower. The rate of descent increased dramatically. As Ray had intended, he had erred on the side of caution – he was sticking with his plan – since he knew that landing short into Jamaica Bay would have been a complete disaster. As a result, they were too high. Ray pushed the nose further down. The airspeed increased. He was diving the airliner toward the threshold of the runway.

"Ray! Airspeed!" Linda shouted. They had gotten up to 200 knots and the airspeed was on the rise. But the end of the runway was now visible again over the nose, and their altitude was less than 1,000 feet. The distance to the runway threshold was hardly more than one mile ahead.

Linda placed her hand on the speed brake lever near the throttles, as they had rehearsed. Four hundred feet. Two hundred feet. One hundred feet. The green threshold lights of the runway sped past beneath them as they continued down. "Speed is two-oh-five," Linda announced. They were too fast. Much too fast.

"Speed brakes," Ray called out.

Linda pulled the lever, but she could tell that nothing had happened. "Nothing — no speed brakes," she announced. She was frightened now, they had completely run out of options.

Ray allowed the airliner to settle on its wheels; he had figured that they wouldn't have enough hydraulic pressure left to activate the speed brakes, but he sure as hell was going to give them a try. The airliner's touchdown spot on the runway was a few thousand feet beyond the threshold, and they were going far too fast to use the airplane's wheel brakes —they were still *flying* more than they were *rolling,* with the tires barely skimming the surface of the runway. At this speed, the wheel brakes would be useless.

"A hundred fifty knots!" Linda looked out the windshield and she could see the far end of the runway looming ahead, and, beyond it, what she knew was Thurston Bay and, eventually, Rockaway Boulevard. "Not going to stop. Not in time. Ray, ground loop," she called out.

As far as Linda could see, their only chance was for Ray to try a sudden change in direction, to try to get the airliner to spin out left or right so that it was pointed away from the dangers immediately in front of them. It would break the landing gear off, but they had little or no fuel onboard, so maybe....

"No! Arrestor bed!" Ray continued to steer the airliner down the centerline of runway 4 Right while he began to use the wheel brakes for the first time.

The arrestor bed! Linda had forgotten about the special overrun area at the far end of runway 4 Right, the 400 foot-long pad of special cellular concrete that had been designed to bring a transport aircraft to a safe stop in a short distance — a runaway truck ramp for airliners. The weight of a car wouldn't crush it, but the weight of the airliner would collapse the concrete and it would be like moving a car through deeper and deeper snow. They had talked about it when they initially reviewed the airport layout, but under the pressure of the situation Linda had let it slip out of her mind.

The only question was, were they going so fast that they would get completely through that arrestor bed before they were totally stopped? If they did get spit out the far side, the airplane would slide into Thurston Bay. Linda looked at the ship's airspeed. "One hundred twenty knots," she said in a deadened, terror-filled voice as the Consolidated 768 ran across the far end of the runway and onto that special concrete area.

The deceleration was very rapid — but also coming up rapidly was the sight of darkness that she knew was Thurston Bay. Linda could not take her eyes away from the sight of the far end of that special concrete area as it disappeared beneath the airliner's nose. Beyond it was the dark outline of where the bay began.

And then, with one final rocking jolt, Trans-Continental Airlines Flight 3 came to a complete stop, its wheels buried deep in the final few feet of the arrestor bed's special collapsible concrete.

The rocking motion stopped. A few seconds after that, Ray let go of the control wheel and sat back in the captain's flight chair. The cockpit was silent, and he could hear the shouts of joy that were coming from the cabin, and he could see an endless array of red and yellow and white flashing lights as airport and emergency vehicles of all sorts were headed toward them. Ray let out a long and deep breath and then looked at Linda.

"That was incredible," Linda said. Her voice was trembling, but she had a broad smile on her face — it was, she knew, the biggest and the most sincere smile of her life. "I knew you could do it! I knew that you could!" Linda reached out and grabbed his hand. "Goddamnit, that flying was nothing less than...magnificent!"

Ray wrapped his fingers around hers and the two of them sat silently, holding hands, for several long seconds. Finally, Ray cleared his throat so that he could say the one thing that he'd been planning, the one thing that he'd been hoping and praying that he'd get the opportunity to say. "Linda..."

"Yes?"

"...there's something I wasn't sure we'd be able...something we might never get to hear." Ray exhaled deeply.

"What is it?" Linda asked.

Ray turned more in his seat to face her, then gripped her hand even tighter. "Somehow we managed to get us home again. Finally. You and me. One hell of a ride, but we did it. Together." Ray shook his head, smiled, then added, "Welcome to New York. It's time to start on those drinks."

Epilogue

Saturday, January 23rd
Trans-Continental Airlines Hangar, JFK International Airport,
New York
9:20 am, Eastern Standard Time

T hey were using the conference room in the Trans-Continental maintenance hangar as their office today, and it was where the final arrangements for the day's activities were being choreographed. Al had a clipboard in his hands and he made several additional notes on the top sheet.

Al glanced around the conference room. It wasn't bad, all things considered. He had set up three special presentations at the hangar not only because it was big enough to accommodate them, but also because it sent the proper signal to all concerned that this airline was going to return firmly to its roots — to what had made it great in the past. Al had made a convincing argument to the Board of Directors at the emergency meeting two days earlier that airline managers — even those at the very top-end, hell, *especially* those at the very top-end — belonged at the airport. It was the only way for them to stay in touch with what mattered.

Al glanced at his clipboard. He had scheduled the three separate meetings with two hours between each, beginning at 10:00 am. The first one should be a short presentation with a small group, but the second meeting at noon would be jammed with the media and god knows who else — it was the open press conference to provide the details about the Flight 3 incident this past Wednesday. George Fisher was presiding over that one, with Ray Clarke, Linda Erickson, Jack Schofield and Tina Lopez answering the media questions. George was going to keep a tight rein on it, and he wasn't going to allow that conference to go past 1:30 since they had the special Board of Directors agenda – the newly elected Board of Directors – of announcements scheduled at two o'clock. As he finished reviewing his notes, Al saw Jennifer enter the door from the hangar and head toward him.

"Al, I did find the sound man from that rental place," Jennifer said. "The guy promised me that the audio system now checks out fine with those extra speakers at the back. He absolutely swears that you'll have good coverage for everyone in the hangar, no matter how big the crowds are."

"Great."

"Here's more coffee for you." Jennifer handed him one of the two coffee cups she had brought across the room. "This one is yours. Drink up, it's cold outside."

"Thanks." Al reached for his coffee, took a sip, then laid it on the table and glanced at the clipboard again.

As Jennifer watched him, she found herself smiling. As she had seen repeatedly these past few days, Al was launching on what she considered a difficult assignment, and he was doing it with his usual grace and charm. Another factor in the mix was how organized he was, which invariably meant that everything would work out. "Al, have I mentioned that I'd really like you to straighten out the files in my writing office?" Jennifer grabbed his arm with her free hand. "Those files are a real mess. Needs your touch."

"Maybe." Al answered. He took another sip from his coffee, then put the cup down. "What's the pay?" he asked.

"Time with me."

"You're overpaying for the job." Al lightly touched his finger against her cheek. "That's bad policy."

"So, you decline?"

"No, I accept." Al paused. "Got one more item to show George. Just came in." With that, Al gently unwrapped her arm from his and walked across the room.

George Fisher was standing on the other side of the room, talking to Ray. Al approached them but stood silently as George continued with his conversation.

"According to that software engineer on the phone," George said, "the thinking at Consolidated is that somehow the corrupted date coding information in that particular software revision managed to migrate into the powerplant performance database. Because of the interconnect of their engine computer control systems with the airplane's onboard satellite navigation units and the actual time-and-date stamping that those satellite units were passing on, the corrupting software was held off on

Flight 3 until that effective time and date got closer. Then the corrupted software overpowered the operating software."

"Which is why the test airplane on the ground had its software failure much sooner than we did?" Ray asked.

"Apparently." George nodded, then added, "It's too byzantine for me, but that's what they said. At least I think that's what they said." He paused, then added, "These fucking computers. The more we need them, the more they fuck us up."

"Right."

"Anyway," George continued, "Their guess is that any Consolidated 768 that was started after midnight would have had its double engine runaway almost immediately."

"Incredible." Ray shook his head. "Basically, those engine computer boxes were infected with the granddaddy of computer viruses. The virus was controlling the engines."

"Exactly. The next morning we would have had a dozen catastrophic crashes before anyone figured out the connection. Maybe more." George turned to Al. "On a related note, do we have that official response from Boeing, the one that I'll read at the Board of Directors conference? I don't want to be making shit up."

"Holding it in my hand." Al handed over a piece of paper that he had just received. He gave George a moment to read it, but he knew what his response would be.

"Excellent. Boeing couldn't have been more positive." George waved the paper. "Phrased it beautifully. They could have been far more difficult on this airplane-conversion crapola, but they weren't. Good people. When I make the announcement that we're grounding our Consolidated 768 versions that Kyle got us involved with and we'll turn them back into straight Boeing 767s, I'm going to be a happy man."

"Not as happy as I'll be when our new Board of Directors announces that both Brandon Kyle and William Wesson have elected to leave the company to find employment elsewhere," Al said. "Should be a real crowd-pleaser."

"Don't know how they'll find time to job hunt with the Federal investigation into Kyle's statements," George said. "I couldn't believe what I was hearing when Steven Chew from the TSA told me what Kyle and Wesson had said about the hijacking and, in particular, what they had said about Ray. A straight lie. A company psychologist, for chrissake. Can't figure out why he was saying that crap."

"The world of high corporate intrigue weaves a tangled web," Al answered. "Even though his conversations on that hotline to the TSA were being recorded — hell, it says that in bold print in the emergency notification handbook, if they had bothered to read it — most of what Kyle said was ambiguous, or he will claim that he was misinformed. Kyle certainly will not admit fault. The end result is that we get rid of Kyle and his band of crooks from the Board."

"Right." George paused, then said, "I was surprised at how many of the Board members were opposed to Kyle's plans, but, individually, they didn't feel they could stop him. Some of the Board members told me that the opposition view had no clear-cut leadership for going head-to-head against Brandon Kyle, that was the basic problem. Hell, if it were up to me, I'd throw a noose around that bastard's neck and hang him from the highest beam in this hangar."

"Well, unfortunately, that's probably not going to happen," Al said with a smile. "The Feds will make Kyle squirm, but there's probably nothing actually *illegal* in what he said or what he did."

"His involvement almost kept us from getting Flight 3 back," Fisher said. "And that sure does piss me off. Not to mention what he was trying to do to the airline itself. Brandon Kyle is one incredible and self-serving sonovabitch."

"So noted, George." Al nodded, then said, "Before I forget, I need to know how you want to handle the questions about Peter Fenton during the noon press conference. You've been vague on that."

"I'll deal with those questions," George answered. "The bottom line is that the discharge of the TSA-supplied handgun occurred during the portion of the flight that was involved in a series of violent and uncontrolled maneuvers."

"Certainly," Al said. He suspected that this would be George's response.

"Right," George continued. "The discharge of that pistol was an accident, pure and simple. That's the story I've been told. It was told to me by everyone who was in a direct position to know what happened out there. The members of that flight crew have a comprehensive explanation of what occurred over the North Atlantic, so why would I want to say anything different? I wasn't there."

"That's how it happened," Ray said. "An accident during those violent maneuvers while the First Officer was putting his sidearm away before his scheduled rest break in the cabin. It was bad timing, that's all. Linda, Jack and I remember it clearly. Peter got the mistaken idea that a hijacking was involved during the initial moments of chaos. That idea was reinforced later on when Linda and I wouldn't let him back into the cockpit. We knew that he was in shock and he'd been sedated, and I didn't think he could contribute anything useful under those conditions. I sure as hell didn't want the distraction of dealing with him in the state that I figured he was in."

"The passengers heard Peter saying those things about a hijacking," George said. "Hell, he told everyone who would listen, and a gang of them eventually went along with it. There's no way to pretend otherwise."

"No need to pretend otherwise," Ray said. "Peter was suffering from shock because of the gunshot wound and was very much under the influence of the sedation that the doctor had administered. That's why he wasn't thinking straight, and why he wasn't remembering what really happened. That's the whole story."

"Understand," Al said. "Makes sense."

Ray lowered his voice. "We also agree that there's nothing to be served by coming down on Peter. His fear got hold of him during the worst of it and he didn't know what he was doing, but he thought he was doing the proper thing. We spoke with Doctor Frankel about this." Ray glanced at George, who gave a small nod before Ray continued. "The airline has hired Lee Frankel to be Peter's counselor. Peter's going to need help, some guidance, to get over this." Ray then added, "I don't have to tell you how much respect I have for Lee, considering what he did on that flight. We owe him a great deal." And Ray also knew that, in particular, he did, too.

"Those details about Frankel and Fenton are not for public consumption," George chimed in. "Confidential medical information."

Al nodded. "What, eventually, will happen to Peter Fenton?"

"He'll have a job at the airline as long as he wants," George said. "But not a flying job. Don't mind being generous, but I sure as hell don't intend to be stupid. Fenton's well qualified to do lots of things around here, but I don't want the airline testing his piloting abilities in the future."

"Good choice."

"Right."

Al pulled his gold pocket watch out and looked at it. "Time to go out. I expect a small crowd so they should be seated near the speaker's platform. That'll make this a little more intimate."

"Here we go, folks. Let's get Lucy over here." George began to lead the way and, as he did, he motioned for the people across the room to escort Lucy over. As he approached the door, George leaned over to Al. "Do you have another of the printed programs? I left mine on the table."

"Certainly." Al handed over one of the elegantly engraved cards that he had made for this, the first of the day's activities at the hangar.

George took the card and looked at it one final time before he opened the door that would lead them out to the hangar floor and directly to the speaker's platform that had been erected against the far wall.

Trans-Continental Airlines Hangar, JFK International Airport
Saturday, January 24th
10:00 AM
Captain Maynard Lyman Memorial Service

(order of the speakers:)
Albert DeWitt: Opening remarks
Captain George Fisher: The long and wonderful history of Captain Maynard Lyman.
Captain Ray Clarke: My early flights with Captain Maynard Lyman.

Mrs. Lucy Lyman: Some final words about my beloved husband.

When George opened the door that led to the hangar floor, he was astonished. Instead of the small group of friends and fellow workers of Maynard's that he was expecting, the entire hangar — from one end to the other — was totally filled. As George and the others approached the speaker's platform, they could see that the crowd contained every possible cross section from the employee groups of the airline. It also contained nearly all the passengers who had been onboard Flight 3, and, seemingly, all their relatives, too. In a word, the hangar was absolutely, completely packed.

The crowd was hushed as George led the group of those who would be speaking onto the platform. He glanced down and saw, in the first row, Captain Jack Schofield in full uniform, but with his arm in a sling. Second Officer Linda Erickson was beside him. Next was Flight Attendant Tina Lopez, with Doctor Lee Frankel standing beside her. Finally, Jennifer Lane had taken the last empty seat in that front row.

Everybody sat as Al provided some poignant opening remarks. Then George got up and spoke for several minutes about his good friend Maynard, and about Maynard's long and illustrious career at Trans-Continental. After that, Ray rose and gave a short talk about his early flights at the airline when Captain Maynard Lyman had taken him under his wing and had taught him so very, very much.

Finally, Al introduced the wife of Maynard Lyman to the hushed crowd. This tall, thin woman with her soft and flowing grey hair and her very elegant and keen face moved to the microphone in the center of the speaker's stand.

"When I first met Maynard," Lucy began in her small but crystal-clear voice, "he was a twenty-two year old new co-pilot and I was a twenty-one year old receptionist right here at the airline. It was love at first sight. We were married seven months later." Lucy paused. "We were married for over fifty years," she said, her voice trailing off.

Lucy cleared her throat, then smiled at the silent crowd, all of them seemingly hanging on her every word. She continued, "After his second heart attack, Maynard told me what we both knew — that he was on borrowed time. But he also told me something else," Lucy added. She paused for a moment as she allowed her eyes to sweep across the endless sea of faces of those sitting in the countless rows of chairs assembled directly in front of her as far back as the distant hangar walls, and the people who were standing behind those seats.

Lucy's amplified words, which were coming through quite distinctly, drifted effortlessly across the hushed crowd. "Maynard said that he had come to realize something — that borrowed time is like borrowed money. Once you borrowed it, you hoped that you were doing something useful and necessary with it." Lucy paused again, then finally added, "Then, it would have been well worth whatever the interest charges might be, well worth the price that you've paid."

As her last words were spoken, they seemed to hang motionless above the crowd. As the echo of those spoken words finally dissipated, not a single person in the enormous crowd made a sound or moved a muscle. All eyes were fixed on her.

Ray was the first to move. He rose slowly from his seat on the speaker's stand, then turned and faced Lucy directly. Their eyes locked together. Once they had, Ray began a slow, rhythmic clapping.

And then George Fisher, and then Al DeWitt. And then, in the first row, Jack Schofield, and then Linda Erickson, and then Tina Lopez and then Lee Frankel and Jennifer Lane also rose from their seats and joined in with the slow, rhythmic applause.

Finally, in a moving wave of symbiotic human activity, those who were seated in those hundreds and hundreds of chairs inside the cavernous hangar began to rise to their feet and also began to clap, and those who were standing behind them and across the back walls joined in, first with clapping, then, suddenly, with cheers and then with yells and shouts in what had become a genuine outburst of recognition and sincere appreciation for a truly selfless act that had touched each and every one of them.

As Jennifer would later say in her special press coverage about the Flight 3 saga — press coverage that was eventually syndicated around the nation and around the world — the thunderous round of spontaneous applause and cheering that swept across everyone who was part of that crowd on that cold January morning in New York could be heard far beyond the airline's hangar. It could be heard far beyond the airport itself, and even far beyond this enormous city.

It could be heard, quite loud and clear, as far as the Heavens.

The End

Thomas Block has written a number of aviation-oriented novels, many which have gone on to acquire best-seller status in numerous countries. His novel writing began with the publication of "Mayday" in 1979. That novel was rewritten with his boyhood friend, novelist Nelson DeMille in 1998 and remains on DeMille's extensive backlist. "Mayday" became a CBS Movie of the Week in October, 2005.

Several of the other novels by Block include "Orbit" (a top bestseller in Germany, among other nations), "Airship Nine", "Forced Landing" (also done as a radio serialization drama in Japan), "Skyfall", "Open Skies" and "Captain". Thomas Block is still writing both fiction and non-fiction, and has edited and updated his earlier novels into ebooks in all the major formats and also into new full-sized (trade soft cover) printed versions.

Block's magazine writing began in 1968 and over the next five decades his work has appeared in numerous publications. He worked 20 years at FLYING Magazine as Contributing Editor, and as Contributing Editor to Plane & Pilot Magazine for 11 years. Block became Editor-at-Large for Piper Flyer Magazine and Cessna Flyer Magazine in 2001. During his long career as an aviation writer he has written on a wide array of subjects that range from involvement with government officials to evaluation reports on most everything that flies.

An airline pilot for US Airways for over 36 years before his retirement in April, 2000, Captain Thomas Block has been a pilot since 1959. Since 2002, he has lived on a ranch in Florida with his wife Sharon where they board, compete and train horses. Complete information (including direct links to booksellers) is available at http://www.ThomasBlockNovels.com or through the author's additional website at http://www.FlyingB-Ranch.com. For Facebook users, complete information about Thomas Block Novels can also be found at two interlinked Facebook sites:
http://www.Facebook.com/Captain.by.Thomas.Block
http://www.Facebook.com/ThomasBlockNovels.

Take the Captain Reader Survey and see 'insider' information on the writing of the novel. The online survey takes 10 minutes - there's a small ebook prize waiting when you finish! To access, go through any of the author's websites or Facebook sites listed above, or go directly to http://www.SurveyMonkey/S/Captain.

Made in the USA
Lexington, KY
26 October 2012